ACROSS THE SEASONS

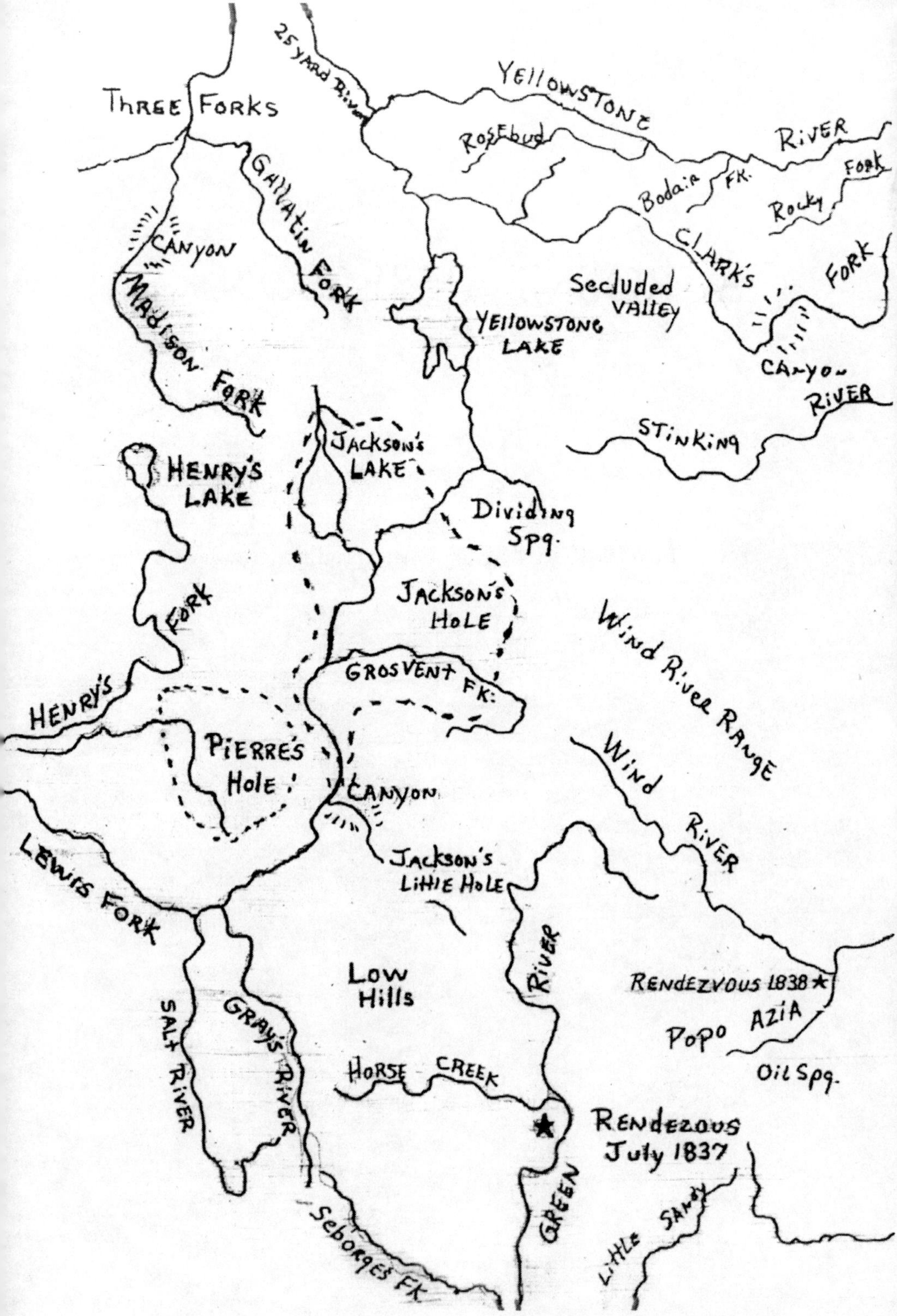

Three Forks
25 Yard River
Yellowstone River
Rosebud
Bodair Fk.
Rocky Fork
Clark's Fork
Secluded Valley
Canyon
Gallatin Fork
Madison Fork
Canyon
Yellowstone Lake
Stinking River
Jackson's Lake
Henry's Lake
Dividing Spg.
Jackson's Hole
Henry's Fork
Grosvent Fk.
Wind River Range
Wind River
Pierre's Hole
Canyon
Lewis Fork
Jackson's Little Hole
Low Hills
River
Rendezvous 1838
Popo Azia
Oil Spg.
Salt River
Gray's River
Horse Creek
Rendezous July 1837
Green
Little Sandy
Seborges Fk

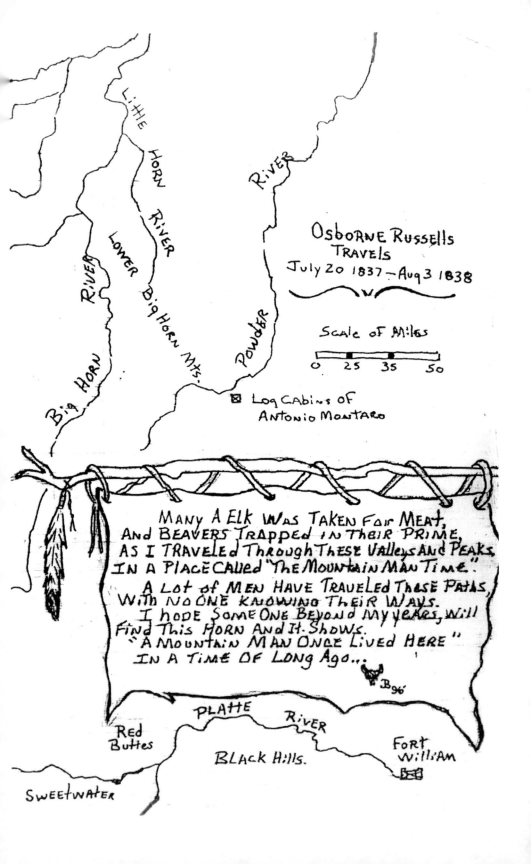

Osborne Russells Travels
July 20 1837 — Aug 3 1838

Scale of Miles
0   25   35   50

⊠ Log Cabins of Antonio Montaro

Little Horn River
Lower Big Horn Mts.
Big Horn River
Big Horn
Powder River
River

MANY A ELK WAS TAKEN FOR MEAT,
AND BEAVERS TRAPPED IN THEIR PRIME,
AS I TRAVELED THROUGH THESE VALLEYS AND PEAKS,
IN A PLACE CALLED "THE MOUNTAIN MAN TIME".

A LOT OF MEN HAVE TRAVELED THESE PATHS,
WITH NO ONE KNOWING THEIR WAYS.
I HOPE SOME ONE BEYOND MY YEARS, WILL
FIND THIS HORN AND IT SHOWS.
"A MOUNTAIN MAN ONCE LIVED HERE"
IN A TIME OF LONG AGO...

B 96'

PLATTE River
Red Buttes
BLACK Hills.
Fort William
SWEETWATER

ACROSS THE SEASONS

BY
LAURA RUGEL GLISE

Trafford Publishing
Victoria

Printed in Canada

FIRST EDITION

Front cover: *Carson's Men*, Charles M. Russell courtesy The Thomas Gilcrease Institute of American History and Art, Tulsa, Oklahoma. Limited portions of this novel quoted from Osborne Russell's *Journal of a Trapper* by permission from The University of Nebraska Press. Map illustration: Bobby Lee. Back cover photograph: Lanney R. Ratcliff.

National Library of Canada Cataloguing in Publication Data

Glise, Laura Rugel,
  Across the seasons

ISBN 1-55212-625-0

I. Title.
PS3513.L68157A72 2001   813'.6   C2001-910169-4

TRAFFORD

This book was published *on-demand* in cooperation with Trafford Publishing.
On-demand publishing is a unique process and service of making a book available for retail sale to the public taking advantage of on-demand manufacturing and Internet marketing.
On-demand publishing includes promotions, retail sales, manufacturing, order fulfilment, accounting and collecting royalties on behalf of the author.

Suite 6E, 2333 Government St., Victoria, B.C. V8T 4P4, CANADA
Phone   250-383-6864   Toll-free   1-888-232-4444 (Canada & US)
Fax   250-383-6804   E-mail   sales@trafford.com
Web site   www.trafford.com   TRAFFORD PUBLISHING IS A DIVISION OF TRAFFORD HOLDINGS LTD.
Trafford Catalogue #01-0027   www.trafford.com/robots/01-0027.html

10   9   8   7   6   5   4

For Sayward
Follow your bliss

Acknowledgements

Thank you to those who made the journey Across the Seasons with me; my family, and my friends Melissa, Debbie, and Kathy. And Evelyn, whose long-playing friendship provided me with fact more interesting than fiction.

Thank you to Bobby and Carolyn Lee, my first teachers, and J.R. and Eileen Watson for always making a place for me by their fire.

Thank you to Lanney R. Ratcliff, for acting as my subject-matter-expert and helping me find plausible explanations for historical science fiction.

Thank you to the Rendezvous Association of 1838, Riverton, Wyoming, for their diligent efforts preserving the original Rendezvous site. Lastly, thank you to the American Mountain Men for making it possible for me to travel back in time when I visited their encampment on Dry Cottonwood Creek.

The song "Foolish Royal Tragedy," is the property of Sean Murphy.

I.

There is no past,
Present or future.
Using tenses to divide
Time is like making
Chalk marks on water.

Janet Frame

Chapter 1

How many times have I walked the beach? Walking east. Walking west. Hoping one day I will find what I am looking for, or find what I have lost. Only a handful of walks have been made before sunrise. In the early years, the novelty of our family owning a beach house in Destin, Florida inspired early morning or midnight walks. We combed each dune, studied each wave, searching for treasure the Spaniards might have left.

The last day of a visit home always filled me with urgency. I stared out to sea noting the subtle colors of the water and each gentle reverse of the wind. Standing alone at dawn, my toes licked by the cold surf, I slowly and sweetly savored one more journey home, one more chapter in my life.

Over the years the house in Destin became a home for the four of us when we scattered after college, and a home that served as a gathering place for aunts and uncles, cousins grown and married, and for friendships that lasted over the years. My cousin Harold visited in 1983 and walked the beach to decide whether or not to accept an appointment from the Air Force after his four years of college were completed at the Academy. My cousin Royal came in 1992 on his honeymoon. Royal, the youngest of ten cousins, once the baby in the family photographs, was now a man with three children of his own. When I was 20, my best friend, Patricia, and I sneaked to the beach at sunset and took photographs topless; our bodies young and beautiful in the last golden light of day.

Gordon Reese, a family friend and business associate of my father's, died here in 1985. He suffered a heart attack and died in my Mother's arms on the blue ceramic tile of the bathroom floor.

Today was a new day. A new sunrise. The sugar-white sand had shifted. It had been carried out to sea and back to the shore. The countless footprints of those who had walked here through the years were gone and on this day, I was the first. I was the last.

At sunrise the light comes before the color. Each minute of daylight paints the sky with golden hues and pale pinks. The summer morning palette reflected brilliantly on the surface of the sea. Today the surf was as calm as the water in a pool before the swimmers arrive, the sound of the

1

waves more a whisper than a roar. I wouldn't come down again today. Once I showered and packed, I would become less nostalgic and my mind would focus on the five-hour drive to Atlanta and the work week ahead.

As I left the beach I saw the tall gables of our stucco house with its turquoise trim. The last three years my parents' home had become my sanctuary and retreat from the world. By the time I walked the 100 yards from the beach, the black asphalt had already started to warm in the early June sun. Walking up the driveway I counted the shells and the rocks my Mother insisted the contractor embed in the concrete when our house was built. My Mother could have taught Rachel Carson a thing or two about being a naturalist.

Inside the house was still. I made coffee and went outside on the deck and waited for my parents to awaken. With the passing of a few more days the blazing summer sun would make it impossible to sit on the deck after 9 a.m., even under the shade of our bright floral umbrella. The purple martins darted in and out of their home high atop a pole. Two taupe-feathered Mexican doves dined at the other end of the deck; Mother fed them religiously each day on an old, badly scratched Teflon-coated cookie sheet.

I noticed Tom Canale, wearing a red tank top and navy running shorts, walking his two female Dobermans. He had shoulder-length black hair and tanned olive skin. He smoked long, thin imported cigars as he walked his dogs every morning and every evening. He intrigued me, although I had never met him. He was extremely attractive in a European way. Rumor had it he was a professional gambler. I had a dream about him a few years ago. As I watched Tom Canale, he had no idea how much my subconscious mind had enjoyed him that night as I slept, and how much my waking mind had enjoyed him each time I remembered the erotic dream.

In my dream I was walking on the beach. I met Tom for the first time and he invited me to his home to watch the sunset and to have a drink. When I arrived that evening, I handed him a new box of tempera paints and a thick red sable brush with a long black handle. I asked him to paint my buttocks. I raised my denim skirt and leaned across his kitchen table. The smooth wooden table top was cool on my stomach. One by one he took the lids off the jars arranging each color, just so, on the table. Red. Yellow. Blue. Green. Black. White. He began to paint my ass with slow, deliberate brush strokes until it was brightly colored like a psychedelic poster. When the painting was complete he softly blew on my skin until the paint was dry, then he lowered my skirt over my legs. We didn't have sex. I have always believed, and found from experience, that fantasy is almost always better than reality. Some of life's sexiest moments come without consummation.

"Why are you up so early, sweetheart?" asked my Dad as he stepped through the sliding glass door onto the deck. He bent over to kiss me good morning.

I smiled and looked out to sea, spotting a shrimp boat on the horizon. "Oh, you know how I am the last day of a visit home. Soon I'll be wrapped up in packing the truck and getting off on time. I wanted to stretch my day a little longer by getting up early."

Daddy brought us a mug of hot coffee. The first cup of the morning always smells the best and tastes the best. We sat in silence. The temperature continued to rise. He read the paper; I admired the water and how it turned from a beautiful green to a deep teal blue. I watched the deep-mouth brown pelicans skim over the glassy surface. I could have sat with him at that table forever.

He cooked bacon and eggs for breakfast. As long as I live the smell of bacon frying will take me home.

"When will you be back this summer?" asked my Mother, her hair still damp from her morning shower.

I picked up my orange juice and began to rotate the bottom making small circles on the glass table top. "I probably won't be back until right before school starts."

"Why not? Where are you going this summer? Are you going to Europe without me?" My Mother fired the questions in rapid succession and an unjustified sense of guilt began to rise within me.

"No. I'm thinking about going to New Mexico to spend the summer at the Crow Canyon Archaeological Institute. I've mentioned it before. It's in the Four Corners area of New Mexico, Colorado, Arizona and Utah." I hurried though my explanation without pausing. "I've always wanted to go, and the director has offered me a wonderful summer position as art historian in residence."

"She can't spend every spring and summer break with us, Catherine. She needs a new life of her own, but you could wait and leave this weekend," he smiled and tempted, "We'll take you to lunch at the Bay Cafe in Ft. Walton." My Father was my first hero and he continued to hold the title throughout my life.

After breakfast I made the last sweep of the house, scouting for a book, shoe, or bottle of shampoo I forgot to pack.

"Be careful."

"Drive safely."

"Call us when you get home."

The warnings were always the same as I backed out the long driveway. The outpouring of love and concern from my parents was as strong as the first day I started school. Mother and Daddy stood hand-in-hand in the driveway. They always waved until I was out of sight. I sometimes wondered what they said to one another during those moments. I drove to the end of the street. Today a honk and a quick wave out the window didn't seem enough. I stopped the car, got out, and waved frantically. I began to cry.

When I arrived home I remembered Margaret had gone to Portland for a three-day humanities conference and she wouldn't be home until Sunday night. The weekend stretched endlessly ahead of me with limitless opportunities for leisure and loneliness. I picked up a pencil and paper and began to make my "To Do" list.

Rake the yard. Fertilize the plants. Repaint the bathroom. Get out the summer clothes. Pack the winter clothes. Buy a new telephone cord. I cursed aloud and threw my pencil across the room. Maybe I should have stayed in Florida in the seclusion and protection of my parents' home.

There had been a time when I was good company for myself. But now I viewed myself as the type of controlled, organized, and predictable person I used to critcize and detest. I walked across the room to retrieve my pencil and to ask the Lord's forgiveness for my short temper. I caught sight of my reflection in the mirror across the room.

No one at the university would recognize me in faded jeans and a denim work shirt. At work I hid in a strict disguise of navy, gray, and black tailored wool suits. Strictly business and strictly professorial. I leaned close to the mirror and ran my fingers across the planes of my face. I noticed the lines the years were beginning to finely etch in my face and the way my hands were beginning to weather. Soon I wouldn't be thirty-something; in two years I would be forty-ish. As the Greeks would say, mutability was setting in. That's not to say I wasn't attractive. A tall, shapely woman with hair the color of wheat turns heads when she walks in a room, no matter her age. I had physical power. I knew it. I ran from it.

It was finally six o'clock. I walked through the living room to the kitchen and poured myself a large glass of red wine. I brought the first sip of the night to my lips. I leaned against the sink. The open window sill was filled with votive candles, sea shells, small carved wooden animals, and a tiny ceramic frog with a gold crown. There was also a vial of dirt from Frank Lloyd Wright's Talisien West where I had been a guest two years ago. I looked out the kitchen window at the small lake bordering the back yard. The new foliage on the trees obscured most of the lake. Each summer I vowed to clear the honeysuckle vines and new saplings by the lake and erect a gazebo. But fall came, and winter came, and spring came, and the underbrush grew thicker until it was time to make the same vow again. A dozen mallards and a seasonal heron nested in the ground cover. The downed limbs in the water were a perfect refuge for bass and bream on a hot summer day. Our property was a favorite for fisherman since it was the most natural habitat on the lake. Two men in a small boat were casting toward the shore. How long had it been since I went fishing?

Why wasn't Margaret home? Why hadn't I remembered to get a number where I could call her? I depended on Margaret. I needed her. I had a handful of good friends but it would take me a good hour and two or three glasses of red wine before I could come close to admitting how empty I felt. Margaret was the vault where I hid my secrets.

Seventeen years had passed since we were students in the art department at the University of Memphis, in our day, Memphis State. Time had blurred my recollection of where and when we first met. My first real memory was an evening in November. Margaret unexpectedly entered the sculpture studio with a camera and took a black and white photograph of me. From time-to-time over the years Margaret will unexpectedly hand me the spontaneous photograph. I always look curiously at my face as a young woman. Is the girl in the faded photograph really me? The girl with the careless, smiling manner beaming back at the camera lens. It is an odd pose. Sitting on a pile of wood I playfully picked up a thick tree limb and cradled it in my arms like a baby. The baby I always wanted. The baby I would never have.

There wasn't an early photograph of Margaret. It was Margaret, rendering her likeness in a drawing class self-portrait, that came closest to capturing her mood in the early years: long, straight, dark hair, wire-rimmed glasses, denim shirt, and faded jeans. One of Margaret's lovers criticized the portrait because of her moody facial expression. It was the phallic symbolism of the Champale beer bottle, and Margaret's hand positioned casually near her crotch that made first-time viewers uncomfortable. I loved the picture. Not only did the drawing her display artistic talent, but it reminded me of Margaret when she was young and rebellious.

That first night at Memphis State; the photograph and the new friendship that would stretch across my lifetime, that was the night Margaret confided she was a lesbian.

The drive from my home in Newnan to the Emory campus took an hour. The Emory campus was like an anthill, some part of it was always in motion. Clifton Road bisected the campus and boasted a smorgasbord of prestigious medical facilities; the Center for Disease Control, Emory University Hospital, and Yerkes Primate Research Center. Although the university was highly respected for my department, Art and Archaeology, we were dwarfed by the long shadow cast by the medical profession.

It was hard to believe it was summer. Fall quarter, and the start of a new academic year, would begin in of a couple of months, then it was a downhill slide to Christmas. Life seemed to be accelerating. Today the campus was crowded with eager freshman entering the university a few weeks after their high school graduation. New-student orientation was in full swing and anxious parents and their equally anxious children toured the campus trying to find their bearings and calm their fears. They were like puppies, desperately eager to please, tails wagging, young and vulnerable. The faces of the young girls were like perfectly sculpted masks without flaws or age. How much more interesting were the faces of the older women students whose faces were etched with wonderful stories, too much sun, and too much responsibility.

I loved the Emory library and its quirky architecture, but I loved any library. They recalled memories of my childhood and summers spent with my grandparents in Harlingen, Texas. Their home was not air-conditioned and summer days in the Rio Grande Valley were long and torturously hot. My grandmother took my sister and me to the library every week. It was air-conditioned and freezing inside compared to the unbearable summer heat. It seemed to me all the books were kept under refrigeration which produced a wonderfully distinctive smell. It was a place to linger, carefully considering which books we would take home to read.

In the Emory library I always worked on the fifth floor. My private corner had a long table which allowed me to open up as many books as I needed to study, compare, and evaluate. I took off my heels and paced from one end of the table to the other. I was totally engrossed in making comparisons and recording my observations for an article I was writing on Picasso and Braque. I was trying to determine the truth of what had been written over the years in regard to their exploration of cubism and collage. Braque and Picasso painted like Siamese twins in a type of symbiosis, and believed painting was not a mirror that reflected society, but a language. Braque, a devoted admirer of Cezanne, was a craftsman of the language, but it was Picasso who possessed the sculptural vision to create true dimension on the flat surface of his paintings.

For most individuals, time passes slowly at study, but for me it had always been an indulgence. Being an art history professor allowed me to explore ideas, concepts, and theories of art, music, sociology, and history and how they were all woven together to form a collective tapestry of intelligence. It was not easy to convey to students that art was not about the expression of talent or the creating of lovely things. Art concerned itself with the preservation and the containment of the soul. A great work of art, a symphony, or a poem, arrested life, transformed it, and made it available for others to enjoy. I sometimes smiled about the art historians of the future and the confusion that might arise when they furiously debated whether the golden arches of McDonalds were an "M" or a "W," or whether Barbie was a twenty-first century fertility goddess.

Twice during a trip to Greece, I felt I became a part of art history. The first time was in the National Museum in Athens. In one of the glass cases I saw a hair pin. I was hurled back in time to a small city-state in Greece where each morning a woman pinned her hair with this simple and beautiful ornament. Had it first been her grandmother's and then her mother's, passed down from generation-to-generation and lost in the earth for centuries to be discovered by an archaeologist on a dig?

The second time was at Phaistos, on the island of Crete. As I looked across the hills beyond the ruins of a once magnificent palace, I left my place in time and moved into that shadowy realm where feelings are more important than facts. I had connected intellectually to the grandeur of the Parthenon and the mystery of the Minoan Palace at Knossos, but at Phaistos I connected emotionally. How joyously the people must have lived, surrounded by the Mediterranean Sea and the splendid landscape. I have always believed that time is not a line that begins at the left and, adding years, moves to the right. I believe time is like a stack of cards and that all history layers upward into one eternal flame. At Phaistos, while I watched the swallows hover motionless in the strong Cretan winds, I hovered motionless as well, as a passerby perhaps, or a distant onlooker, but I inhaled Crete's long ago mysteries as effortlessly as I inhaled the fragrant island breeze.

The laughter of a young couple playing chess across the room pulled me back to reality. The chess board was just an excuse for sitting intimately together in a quiet, undisturbed corner of the library. The real game they were playing was courtship; where a man moves two steps forward and a woman moves one step back. As I watched them laugh and tease I smiled, envying the careless abandon with which they were falling in love. They were oblivious to what tomorrow might bring; a detail that becomes a major consideration as the impetuousness of youth is replaced by the reason of age. The boy reached across the table to hold the girl's hand. Their intimacy made me feel suddenly and desperately alone.

I sat, expressionless, staring at the books on the shelf. I began to think of Morgan.

Margaret got off the elevator as the two lovers were leaving. She walked over to my table and sat down.

"How did you know I'd be here?"

"Sarah Hanley, you've become predictable, and I say it with all love and affection." There was no escape. Margaret was going to speak her mind, no sugar and spice, no polite conversation, no pretense or niceties. I bit the right inside corner of my mouth, a habit I had developed over the years that surfaced whenever I was nervous or deep in thought, but mostly nervous.

"Predictable?" I repeated the term once abhorrent to me, but which was now a pretty damn good description. I looked straight into Margaret's eyes and, resigned that she was right, said nothing more.

"Name three things you used to do that you don't do anymore."

"Only three? The list is endless! Do you want them in order?" Thoughtfully, I answered. "Have sex with strangers. Go without underwear. And drink Jack Daniels straight from the bottle."

"Why not?"

"In the words of Shirley Valentine, I'll soon be 39 not 22. I'd be just another stupid woman looking for adventure and the time for adventure is over."

"No, you simply assassinated the woman whose first and last name was Adventure — yourself. You've become a child of Saturn."

"What, pray tell, is a child of Saturn?"

"Depressed. Five hundred years ago people chronically disposed to melancholy were identified with the Roman god Saturn, and known as 'children of Saturn.' But, on a more positive note, Saturn locates identity deeply within the soul, not simply on the surface of the personality."

Margaret was right, but Margaret loved me anyway. To the rest of the world I was intelligent, accomplished, capable, and professional. Everyone seemed to prefer me this way. Neatly tied down and matured, rather than the loaded gun that used to chase shots of tequila with beer and jalapenos, jump in fountains, and attract lovers like swarming fireflies.

"How many times are you going to read that book?" She pointed to the shabby paperback inside a ziplock bag.

"I can't explain it, but every time I read Osborne Russell's *Journal of a Trapper*, it's comforting somehow."

"Comforting, my ass. You've had a crush on Russell since I met you twenty years ago. I'm not a psychiatrist, but I don't think it's healthy to be in love with a man that died over a hundred years ago."

"You're right, you're not a shrink."

"Sarah, I want you to go someplace with me." Margaret leaned forward and lowered her voice as if she was going to tell me a secret. "I want you to go to St. George for the annual Cherokee powwow. Remember, we had planned to go a few years ago."

"Oh, please, Margaret! Things were different then." I threw up my hands in an attempt to convey my position of resistance. I hated myself for it, but I began to whine in protest.

"When was the last time you went camping? You used to love to pitch a tent in a campground, or in a field, or what about the time you camped in Miriam's front yard in midtown Memphis in the middle of the winter?"

"Things were different then."

"Sarah, you were different then, you weren't so . . . "

"Predictable?" I interrupted.

Margaret nodded. I knew she was right. I had no where to hide. She knew me too well.

"The powwow is this weekend."

"Margaret, I just got back from Florida."

"What does that have to do with this? You used to jump in the car even if it was to ride to the grocery store to get a quart of milk. This will be fun! Remember Ruth Woolrich? I introduced her to you at the luncheon the day you received the Governor's Award in the Humanities. She's a member of the Cherokee nation. She'll be there and she can introduce us to people you would never meet in a classroom."

"I don't know where my camping stuff is."

"I'll bring everything, even a couple bottles of Bulls Blood."

"You and that Hungarian wine."

"We'll leave at 3:00 o'clock Friday."

I didn't answer. I didn't tell her it was too hot for a campfire. I didn't tell her I hated the smell of inspect repellent and that the mosquitoes would be thicker than fleas on the Georgia/Florida line. I didn't tell her rattlesnakes partied in the dense palmetto this time of year. I didn't tell her I was too tired, or I needed to clean my house. I didn't tell her because I didn't want to further embarrass myself.

"Okay, I'll go.

Chapter 2

Margaret was impressed with my punctuality. We left at 3:00 p.m. for St. George as we had planned. I arrived with one overnight bag, and my pillow. The trip would take a good seven hours and we would have to set up camp in the dark.

"What are you teaching this fall?" asked Margaret.

"Intro to Art, Northwest Indian Art, and Architecture as Sculpture."

"It seems like yesterday we were the students. I guess it's like Indiana Jones says, 'It's not the years, it's the miles.'" She looked at me with a sly gleam in her eyes. "Feel like reminiscing about our past?"

"Okay, I'll play." I took her challenge, "See if you can remember something we've done together that I've forgotten."

"That should be fairly easy considering the brain cells we've destroyed over the years. What about the time we were in Emily's sexual response research project at the University of Tennessee?"

"Ah, yes, I remember proudly announcing to my close friends that I was going to masturbate for science! How much did we get paid?"

"I think they paid us five dollars, but we weren't exactly doing it for the money."

"Didn't we get a certificate?"

"No, we didn't get a certificate! What would it have read? I can see it now on your office wall with the rest of your awards and degrees."

And so we began. Retort for retort, shot for shot. It was the joy, and it was equally the danger of sharing a past with someone who knew entirely too much.

"What about the time you were a guest speaker at Georgia State?" Her mouth was stretched in a tight thin line. She knew exactly what I was going to say. "We got a cab after the conference and asked the driver to go through the window at McDonalds, and then we went to that lesbian bar. What was it? The Sports Page? I don't think it's in business now." I paused determining just how ruthlessly to proceed. "In thirty minutes you had a woman that sold real estate, insurance or something like that, madly in love with you, and a middle-aged man hitting on you at the bar."

"He was somebody's grandfather."

"Oh, was that the fascination? Did he show you his AARP membership card before you disappeared to the parking lot and into the backseat of his car? You were out of your mind!"

"I was drunk." It was a lousy defense.

"Your sexual experience with men is limited to losing your virginity to Greg DeVane and having oral sex with somebody's grandfather . . . you know, there are other options."

"If I could have found a man like Morgan, well, I can't say. There aren't many men like him around. But you know that, that's why you married him."

We fell into silence, each remembering how much we loved him and how much it hurt to have him gone. Hot tears filled my eyes. I didn't want to cry.

Margaret tried to stop my inevitable flood of emotions,

"Sarah, Morgan was a soldier, he died a hero."

Morgan died a hero, and everything died with him. Our marriage had never been one of dependency, but his death amputated my spirit. We had a passion for one another. He loved me dearly. He was the kind of man that passed the time in a bookstore instead of in a bar. He wouldn't approve of my present behavior. If he was looking down on me tonight, I knew he would want me to assassinate the impostor that had taken control of my body and withered my heart.

I said nothing. I felt as if a rope was tightening around my neck, the emotions were so strong. My grief washed over me in waves. I remembered the first time I realized I had gone an entire day without crying. I was riding home to Newnan from Atlanta about 9:30 at night when I thought, My God, I haven't cried today. Even three years later my sorrow often disabled me.

Margaret gave me privacy to resurrect my feelings of loss and abandonment, but resumed the conversation saying, "Sarah, I think you should start dating. Morgan died more than three years ago. You need to start living again. You're trapped in a bardo state."

"I don't have the vaguest idea what you're talking about."

"The *Tibetan Book of the Dead* describes the time between incarnations, the period before the next birth of life, as bardo. You've imprisoned yourself in a dead, cold, unrelated world. You don't want to participate in life. You're between lives, Sarah. Get in the game for God's sake. You're certainly not the woman I once knew." Her last remark was uncalled for and she knew it, but she let it lie.

We rode for miles in silence. I knew she was right, but I also knew she would always stand by me. The sun was casting long shadows across the landscape. The clouds stretched like flimsy gauze across the violet sky. The soft golden light of sunset reflected on Margaret's face. How unconventionally pretty she was. The long, dark straight hair of her youth had been cropped short and was now salt and pepper gray. Her face was full and soft.

I took out the road atlas to check our progress before daylight was gone. "A couple more exits and we'll get onto highway 376 to St. George."

"Next exit I have to go to the bathroom. Do you want me to drive?"

"No, I can make it another hour. Besides, you don't like to drive at night." Margaret pulled off the Interstate at the next exit.

"I'll pay for the gas. What do you want to drink?" I asked.

"Get me a Yoo Hoo." She got out to pump the gas.

"A Yoo Hoo? Do you want a moon pie to go with it?" When I returned to the truck I was aware of the loud sounds and the heavy smell of Interstate traffic, exhaust fumes, and gasoline. I handed Margaret her Yoo Hoo and pulled one of two quarts of Budweiser from a brown paper bag.

"Thirsty?"

I filled my mouth with ice cold beer and swallowed. "Did I ever tell you about the bar in Memphis that only sold beer in quarts?"

"No, I'm intrigued. I find it hard to believe you have a story in your repertoire I have never heard before!"

"When Morgan and I lived downtown in Memphis at 99 North Main, on the weekends we would explore the ends of the Mid-America Mall. The east/west ends of downtown were far more interesting because the developers hadn't moved in yet. This was long before anyone ever thought of the Pyramid, or condos on the Mississippi River, and A. Schwabs was the only business not boarded up on Beale Street. Anyway, Morgan and I went inside this bar in Pinch, on the west end of Main Street, that was certainly not included in the Chamber of Commerce's *Visitors' Guide to Memphis*. The only two people inside were black, as was the case in most of the really interesting and authentic places in downtown Memphis. It was empty except for an elderly man behind the counter and a really good looking middle-aged woman, sort of a Tina Turner look-alike. Eight or maybe ten tables and metal chairs with torn red vinyl cushions were arranged in the back half of the room. In the front of the room was a juke box and lots of empty space so people could dance. There were no windows and the only exit I could see was the front door. The menu was painted on the wall behind the counter, where the food was cooked for the world to see. There weren't any words but primitive paintings of bacon, eggs, and toast, cheeseburgers, fries, pie, and a bottle of beer with the prices beneath. Under the bottle of beer was written, *Our beer so cold you have to put it in the oven before you drink it* and another, *Our beer's colder than your ex-wife's heart.* We ordered two beers and the man brought two quarts.

"My kind of place," said Margaret.

"Morgan went to the juke box to play some music and break the tension. After awhile the woman came over and asked me to dance. I was shocked by her invitation but Morgan said, "Sure, she'll dance with you.""

"And did you?"

"Of course I did, and not just one dance, but two or three. Morgan knew he could overpower the old man behind the counter, but I don't think he was sure about the woman."

"That's a great story. I can easily picture Morgan offering you as a sacrifice."

"He thought it was highly amusing."

We crossed the state line from Georgia into Florida. The map showed that we reentered Georgia in about twelve miles.

"We need to look for signs to show where to get off the highway. June said the signs might be hard to spot in the dark." Within fifteen minutes we pulled off highway 94 onto a deserted dirt road. We turned into a field at hand-painted sign that read *PowWow.*

Our headlights followed the tire tracks of other cars, but there was no one in sight. Three deer jumped back into the tree line and palmetto. It was eleven o'clock at night. Almost two hours after sunset, the early summer heat was still clinging to the land. The heat released the sweet, woodsy smell of the earth. The night was filled with the sounds of insects and the unmistakable hum of human conversations somewhere ahead in the dark. Within a few minutes our headlights shone on a great gathering of tents, trailers, cars, and trucks, where those still awake sat in lawn chairs illuminated by Coleman lanterns and an occasional campfire. The harsh brightness of our headlights invaded their privacy and the intimacy of their late-night conversations. It took ten minutes to find an area where we could camp and have the privacy to relieve ourselves without walking to the portable johns down the road.

Margaret and I moved quietly, whispering as we set up our tent by flashlight. The stars were incredible. It was one of those rare nights when it seemed we were experiencing the heavens for the first time. The infinite canopy of darkness was ablaze with millions of stars burning fiercely; red, blue and hot white. There was a feeling in the night. The air was warm, heavy, and humid like a soft wool blanket wrapped around my shoulders, hips and legs. As I breathed I felt I was inhaling something living. I looked at Margaret. I wondered, "Can she feel it?" I was too tired to put words to the high electricity of emotions I was experiencing. I felt as though I was a radio receiver and waves from a far away and timeless place were trying to communicate with me.

We crawled on our hands and knees into the tent. We slept in our t-shirts on top of our sleeping bags. I lay motionless for a long time, listening to the night.

I whispered, "Margaret, thank you for making me come this weekend."

She was already asleep.

Chapter 3

Saturday was filled with ceremonial dancing, singing, and a loosely structured program of speakers and activities. The genuine charm of the powwow was that it had the spontaneity and warmth of a family reunion. Ruth Woolrich spent the morning with us but Margaret and I went our separate ways after lunch. I wanted to wander and meet some of the artists who had brought their work on display.

At one time the state of Georgia had included land that is now Mississippi and Alabama. In 1835 gold was found on Cherokee land and they were forced to cede their lands to the United States. In 1838, the Supreme Court ruled that Indians had the legal right to stay in their ancestral homes, but President Jackson disagreed. To drive the Indians out of the state, Georgia offered to give up almost two-thirds of its land area. The federal government accepted the plan and more than 18,000 men, women and children were herded out of the state on the Trail of Tears. Many fled into the swamps of north Florida and for generations, did not admit their heritage. This annual powwow, held near the Florida-Georgia line, was close to the swamps where many Cherokee had taken refuge.

About five o'clock, hot and thirsty, I made my way back to our campsite. The sky was overcast and the air was steamy and humid. I spread a blanket in the shade of the truck, and opened the ice chest to retrieve the second quart of beer. I placed the bottle against my throat. Pieces of ice dropped from the brown bottle, slipped into my shirt, and fell on my breasts. It brought back the memory of John Henson and the most erotic moment in my life. I hadn't thought about him in years.

John, Evan and I were in college together. I was 21 and Evan and John were 20. I had known Evan a couple of years. He was a slender 6' 3" with long hair the color of a raven at midnight. He would enter the Memphis State cafeteria wearing a red Hudson's Bay blanket draped around his broad shoulders and all eyes would turn to watch him. The blanket was tied in the front with rawhide thongs wrapped around two smooth river stones tied under the wool. We would sit for hours talking about the West and about a summer trip he and John were planning to Wyoming. They planned to travel across the Wind River Mountains on horseback living as mountain men, before the opening of the Oregon Trail.

John was 5' 10" and as blonde as Evan was dark. He would occasionally mimic Evan's Indian costume or wear the leather shirt and leggings he had sewn for their trip. He looked better in blue jeans and a denim work shirt than most men looked in tuxedos. For eight weeks the three of us were inseparable. We went to bars, to concerts, and to street parties in Overton Square. They taught me how to enter a room with a presence so strong that everyone within seventy feet would turn to look. It was a sweet power. I was attracted to Evan and John not only because of their arresting handsome physiques, but because of the drama with which they lived their lives.

Evan and John were going to Wyoming mid-June. I visited the student employment office on campus to find a summer job. I saw a brochure posted from the Girl Scout Council of Texas. They needed a unit leader for Peachcreek Ranch, a primitive camp outside Houston, that offered horseback riding for girls age seven through twelve. On the application I was asked to list my expertise in knot craft, horseback riding, cooking in a fire pit, swimming, orienteering, plant identification, first aid, canoeing, and camping. I checked every box, claiming I had skills in all areas when, in fact, I could only swim to save my life and, to my credit, ride a horse with the best. I had never even been a Girl Scout! But they hired me and that was the summer I grew up.

Had it been so many years ago since the three of us parted for our separate summer journeys: Evan and John to Lander, Wyoming, and I to New Caney, Texas? In early July, I received a letter from them asking me to come to Wyoming and make the return trip from Jackson to Lander. In August, with only one two-week session of camp remaining, I quit. I sent my parents a postcard saying I was leaving camp to go to Wyoming. I omitted I was going to hitchhike from Austin.

My last hitch was from Rock Springs to Jackson. I got out on a corner of the town square. On each of the four corners of the square were hundreds of elk antlers lashed together to form four huge archways. Sitting on the grass in the hot summer sun, as if my arrival had been scheduled, was Evan. Exhausted and sunburned, I had hitchhiked 2,000 miles in three days and two nights. It was as if I was being driven by an invisible force, and I couldn't distinguish whether the force was within me, or outside of me. I never found out. My journey never happened.

Their invitation to join them was written before they started their trip over the mountains. By the time they crossed the Continental Divide and arrived in Jackson they had nearly starved to death, been kicked by their horses, eaten alive by mosquitoes, and lived in pure Hell to hear Evan tell the story. I recalled a highly romantic comment they made one spring night before they left Memphis, "What is life without horses?" By the time I reached Jackson, Evan was considering shooting his horse rather than taking it back across the country.

Someone, I think his name was Jim, came to Jackson and drove Evan and me back to Lander. John had gone ahead to find work while Evan waited for me. We were stuck in Lander. Evan and John had been brought to Wyoming by John's brother who had long since returned to Memphis. We had little money, so we accepted an invitation to stay with Jim, his wife, and their three-month old baby in a two-bedroom apartment in a housing project.

I was furious. I had hitchhiked across the country to ride horseback across the Continental Divide, but instead drove by the Tetons like a damn tourist. I was angry my dream was not going to come true. I was still angry, years later, because I never confronted either of them. I didn't have the resources, the knowledge, or the confidence to make the trip over the mountains alone. I despised myself for my stupidity.

We returned from Wyoming Labor Day weekend. In late September John called and asked me to celebrate his birthday with him. We made plans to go fishing in Arkansas for the weekend. I had never been alone with him. We left Memphis after dark Friday after he finished work. After driving a couple of hours we reached our destination. I remember John put a blanket on the ground; no pillows, tent, or air mattress, we simply lay down together and he wrapped his arms around me. His chest was pressed tightly against my back. The sexual tension between us was so intense I didn't think I could possibly fall asleep. We lay in the dark not saying a word.

The next morning we drove to town to buy fishing licenses and to buy bait. The small country store kept crickets and minnows in old soft drink coolers in the women's bathroom. It was too hot for the fish to bite. In retrospect, I don't remember ever fishing; maybe we did. We camped by a small stream back in the woods and away from the main road. Even though it was late September, it was unbearably hot and we were miserable. We spent most of the afternoon talking about how much Evan hated Wyoming, and about the people we met during the summer.

John opened the ice chest to get a beer. Without saying a word, he untied the blue bandana from his neck and dropped it into the ice and cold water. I was seated across from him, cross-legged on the ground. Leaning forward, he reached for my shirt. With both hands he slowly unsnapped the white pearl buttons on my faded burgundy western shirt. I was stunned. I sat motionless in the hot sunlight, before a man I had desired since the day

I met him. My breasts were wet with perspiration. John reached into the ice chest for the bandana. He moved the wet, frigid cloth across my face, my throat, around my neck, and across my breasts. I gasped as he touched me and he saw my body for the first time. After a couple of minutes he buttoned my shirt, kissed me lightly, and retied the bandana around his neck.

That night we slept close together as the night before. I assumed his sexual overture earlier in the afternoon foretold our lovemaking by the campfire that evening, but it was many weeks before we made love.

The heat of the day, the beer, and the languid memory of John lulled me to sleep. I awakened with a chill. The sun had set and the earth was gradually giving up its heat to the onset of night. Earlier in the day Margaret had given me instructions where to join her for a women's storytelling session. With flashlight in hand, I made my way past a half a mile of trailers and tents before I identified the grove she had described. A group of fifty women were gathered in a field fifty yards away near the tree line. Even at a distance I could see the outlines of their bodies against the amber glow of the campfire. As I approached, I heard soft singing and chanting rising high above the tree tops like smoke rising to the sky. I walked around the circle of standing women, trying to find a break in the crowd to enter the group.

I took my place in the circle and looked inside. Standing in the center was an old woman. Golden light emanated from her body. It was as though her spirit, weathered and mysterious, illuminated everything around her with its divinity. Her hands were like the roots of a great tree where they meet the earth. They were crooked and strong as if they had courageously clung to the earth many times to avoid being uprooted by great violent storms. Her hands were raised to the night sky, and she spoke of an ancient time when women shared their knowledge to bring balance, wisdom, and truth to their people. There was a joy and a peacefulness in her voice that poured into my ears and filled my consciousness. I felt like an insect furiously beating my wings and flying blindly into the bright light. My heart was racing. I could not move. I could not breathe.

I don't remember how many stories she told, or how much time passed. I suddenly realized the circle had collapsed and the women were dispersing and moving away. I could not understand the complacency with which the women accepted the phenomenon. Where was Margaret? The old woman turned and moved slowly and gracefully across the field. I could not understand why this magnificent Light Being was coming toward me. We stood alone; the wide expanse of the recently mowed field before us, and the secretive darkness of the forest behind us. My body was frozen with wonder, amazement, and disbelief. Calmly, and sweetly, she took my hands. Without speaking we looked into one another's eyes. Standing close to her I could tell she was very old, and yet she stood powerful and erect. Her face, weathered, soft and joyful, resembled an Alfred Steiglitz portrait of Georgia O'Keefe where each of life's sorrows and responsibilities had been magnificently etched.

"I have waited for you all of my life," she said. "When I was a young girl my great great grandmother, a member of the Bannock tribe, told me someday you would come, but I am an old woman, and I had almost given up hope."

"I don't understand."

"I recognize you by the golden light that fills and surrounds you. We all radiate the same light, but most choose to go through life asleep, and their light does not shine." Reflected in her dark eyes like a mirror, I saw my illuminated aura.

We walked slowly, her hand on my arm, until we reached her camper. Her grown children, and her grandchildren played dominoes on a metal folding table under the light of a Coleman lantern. They smiled, and nodded as if they understood why I was there. The two of us sat in blue plastic lawn chairs, away from the others and the harsh light of the hissing lantern. I didn't know what to say, so I waited for her to begin.

"I told many stories tonight. But there is one story I have kept since I was a little girl. It is the story my great great grandmother gave me. She said one day I would meet a beautiful woman filled with the golden light of the first rays of the sunrise and surrounded by the golden light of the last rays of the sunset. She told me to hold the story in my heart and to share it only with you." Once again she took my hands in hers as though we were both links in a supernatural chain. I hung on each word she said, hoping one of them would force me back to reality. I wanted to understand what I was seeing and hearing, and what was happening inside of me.

She began. "Our life is a path. All of life is a journey. We all make the journey, some journey for a short time or, if they are fortunate like me, for many years. As we each make our journey, we carve our trail into the side of the mountains, but sometimes we stray from the trail we are meant to travel. You have become lost. Your face has come from beneath the ground many times, but you have strayed from the trail that belongs only to you. My great great grandmother said I must tell you there is a spirit blanket that allows a horse and its rider to travel across the seasons. You must find the blanket and ride across the seasons. Until you make this journey, you will remain lost and unable to fulfill your destiny. Do you understand?"

"No."

She smiled at me as if she was my own great great grandmother. "There are no more answers for you," she said softly, squeezing my hand to comfort me. "You have heard the story I have carried throughout my life for you. The story is where you begin. Your destiny possesses a richness you can't imagine. May the Creator bless you."

Before I could structure a question, two of her children came to help her into the small camper. I stood awkwardly not knowing what to do or where to go. She turned to me and raised her hand in a gesture of a blessing. Her children resumed their domino game. I tried to remember how to get back to our camp.

Margaret listened to my story when I returned to camp. How could I expect her to believe the incredible events that had happened? She hung on my words as I told her the surrealistic circumstances of the evening. About the golden light around the old woman, and the golden light she said surrounded me. About the prophesy of her great great grandmother, and the story about the blanket that would take a horse and its rider across the seasons. She told me I must find it? Where would I find such a blanket even if one was to exist?

Our tent was suffocating. I took my blanket and pillow into the bed of the truck and looked heavenward into a sea of stars. I felt vulnerable, confused, and aggravated that I was left without answers to my many questions. It was crazy, absolutely crazy. And yet, there was a voice within me that was singing after having been silenced for many years. A voice I had outgrown and abandoned. An inner voice that was very much at home in a sense of time that reached beyond the limits of ordinary life and into the great mysteries of the eternal. I thanked God for my life and, as I did every night, asked Him to use my life to His glory.

At the first sign of daybreak, I awakened Margaret and we went to find the old woman to ask her the questions that had haunted me during the night. It was Sunday morning and many families were packing to leave before the heat of the day became oppressive. When we finally found her campsite it was deserted, and her family's camper was gone.

"My God, Margaret! I can't believe she's left." I stood frozen in the vacant spot where we had talked a few hours before.

"Did you know her? The old one?" A middle-age woman in denim shorts and a NASCAR t-shirt joined us.

"I met her last night. We sat here together."

"Her long journey was over. Her family took her home early this morning," said the woman. "She died last night."

Chapter 4

We arrived in Atlanta late Sunday. Margaret encouraged me to spend the night. I didn't argue. By the time we unloaded her truck and put away the camping gear, the sun had set and it was that in-between time before day ends and night begins. We spent the evening in her garage studio drinking Jack Daniels out of coffee cups while she glazed her pottery.

"What time is your first class in the morning?" asked Margaret.

"Eleven. What about you? Do you have to be at the humanities council at 8:30?"

"Nope. I got a break from Dr. Leonard. I'm scheduled to conduct a grant writing workshop in Macon. I don't have to leave until ten." She held a small ceramic box incised with beautiful curvilinear shapes on its four sides and the lid.

"Sarah, are you going to tell anyone what happened this weekend?"

"Are you kidding? Who would I tell? And what would I tell them? Hey, you won't believe what happened to me this weekend! I went to a Cherokee powwow and met an Indian woman who was ninety years old, give or take a few years, and she told me she'd been waiting for me all her life. It seems her great great grandmother told her one day she would meet me. And, pay close attention because this is the really good part, she was kind of different! She glowed in the dark! She told me I was the one her great great grandmother had spoken of because I glowed in the dark, too! She also told me I had to find a spirit blanket that would take a horse and its rider across the seasons. She said I had to find this "magic" blanket and make a journey, that, and here I pause with dramatic emphasis, "Is My Destiny!" Does that just about sum it up? Have I left anything out? Oh, excuse me, yes, I did. I forgot to mention that the next morning when I went back to talk to the woman I learned she had died during the night! Who would believe such a story, in fact, it's amazing that you believe me!"

I held my head in my hands. I was exasperated. I picked up the bottle of Jack Daniels. "Do you want another drink?"

"Nah, I'm not the woman I used to be," apologized Margaret.

"Well, neither am I, and occasionally that fact alone drives me to drink." I poured the caramel colored liquor into my coffee cup. Its strong, familiar smell filled my nose. It was warm in my mouth and it burned the back of my throat. I could taste it on my tongue, the sides of my mouth, and in my nose.

"Drink all the Jack Daniels you want, Jack Daniels makes you cry, but it doesn't make you crazy. Tequila makes you crazy."

"Tequila? Never again! My thirtieth birthday party cured me of that dangerous habit. Ten shots of tequila chased by ten bears."

"You mean ten beers, not ten bears."

"Whatever. Ten shots of tequila, chased by ten BEERS, and five jalapeno peppers stuffed with cream cheese. The next day I felt like some-one had given me a lobotomy with a rusty can opener. It took me three days to recover. Tequila! Never." I raised my right hand and solemnly made the vow again.

"One night I was drinking tequila before I went backpacking on the Appalachian Trail for thirteen days. I spent the night at a friend's farm before leaving for Knoxville the next morning. We started playing cards and whoever drew the low card had to drink a shot of tequila. I forgot I was heating Snow Seal on the stove to waterproof my hiking boots and I set one of the kitchen cabinets on fire."

"Ah, the things we omit from our resumes! If the rest of the world only knew you like I do! Pour me another drink., I can see where this is heading. One of us will be cussing or crying before the night is over."

My eyes were fixed on Margaret as she worked. I noticed how delib-erately she selected the glazes and how patiently she applied each color. How many times since we were young women had I passed the time talk-ing to her and watching her work, mixing the clay, mixing the glazes. Her strong hands sculpted the clay, the earth's body, to her artistic will.

Her sketches and her old photographs were thumb tacked to the walls of her studio. The unpainted wooden shelves we built together looked like an apothecary store with each Mason jar precisely arranged with the differ-ent glazes and chemicals. They were flanked on each side by worn and stained textbooks that we had paged through year after year like ancient alchemists. The battered trash can we used to raku our pots stood in the corner. To me her possessions were priceless artifacts that should be pro-tected within the tight security of a museum. I walked to the trash can, removed the lid, and looked inside the charred cavity.

Margaret smiled and went back to work. My memories had taken me far away from her studio. I privately reminisced about the first time she asked me to gather sticks, leaves, and pine cones and place them into the garbage can. I didn't know what on earth she planned to do with them, but it was all of great interest to me. After we filled the can we put on heavy asbestos gloves and used long steel tongs to carefully remove the fiery red ceramic sculpture from the blazing kiln. When the glowing sculpture was placed in the garbage can the intense heat burst the organic matter into flame. Replacing the lid extinguished the fire, but the smoldering leaves and sticks burned the body of the clay a sensual, smoky black. The smell was supremely wonderful and its odor always lingered in the can. Like the familiar smell of the whiskey in my coffee cup, it brought back memories of the sisterhood she and I had forged of clay and steel, Jack Daniels and raku.

I noticed she had stopped working. "What are you thinking?"

"Sarah, what if we . . ."

"What if we? What?" I moved across the room and sat in a wooden folding chair.

"Maybe we're looking at your encounter all wrong. What if we look at this weekend without using our twenty-first century, high-tech minds? What if we assume everything the old woman said is true and everything she said could really happen. What if we focus on the possibility and not the impossibility? Have you ever read Thomas Moore's *Care of the Soul*?"

"No."

"Moore wrote that the infinite inner space of a story is its soul. If we deprive sacred stories of their mystery, we are left with the literalism of a single meaning. But, when a story is allowed its soul, we can discover our own depths. It's true that if you told anyone the version you repeated to me, they would think you were mentally unbalanced. But the inner space of the story is that this weekend you met a woman of incredible spirit, and somehow the two of you are connected in time. She shared her vision with you, a story she had guarded for you since she was a child, and she told of a journey you have to make. As for the light you saw, auras are not an uncommon phenomenon among people who are psychically sensitive. Don't deprive your story of its soul."

"Believe her story is true and believe it could happen? Are you really saying we should believe there is a blanket that will take a horse and its rider across the seasons? Across the seasons where? To jump from New Year's Day to the Fourth of July? To change the future? To change the past? It's impossible."

"Why do we need to expose everything that's hidden? To understand all mysteries? We don't know whether we'll make it home tomorrow. We each have our individual faiths, but neither of us can explain what happened to Morgan when he died. We don't have any answers or any guarantees but we go on living every day. We go on because of the 'possibility' that the dreams we dream and the things we want for our lives will come true. And, even when they don't come true we still go on."

She waited for my response. Of course, she was right. I believed there were mysteries beyond the scope of reason. The inexplicable alternative seemed strange, but it was wildly appealing to my "shadow," the person I had not become because of the choices I had made in my life. The physical world with its death, violence, grief, and cruelty, was the reality that should be impossible. Magic, the spiritual, the supernatural, the invisible, and the unexplained were much more palatable.

"Well, I don't know why I'm making such a big deal out of this. I believe in Santa Claus, the Easter Bunny, and the tooth fairy. It seems like a blanket that can take a horse and its rider across the seasons shouldn't be that much of a stretch for me."

"You're drunk, Sarah, but you're absolutely right"

We sat in silence for a couple of minutes. "Margaret, I don't know if I ever told you this. It's always been difficult for me to verbalize, so I doubt I've mentioned it." I realized I was rambling. "Besides, as I've gotten older, it doesn't seem to matter anymore."

"Well, you certainly have my attention now."

"Since I was a young woman, maybe 19 or 20, I've always felt I was here on earth for a very special reason, a very particular reason. Perhaps it's egocentric to think such a thing, but I have always intuitively felt there was *Something* out there ahead of me, waiting for me. It's hard to explain. Maybe *It* is something that will happen to me, or a door I will go through, or maybe a person I will meet. But *It* is *Something* in time meant only for me." I shook my head to offer an apology for such nonsense but I continued.

"Over the years I've become frustrated it was all a hallucination. I thought I had simply invented the idea, and there wasn't *Something* magical or special ahead of me. Maybe I just imagined the whole thing." I was embarrassed to speak my thoughts aloud, even to Margaret.

"I had a strange dream ten years ago. In my dream there wasn't any background or foreground, or sky, only an immense horizon. It wasn't day or night, or inside or outside. The dream didn't have any of those physical reference points we use to determine where we are. I was standing in a long line of people of different races and ages. They were talking to one other and visiting. The line moved very slowly. I noticed a large oak table at the end of the line. As each person got to the table they were writing something in a book. I had no idea what they are doing, or why we were standing in the line. I turned to an elderly woman behind me, I'll never forget her face, she looked familiar to me, but I had never met her before. I asked if she could please tell me what they were writing in the book. She said simply, "God says in the Bible, in My house there are many mansions and I go to prepare a place for you. We live many lives on our way to eternity. God is asking us to write who we really are; the name of our true soul." Then she resumed talking to the people behind her. As I got closer to the front of the line I became more and more agitated because I didn't know what name to write. I didn't know who I was or who else I might have been, but when it was my turn, my hand automatically picked up the pen and wrote a name on the page. I recognized the name and was shocked to see who I really was. When I awoke I didn't remember the name I had written."

"What an incredible dream. I wonder what I would have written."

"I believe the dream was trying to show me God's plan for our lives is infinitely more complex than we can imagine or intellectualize; so you're right. I will try to focus on the possibilities and not on the impossibilities."

"Maybe the journey the old woman said you must make is what has been waiting for you."

"Maybe, but maybe it's just a myth I created."

"Joseph Campbell said the myth is the public dream and the dream is the private myth. Myths are a way of imagining and they're not concerned with fact. Mythologies often begin with physical evidence but they're not concerned with literal causes; they're concerned with insightful imaginings and the truths of human life. That's enough for tonight! What time is it anyway? I'm tired, let's clean up."

I didn't argue. It was only the adrenalin of the weekend keeping me awake. Margaret carefully washed each brush and I sealed the jars of glaze. The studio was tidy when we locked the door. As we walked the thirty yards from the garage studio to her house, we both noticed the sky ablaze with stars. We didn't speak, we just looked at the black expanse of sky. We listened to the sounds of the city crowding in around us; the muffled voices from the neighborhood houses, the cars from Interstate 285, and the symphonic orchestra of insects. We smelled the fresh fragrance of recently mowed summer grass and the sweet honeysuckle growing on the chain link fence.

"You know, Sarah, it's absolutely amazing how much a life can change in twenty-four hours."

I went to bed but I couldn't sleep. I tossed and turned a couple of hours. I felt the ceiling, the walls, and the floor closing in on me. It was suffocating. I impulsively pulled the blanket off the bed and wrapped it around my shoulders. I left the house. I paced back and forth in the deep field behind Margaret's house like an animal trapped inside a small wire cage. My thoughts raced and flew before me like subliminal messages on a movie screen. I lay down on the ground turning my face and my thoughts to the heavens.

Where is Morgan? I wondered. Is he on the other side of the night and is the darkness simply a veil that keeps us apart? Can he see me? Are the stars pinholes in the heavens where God's light shines through and allows those who have gone before to see those of us who are left behind?

I recalled one storyteller at the powwow referring to the Milky Way as a river strewn with shining rocks. What beautiful imagery! Are the seasons of which the old woman spoke seasons of the year or seasons of a greater time? And where was she now? What name did she write in God's book when it came her turn at the head of the line?

I thought of one of the stories the old woman told in the sacred circle. It was the story of where the buffaloes began, deep beneath the waters of a great lake. I must have fallen asleep because I dreamed I stood on the lake's shore as the buffaloes came up from the lake; the water shining on their dark shaggy coats, their black horns gleaming in the moonlight. I dreamed of the ageless stories Margaret had told me over the years of the daughters of Copper Woman.

The earth beneath me was supple and soft. I felt gently cradled as I pressed my body into my Mother Earth. My fingers tightly clenched the wet grass and my body took root in the earth to find the courage and strength I had lost. The night roared in my ears. I prayed and placed myself in a bubble of Christ Light.

I fell asleep.

The early morning sky was filled with clouds and splendid color. The robins were hard at work raking up the earth with their sharp feet to find their breakfast. The rye grass stood high around me. The wet and the cold made me shudder, but it made me feel very much alive! The morning sky seemed to shimmer and vibrate. How wonderful to be alive. I was at peace; serenely, calmly, and joyfully at peace, as I lay in the open field. For the first time since I heard the old woman's story, I didn't feel the need to struggle to find the answers. The tree branches resembled black lace against the breaking dawn. The sky resembled a landscape. A bank of deep indigo clouds rose in sharp contrast to the golden sky that stretched endlessly beyond. I watched the panorama shift and change. The contours of the clouds were sharp and angular. The shapes were familiar to me.

"What is that silhouette in the clouds?" I studied the sky.

Suddenly it was as clear to me as if God had whispered in my ear. Could it be this simple? Was this my imagination? The inky blue clouds, sharp and angular, silhouetted against the soft gold of the early morning sky were the unmistakable peaks of the Grand Tetons. With every instinct I possessed, I knew the journey I had to make was to cross the Wind River Mountains on horseback. The journey I was promised as a young woman. The journey that was stolen from me. It did not matter that the details had not been revealed to me. Perhaps to ride across the seasons simply meant to go back and complete the history that should have already been a part of my past. In my life of predictability, I heard a distant echo or perhaps it was a siren's song that sweetly and seductively called to me. I instinctively reached out my hand to grab Ariadne's magic thread to guide me safely out of the dark labyrinth within which I had abandoned my soul.

I heard the concern in Margaret's voice as she shouted from the back porch, "Sarah, are you all right?" I sat up in the grass and then stood and waved to reassure her.

"Yes, I'm fine. Come here."

I anxiously looked overhead. I wanted confirmation that she also recognized the distinctive summits of the Tetons in the clouds, but the mirage had changed as quickly as it had formed. Margaret stood beside me concerned about my odd behavior and appearance. She saw the tears on my face, the pieces of wet grass clinging to my legs and arms like long, green strands of cellophane in an Easter basket. My blue cotton gown was laminated to the contours of my body by the dew.

"Margaret, I know the journey I have to make. I'm going to Wyoming and cross the Wind River Range on horseback and make the journey I dreamed of when I was young. I'm certain it's the journey in the old woman's story."

"My God, Sarah, I think you're beginning to live again."

Chapter 5

My classes dragged on forever. I felt guilty rushing through the final review before exams, but my mind was far from art history. Even at 3:00 in the afternoon the drive from the Emory campus to Newnan took over an hour. I left my briefcase, slide carousels, and paperwork in the car and rushed onto the porch to unlock the front door. I wasn't sure whether I was afraid, or whether I simply didn't know what I should do next; for a few minutes, I stood at the door.

I found the road atlas downstairs in my studio on a shelf under the drawing table. I turned the pages of the atlas to Wyoming. It was big and wide, not one of those oddly shaped states, but a nice sturdy, rectangle. And one hell of a state! Its name was derived from the Delaware Indian word meaning, "upon the great plain." Three of the great pioneer trails of the United States crossed Wyoming: the California Trail, the Mormon Trail, and the Oregon Trail; all went through South Pass. It took four treaties, more than any other state in the United States, to get the rights to the land that made up Wyoming. To this day it is known as the "Equality State," because women were the first in the United States to vote and to hold public office. The first woman governor was elected in 1924.

Forests comprise 50 million acres in Wyoming; one-sixth of its land area. Lander is located in the Shoshone Basin, between the Wind River Range and the Rattle Snake Mountains. It is in one of the state's broad, flat, mostly treeless basins, dotted with rugged and lonely towers of rock. Because the basins get less rainfall than the mountains, the vegetation is short grasses and low plants which grow like carpet in soft, muted colors of celery, taupe, and rust. Just north of Lander, near Riverton, is the Wind River Indian Reservation, where half of Wyoming's 7,000 Native American population live.

I called Sinks Canyon State Park in Lander, Wyoming. A male voice answered.

"Hello. I'd like some information about the Wind River Range."

"Well, I can try to help you. What would you like to know?"

"I'm planning a pack trip across the Continental Divide. I'd like to know where can I get a map of the Bridger-Teton Forest that shows the horse trails?"

"You can get maps from the U.S. Forest Service in Lander, I'll be glad to give you their number. There is a snow plow route over the mountains to Jackson, but whether or not you could get permission to use it as a trail, I don't know about that. You really should talk to an outfitter. They could probably help you more than I can. There are lots of outfitters around, but I'd recommend a guy at Half Moon Lake in Pinedale, let me give you his number."

The ranger gave me Frank Deede's name and suggested I call him late in the evening since it was hard to reach him during the day. He gave me the telephone number for the forest service.

The intensity of the past three days began to take its toll. I was too tired to make a plan or to try and interpret the significance of what was happening in my life. I went into the bedroom and lay down. Our immense library was in our bedroom. Morgan built bookcases around the walls surrounding our bed. It would be impossible to replace the collection of art history, military history, and literature we had collected over the years. My eyes scanned the book titles: *Mummies made in Egypt, Architecture through the Ages, Shogun, Madame Bovary, Civil War Generals, The Bride and the Bachelors, How Thing's Work, The Poetry of Edna St. Vincent Millay, John Henry, Aida, The Killer Angels, Sources of the River.*

I sat up in bed. I had a book to help me plan my trip! I had a map of the Wind River Mountains. I raced out to my truck and found Osborne Russell's *Journal of a Trapper*. It was inside a ziplock bag and held together by a red rubber band. I lovingly held it in my hands, turning its soft worn pages. On the cover was the painting, *Carson's Men*, by Charles M. Russell. Inside the book was a carefully folded piece of notebook paper. It had been a long time since I read the poem written by Sean Murphy, the soulful blonde songwriter I met on the train on my way to New Caney, Texas that summer long ago.

A Foolish Royal Tragedy

There lives here a Princess lost on a Prince.
She loved him one night and ain't seen him since.
She works in the city and dreams of the wood.
Give it all for him if only she could.
But he's living on mountains proving his "bluff."
Looking for dragons and all that Prince-stuff.

And she wears a smile to protect her frown.
Getting high off good whiskey and getting let down.
Trying to keep busy and filling her mind,
with plans for the future to eat up her time . . . .
There once lived a great Prince he roamed through the land.
Performing great deeds with the slight of his hand.
And he felt her love but he followed his calling,
Which led to the Road, which led to his falling.
She dreamed of his young face.
She dreamed of his dangers.
She dreamed of him mostly when she slept with strangers.
Now the Prince always said he'd return to her one night,
When the dragons were dead, and all the wrongs were all right.
But that takes a long time and time has the key,
For changing a strong love into a sad memory . . . .
The crowds they all cheered him and they begged for a song.
But his heart wasn't in it.
His Princess had gone . . . .

I had carefully placed the poem in Russell's book because I knew within its cover the poem would always be safe. I would never part with this extraordinary journal, inexplicably, Osborne Russell was a part of my life.

When Evan and John first began planning their trip to Wyoming, they used Russell's book as a guide and as an inspiration. Russell was an exceptional mountain man who traveled extensively between the Wind River, Yellowstone, the Great Salt Lake, and Bear Lake, Idaho during the years 1834-1843. His journal had become one of the definitive accounts of life in the Rocky Mountains. It was published years after his death. I, too, decided to use Russell's book as a guide. I strongly felt as though I knew this extraordinary man from the past. His words and his thoughts were so eloquently preserved in this modest account of his life.

Evan gave me his copy of the book before he and John left for Wyoming. When I left Memphis that summer for Peachcreek Girl Scout Ranch in New Caney, Texas, Osborne Russell's book was the first thing I packed. Peachcreek featured primitive camping and horseback riding. Primitive was an adequate description since the latrines were fifty yards away from the counselors' tent. The counselors and the campers slept in canvas Army tents that had been waterproofed with kerosene in which paraffin had been dissolved. At night we heavily sprayed ourselves with insect repellent and rolled up the sides of the tent for ventilation in the hot and humid Texas summer heat. I read Russell's journal by flashlight and thought about John and Evan riding horseback over the mountains.

During the first two-week session of camp, it began to rain. It rained and it rained and it didn't stop raining. After three days the novelty of the rain hikes and the mud races wore thin. The children's clothes were wet and muddy. We took their clothes, not to be washed, but to be dried in the two dryers in the multi-purpose building. The children began to get athlete's foot. The creek, beneath the huge orange bridge that connected the two sections of the camp, began to rise. There was no swimming, canoeing, horseback riding; just endless walks in the rain.

On the fifth day, the camp director agreed to my request to bring my ten-year old girls from our campsite, Horseshoe Bend, to the multi-purpose building to spend the night. My unit was the closest to the creek, and although the counselors' tent was a good 75 yards away from the rising water, some my girls' tents were as close as twenty-five yards. In the middle of the night we were awakened by the camp nurse, the water had risen rapidly. We had to evacuate the children immediately, before the water got higher.

We left the building with only our flashlights and formed a human chain. I don't know who was the most afraid, my 18 year old co-leader at the front of the line or me at the end. The dark, rising water was waist deep on me and chest high on most of the campers. As limbs and debris passed in the swift current, I could only imagine what I would do if one of my children panicked, broke the chain, and was swept away in the night. When we reached high ground we were evacuated in boats. We were registered by the Red Cross at a nearby school. I thought about life in a very different way after the experience. I said a prayer of thanksgiving that my life and the lives of my children had been saved.

When the counselors returned to camp three days later there was no water. There were health department warnings about rabid animals and swarming hordes of insects and snakes. It was the nastiest, smelliest mess I have ever seen. Our tents had been swept off their concrete blocks by the flood water. Children's clothes, letters, cameras, and other belongings were surrealistically hung in the limbs of the trees or were buried in the thick, foul mud. Everything I owned was gone. As I walked alone in the woods, almost half a mile away from where our tent had stood, I found Russell's *Journal of a Trapper*. The book was soaking wet, and covered with slime and silt. I held the book tightly against my body. No one would ever understand the fear and self-doubt I experienced when I held a tiny hand in mine and ordered my children out into the darkness, into the rising flood water, and into an uncertain future. Alone in the hot, piney woods of Texas, I began to cry.

It seemed to me, Osborne Russell held my hand.

Chapter 6

The realization my journey was to cross the Wind River Range on horseback was simple compared to preparing for the trip. My camping and outdoor skills, as well as my knowledge of genuine survival, were rusty and timeworn. What's more, I hadn't been on a horse in years. In planning my trip, I kept strictly to the practical with one exception. I packed my J. Peterman horseman's duster. The coat was designed to protect the rider, his rump, his saddle, and his legs down to the ankles. The coat was the epitome of western romance; it stood right up there with John Wayne's cavalry denim blouse.

After several attempts I reached Frank Deede at Half Moon Lake in Pinedale, Wyoming. He told me he was hired regularly to set up drop camps for hunters, fisherman, and outdoor enthusiasts. His standard fee was $75 per day per riding animal and $65 per day for a pack animal. There was also a trailer fee of $1.75 per mile to get the horses from Pinedale to the Tetons. He agreed to outfit my trip but he insisted I come to Pinedale for at least three days and judge for himself whether I was prepared to make the crossing alone. I agreed to his request.

My most serious problem was trying to read the four maps I received from the U.S. Forest Service. I spent hours trying to understand how the maps fit together. The scale was 1:126 on all the maps, but only two were true topographic quadrangle maps. The contour interval was 50 meters. The conversion table instructed me to convert meters to feet by multiplying by 3.2802. To convert feet to meters I had to multiply by 0.3048. Yeah, right! What the hell was a meter? My Ph.D. was useless in trying to find the best route, and follow it, over the mountains. I folded the maps. I cut them. I taped them back together again. Morgan tried to teach me orienteering. He insisted if I was going to camp alone, I needed to know how to read a map. I pretended to be interested, but I wasn't, and I deeply regretted it now. As I spent hours pouring over the topo maps of Wyoming, I developed an even greater respect for Russell. I wondered what sort of a man he was. I knew the particulars of his life, but it was the subtleties that intrigued me.

Osborne Russell was born in a small village in Maine on June 12, 1814. He was one of nine children. Maybe that's why he ran away from home at sixteen to go to sea. He deserted his ship in New York and went to work for the Northwest Fur Trapping and Trading Co., which operated in Wisconsin and Minnesota. He joined Nathaniel Wyeth's second expedition to the Rocky Mountains on April 4, 1834, at Independence, Missouri. In 1822 William H. Ashley placed the following advertisement:

To Enterprising Young Men

The subscriber wishes to engage ONE HUNDRED MEN,
to ascend the river Missouri to its source, there to be employed
for one, two, or three years — For particulars, enquire of
Major Andrew Henry, near the Lead Mines, in the County
of Washington, (who will ascend with, and command the party)
or to the subscriber at St. Louis.
February 13   Wm. H. Ashley

Russell was hired for a period of eighteen months by Wyeth's Columbia River Fishing and Trading Company, at a wage of two hundred and fifty dollars. He must have been filled with a great sense of enthusiasm and adventure as he began his journey westward. It was at this time he began: *Journal of a Trapper Or Nine Years Residence among the Rocky Mountains Between the years 1834 and 1843.*

The title page of his Journal read:

Journal of a Trapper
Or
Nine Years Residence among the
Rocky Mountains
Between the years of 1834 and 1843 Comprising
A general description of the Country, Climate,
Rivers, Lakes, Mountains, etc The nature and habits
of Animals, Manners and Customs of Indians and a Complete
view of the life led by a Hunter in those regions
By Osborne Russell

I envy no man that knows more than myself
and pity them that know less: Sir T. Brown.

Spread before me in the maps of Russell's journal were the "wild regions of the Rocky Mountains." The Continental Divide wound through Wyoming from the northwest corner to the south central edge of the state, separating the waters of the Atlantic and the Pacific Oceans. Each lake, peak, creek, and canyon had been carefully and wonderfully named; Upper Cathedral Lake, Fire Hole Lakes, Lake Solitude, Elephant Head, Angel Pass, Pyramid Peak, Bears Ears Mountain. The legend of the U. S. Forest Service maps credited the Geometrics Service Center in Salt Lake City for the geographic information. But I knew it was men like Osborne Russell, Jim Bridger, John Colter, Hugh Glass, Jedediah Strong Smith, Joe Meek, and Bill Williams that had bravely and lovingly charted the wilderness. The lives of these extraordinary men alternated between plenty and starvation. While it seemed strange to others that these men found so strong and fascinating a charm in their nomadic and dangerous lives, it had always held great appeal for me. I remembered reading A. B. Guthrie's, *The Big Sky*. Boone Caudill, the tragic and adventurous hero, stated, "I ain't hankering to live in no anthill." Although I lived in an anthill, I was repelled by my ordinary environment: the monotonous life of the settlements. I had become tame. I couldn't explain the dichotomy between the life I led, and the life that called to me from a far away and nameless place.

Russell was estranged from the comforts and privileges of civilization. He faced peril, danger, loneliness, want, and lawless freedom. Russell possessed the courage, cunning, and extraordinary skill to stay alive for nine years in the Rocky Mountains. He lived a strange, wild, hard, romantic, and exciting life, and he wrote about it as if he was a poet.

There weren't any known photographs of Russell. There had been one, in the possession of his great nephew, that was destroyed in a fire started by vandals. I could sense the strength of Russell's character in his vivid and rich description of Wyoming's dark forests, summits, and jagged cliffs. Jim Bridger described him as a "competent journalist." In my mind's eye I could see Russell, poised and frozen in time. He was sitting on his horse early in the morning when the clouds lie down around the shoulders of the great mountains, and the air smells as if God has just created the earth. There, quiet and still, I could see him listening to the symphony of the wilderness and dreaming of the trail that was his destiny to carve across the mountains.

It seemed impossible that it had been three weeks since Margaret and I attended the powwow, and the old woman told me the story that had rerouted my life. Margaret agreed to come to Newnan to stay with me the night before I left. I was impatient for her to arrive. I went outside and looked inside my truck. I had repacked four times. How did the women on the Oregon Trail manage? There were sixty-nine adults and children when the first covered wagons crossed the trail in 1841. Just four years later in 1845, "The Great Migration," began as more than 5,000 pioneers left Independence, Missouri for the Willamette Valley on the Columbia River in Oregon after the highly publicized expedition of Fremont's exploration of the Rocky Mountains. What indomitable spirits the pioneers must have had to pack their most cherished possessions in a canvas-covered wagons and set forth for Oregon and the promise of a new life. They traveled across the endless plains and over the foreboding mountains, and I was driving across the country in an air-conditioned Tahoe with a CD player. I would start my trip across the mountains with two sound horses and my food secured in ziplock bags.

My Mother sent me a back issue of Martha Stewart's *Living* magazine, June, 1995. The magazine contained an article entitled, "ah Wilderness: Backpacking in Wyoming." The article included recipes for breakfast scones, quesadillas, and cold noodles with pan-fried trout. I wondered how much Martha would charge to tag along and cook for two weeks? I planned to eat more simply. I packed grits and homemade pancake mix. My seasonings included liberal amounts of cumin, red cayenne and cracked black pepper, and a braid of garlic to season dehydrated red, black and pinto beans, and long-grain wild rice.

Morgan's military-supply closet was the next best thing to a trip to an Army surplus store. His supplies proved invaluable. Morgan was a preferred customer at Ranger Joe's and the Cavalry Store in Columbus. He could have outfitted a squad from the 75th Ranger Regiment with the phenomenal supply of equipment he purchased during his military career. In a wool blanket at the bottom of the closet I found a Lorrance Global Position System with 21 AA batteries. Inside an olive drab green waterproof stuff bag I packed a Khyber hunting knife, a Gerber multitool with pliers, screwdriver, and saw, my Swiss Army knife, 120 feet of cotton rope, a compass, and space blanket. I was taking a Smith and Wesson .44 Magnum wrapped in a flannel pillowcase, and six extra cartridges in a purple Crown Royal bag.

Morgan despised camping; too much of his military job description was spent in the woods. He wouldn't camp unless he was getting paid. He balked at anything more than a picnic and an all-day hike around a Civil War battlefield. On the rare occasions he would concede to go, he camped like a "dude" rather than an infantryman. On one particular trip, he purchased four lawn chairs, bought a new Coleman tent that slept six, another screened tent to avoid being eaten by insects, and a 9 x 12 foot piece of astroturf. It was downright embarrassing. Each evening he ritualistically set up the four chairs on the astroturf. One night a European couple arrived in a small rental economy car. There was nothing in their backseat, no luggage carriers strapped to the top of their car, or bicycles hanging off the back. They quietly set up their two-person tent. They didn't build a camp-fire, they didn't have lanterns, they simply ate their dinner, read quietly at their picnic table until sunset, and then went to bed. In the morning, the Europeans were long gone, but it took us over an hour to break camp and repack the truck. Despite the complicated and rather artificial nature of our camping trips, the times were good. We made love quietly and covertly leaning against trees and in deserted bath houses.

This summer I was going west like the Europeans.

I wanted to take something of a personal nature with me, besides Russell's book. It couldn't be too large, too heavy, or too fragile. The day before I left I chose William, a blue faience Egyptian hippopotamus that was the Metropolitan Museum of Art's unofficial mascot. The ancient Egyptians believed the hippopotamus was endowed with supernatural powers. Christmas, the year before Morgan died, I found William in my stocking. He was only two inches long, and he was the most exquisite turquoise. His sides, head and back were delicately incised with lotus petals decorations reminiscent of his marshy Nile habitat. He held the highest place of honor on my desk. After Morgan's death, my sister, gave me a copy of Joan Grant's beautiful Egyptian fairy tale, *The Blue Faience Hippopotamus*.

Margaret arrived at my door with a smile, her arms filled with paper grocery bags and brightly wrapped packages. We embraced.

"What did you bring?" I asked. She opened the bags and showed me cartons of three-pepper hummus, tabouleh, feta cheese, and sourdough French bread. "Let's go down to the lake and eat at the picnic table. It won't be too hot under the trees. What did you bring for us to drink?"

"Two bottles of red wine. What would a vision quest party be without red wine?"

"Go through the gate, and I'll meet you in the back." I went into the house and grabbed my Swiss Army knife, a tablecloth, two forks, plates, and wine glasses. I also grabbed the J. Peterman duster which Margaret had never seen. From the window I saw her standing at the edge of the lake watching the fish strike at the water bugs on the surface of the dark green water. We had spent many afternoons fishing, reminiscing, dreaming, bitching. How could either of us foreseen, years ago as young women, we would form a bond that would strengthen and comfort us throughout our lives. Our spirits recognized the hidden treasure within one another and forged an alliance that developed in accordance with its own natural laws.

"If you don't get down here, I'm going to start singing," Margaret began belting out *Sweet Betsy from Pike*. "Out on the prairie one bright, starry night, they broke out the whiskey and Betsy got tight. She sang and she shouted and danced o'er the plain, and showed her bare ass to the whole wagon train."

I hurried before she could begin a chorus of *Root Hog or Die*.

"First we toast, then we open the presents," ordered Margaret. She opened one of the bottles of red wine and filled our goblets to the brim.

"Are you the designated drinker tonight?"

"To you both, Sarah, the friend I love and her dark shadow. May the two of you wrestle sweetly in the wilderness, and may the best woman win."

The wine was aromatic, dry, and full bodied. It felt like delicious red velvet filling my mouth and throat. Just one drink elevated my body temperature and I began to perspire.

"Open this one first!" She pushed a box wrapped in blue-green foil across the table. Inside the box, beneath confetti-printed tissue paper were three brown leather wine skins with red piping. I removed one of the hand-carved wooden red stoppers and raised the neck to my mouth. I recognized the familiar aroma of Jack Daniels.

"To be politically correct you're supposed to squirt it into your mouth," said Margaret. I squeezed the wine skin forcefully from the bottom and a thin stream hit the corner of my mouth.

She placed the next package, a large box wrapped in brown kraft paper tied and knotted unceremoniously with twine, on the table. She handed me the knife. Rolled up inside the box was a red and gray saddle blanket. She reached into the box, carefully lifted the blanket and, without speaking, placed it before me on the table. Her motions were reverent and deliberate; her manner reminiscent of an ancient priestess preparing an altar. She looked at me and nodded, I unrolled the saddle blanket to find three small packages.

The first gift was a small silver bell on a silver chain. Margaret placed it over my head. "Nooka Indian women believed that when a woman went into the mountains she should wear a bell so the bears know she is their friend."

The second gift was a beautiful herkamer crystal. "It is a traveling crystal," said Margaret, placing it in my hand. "It will protect you on your journey and will bring you back safely."

The last gift was a pouch of tobacco. "The tobacco is to make offerings to the spirits that are asleep in all the named and nameless things." She refilled our wine glasses. "And, tobacco spit on bait is like an aphrodisiac to fish," she added smiling.

"Thank you, the gifts are wonderful. I'm going to miss you."

"Just promise me that you'll get back here safely so I don't have to tell your parents all the things that you've left out."

"I promise, now let me show you my coat. I turned and pivoted, modeling as if I was walking down a runway in Paris or Milan. "What do you think?"

"I think it's too damn clean."

"Well, of course it's clean, I've only worn it once."

"You look like a dude."

"It's going to get dirty when I wear it."

"A dude."

This was certainly not the response I had anticipated. Between the red wine, the heavy canvas coat, and the June heat, I was perspiring heavily. I spontaneously raised my wine glass and solemnly offered a toast.

"To White Buffalo Calf Woman." I turned up the glass and drank, placing the empty goblet on the table. I turned away from Margaret and walked into the lake.

She began to hoop, yell, and laugh hysterically. I waded waist deep into the water, spread my arms, and fell backward submerging my body and head in the still green water. The coat soaked up the water like a sponge, and my body sank like an anchor. Margaret's face filled with surprise and disbelief.

"Now do I look like a dude?"

Chapter 7

I began the journey that had been waiting for me. The life I was destined to live was once again in my path. I felt by running away from the shopping malls, the fast food drive-up windows, and the telephone, I was running home. I would soon be beyond the roads traveled by eighteen-wheelers, Suburbans, and Honda Accords. Before leaving I clipped a black and white photograph of Margaret to my visor. She was standing in a cornfield in jeans, a denim work shirt, and a bandana tied loosely around her neck. Margaret's image smiled reassuringly as I made my way westward. Mary Chapin Carpenter's song, *Passionate Kisses*, blared from my CD player.

On the passenger visor I clipped a postcard I received from my Dad the week before I left. On the front was a photograph of a Destin sunset, brilliantly hued with pinks, violets and indigo blue. On the back he had written a poem by Kipling, his favorite author:

> *Something hidden. Go and find it.*
> *Go and look behind the Ranges —*
> *Something lost behind the Ranges.*
> *Lost and waiting for you.*
> *Go!*
> *Have I told you lately that I love you? Daddy*

It was a long trip west from Atlanta. I stopped for the night in Oregon, Missouri. On the door of a convenience store was a purple flyer advertising a concert on the town square. At sunset, I left my motel and walked a quarter mile to the center of town. The warm summer air had cooled slightly, and the street lights came on one at a time to illuminate the stage, a flat-bed trailer pulled up in front of the courthouse. The square was roped off with the police department's yellow plastic crime-scene tape.

A seven-piece band played country music while children played on the courthouse lawn. The townsfolk sat in gray metal folding chairs with First Methodist Church of Oregon stenciled on the back. The band members, ranging in age from 18 to 75, played mostly instrumentals with an occasional *Maybeline, Achey Breaky Heart*, or *Folsom Prison*. It reminded me of growing up in Texas. Everything was simple. My life revolved around my family; brother, sisters, cousins, aunts, uncles, grandparents. Christmas past was filled with memories of my grandparents arriving with their car trunk packed with gumdrop trees, flocked wreaths made from tumbleweeds, popcorn balls, and coffee cans filled with iced ginger cookies, homemade breads, and candies. I sensed this small town still observed the same values that were the framework of my Texas upbringing.

The crowd clapped generously and with sincere appreciation after each song. The local banks and funeral home had set up small tents to protect the crowd in case of a sudden summer shower. I sat on the courthouse lawn, leaning against the base of a bronze historical marker honoring Lewis and Clark. Four men sat at a folding card table and played dominoes the toes of their scuffed cowboy boots tapping in rhythm to the music. I enjoyed the night and looked forward to the days ahead.

People from all over the world come to Mount Rushmore. The flags of the fifty states line the sidewalk leading to the park. There is no way to describe the visual impact of Rushmore. The color photographs in the travel brochures, history books, and even PBS specials, left visitors unprepared for the startling vision of Presidents Washington, Lincoln, Jefferson, and Roosevelt, carved in stone high above the Visitor Center. Even mid-summer, the air was cold when the wind blew. I stopped for coffee in the restaurant where Cary Grant and Eva Marie Saint conversed with James Mason and Martin Landau in the famous scene from Hitchcock's *North by Northwest*. I went into the gift shop to buy postcards to send to my family, and studied a rack of brochures featuring local tourist attractions. The Mitchell Corn Palace. Done that. Walls Drug Store. Done that. The Tetons. Going to do that. Crazy Horse Memorial? I opened the brochure and found it was seventeen miles from Mount Rushmore. I decided to check it out.

I knew from my studies of Native American history and culture that His Crazy Horse was a chief of the Oglala Sioux Indians. When the U.S. government ordered the Sioux Indians to enter a reservation they refused. In our history books his greatest recognition was the Battle of Little Bighorn, where Lieutenant Colonel George Armstrong Custer and his command were killed. The directions in the brochure were easy to follow. It didn't take long to arrive at the entrance. As I turned off the highway, I took my place in a long line of cars. Even from a distance, without any knowledge of the monument's history, the sculptural image was hypnotic; the strong profile of Crazy Horse and his powerful steed rising from the mountain. He pointed to the mountains before him.

The monument reminded me of the Ute Indian legend that, at one time, all Utes were giants. A hunting party left a lone brave to stand sentry over the land until they returned. Centuries passed and the brave fell asleep. The Creator became angry and reduced all Utes to human size. The sleeping sentry was transformed into a mountain to stand eternal guard over the land. The legend stated that one day the sleeping Ute would rise up from the earth and rescue his people in a time of great danger.

As I left the Crazy Horse Memorial I saw a sign that read "Trading Post: The Best Place to See the Monument." I pulled into the trading post and had to agree, that if a "look" was the only thing a tourist was interested in enjoying, the post was a find. They certainly had enough plastic tomahawks and elasticized Indian beaded headbands made in Taiwan, to add up to the admission charge at the memorial. I bought a bottle of water, some pretzels and turned to the business of finding a place to stay for the night. As I pulled out of the parking lot I saw an old trailer at the northeast corner of the property. A man in a plaid shirt, cowboy hat, and jeans sat motionless in a lawn chair beside a hand-painted sign that read: *Indian Julery, Potery, Blankets*. I made a left turn onto the highway and drove away.

Then I got that feeling. That eerie feeling. That irrational, I know that I'm crazy feeling but I have to go back. I have to turn around and go back to that trailer. I hate that feeling. I always tried to talk myself out of listening to the voices in my head. I glanced at the photograph of Margaret and I turned around.

The man didn't move when I pulled up beside his small untidy trading post. There were used tires behind the trailer, old bicycles, and metal drum containers filled with scrap pieces of lumber. Old wooden ammo crates, with hemp rope handles, were stacked by the trailer door.

"Good afternoon," I greeted him as I got out of the car. "You have a great view."

"Yes, it is an ever-changing view." His voice was quiet and deep. His long, silver hair was tied back, his straw cowboy hat had seen better days. I noticed his trailer and his chair faced the monument, as if Crazy Horse was pointing to him. I looked around, not knowing if I should go inside or if the trailer was his home. In the window hung a faded yellow gauze curtain held back by a large feather.

"What are you looking for today?"

"A blanket."

"What kind of blanket?"

Without thinking I blurted, "A woman told me a legend of a blanket that can take a horse and its rider across the seasons. Have you ever heard this legend?" I felt awkward and stupid. He looked down at his hands which were the color of polished copper.

"I know the legend. The story she told you is true." He waited. After what seemed an eternity, he stood. He was taller than I imagined and he stood straight and erect. He gestured for me to sit down in a green and white aluminum lawn chair. I accepted his unexpected hospitality and sat cautiously and slowly. The chair was missing two of its plastic straps and I was afraid it would not hold my weight. He disappeared inside the trailer and returned with another lawn chair, and two cans of Pabst Blue Ribbon beer. He walked slowly but without hesitation or infirmity. His movements conveyed the elegance of a Japanese warrior performing a kata. He placed his chair beside mine and handed me a beer.

"Your eyes are green. They are the sign of an old soul reborn." He gestured toward the monument. "When His Crazy Horse was a boy his name was Curly. After his first great war deed his father, who was also named Crazy Horse, gave him his name. Crazy Horse was called the "Strange One" by his people because of his unusual spiritual powers. He was special. You, too, are special. Some who are special are chosen at birth, the others are found when it is time. They are found by attitude and skill, sometimes they are found by accident."

"I expect if I am special, I was found by accident."

"Do not talk from your mouth. Ask me questions from your heart, and my heart will answer you," he said.

"The woman told me I must find the blanket that takes a horse and its rider across the seasons. She said I must find the blanket and make a journey. Do you know where I might find this blanket?" The warm, late afternoon wind blew across my face.

"I have your blanket. The blanket to ride across the seasons, but money cannot buy it."

I began the intellectual struggle I experienced when I first heard the old woman's story. In this technological and scientific age, in this age of the Internet and heart transplants, how could I accept, on faith, such a blanket existed?

"The blanket must be earned by trading something of yourself. You must decide what you will trade for the blanket."

"Do you mean give you something of mine?"

"No. Trade something of yourself. You must trade something of great personal value to you." He gestured toward my truck. "Perhaps you should look to see what you have brought on your journey that would be worthy of such a trade."

For a moment I just looked at him, surely appearing stupid in my delay and confusion. I understood the blanket was not for sale, but trading something of mine for a mythological blanket whose powers had now been extolled by two persons? How could it be real? Doing as he instructed, I walked to my truck and opened the back doors of the Tahoe. My gaze traveled across boxes of food, my two small stuff bags, my cooler, flashlights, and Duraflame logs. I looked again. Canvas bedroll, four gallons of water, a blue plastic tarp. Nothing here. Nothing of myself, just stuff.

I closed the doors and looked in the driver's window. Road Atlas, CDs, the black and white photograph of Margaret, the postcard from my Dad, my leather bag with my wallet and makeup. I looked at the brown beaver beanie baby, *Bucky*, hanging from the rearview mirror. I bought him at the Mitchell Corn Palace in Missouri, probably much too new to be interpreted as highly personal. Perhaps Margaret's gifts; the silver bell or the herkamer crystal? I walked to the front passenger door, opened it, and climbed into the seat, scanning my belongings for something of deep personal value. I looked to see if the old man was watching but he had gone inside the trailer, maybe to see which rag-tag blanket he was going to pass off as authentic.

I looked toward the trading post. A constant stream of tourists entered empty handed and left carrying plastic bags bulging with souvenirs. They were so proud of their treasures, you would think it was the Metropolitan Museum of Art gift shop. My left hand moved hesitantly to the storage console between the two bucket seats, and rested on the latch. I looked inside for the only item in my possession that was priceless to me. Wrapped in a black velvet drawstring pouch was William, the blue faience hippopotamus Morgan gave me the Christmas before he died. How beautiful his turquoise color. How elegantly the ancient Egyptian craftsman had delicately incised the lotus blossoms on his back. How charming to see such a powerful and monumental animal rendered in such a diminutive size. I smiled tenderly remembering the gift and its giver.

My mind began the battle between the logical and the illogical: the possible and the impossible, the intelligent decision and the irrational decision. How could I possibly take the last gift I received from Morgan and give it to man I didn't know for a blanket that couldn't possibly exist? The cinematic image of Indiana Jones in *The Last Crusade* jumped into my mind. In his quest for the Holy Grail, Jones' father had been shot and Indiana faced three tests to reach the Grail. Passing the first two, he found himself at a huge precipice impossible to jump. It was at this point Jones realized it was a leap of faith which, looking below, appeared to be inevitable suicide. Hearing the cries of his dying Father behind him, he said a prayer and stepped into the abyss. He discovered a camouflaged bridge that allowed him to pass to the other side, find the Grail and save his Father's life. I thought of my Father and his Texas witticisms; "Don't build a bird's nest on the ground, Don't be a dog-in-a-manger, Don't bite off half a bullet, Don't shake a scared stick." Faith was illogical, one either had it or not. I decided to bite off the whole bullet.

The old man didn't ask a single question or make a any comment when I returned to the trailer and handed him William. He disappeared inside the trailer and returned with a brown paper bag tied with twine. He handed me the package and a small sandwich bag filled with cornmeal.

"The night before you place the blanket on your horse light a fire. Make an offering in the four directions of the wind: north, south, east, and west. It will help you return safely. Do not forget. His Crazy Horse made his journey across the mountains, and now you must make yours."

"I won't forget. Thank you, and thank you for the cold beer." I turned to leave and stopped at the sight of the sculpture of His Crazy Horse, gloriously painted in the pinks, yellows, and crimson of the evening sunset; the empty South Dakota sky high above him. The rock looked alive. Illuminated and strengthened by the sun, it seemed Crazy Horse could easily break free of his granite prison and ride into the warm summer night on his mighty horse.

I placed the package on the seat. My overwhelming curiosity was delayed by the reality that it was the peak of the tourist season and I had no place to stay. At each exit I was tempted to pull off the Interstate, untie the bundle and look at the blanket. I had to drive to Spearfish, South Dakota before I found a small mom-and-pop motel with a vacancy sign.

The room was small and smelled of mildew and Pinesol. I put the package on the dark green bedspread printed with hunting scenes, and went outside to find one of the wineskins. Returning, I sat in a worn chair beside the double bed. I removed the cap and generously filled my mouth. I held it for a moment, its strength burned the inside of my mouth. I hesitantly untied the twine and unwrapped the brown paper bag.

Inside I found a worn chestnut brown and tan saddle blanket folded in a square. The wool smelled strongly of smoke, and stains of dirt and charcoal made some of the fabric dark. There were several tears which had been carefully and meticulously mended, and a rust-colored mark that appeared to have been painted on the blanket. I ran my hands back and forth across the soft wool. Who wove it? Who did it belong to? Was it a gift from a mother to her son as he rode out for the first time to hunt buffalo, to steal a horse, or to make coup on an enemy? How did it come into the old man's possession? And when I put it on my horse what would happen? Nothing?

Something? And if Something, what? Where was, across the seasons? I stared at the blanket. Could this nondescript wool blanket be magic? My fingers felt something inside the folds; maybe more cornmeal to make the offering to the four winds?

I opened the blanket. Inside was William.

Chapter 8

After passing through Pinedale, Wyoming, Half Moon Lake was a left-hand turn past the Museum of the Mountain Man and up Fremont Lake Road. The staggering vision of the Wind River Range was thrilling and intimidating. The vista stretched as far as I could see from the left to the right. A small hand-painted sign pointed the way to Half Moon Guest Ranch. After a quarter mile I saw a small crescent-shaped lake far below me, its waters were a deep teal blue. It took me ten minutes to make the downhill descent on the unpaved road. Signs directed me to the office and to the restaurant. As I approached the buildings I saw two employees on the roof sitting on plastic milk crates in a makeshift outdoor break room. The office was built of logs and painted with Rustoleum red primer. The dining room, connected to the office by a short covered walkway, was also made of logs but had a natural-roughhewn finish.

Inside I found two young women, seventeen or eighteen years old, who were quick to tell me they rarely met anyone new at the Half Moon Guest Ranch. The resort attracted a steady stream of local townsfolk who made the fifteen-minute drive from Pinedale for breakfast, lunch, or dinner. While registering, I was told Frank wouldn't be in until late, and one of the girls asked if I wanted to be taken to my cabin, or if I wanted to eat dinner first. The ranch, on the American plan, included three meals a day in the cost of the cabin. I was starved. I ordered a glass of red wine and walked outside onto the deck which was the length of the building.

The dining room had several large bay windows on both the front and back which gave a clear view through the dining room to the deck, and the lake on the other side. On the deck were several green wooden picnic tables and chairs for guests to sit and enjoy the beauty of the jewel-like lake. Two ruby-throated hummingbirds were attacking each other as they fought for nectar at a red feeder. Their wings made a loud whirring as they flew overhead. As they challenged one another for the territory they made a squeaking sound like a mouse. Clay pots of red begonias were hung on the deck railing. The wind was up, and the cold temperature made it difficult to believe tomorrow was the first of July.

I was joined by a one-eyed gray and black Australian cattle dog. He eyed me suspiciously at a measured distance. We stared one another down, he lost interest, and trotted off. There wasn't a house as far as the eye could see. The last ray of sunlight disappeared behind the mountain turning the water the color of India ink. A float of spare tires and white Clorox bottles bobbed in the rough water. The white caps frothed like stiff meringue in the strong wind.

"Here's your wine, Dr. Hanley."

"Thank you, but please, call me Sarah."

"Okay. I'm Kathy."

"What are the Clorox bottles for?"

"There's a big rock out there, so Frank anchored that mess together to keep boaters from hitting it."

"Good idea. It's so beautiful here."

"It is beautiful, but not very exciting. The most excitement we've had lately is when a tourist lost the keys to his rental car on a trail ride and had to borrow a car and drive all the way to Jackson to get another set."

"Remind me not to make the same mistake. What's for dinner?"

"Chicken fried steak or spaghetti and meatballs, they're both excellent. Ron's a fantastic chef."

I decided on the chicken fried steak. I heard voices behind me as guests entered the restaurant. I'm sure they could tell I was from out-of-town since I was outside in the cold when any local would have come inside when the sun went down.

Kathy called me to dinner. The chicken fried steak had thick gravy gravy and a poached egg on top, whole green beans, baby carrots with almonds, a dinner salad, and homemade French bread. It was delicious. Chef Ron came to personally ask if I enjoyed my dinner. He looked more like a gunfighter than a chef. He was small, wiry, and had a short black moustache. He wore a white chef's coat that appeared to have been tie-dyed with spaghetti sauce and grease.

"Would you like dessert now?"

"Oh, no, I couldn't possibly eat anything else. It was wonderful!" He seemed pleased by the compliment.

"Well, take some cookies to the cabin with you." He walked across the dining room to a round table in the corner with an enormous cookie jar. He took three large cookies from the jar, wrapped them in a napkin, and brought them to me. "They're macadamia nut, a secret recipe of mine. The Spring Water cookie jar is always full!"

I thanked him and went outside to meet Kathy who had gotten on a three-wheel all terrain vehicle to lead me up the road to my cabin. The furnishings of the small cabin were modest. There were two rooms; a bed-room and living room with a worn couch and a formica-covered dining room table and four chairs. There were cheaply framed cardboard paint-ings on the walls and moths in the bathroom. After Kathy turned on the lights in the cabin she told me good night, and walked to the cabin door.

"Kathy, what's Frank like?"

She laughed, "You'll see tomorrow."

I entered the dining room at nine the next morning. The only other guests were a family of four. The mother was meticulously cutting sausage into bite-sized pieces for her three-year old in a red booster seat.

"Good morning, Dr. Hanley," greeted Chef Ron, still wearing his stained chef's coat. "How was your first night?"

"Great," I replied, too polite to mention the moths in the bathroom and the water that smelled like pond scum.

"What would you like for breakfast?"

"I'll start with coffee and go from there." He brought me a large white mug of coffee and began to grill me about where I was from, what I did, if I was married or divorced, and how long I would be staying. I tried to be polite remembering that my being from out-of-town stirred everyone's cu-riosity. Eventually, I changed the subject by talking about how hungry I was. I ordered the blueberry buckwheat pancakes. The dining room smelled like my Grandmother was cooking in the kitchen.

My plate arrived with six huge pancakes, hotcakes, my PaPa called them when I was a child. Butter. Hot Vermont maple syrup in a small white pitcher. Two eggs over easy and four slab-cut strips of pepper bacon I had not ordered.

"You'll need your energy for where Frank will take you today."

"What's Frank like?"

Chef Ron smiled broadly and laughed, "No easy way to describe Frank. You'll have to see for yourself!" The pancakes were awesome, and strongly flavored with buttermilk. I proceeded to fill my mouth with a generous bite of everything on the plate.

"Dr. Hanley, I'm sorry I wasn't here when you arrived."

I looked up from my feast, my mouth full of pancakes and bacon, and saw a man, I presumed was Frank Deede, standing before me.

"May I join you? Ron, how about some coffee over here?"

He sat down at the table. I was chewing quickly trying to disguise my lack of table manners. Chef Ron emerged from the kitchen with a mug and a pot of coffee, which took some of the pressure off me to answer Frank's question with a mouth full of pancakes.

"What time did you get in Frank?"

"Five this morning. It's a damn good thing Lestat knows the way home. I fell asleep in the saddle about three." Ron filled Frank's mug, refilled mine and hurried into the kitchen.

"Well, Dr. Hanley . . . "

"Sarah."

"Sarah. I've certainly been looking forward to meeting you since our first telephone conversation. I must say you're not what I expected."

"What did you expect?"

"I expected someone younger, and I expected someone less attractive."

It seemed a backhanded compliment.

"What I mean is, it seems like you are old enough to have more sense about you than to go into the mountains alone."

"It's personal."

"Must be very personal if you're willing to risk your safety. No offense, but even though you're paying top dollar to lease two of my best horses, I don't feel comfortable sending you across the Continental Divide until I know you can handle yourself. It wouldn't be very ethical."

I nodded, trying not to stare at the burn scars on the right side of his face and his forearms.

"You have never owned a horse, and the last time you rode for more than three hours was 15 years ago?"

"That's correct."

"Well, Dr. Hanley, Sarah, you're crazy or headstrong, or maybe both. I'll meet you at the stables in an hour. Wear a hat. Bring your canteen or a water bottle, and I'll take you out with some of my regulars, a retired Air Force Colonel that lives at Fremont Lake and his family."

I agreed.

He finished his coffee and rose to leave. "Mosquitoes are real bad when the wind quits blowing, so spray yourself." Two families entered the dining room. Frank crossed the room with long strides, shook hands with the men and hugged their wives and their children. I could not hear what they were saying.

After Frank left I waited a respectable amount of time and then returned to my cabin. I pulled back my hair and stuffed it under my Panama hat. I brushed my teeth, applied sunscreen, and repellent. I wondered how Frank was burned; even with scars pulled tight across his face and arms, he was very handsome. I wondered how much of his body was burned.

I went outside and sat in one of the wooden chairs on the shallow cabin porch. The exquisite lake below was surrounded by dark evergreen-covered mountains. Butterflies traveled across the dense sagebrush from wildflower-to-wildflower. Kathy arrived on the three-wheeler to water the red and white petunias in a large whiskey barrel on the porch.

"Are you going on the trail ride with Colonel Henderson?"

"Yes, I'm just killing time. To get to the stables I keep up the road to the left?"

"That's correct."

"How far will we go today?"

"Well, at least four hours, maybe five. Let me put it this way, you'll be ready for bed early tonight!"

It was less than a quarter mile from my cabin to the stables. I was embarrassed I drove instead of walking; it sent a poor message. I inhaled the the smell of the horses; the odor of their bodies, their feces, and their lather. I remembered all the good times and forgot the rides when a horse tried to drown me or buck me off under a low-limbed tree.

Frank was busy saddling the horses. He moved back and forth between the tack room and the hitching post, talking with the Colonel and his family who arrived before me. The colonel was a distinguished man in his late sixties. He was wearing jeans, a light jacket over a red plaid shirt and a navy USAF baseball cap embroidered with gold braid. His son, in his mid-thirties, looked like an accountant; his father much more dashing at twice his son's age. His granddaughter, a cute girl of ten or eleven, attentively watched everything happening around her. They seemed surprised at my arrival. I got the impression Frank had omitted the news I was joining them for their ride.

"Jerry, this is Sarah Hanley, she is a college professor from Atlanta," remarked Frank, without stopping his work to complete the introductions.

"Glad you're joining us, Sarah. This is my son, Jonathan, and my granddaughter, Maggie." Everyone smiled, nodded, and said hello. I filled the awkwardness by thanking them for allowing me to join their family.

"Maggie, have you ridden much since last summer?" asked Frank as he finished cinching up a bay mare.

"No, Sir."

"Well, come over here and let's see how these stirrups fit." She walked down the steps to join Frank.

"What's her name?"

"Her name is Minnie, just like Minnie Mouse. She's a good saddle horse, but you have to make sure she knows you're the boss. Okay?" He adjusted her stirrups and continued our assignments.

"Jonathan, you'll ride Pete." Frank slapped the buttocks of a dark brown horse with two white fetlocks. "Jerry, you get your favorite, Loco."

"Why is his name Loco?" asked Maggie. "Is he crazy?"

"No, it's because he runs like freight train that's jumped the tracks, but Jerry knows how to pull rank on him."

"And I've had to a time or two, haven't I, Frank!" Jerry untied the reins from the hitching post and confidently mounted Loco standing up in the stirrups to test their feel.

"Dr. Hanley."

"Sarah."

"Sarah. This is Cocoa. She's the most surefooted horse I've got. She can get you safely down a mountainside of glass, but you've got to trust her. Let her be in charge when you're not. Work with her. You'll know when its coming together between the two of you."

Cocoa was the color of a cup of Starbuck's semisweet hot chocolate with whipped cream. She was big with a broad rear and wide back. I grabbed the saddle horn and the back of the saddle and raised my left foot to reach the high stirrup. I pulled myself up, right leg over, and took my seat. I knew that Frank was watching as I mounted her.

"You look good up there Dr. Hanley," he complimented, his mouth in a half smile and the look of good-hearted mischief in his eyes.

"The saddle feels a little loose," I commented, rocking from side to side standing in the stirrups.

"You'll get used to it. Just stay in the middle." He got his blue jean jacket from the tack room and put it on over his Half Moon Lake t-shirt. He quickly untied his horse and mounted.

"What do you feel like today, Jerry?"

"We paid for a two-hour ride.

"I know what you paid for, Jerry, I asked what you feel like." He smiled broadly, his scarred skin pulling tight across the right side of his face. He was extremely masculine and handsome despite what some might consider his disfigurement. He led the way out of the gate.

"Understood, Frank. I think four hours is the maximum we should stay out. This is Maggie and Jonathan's first ride this summer."

"All right then, let's follow Pole Creek to Fayette Lake, head up the mountain and cross over to Sweeney Creek and then back down."

"Sounds good."

I allowed everyone to move out in a line ahead of me, preferring to be at the end of the string, and opting for limited conversation as we rode. The ride was enjoyable and it built my confidence. Most of the time we walked single file but there were times that required polite conversation when I would find myself beside Maggie, Jonathan or Jerry, but never Frank. I had retreated into my own world. Once again, I was seeing the world from the back of a horse, and I found deep pleasure in the view and in the companionship with the animal. Cocoa shook her head and swung her tail to drive away the swarms of mosquitoes that came and went as the wind died down and picked up again.

The Wyoming sky was as brilliant as a blue bird with thick white clouds that looked like heaping spoonfuls of marshmallow creme. The landscape fluctuated between stream beds, rocky hillsides, open meadows, and dense forests with fallen trees strewn like giant pick-up sticks. From time-to-time we had to dismount and walk our horses through the maze of deadwood. Although we rode at a high elevation, the Wind River Range, the backbone of Wyoming's Continental Divide, rose even higher in the distance. I couldn't help but wonder what it would be like when I rode off alone. My fear excited me.

When we moved from the ridge line and reached a clearing, Frank moved his horse into a canter, signaling, without words, the go ahead for the rest of us to do the same. He sat erect in the saddle, his right hand extended to balance himself as he rode away.

"Okay, Cocoa, let's go," my voice and my legs gave approval for pursuit. I felt her physical intelligence and her confidence as she ran. She was not obsessed to overtake the others, but happy to join in the run. I remembered Frank's advice to stay in the middle so I concentrated on staying centered in the saddle. The gap narrowed between our band. Frank stopped and looked back to see where we were. With a shift in my weight backward, Cocoa gently slowed to a halt. I hoped Frank would allow me to take her as my saddle horse. I felt with Cocoa's physical strength and power, that if a blanket could not take me across the seasons, she could.

When we caught up to Frank he told us we were thirty minutes away from the ranch. It didn't seem we had been riding three hours. He said we were going to take a short cut and head down the side of the mountain. He couldn't mean this mountain! Although the mountainside was not wooded, it had an incline similar to a scene out of *The Man From Snowy River*. Jerry must have been accustomed to Frank's trail blazing. No one spoke; only Maggie and I looked wide-eyed at the rocks below.

"Maggie, don't pull back on the reigns. Minnie knows the hill and she'll get you down safely. Just take it slow and lean back. Don't pull back, just lean back. Understand?"

"Yeah," answered Maggie hesitantly.

"Yes, Sir," corrected the Colonel.

"Yes, Sir, " she replied, responding to the order to correct her manners because of her grandfather's command.

"Sarah, are you okay with this?" asked Frank.

"Yes, Sir," I replied, smiling at Maggie to ease the anxiety we were both feeling.

Frank started down first, followed by Jerry. Maggie was instructed to start next. Her Dad followed to keep an eye on her, although I wasn't sure how much help he would be in an emergency. I waited until he was about twenty yards down the side. God, it was incredibly beautiful up here. I nudged Cocoa. She lowered her head and began to pick her way across the rocks and down the mountain. The incline was so steep I felt like I was reclining, my feet in the stirrups close to her neck, and my head almost touching her rear. My reigns were so short I had to extend my arms as far as I could to give Cocoa her head. I didn't know my body would still bend like this! Her hoofs slipped on the smooth rocks but she never stumbled. We slowly made our way down the mountain in what seemed an eternity. Jonathan called to Maggie three or four times reminding her not to pull back on the reigns. As Frank promised, we got back to the stables within thirty minutes, the horses were as sound as when we left. I couldn't speak for the others but I was stiff-legged and sore when I dismounted.

"Thanks, great ride, Frank. See you later this week. Is Saturday good for you?"

Frank looked at me and then answered, "Let's make it Sunday, Jerry. I'm taking Dr. Hanley to Jackson Saturday to begin her trip."

"Fine, Frank. Sarah, good meeting you. Have a good trip."

"Good to meet you, too, Jerry. Maggie, you were my inspiration." She smiled shyly. Within minutes they left.

I lingered awkwardly. "Why don't you let me help you unsaddle the horses?"

"Okay. Unsaddle Cocoa, then Minnie. Put their tack inside. You'll see their names on the wall. How did you like her?"

"She was great. After coming down the face of that mountain, I trust her completely."

"That wasn't a mountain!"

"That wasn't a hill!"

"Well, I guess everything's relative," commented Frank, ending the debate. After we unsaddled the horses we brushed them and led them into the corral. "How do you feel?"

"The joints in my knees are sore."

"Tomorrow we'll let your stirrups down a notch. That may help. Maybe not. You may just have to get used to it. You rode well, today."

The wind had died, and the mosquitoes swarmed around our faces and hands looking for any opportunity to light.

"It will be better down by the lake, wind always blows on the water. Are you hungry?"

"No, not really."

He looked at his watch. I looked at the scars on his right forearm. "It's 4:30. I'd like to see the route you're planning to take across the mountains. Why don't you meet me at 6:00 on the deck, bring your map, we'll talk more about your trip."

"All right. Frank, may I take Cocoa?"

I think he intentionally made me wait. "Yes, Dr. Hanley," he grinned, "you may take Cocoa."

At the cabin I showered in the foul-smelling water and I washed my hair, but I vetoed shaving my legs. I changed into clean jeans, a denim shirt, charcoal-gray wool sweater and my blue polar fleece jacket. I wanted to wear my J. Peterman duster but I decided it was too theatrical for Frank, Chef Ron, and the locals. I considered walking the sketchy trail from my cabin to the dining hall, but reconsidered after I evaluated my physical condition, and the fact I would be returning after dark.

I arrived promptly at 6:00. The gray and black cattle dog was asleep in a flower bed filled with purple and white petunias. He opened his one eye dispassionately and returned to his dog dreams. Through the large glass bay windows I could see through the dining room to the deck. Frank was sitting at one of the round tables. He had changed and was wearing a blue plaid wool shirt and a down vest. The dining room was empty except for the kitchen crew setting the tables and refilling the cookie jar. I walked around the left side of the building between the office and the dining hall to the deck. Frank stood when he saw me.

"Good evening, Sarah."

"Are there ever any bad evenings here?" I asked, unable to imagine conflict in the midst of such beauty.

"Well, it turns bad real quick when Ron and his wife aren't getting along. They say too many cooks spoil the stew? It's a cook unhappy with his wife that spoils everything!"

"Temperamental?"

"Whoa! When the man lets the cookie jar stay empty for three or four days, we might as well close the place. Luckily, it doesn't happen with too much frequency!"

Kathy came out the door carrying a tray with a can of Budweiser and a glass of red wine. She set the tray on the table. "How was your ride today? Are you sore?"

"Well, yes. Sore is a four-letter word that could be used to describe my physical condition."

"Frank said you did real well. Let me know when you're ready for dinner. Frank, is it okay if I take my break now before we get busy?"

"Sure." Kathy left for the outdoor break room on the roof.

"Hey, Frank," yelled Chef Ron from the kitchen door. "You've got a phone call."

"Excuse me."

I was left alone with a landscape so beautiful that I wanted to whisper, afraid that any loud sound I made would break the magic spell that had been cast on this beautiful crescent-shaped lake. How could I have forgotten the magnetic pull the mountains had on me? Why did I stay in Georgia after Morgan died? A job I loved? Maybe. But maybe it was really because the gypsy in me had died somewhere along the way.

Although it wouldn't be dark for awhile, the sunlight was gone and the wind made the evening seem colder than the actual temperature. In the distance I could hear the hum of a motorboat and the sound of the water hitting the rocks on the shore below. I opened the *Wyoming Atlas and Gazetter* I bought at a convenience store off the Interstate. After all my cutting and pasting of the Forest Service maps, the DeLorme Atlas had topo maps of the entire state laid out in grids. With a yellow highlighter I had marked the trail that I believed trappers had used to travel from the Tetons, across the Continental Divide, to the Wind River. The trails were numbered on the map, but I wasn't sure how they would really be marked. The longitude and latitude were on each grid. I planned to use the GPS to check my position by satellite each morning. It was downright embarrassing to rely on a satellite in space to navigate country that had explored by mountain men in the early 1800s. North would always be north, but how long would satellites rotate the earth?

Frank returned and sat next to me on the bench. The strong wind blew the pages of the atlas. I had to use both hands to keep it from blowing away.

"This isn't going to work. Get the atlas, I'll get our drinks, and let's go inside. Ron built a fire in the sitting room at the other end of the dining room. It will give us some privacy so you won't have everyone eating dinner here tonight giving you their personal version of how they think you should cross the Divide." I nodded and followed him inside. Only two families were eating and Frank seemed unacquainted with both. He pushed a table and two chairs from the dining room in front of the roaring fire. We sat down and discussed the route I had highlighted. His tone was supportive. He told me most of the unimproved roads and the creeks were marked. He said I had done an excellent job selecting a way to cross the mountains, and asked if anyone helped me plan the trip. I told him about Osborne Russell and *Journal of a Trapper*. We spent the next hour talking about how to anticipate weather conditions, storms, what to do if I got lost, or came across a grizzly bear. I told him about the red pepper grizzly bear repellent I bought from a mail order catalog before I left, and showed him the silver bell on the chain around my neck.

"Grizzly bear repellent? Let me guess. It's like hornet and wasp spray, it shoots out to twenty feet, I bet."

"Right."

"Fine, Sarah, you take your bear repellent if it makes you feel safer, but if a charging grizzly bear gets within twenty feet of you, you'd better spray and pray! That stuff will burn the bear until you are dead. You are taking a firearm?"

"A Smith and Wesson .44 Magnum."

"That's a better bear repellent. It's effective past twenty feet."

At dinner we talked about forest fires and how far and how high to hang my food from camp to deter curious bears. He asked me to leave him emergency numbers. We studied the map and further discussed how far I wanted to ride after I crossed the Divide. We developed a plan for me to get in touch with him after my trip was over, and how soon I could expect him to arrive.

"Do you want me to go ahead and pay you for the horses?"

"That would probably be good business, but it's up to you."

"I'll go ahead and pay. What do you want me to do tomorrow?"

"First thing in the morning I'll introduce you to your pack horse, Walmart, and show you how to rig the pack saddle. Bring all your gear and we'll practice. I'll mark a route I want you to follow. You need to get a feel for leading a horse, it's different than what we did today. I want to see if you can find your way without a guide. Do you have gloves?"

"Yes, but what if I get lost, Frank?"

"You won't get lost. May I ask you a personal question?"

"Why am I afraid to say yes?"

"Why are you going out into the mountains alone? Why isn't a man making this trip with you? You're a fine-looking woman, Dr. Hanley."

I blushed at his unexpected compliment. "Let me see, how did you so eloquently phrase it when we met . . . you were expecting someone younger and less attractive?"

"Well, now I can't remember anyone ever describing me as eloquent."

"My husband died three years ago. There was an accident."

"I'm sorry. I didn't mean to pry. I hope I didn't offend you."

"No, Frank, you didn't offend me. Thank you for the compliment. I haven't had a man treat me like a woman in a very long time."

"I meant every word."

The evening, the conversation, the planning together, and the dinner with Frank was enjoyable. We talked long after the fire had died and the kitchen staff had left for the night.

The next day I ran Frank's gauntlet to his satisfaction. I packed into the mountains and followed the trail he assigned me and never once thought about using a satellite signal to find my way. When I returned I recited the endless instructions he had given me about taking care of the horses, what to do in case of a sudden thunderstorm, bear encounters, or if I got lost.

I passed Frank's tests.

At six a.m. on July fifth, Frank and I left Half Moon Lake, horse trailer in tow, for the two and a half hour drive to Jackson.

Chapter 9

We arrived in Jackson at nine in the morning. Jackson hadn't changed over the years. It was the same tourist anthill I remembered, only bigger. Neon hotel signs, billboards, and other garish detractors disfigured the country-side. The sidewalks were wooden and the streets were lined with designer stores; Ralph Lauren, Orvis, Eddie Bauer, even the ice cream, Häägen Daz, was designer. The windows of the retail stores, which called themselves galleries, were filled with displays of kachinas, turquoise, crystals, and Pendleton blankets. The Million Dollar Cowboy Bar faced the town square. At each of the four corners of the square were huge archways made of hundreds of elk antlers lashed together. At the east end of the square tour-ists, eager to see Jackson western style, waited to board a stagecoach pulled by a team of Palomino horses. The streets were filled with Suburbans, jeeps, and cars rigged with racks of bicycles, kayaks, and camping gear. Pedestri-ans ignored the flashing *Do Not Walk* traffic lights and dashed in front of oncoming cars to cross the street. At the Teton Theater *Star Wars: The Phantom Menace* was on the marquee.

A charter bus of Japanese tourists, headed north for the Teton Na-tional Forest, pulled in front of Frank. Just outside town, past the National Wildlife Museum on the left, the Tetons seemed to appear out of nowhere. Their ragged peaks hung in the morning mist as if they were magically suspended above the earth. Mountains possess the extraordinary power to awaken a sense of the sacred within us. It is clear why the Greeks placed the thrones of their gods high on the dangerous summit of Mount Olym-pus. High above me in the Wyoming sky I saw an eagle, the symbol of our country, the bird of Zeus. This was where I would begin. This time I was not a tourist. I was a sculptor setting out to carve my own path across the mountains.

As we drove into the park I stared at the mountains, entranced by their overwhelming beauty. There was a presence in the Tetons that was arresting. Their dark granite, snow-covered faces formed a fortress on the west of the park. Trees grew up their slopes from the valley floor as far as the snow and the rocky cliffs would allow. I traced their outline refamiliarizing myself with their unique silhouette. It was the silhouette I saw in the mirage of clouds at Margaret's, clouds painted by the rising sun with colors yet unnamed. Park visitors pulled into the first scenic overlook to marvel at the extraordinary view. They were bundled in polar fleece and down vests, their cameras hanging around their necks.

We drove a half mile farther and Frank turned to the right on Gros Ventre Road. We turned away from the Tetons and drove east into the hills. The road was lined with split rail fences. The warmth of the sun awakened huge flying insects which filled the air. The Gros Ventre River ran along the road to the right.

"Frank, will you pull over a minute?" He didn't hesitate and carefully moved the truck and trailer to the narrow shoulder of the road.

"Is something the matter?"

"I forgot this is the only time I'll see the Tetons, I'll be going in the opposite direction. Could we stop for a few minutes?"

"Sure thing."

I opened the truck door and walked to the back of the trailer. After a few minutes Frank joined me. He pointed to the mountains. "Do you see the Teton Glacier?"

"Where?"

"The highest peak is the Grand Teton. Below the lower ridge line to the left there's a stomach-shaped area of snow; the Teton Glacier. It's hard to imagine but during the Ice Age southward-flowing ice, more than 3,000 feet thick, filled the valley overriding the surrounding mountains and buttes; only the higher Teton peaks protruded through the ice."

We stood together leaning against the trailer, the smell of the horses grew stronger as the temperature rose. The trailer moved as they shifted their weight.

"Sarah, you don't have to go down this trail alone. I know you have personal reasons for this journey, but I can show you places in the mountains where you'll feel that you're the first person to ever see them. I'll take you, and I'll leave you. You can have all the privacy you need. I won't come back for a month, for two months, if that's what you need."

"Frank, I do have to go down this trail alone." There was an inexplicable feeling of trust between us. Standing beside him in, the bright morning sun, I shared the unusual story of the spirit blanket. After I finished, I couldn't tell by his facial expression what he thought of the tale.

"And, did you find the blanket?"

"Yes, I found it and I traded for it. I'll show it to you when I saddle up."

"Are you going to put it on Cocoa today?"

"No, the old man told me I had to make an offering in the direction of the four winds the night before I put the blanket on my horse to insure my safe return."

We stood for a few more minutes in silence, both appreciating the grandeur of the mountain faces. A huge RV with a license plate reading, *The Godleys*, pulled past us and up the road.

"How far can they go up this road?"

"Not much farther. The road turns to gravel past Atherton Creek Campground. It's the last campground with any facilities. Crystal Creek, where we'll unload doesn't have any showers and only one toilet. After the hot water runs out the tourists are few and far between. Are you ready to go?"

"Yes."

"Okay, I can see your mind is set. Let's do it."

We passed a small collection of buildings and houses on the right of the road.

"See the name of that store?" he pointed to the right. "The Slide In." You'll understand more about the significance of this town when we reach the Gros Ventre Slide. This town, Kelly, is the only town between the Teton range and the Rocky Mountains."

A few miles ahead we pulled off to the right of the road at an overlook of the Gros Ventre Slide. "You've got to see this," said Frank turning off the engine. We walked over to the Forest Service sign and I read:

Before you lie the remnants of one of the largest earth movements in the world. On June 23, 1925, earth, rock and debris moved rapidly from an altitude of 9000 feet, across the valley bottom and up the slope of the red bluffs behind you. The action lasted only minutes but a river was damned and the landscape changed.

Frank told me the slide dammed the river, but two years later the dam broke and sent a wall of water flooding downstream. It took the town of Kelly unaware; six people and hundreds of animals drown. It was hard to that imagine the Gros Ventre River, which flowed below us like a liquid current of diamonds, was the force responsible for such terrible tragedy. The slide looked like a rocky scar. Dark green pine trees grew up to the edge of the slide trying to secure and reclaim the mountainside.

As we drove further up the road the red hills looked as if they had been airbrushed. The sagebrush grew thick along the road and hugged the hills like a carpet. The vegetation was pastel colors: pink, green, and tan. The river changed, running deep and then a few miles further, running shallow. Signs warned of deer crossing and declared the area an open range. Once during our drive we passed a man on horseback herding a few head of cattle with his dog. The cattle obediently moved off the road as the cowboy raised his rope and the dog lowered his head. The road was dusty, and the farther we drove, the more narrow it became and the cars less frequent. We passed Red Hills Ranch whose boundaries were marked by a weathered split rail fence. Occasionally I saw the Tetons in the side view mirror. What must it be like to own a part of this beauty and call the Bridger-Teton National Forest your home?

Within thirty minutes up the dusty road, we reached Crystal Creek Campground, named for the pristine creek that flowed beside it. The National Park Service's steel box for camping fees was the only visible sign that distinguished the site as a campground. I saw only one campsite; a pop-up tent on the rise beside the creek. A woman wearing a large straw hat was sitting in a lawn chair reading a book, and a man in olive drab waders was fly fishing in the creek.

"This is it." He pulled off the road, turned off the motor, and got out the atlas. "We're here," he pointed on the map. "I think you should take it slow today. Get used to leading your pack horse. Pay attention to everything around you. The horses are the best but they'll still react if they're spooked. It's a horse's nature to run away and then look back and see what the matter was."

It was ironic. I had envisioned heading out on an unmarked trail not a gravel road. My original apprehension seemed foolish.

"The places we rode at Half Moon are more primitive than what's ahead of you, but there are plenty of things to be afraid of, even though it's not quite the wilderness you might have expected. The danger of grizzly bears is not a myth, nor are attacks on women in national forests by other backpackers. I'm not going to try to guess when you'll come out. You'll see places you may not want to leave for a few days. And remember, this isn't a race. How do you feel?"

"I feel alive."

"Best way to feel."

We got out of the truck and unloaded the horses and my few articles of gear. I took Cocoa and Walmart to the creek for water. The sun moved higher in the eastern sky. The wind blew just enough to make the leaves on the trees quiver. I, too, was quivering. I was anxious for Frank to leave so I could drop my outward appearance of confidence and capability. I was ready to go. I was ready to make my offering in the direction of the four winds and place the spirit blanket beneath Cocoa's saddle. Frank watched silently while I saddled the horses and secured my gear. I keenly felt the spontaneous friendship that had grown between us so effortlessly. A friendship initiated by feelings and no facts. He didn't know many specifics about me, nor I him; but I knew if I asked him to come with me now, he would get on a horse and come. A good wind blew between us. I could feel his eyes on me as I moved, checking my work. The horses secured, I walked to the passenger side of the truck and got my canvas bedroll from behind the seat, and carried it to Frank.

Neither of us spoke as I unrolled the package to reveal the faded woven artifact within. We held the blanket between us. Frank ran his fingers across the cloth touching its worn texture, tracing the irregular shape of the rust-colored mark. As the wool was exposed to the morning air, we smelled its distinctive odor. I waited for his reaction.

"Across the seasons . . . I wonder what it means?" His eyes were locked on the blanket's simple pattern. With the exception of Margaret, I had revealed the mystery to no one. "Well, be back by October or the rates go up." His humor shattered the tension.

"What are you worried about, Frank? You have my credit card and my Mother's telephone number. I'm your prisoner."

He began the sermon he had repeated at least twice before. "If a rancher gives you a hard time, be sincere, but I don't think anyone's going to hassle you for passing through. If you get lost, just stay where you are. You have plenty of supplies. Someone will come along. And don't forget to wear your gloves or you'll tear up your hands."

"Yes, Dad."

"Oh, that's cheap. Saddle up and get on your way."

We rolled the blanket back inside the bedroll and tied it on the back of my saddle. I pulled the reigns over Cocoa's head, holding them in my left hand on the saddle horn. I pulled myself up and threw my leg over her rump in one easy motion. Frank walked behind me, untied Walmart, and handed me the rope.

"Good bye, Dr. Hanley, fair weather to you."

"I'll see you down the road a piece. Thank you for everything."

He smiled and tipped his hat. "It was my pleasure, M'am."

"Come on Cocoa." I urged her forward with the sound of my voice and my heels into her broad body. She moved forward with such physical strength that I didn't feel I was beginning my journey alone. She turned into the direction of the wind and started up the road. I didn't look back at Frank, but similar to times before during the past week, I could feel him watching me as I began my adventure of the spirit. I knew he would stay until I was out of sight.

The soil was rocky and dry. Within thirty minutes I was thirsty from the heat, the dry air, and the dust from the road. The wildflowers were beautiful. I remembered some of their names from our ride at Half Moon Lake: lupine, yellowbells, wild buckwheat. Regardless of their names they were elegant. They grew close to the ground for protection from frost or late snowstorms. They covered the ground like brilliant cushions of yellow, blue, red, purple, and white. As I looked ahead I could not believe a brown UPS truck was coming down the lonely road. The horses hoofs created a steady rhythm as they hit the surface of the road. My pace was a clip and a clop, an easy transition from the world on the ground and the view of the world from the back of a horse. With each step I deepened the gulf between me and the rest of the world.

After riding five hours I decided to stop, taking Frank's advice to take it easy my first day and not make the trip a race. I was not sure of the time of day because I had made the decision to leave my watch behind. I moved down the hill to set camp about half a mile off the road by the river. The landscape was beautiful. Orange and black butterflies, the color of tigers, and small blue butterflies leisurely flew from flower-to-flower. The pine trees were much different than Georgia, the cones were smaller, and the limbs grew much closer to the ground. My legs were stiff and my knees creaked like the Tin Man when I dismounted. Frank had assured me repeatedly that Cocoa would not stray, and Walmart would stay with her. I unsaddled both horses, removed their bridles, leaving on only their halters. I held my breath, hoping they wouldn't flee at their first opportunity. Cocoa vigorously shook her body from head to tail and walked to the water. Walmart, rid of his burden, rolled in the dirt, then followed her obediently.

I stood, staring rather stupidly, at my few bundles of gear. For the first time I realized how little I had. Traveling across the country there was always the truck and its compartments filled with my belongings. There was my purse with my money, credit cards and identification, extra clothes and a couple of paperbacks I intended to read but never got around to. I had my saddle and a pack saddle loaded with absolute necessities; no Coleman lanterns, stoves, coolers, folding chairs, or Australian showers.

I placed the door of my tent toward the east. In the morning the sunlight would pour in the door and awaken me. The Sioux held their pipe to the sun so the sun could take the first puff, then to the four directions, as I would do tonight when I made my offering. I located a tree 100 feet from the river to hang my food. One of the forest service signs I passed earlier warned that I was in grizzly bear country. Terrifying graphics, showing the difference between the size of a black bear claw and a grizzly bear claw, rekindled the apprehension I first experienced when I received my brochures in the mail from the Interagency Grizzly Bear Committee. The fluorescent green brochures described what I should do in almost any situation. Keep calm. Avoid direct eye contact. Back up slowly. Speak to the bear in a soft monotone. Never turn your back. Never kneel. It gave the locations bears frequent most often. The pamphlet, *Women in Grizzly Bear Country,* assured me that, although bears are attracted by odor, there was no evidence grizzles are overly attracted to menstrual odors more than any other odor, and there was no statistical evidence that known attacks were related to menstruation. Nonetheless, I was relieved my period was over before I arrived at Half Moon Lake. I planned to sleep with my Counter Assault Oleoresin Capsicum Red Pepper Spray in hand tonight. I hoped the capsicum red pepper was more effective on grizzly bears than it was on my squirrels last spring. I mixed red pepper with the bird seed to keep the squirrels out of the bird feeders. It didn't work, I had created salsa for squirrels!

It took me thirty minutes to find an ample supply of wood for my fire. While looking for limbs and larger logs I found an old rusty horseshoe. For some reason I regarded it affectionately and found myself wondering about its origin. I laid the fire, set up my small two-person tent and decided on yellow rice and salsa for dinner. Before starting the fire I walked the 100 yards from camp and hung the rest of my food, in its canvas stuff bag, fifteen feet off the ground and four feet from the tree trunk.

What seemed would be a long time until sunset, passed quickly. I ate out of the pot, and finished every grain of rice. As the sun set I tied and staked the horses. It was time to make my offering. I stoked the fire, moved closer, and sat cross-legged on the ground. I untied the canvas, removed the spirit blanket, and placed it before me. With my knife I drew a circle placing myself and the blanket inside. Absent from the night were the sounds of dogs barking, traffic, and televisions. At first I only heard the loud roar of the river and the sound of the fire sizzling deep within the wood, but as I listened I gradually became aware of the night's more subtle sounds: trees being shaken gently by the wind, a coyote's cry, and faraway the hoot of an owl. The temperature fell quickly. I stared, hypnotized by the mystery of fire. I looked inside the flames. The coals seemed to breathe. I was not exactly sure what to say for my offering. I opened the ziplock bag with the cornmeal. I dipped my hand inside and felt the cool coarseness of the yellow grain. The Sioux gave the first puff of the pipe to the sun, but the sun had set, so I gestured toward the moon and tossed a generous handful north.

"God bless my trip, use my life to your glory, bring me home safely."
I repeated my prayer in the three other cardinal directions. I placed more
wood on the fire. The night wind rushed across the coals and yellow, orange, and blue flames licked upward through the new logs. I remembered
Joseph Campbell's observations in *The Power of Myth*; that a hunter is an
individual in a way no farmer will ever be. I had been a farmer toiling in
my scholarly fields, now I was going off on a hunt. I aspired to be what
Campbell referred to as the *Hero with a Thousand Faces*. I was going on a
vision quest, leaving the world in which I lived, going into the mountains
to discover what had been missing within me. I looked upward into the
night sky strewn with millions of stars that appeared to be a celestial necklace around the goddess earth. I could hear my heart pounding wildly in
my chest, in my ears, and through my body like an ancient drumbeat. I
wondered, after we die do we become stars in the heavens, guiding travelers,
seducing lovers, and inspiring poets? As we achieved higher spirituality do
we outgrow the physical pleasure of lying on the green grass in a spring
meadow, the cool refreshment of water splashed on our faces on a hot summer day, the childish joy of the first snowfall of winter, or the contentment
of sleeping in a lover's arms? Do we go gently into that good night, content
to leave our flesh behind for a higher consciousness? Which star was the
old Indian woman who had sent me on this journey? I picked one, and
wished her God's speed and good night.

I placed the spirit blanket under my head. It was uncomfortably hard
but it raised my head into a better sleeping position. I rolled onto my right
side and looked into the fire. I inhaled the smoke from the fire, and I inhaled the smoke from deep within the weave of the spirit blanket. The
smoke within the blanket came from a distant fire. The smell was comforting and familiar. I fell into a dream.

Sisiutl had come for me. I swallowed the sun and it began to pass
through my body. I was standing on the moon and could see the earth rising. I had seen pictures of the earth from the moon, but a photograph could
never capture the mystery of the moon's psychic landscape. I felt like Chagall
hovering lyrically over the earth. I was naked except for the spirit blanket
wrapped around my shoulders. I admired the alabaster-blue moonlight reflected on my breasts, belly, hips, and legs. My body was beautiful and
glowed luminously; the earth's second moon. I was leaning against an oak
tree whose branches were divided in two directions. Half of the branches
reached toward the earth as if the earth was its sun and the tree's source of
nourishment. The other branches were longer and strained backward dis-

appearing into the darkness of space. The letter "*V*" was deeply carved into the tree by a sharp butcher knife which was stuck in the gnarled trunk.

I turned away from the earth and pressed deeper into the silence, deeper into the darkness.

The stars looked like candles that had been carefully lit by the sun. I felt the moon rupture violently beneath my feet. Its surface opened and a thick boiling column of silver smoke twisted itself around me and pulled me further into the dream world of de Chirico and Barlach; into a spirit world dominated by the unseen forces of the subconscious. I heard a distant bell ring nine times. I held tightly to the blanket wrapped around my shoulders, but a thread caught on a sharp branch of the oak tree and the blanket began to unravel. I pulled frantically at the thread and the blanket began to dissolve into a red liquid that fell through space like a waterfall pouring into the sea.

I heard the singing of the morning stars. The sun was delivered from my body. The dawn appeared and I awoke.

II.

The myth is the public dream.
The dream is the private myth.

Joseph Campbell

Chapter 10

When Sarah awoke the coals were still smoldering in the fire, the full moon lingered in the early morning sky. The shifting sunlight slowly illuminated and colored the landscape. The mountains to the east caught the first light of morning. The high white snow was fluorescent against the gray mountain face. The dark evergreens hugged the mountains like moss growing on a rock. She sat for a moment thinking how beautiful and peaceful the world was today. It was difficult to imagine it could be more beautiful farther down the road. Cocoa and Walmart stood together calmly, their breath collecting in clouds of steam around their heads.

Sarah rose stiffly to her feet, reminded of Robert Redford's line in *The Electric Horseman*, that in the morning some parts wake up before others. It was much colder than she had expected. The high wind cut through her clothes like a laser. Cooking breakfast seemed too much trouble, but she rebuilt the fire. She searched through her stuff bags and found her polar fleece jacket. A big cup of coffee would be nice if the Hardee's drive-through window was open. She took a ziplock bag of walnuts, dried cranberries, and Turkish apricots down to the river. The sunlight was blinding as it reflected on the river's surface. She watched the water rush over the smooth, round rocks in the river. Some of the rocks looked like dinosaur eggs, speckled and nestled in the bed, as if they had been recently laid and were waiting to hatch.

Today was Sarah's first day without electricity, gasoline or telephones. Her mind raced. She had the sensation she was standing apart from Herself, and that her body had risen above the horizon to view the diaphanous landscape. These were not the mountains she had diligently studied on the map, these were the mountains of her dreams. She felt the enormous gulf that existed between herself and the rest of the world. In retrospect the pilgrimage of her life had been one of ordinary experience. Were the mountains of the world a geographic rosary where pilgrims sought forgiveness for their lack of spirit? This morning they looked like the backbone of the world.

Sarah whistled for Cocoa; Walmart followed like a school boy. She scattered the last charred pieces of wood from her campfire. She powered the GPS to check her location and waited for the indicator lights to give her the present coordinates. Nothing happened. She was getting power from the batteries but no reading. "Figures," she thought, fighting the impulse to throw it in the woods, certain the act would be considered littering. She followed the trail by the river rather than return to the road.

The morning passed quickly. Early afternoon Sarah stopped by the river to stretch her legs and water the horses. The sunlight was blinding as it cut sharply through the trees like fine bright thread through the eye of a needle. The light reflected off the rushing river like millions of brilliant crystals. The water roared as it hurried downstream slapping the rocks and digging deep into the riverbed and into the bank. As she knelt, she was unaware she was being watched.

The man eyed her greedily and kept himself hidden in the dark shadows of the trees. He could not believe his good fortune finding a White woman alone, away from the rest of her party. He had been thinking of the pleasures of women for months. He knew that within four or five days he could have an Indian woman but he was impatient and could not let this opportunity pass. He knew the sound of the river would limit her ability to hear him approaching. He took advantage of her kneeling position and caught her off guard, grabbing her from behind, hurling her forward and face down into the riverbed.

Her head struck a rock below the surface; she didn't know if her face was burning from the cold or the blow to her face. Unable to breathe she panicked she was going to drown. She flailed her arms trying to get her knees under her body. It was as if a great tree had fallen and pinned her underwater.

Her attacker did not want her to drown. He grabbed her by the belt and threw her out of the river onto the bank. The earth did not give. She hit the ground with such force she heard her bones crack. The world was a blur. She gasped to breathe, but choked when she inhaled water into her windpipe. She struggled to gain control. She coughed trying to force the water from her lungs. He had thrown her under one of the horses. Looking up she could see its belly. The horse stepped on her forearm as he jumped out of the away. She heard a man laughing cruelly.

"Ah, now, my lady. I'm not going to kill you. I'm just trying to get your attention."

Sarah struggled to sit, pushing the wet hair from her face, trying to focus her eyes in the direction of the mocking, hoarse voice. She breathed rapidly, hurting from the injury to her body and from the cold. Her fears of drowning shifted to fear of the huge man standing in front of her. He stood over her, cornering her, as if she was his prey. She was unable to speak. She had to escape. He lunged to grab her before she could move and scramble out of his reach. Her head was pounding. She tried to get to her feet, stumbled, and tried to crawl away. He impatiently grabbed her again by her belt, jerking her to a standing position and, threw her violently. She hit the ground face down and tasted dirt and blood in her mouth. She could not move.

"Do I have your attention now?" he yelled. She would rather die than lie with this filthy man. He knelt to the ground grabbing her shoulder roughly, turning her over. "You're a fine looking woman even wet. Let's have a better look at what we have here." He threw his knee over her, straddling her, sitting on her stomach. His heavy weight crushed her. She smelled the foul odor of his body. She saw the greasy stains on his worn clothing, and the pieces of food in his matted red beard. He fumbled with the buttons on her shirt.

"Get the hell off of me," she struggled to control his hands.

He laughed and continued to unbutton her shirt, leering as he saw her breasts. He ran his rough, cracked hands across her nipples, grabbing, and pinching her.

"No. No, damn you." The sound erupted from her body and exploded in the stillness of the afternoon. She hit him furiously with her fists and struggled. "Get off me!"

His expression became ugly. He slapped her face and ripped open her shirt. She screamed again, frantically grabbing at the ground with her fingers. Her hands full, she threw dirt and small pieces of gravel in his face. He cursed and grabbed his eyes.

"You damn whore! I'm going to kill you when I'm finished."

"Mister, you're not going to kill anybody. Now get off her and move away, or I'm going to kill you."

Her attacker looked at the stranger who stood pointing a rifle at his head. "Hold on, I'll share her with you. It's a White woman for God's sake." His eyes were red from the dirt and full of tears. He wiped his face with the dirty sleeve of his checked shirt.

"I said get off her, now."

Her attacker got up, raising his hands in a gesture of surrender. Sarah's lungs immediately filled with air when the weight of the huge man was removed from her body. The two men, dressed in the same homespun clothing, began to shout, cursing and threatening one another. She lay on the ground, paralyzed from the blows to her body and unable to move. The men's threats and obscenities continued.

"Get on your way or I'll kill you," threatened the younger man.

The heavy, bearded man lunged toward his challenger. Sarah heard a loud crack and saw a cloud of blue smoke rise from the barrel of his rifle. Her attacker crashed to the ground like a fallen tree. The shooter scarcely looked at his flintlock as he reloaded. He quickly poured a measure of black powder from his powder horn into a brass measure, then into the barrel of his rifle. A long strip of faded gray ticking was tied to the strap of his leather bullet pouch; he put it in his mouth, wetting it with his saliva. He positioned the cloth over the muzzle and followed it with a lead ball, pushing it flush to the opening with his knife. With the ball held tight by the patch, he cut the ends of the cloth. He thrust the ramrod down hard in the barrel, once, then several more times until the ball was seated firmly on the powder charge. He poured a bit of powder into the pan of his rifle, replaced the horn plug and brought the gun to ready, looking anxiously along the river and into the dark shadows of the trees, in case her attacker was not alone.

Everything fell silent. She lay motionless on the ground. After the shooter was convinced her attacker was alone, he checked the body for a pulse. He turned and walked toward Sarah. He put his rifle on the ground and slowly bent at the waist, offering his hand to her.

"M'am, you're badly hurt, let me help you."

Sarah sat, scrambling backward to move out of his reach. Looking down she saw her breasts were bare, her nipples hard from the cold water. She was too frightened to feel embarrassment. She felt helpless, but full of rage as she struggled to get to her feet. She stumbled, falling once before she reached Cocoa. Her hands were numb from the cold water but she found her gun in the saddle bag and pointed it at him. He didn't move. Sarah's eyes darted between the man offering help and the dead man on the ground.

"Get away from me. I'll kill you if you come any closer!" The water from her hair ran into her eyes. She wiped her face and saw blood on her hands.

"M'am, I'm not going to hurt you. Let me help you." He stood motionless, his hands raised in surrender.

God, she wished Frank was here. She quickly glanced at her attacker lying dead on the ground. The man who was trying to comfort her was dressed in the same odd costume. She assumed they were friends traveling together in an afternoon gone bad. One prone to rape, the other prone to murder. Sarah kept the gun aimed at him, wondering under what circumstances she would fire and take his life.

"M'am, I'm not going to hurt you."

"Stay away, don't come near me. I swear I'll shoot you." Her head pounded.

"I don't know that man. I heard you scream for help. Please, put your pistol down. What are you doing out here? Are you alone?"

For the first time Sarah looked closely at the man talking to her, asking her the same questions over and over, trying to get her attention. He was slim and tall. His voice was quiet and sincere. She was terrified. She could feel the pain rising in her body. For the first time she was embarrassed, with her left hand she reached for her denim shirt and tried to cover herself. A man had tried to rape her and he was dead. The man who had killed him was trying to convince her he wanted to help. She was confused. Even with a gun in her hand, she felt defenseless. She was not Campbell's *Hero with A Thousand Faces*, but a child with a thousand fears.

"I'm going to get on my horse and I'm going to leave. If you move or try to come near me I'll kill you." Sarah was shaking and her teeth began to chatter. "I have six bullets in this gun and I'll pour every one of them into you if you try to stop me. Do you understand?"

"I understand. I won't move, but you should let me help you. You're bleeding badly."

Sarah didn't answer. She felt sick. She tried to hold back, but gagged and heaved. Vomit poured out of her mouth spraying the ground. She wiped the drool from her mouth with her sleeve. She tried to whistle for Walmart but no sound came from her lips. Her eyes darted between the horse and the man. Her arm rose and fell, heavy with the gun, heavy with shock and exhaustion. Gathering Cocoa's reigns she led her the few feet to where Walmart stood. Positioning the two horses side-by-side, Sarah threw Walmart's reigns across Cocoa's saddle. She knew she would have to turn her back on the man and lower her aim to mount. She placed her left foot in the stirrup, she tried and failed to pull herself up and over into the saddle. For the first time she began to cry. She heard his voice again softly asking to let him help her.

"Don't move," she said weakly, thankful she was facing away from him and he could not see her tears.

She summoned all her strength and managed to pull herself up into the saddle. The young man watched helplessly, also confused by everything that had happened. It was fortunate he was passing nearby and heard her screaming. She stood little chance of overpowering her attacker considering the severity of her injuries and his size. He understood her fear and confusion, but he knew she would not survive in her condition. She rode slowly into the woods. He decided to follow at a distance, to make sure he would be near if she needed him.

As he watched her a strange physical sensation overcame him. He had been trying to help her out of regard for another person's life, but he now realized he wanted to run after her and hold her in his arms, fearing somehow she might get away and he might never see her again.

Sarah let Cocoa lead. She had no idea where she was going. She held onto the horn with both hands trying to sit upright in the saddle. Her stomach had quieted but her arm, her face, and her head throbbed with pain. She imagined the bleeding was from her head, maybe the right side of her face, because it was her right sleeve that was stained with blood. Cocoa's pace was steady and slow. In a daze she listened to the sound of the horses' hooves hitting the ground. She tried to concentrate and stay alert but she slumped down onto Cocoa's neck, her head throbbing and her body shivering from hypothermia and shock. She drifted in and out of consciousness, the familiar smell of Cocoa, as if a smelling salt, pulled her back each time. She awoke when Cocoa's steady rocking stopped as the horse stood to urinate. Sarah struggled to push herself off the horses' neck into a sitting position, but as she did the world began to spin around her and she lost her balance. As she fell from the saddle and hit the ground she opened her eyes and saw the young man riding up behind her. He jumped from his horse and knelt beside her, gently lifting her head and cradling it in his arms.

"Please, help me."

When Sarah awoke it was dark and the sounds of the night filled her ears. There was a fire burning and the strangely dressed young man was sitting on the other side of the fire a few feet away. It looked like he was writing. She lay on her right side, motionless, not wanting to call attention to herself. Her eyes searched the perimeter to find the horses. She saw Walmart standing in the shadows with four or five other horses and assumed Cocoa was nearby. Her head hurt so violently that she was afraid to sit up. Remembering her torn shirt she grabbed her chest. The familiar fuzzy texture of her polar fleece and denim shirt assured her she was properly covered. He must have dressed her when she was unconscious. He had covered her with a blanket and, it felt to the touch, he had placed the spirit blanket under her head for a pillow as she had done the night before. She watched him, her covert surveillance concealed by the darkness. She remembered the violence of the afternoon, and how he had rescued her and killed the cruel man who attacked her. Her eyes filled with tears. She could not see his face clearly in the darkness, but she remembered the look in his eyes as she rode away. If he had not ignored her commands, she might have died during the night of her injuries or exposure.

She had to go to the bathroom. She was going to have to get up and when she moved she was going to call attention to herself. She didn't know if she could stand. She tried to push herself up, propping her right elbow under her body. Her head pounded as she changed positions. Her movement caught his attention. He sprang to his feet, closing the distance between them, and knelt by her side. He put his hand firmly on her shoulder.

"Take it easy, M'am, you have a bad blow to your head. You shouldn't move. I'll bring you whatever you need."

"I need to go to the bathroom."

"What?"

"I need to relieve myself."

She was embarrassed and she could tell he was embarrassed and not quite sure how to react. He placed his hand on her back and helped her to a sitting position.

"Take your time. Sit up and I'll help you stand." He kept his hand on her back, applying pressure to give her support. She kept her eyes downward. She was self-consciousness thinking of herself half naked, bleeding, and unconscious while he dressed and took care of her. She extended her right hand for him to pull her up. He stood, half kneeling, "Put your arms around my neck." With his left hand still supporting her she put her right arm, then her left arm around his neck. Her face was close to his.

"Are you ready? Just hold on and I'll do all the work." He slowly rose to his feet, his left hand holding her close to him as they stood. When she was standing her arms slipped from around his neck but she leaned against him trying to get her balance. The smell of his body overwhelmed her. It took her back to reunions with Morgan after his two-week summer camps at Fort Stewart. It was the intoxicating odor of a man's body after he has been living in the woods.

"How do you feel?"

"My head hurts. I feel dizzy." She moved away from him and took a step. The world began to reel around her and she began to fall. He lunged forward to keep her from hitting the ground and picked her up in his arms.

"I've got for you. I'm going to take you over here away from the fire to give you some privacy. I'll come back when you call me." He put her down and stayed with her until she got her balance by leaning against a tree. He took a few steps back.

"I'll be all right. Thank you."

He walked back to the fire. In a few minutes she called him and he quickly returned to her side.

"Let me try to walk in case I need to get up in the middle of the night."

"M'am, I don't think it's a good idea. You're in no . . ."

She interrupted him. "Please, call me Sarah."

"Sarah, I don't think it's a good idea."

"Let me try."

He put his arm around her waist and she held his other hand taking small steps back into the light of the fire, but her knees buckled. He had not held a woman in his arms in a long time and the innocent act of lifting her with his arm under her legs excited him. When she was unconscious he tried not to look at her body when he dressed her, but it was impossible not to notice the shape and size of her breasts. She was beautiful even with blood and dirt on her face. It was evident she didn't realize how badly she was hurt. She should rest at least a day and longer if the pain continued and the bleeding started again. Would someone be coming for her? A White woman couldn't possibly be in the mountains alone. The only two White women he had encountered in the mountains were the wives of missionaries, and she wasn't dressed like a missionary's wife. She wasn't dressed like any woman he had ever seen.

He carried her back to the bed he had made for her. When she looked down she noticed he had covered her with a well-worn white wool blanket with three black stripes. He gently lowered her to the ground. She was exhausted by the small amount of physical activity.

"I've always wanted a Hudson's Bay blanket."

"It's been over these Rocky Mountains more than once."

"Will you hand me that green bag?" He had placed her things around her but the green bag was out of her reach. He reached across her and handed her the bag.

"Could I have some water? I want to take some medicine."

He gave her a tin cup filled with water.

"You need to eat. I have some jerked meat."

"Anything sounds good." She found her bottle of emergency medicine. She had packed Percocet in case she burned herself on the trip. The water refreshed her dry mouth. He helped her sit, propping the green bag and a saddle behind her. She sucked on the jerky allowing the juices in her mouth to soften it so she could chew the meat. He refilled her cup with water. She was aware he was watching her while she ate.

"I didn't know the man who attacked you today."

"I realize that now. I just assumed because you were dressed alike you were friends. Are you a buckskinner?"

"No." He didn't know what she meant but he thought it was better to answer no, if she thought her attacker was a buckskinner.

"I don't understand why you are in the mountains alone."

"I wanted to cross the Wind River Mountains on horseback."

"Alone?"

"Yes."

"I can't believe you would consider such a thing. Don't you know how dangerous it is?"

"I don't think I really took the danger seriously until today."

"Which way did you come from?" he asked.

"Up from the Tetons on the Gros Ventre River where the land slide occurred."

"I know these mountains like I know the back of my hand; I don't know where that is."

"The slide happened in 1930 or 1940, I don't remember, Between my headache and the medicine I can't rely on my judgment. But, thank you for saving my life today."

"I'm glad I happened along. Let me help you lie back down." He moved the saddle from behind her and repositioned his blanket beneath her head. She closed her eyes. What did she mean by the Gros Ventre slide and what did the numbers nineteen thirty and nineteen forty mean? She'd think more clearly in the morning after a good night's rest.

Sarah fell asleep for a few minutes and when she awoke he was sitting close, watching and guarding her.

"Can I get you anything else?"

"No."

"Do you want more water?"

"No. I don't want you to have to carry me to a tree in the middle of the night." The throbbing in her head began to slow. She felt dreamy and delightfully numb.

"Are you warm enough?"

"Yes. That man you killed today, don't we have to tell somebody?"

"Who do you want to tell?"

"The authorities. Shouldn't we tell the authorities?"

"Go to sleep. You'll feel better in the morning. We'll talk more then. I'll be sleeping right over there." He pointed across the fire. "Wake me if you need me."

"Thank you again for taking care of me."

"Good night, M'am."

"My name is Sarah." Her eyes were closed as if she was talking in her sleep.

"Good night, Sarah."

"Good night. You never told me your name."

"My name is Osborne Russell."

Chapter 11

Russell couldn't sleep. He'd slept on the ground in the mountains for the past four years, but the ground had never felt as hard as it did this night. He got up five or six times to check her, to be close if she awoke and needed him. She never moved. Once he knelt beside her, leaning close to make sure she was still breathing. He inhaled deeply to get the smell of her. Her scent was different than any woman he had ever held.

He added wood to the fire. The light allowed him to easily see her long silhouette wrapped in his blanket. He wished she would turn over so he could see her face while she slept. Who was she? His mind was full of questions about her and why she was alone in the mountains. There was nothing logical about her presence.

She was alone.

Even Russell, after four years in the Shining Mountains, rarely traveled alone. When she fell from the horse she dropped her pistol. When he picked it up, its feel, its weight, its grip was unlike any he'd seen. He packed it carefully in one of her bags which were strange to the touch. They weren't wool or canvas, and they weren't cotton. He did not go through her belongings; it would not be right. He only looked long enough to find something to cover her and keep her warm. Her dark blue shirt felt like a strange fur.

And the way she talked. What did she mean nineteen thirty or nineteen forty? What did she mean by the Gros Ventre slide? What was a buckskinner? What authorities? She said it was her second day. What were the days before? She smelled different. She talked different. She looked different, her clothes and her possessions were different.

Earlier while he waited for her to regain consciousness he wrote in his journal. He considered whether or not to include what had befallen him, but instead, wrote about the day before and his journey to meet his comrades on the Wind River. He did not write about how a scream led him to a woman being beaten and raped. He did not write about how he felt when she rode away, or how he felt when he looked at her now through the darkness.

It was the longest night of his life.

He must have fallen asleep, because he was awakened by the morning chill passing through his body and the bright sun rising over the mountains in the east. The fire had burned to ash. He needed to get more wood. He doubted she would be in any condition to travel today. He was critically low on food. He thought about going to the river to fish or hunt for game nearby, but he thought it too dangerous to leave her alone.

Mid-morning he walked to the river's edge to get water. As he knelt to fill his blackened tin coffee pot he became self-conscious about his body odor and his appearance. He hadn't shaved in two or three days nor had he bathed. He heated the water, made fresh coffee, and stripped behind a nearby tree to wash himself and change. He combed his hair and wished he had a bigger mirror to determine the damage he'd done when he cut it last spring. He found his cleanest dirty shirt; a faded red flannel that had been torn and poorly mended several times during the year. He didn't have another pair of pants. He was looking forward to resupplying and enjoying the rare feeling of abundance for a few weeks. He put a spoonful of coffee grounds in his mouth, forcing them across his teeth and around his mouth with his tongue, a primitive, but effective cleaner. He returned to their camp, remade the fire, started the coffee, sat down with his rifle beside him, and closed his eyes.

It was the smell of coffee that awakened Sarah. It was one of those comforting familiar smells that had stretched across her life. Coffee and bacon in the morning. Coffee after dinner in the evening. She heard the sounds of the river. She smelled the smoke from the fire and the odor of the horses. When she turned over he was sitting ten feet away, propped up against his saddle. She lay motionless. She watched him, moving her eyes around the landscape and across his body. She vividly remembered his eyes and the kindness she saw in them during the violence of the afternoon and her pain in the evening. She remembered the sense of comfort she felt when he picked her up when she was unable to walk. He had the body of a baseball player. Slim and strong, with long compact muscles that accentuated his height. His hair was light brown, bleached blonde on the ends by the sun, and collar-length in the back. In the light of day she realized how ruggedly handsome he was and, maybe, 32 years old.

She doubted she could get up by herself, but she didn't want to wake him. She couldn't remember his name. She remembered asking him before she fell asleep. She felt so tired. The simple act of breathing hurt as her ribcage rose and fell. She closed her eyes, trying to remember his name, and fell asleep again. When she awoke she saw him watching her. For a moment they both held one another's gaze without speaking. For the first time she saw him smile.

"Good afternoon, Sarah."

"Afternoon? Did I sleep all day?" She spoke deliberately, expressing herself with difficulty. The words in her mind were not the words coming from her mouth. Everything seemed to be happening in slow motion. Could it really be afternoon the next day?

"You just about slept through it." He poured a cup of water and brought it to her. She struggled to sit.

"Whoa, wait a minute. Take your time," he commanded. Uncontrollably tears filled her eyes. She was confused. She was nauseated. He saw her frustration. He didn't know what to do for her.

"I don't know where I am. I don't know what day it is. I don't even know who you are." She breathed deeply trying to control her nausea.

"I introduced myself last night."

"My name is Osborne Russell."

Sarah stared at him dumbfounded. "You're not Osborne Russell," she said weakly. She wanted to bury her face and cry. She felt out of control and disoriented. "I've been in love with Osborne Russell since I was twenty-two years old and first read his journal." She wiped the hot tears from her eyes.

He turned pale as if he had taken ill. He took a few steps back and walked away. He stood with his back to her, staring across the river. Why was he trying to confuse her? He had saved her life. She waited for him to move or speak. He must be embarrassed, or perhaps he was angry. She pulled herself into a sitting position, and, after great effort, she stood. The gash on the side of her head throbbed. When she touched it she found the dressing had come off. She felt the matted blood in her hair.

He did not turn around, but asked, "Do you need my help?"

"No, I believe I can make it."

She shuffled, taking small steps, pausing whenever she became unsteady or dizzy. The twenty-foot distance felt more like a mile. She leaned against a tree, wrestling to pull her jeans out of the way while she squatted. She was not embarrassed at the loud sound of her urine pouring onto the ground. She was hypnotized by the evening sounds around her. It was as though she was experiencing her sense of hearing for the first time. The chirping of the scarlet tanager was a scream, the water racing downstream was a roar in her ears. Even the pressure of the air against her body felt different. She didn't realize that everything she knew about reality was about to change.

Russell was standing a tasteful distance away, his expression was grave. "Let me help you." He moved toward her and took her by the hand, he placed his other arm behind her back to steady her. She was exhausted from the brief exertion and she was cold. The wind was blowing furiously. He settled her on the bedroll. He stacked two saddles on top of one another to support her back while she sat. She was shivering. He wrapped the white wool blanket around her shoulders.

"I'm going to get more wood and check the horses. Do you want some coffee?"

"Yes, and, could I have some water to clean up?"

His expression did not change as he handed her the hot cup of coffee, and a shallow tin pan with warm water, a worn piece of muslin, and a small round mirror.

"Thank you."

He walked toward the horses. She watched him lead them, two at a time, to the river. He stood patiently as the horses bowed their heads and drank. She wondered what he was thinking, and what he would say when he returned.

Sarah drank the coffee as soon as it cooled to her lips. It was warm in her mouth and down her throat. It was strong and bitter like Greek coffee, and grounds floated in her cup. The tiny mirror was less than two inches in diameter. She moved it around her face. Even at arms length she couldn't see both of her eyes at once. Her face was red and her right eye swollen and purple. She was sunburned and her lips were dry and cracked. Her bottom lip was fat and swollen. She couldn't see the cut on the side of her head. She dipped her hands in the warm water. It felt wonderful. Such a simple thing as warm water suddenly seemed a great luxury. She wet the tattered muslin and held it to the side of her head. It stung. The muslin was red, colored by her blood. She was lucky to be alive. She gently pulled her hair back and carefully moved her fingers along the cut. The tear in her skin was about three inches long. The warm water dissolved the rust-colored crusted blood and her head began to bleed again. She used her fingers to comb her wet hair.

Russell returned with an arm full of wood. He arranged the limbs on the fire and the colored flames quickly rose, in the late afternoon sky.

"I need to hunt before it gets any darker."

"I have food. Please, don't leave me," her teeth chattered.

He pulled his blanket around her shoulders. He folded his tall frame and sat by the dancing fire. For a few minutes he said nothing, holding his bowed head in his hands.

"Who are you?" he asked.

"My name is Sarah Hanley."

"Sarah Hanley, no one has any business in the mountains alone. Nothing about you makes sense. The words you use, the way you look, your clothes, your pistol. And I don't understand how you know my name and about my journal?"

She reached for her saddlebag with her personal items and Russell's journal. She noticed he had washed the spirit blanket the old man said would take her across the seasons. The blanket was luminous. There was a blood stain in the corner; she must have bled on the blanket when her dressing came off during the night.

"My blanket looks new, how did you get it clean?"

"That's my blanket. I got it from an Indian woman at Fort Hall last September. I hoped to trade it at Rendezvous. I placed it under your head last night because everything else I own is filthy."

"No, this is my blanket."

"No, it is not."

"Then where is my blanket?"

"I don't know what you're talking about."

"I had it last night, no, the night before last. It was the first night of my trip. I used it as a pillow. The next morning I packed it. I almost put it on Cocoa when I saddled her, but instead I packed it in my green stuff bag." Sarah reached for the bag, but it was out of arm's length. Russell got up and handed it to her. Without looking she somehow knew the blanket was inside. She could smell it. She could feel it. She pulled the blanket from her bag and gave it to him.

Neither of them spoke as he carefully unfolded her blanket; wrapped inside was William, the small, blue faience hippopotamus and, in a large ziplock bag, *Journal of a Trapper. 1834-1843*. He touched the book lightly as if it might suddenly disappear. He looked as if he had seen a ghost. He walked to the other side of the fire and reached into a leather bag lying next to his bedroll. He handed her a book with stiff cardboard covers bound with a leather spine. Inside, on blue, unlined paper were the handwritten words: Journal of a Trapper by Osborne Russell, 1834 - .

He knelt beside her on the ground, the two blankets spread open between them. Even in the fading light of day it was apparent the blankets were the same. One was old, faded and worn, the other new. The old blanket had a strange rust-colored mark and the new blanket had Sarah's blood in the same place. Sarah's hand trembled as she lightly traced the two marks with her fingertips. Russell took her hand. The wood in the fire crackled and threw burning embers out of the fire.

"What year is this?" she asked softly.

"1838. What year is this for you?"

"2000."

"Sarah, how can this be?"

"I'm dead."

Chapter 12

It was impossible. How could she be alive in 1838? It wasn't a dream. It was too real. She couldn't be dead. She hurt too badly. Russell gently touched her wet hair.

"You're not dead. I need to bandage your head, it's bleeding again." She saw her blood on his hands. In the year 2000 no one would touch another's blood without plastic gloves. On her journey across the mountains she found herself with Osborne Russell, a man she fell in love with years after his death, when she first read his journal. Was he really Osborne Russell, or was he an angel sent to save her life and keep her from harm? An angel who had taken the form of someone she would unconditionally trust with her life.

She took a deep breath. She tried to relax. She looked at the two blankets lying on the ground, the old and the new: the same. She looked at Russell kneeling beside her. She said nothing. She did not move. She looked ahead, deep within the fire, and escaped into the white coals, the rising yellow-orange flames, and the circling gray smoke. Russell felt helpless. He was afraid she might go into shock. It occurred to him she might have medicine that might help her and stop the bleeding.

"Do you have any medicine?"

She looked at her blood on his hands.

"Sarah, do you have any medicine?"

"Yes." She pointed to one of her bags. He handed it to her and she clumsily groped inside to find the first aid kit. She opened it and pulled out hydrogen peroxide, gauze, and antibiotic ointment. He touched her lightly, trying not to hurt her or open the wound.

"Pour this over the cut, it will kill the germs."

Russell carefully pulled back her hair. The peroxide foamed as it ran across her scalp. She shivered as it ran down her neck and into her clothes. He blotted her head, applied the ointment, and wrapped the gauze around her head. He didn't comment, but she could tell by the way he handled the plastic bottle of hydrogen peroxide and the tube of ointment, that a thousand questions were running through his mind. How could she begin to describe the events between 1838 and 2000? The Civil War, automobiles, computer technology, the Internet, birth control, nuclear warfare, space travel, microwaves, satellites.

In slow motion the night closed in around them. It was only Russell's words of encouragement that kept time moving forward. Sarah, confused and in pain, would have been content to shut down, close her eyes and awake again, somewhere else. She curled her mind into a fetal position trying to find any explanation for what had occurred, but in the darkness she felt despair. She thought of her parents, her brother and sisters, and Margaret. She had never considered that by following this path she would create sorrow for those she loved.

God is in control of my life. She mentally repeated it like a mantra with mystical power that would anchor her in this storm of time. Her sadness welled within her until she could no longer hold back the tears.

Russell gave her privacy. He didn't know what to say or what to do. He could only imagine what she was thinking and what she was feeling after all that had happened to her. He had never understood some men's propensity for rape. He kept his distance and respected her silence. She sat with her arms folded and her head down on her knees. He left her alone until he saw her body shake and he heard her cry. The sound of her crying rendered him helpless. He wanted to take her in his arms, but he was afraid to reach out and touch her. He hurt for her. He had fought Indians, the fiercest: the Blackfeet and the Crow. He had been nearly starved and froze to death. He had been shot, but his heart had never been wounded. Her crying pierced him like an enemy's arrow.

It was unusual for Russell to travel alone. He and several others trapped and lived together in loose assemblies, primarily for safety, but also because it was lonely in the mountains. It had been four years since he joined Nathaniel Wyeth's second expedition of trappers in 1834. One of nine children, born and raised in Maine, he ran away from home when he was 16 years old. He had lived his life without women, with the exception of a white woman he met in Missouri before joining the expedition of trappers, and three or four Indian women dazzled by the foofarraw he purchased at Fort Hall. Sometimes the loneliness hurt, the ache and desire for a clean, willing woman, but he pushed it down deep inside and got on with things. He had never been in love; the kind of love where you take a wife and repeat vows meant to last a lifetime. And what of her? Sarah? How could her husband or sweetheart, or her father allow her to make such a perilous journey alone?

It was inconceivable a woman from another time had randomly fallen into his life while he was on his way to Rendezvous. He had been looking forward to a new shirt and trousers, to copious amounts of rum, and to the camaraderie and the brief feeling of safety that accompanied their annual meeting. This year the Rendezvous had been kept a secret until the last minute in an attempt by the American Fur Company to outwit the Hudson's Bay Company and leave them out of the financial opportunity that came with a tired, rag-tag bunch of men come to trade a year's worth of beaver pelts for supplies and whiskey. Russell had been headed in another direction when he found a piece of paper fastened to a storehouse door that said he would find the Whites at the forks of the Wind River. Most trappers spent a year's wages at Rendezvous and left in the debt of the trading companies. It wasn't good sense but it was a damn good time. More and more men were absent from the meeting, not because they met with an untimely death, but because they were unable to repay their debts to the companies.

Sarah struggled to her feet and looked around as if she was looking for a way to escape. She walked out of the light of the fire into the darkness. She was disoriented and unsteady. Russell rose to his feet calling after her. He caught up to her as she tripped over a fallen tree limb and stumbled forward. He saved her fall and helped her steady against a tree. Her face was wet with tears and she had the saddest expression on her face.

"Sarah, I don't have an explanation for what's happened, but I'll take care of you, everything's going to be fine. I promise."

"My family," her voice cracked with emotion. She dropped her head to his shoulder and sobbed. He put his arms around her and found the shuddering of her body the most disturbing and yet the most exciting feeling he had ever known. She didn't move away. She let him hold her. Was her Father still alive? Her Mother? Every reality had been ripped from beneath her and she stood in the darkness held tightly by Osborne Russell, a phantom incarnate, saying he would take care of her.

Russell never loosened his embrace. He was memorizing the softness of her body and the smell of her. He was embarrassed that even during her deep sorrow he felt so much pleasure in the closeness of their bodies. He looked up at the night sky. Sarah suddenly became aware of his arms around her. Were they holding her up or were they holding her? She was embarrassed.

"It's clear tonight, maybe six hours until daylight. Here I am promising to take care of you, but I can't feed you."

"I have food. In the new millennium we don't hunt for food, we just add hot water and stir. I'll show you." They walked slowly, his right arm around her shoulder and her left hand in his, as they moved back into the light. Her eyes were swollen and her face blotchy and red. She was the most beautiful woman he had ever seen.

The horses started. Russell's attention shifted. He seated her safely by the fire and moved to his rifle.

"It's probably nothing, but I'm going to move the horses in closer. I'll be right back." He disappeared into the night. She could hear him talking to the horses, calming them with the tone of his voice. One at a time he brought them closer to camp, picketing them within easy sight distance.

I could have given him my flashlight, she thought. No, it would confuse him all the more.

"You have some fine looking horses," Russell remarked when he returned.

"They belong to a friend of mine." She thought of Frank waiting at Half Moon Lake for the call to come get her. Oddly, the sight of the moon reassured her. Perhaps her Mother and Father were sitting on their deck in Florida looking at the same moon rising over the ocean.

"The moon looks like the Cheshire cat's smile," she said. Russell could not possibly have known what a Cheshire cat was, Lewis G. Carroll's *Alice in Wonderland* had not been written. She didn't want to make him feel uncomfortable by not understanding what she was saying. Russell's intelligence had always intrigued her. In *Journal of a Trapper* he frequently made references she did not understand. She had a Ph.D. in art history which included strong emphasis on Greek civilization, but when she read his poem, *Hunters Farewell to the Mountains*, she had no idea who Boreas was. She had to sift through a classical dictionary to learn Boreas was the god of the north wind. But where did he learn about Boreas?

"Osborne, you've been so kind to me. I know this is also difficult for you. I want you to know I appreciate everything you've done. Are you sure you're not my guardian angel?"

He remembered how aroused he became when his arms were around her. "No M'am, I'm no angel."

"If you'll boil some water, I'll show you how times have really changed." Russell hung his copper kettle on a long chain fastened to a tripod of limbs. The water in the blackened pot hissed as it heated over the hot fire. She thought she was beyond hunger, but as she hunted through the bag her saliva glands watered in anticipation. She decided on Zatarain's Jambalaya with match sticks of pepperoni.

"The water's boiling."

She leaned forward and handed him the plastic bag. He looked at the bag curiously.

"Pull the top apart." He tentatively pulled the sides and the bag separated.

"We call them ziplock bags. Zip for zipper." As she spoke she realized zippers hadn't been invented. "Just pour it in, stir, and cover."

He moved the kettle off the fire so the rice wouldn't burn. He shook the empty bag fascinated by its transparency.

"What is this?"

"Plastic."

"What's plastic?"

"Plastic is made of petroleum byproducts."

"What are petroleum byproducts?"

"Dead dinosaurs."

"What?"

"I don't really know." She laughed at how foolish it must seem that a woman from the future couldn't even explain a ziplock bag. He laughed too, and for just a moment, her fear and confusion disappeared. "In my time our way of life has become complicated by our inventions . . . not harder, but more complicated." If she couldn't explain plastic, how was she going to explain electricity and how a plane flies?

"I hope you'll tell me about all of the inventions."

"I will, but I believe I should begin with the story of this blanket." She took a deep breath, exhaled slowly, and began to gradually relax. Perhaps relax wasn't the right word, but she gradually began to lose her panic, and her conclusion she was dead.

"Osborne, hand me your cup." She searched for her dark blue enamelware cup and one of the leather wineskins. He handed her a dented tin cup. She removed the top and poured Jack Daniels into their cups. Its distinctive smell filled the air.

He raised the cup and drank. "It's good to know some things are still around in the future; that's good whiskey." He had never seen a woman drink liquor.

"It ought to be. It's a hundred and" she mentally did the math. "One hundred and sixty-two years old."

"Tell me about the blanket."

"The story really begins with you, Osborne. When I was twenty-two I had a friend who was enamored by the fur trade "era" as we call it. He read *The Big Sky* by A. B. Guthrie, *Men to Match my Mountains* by Irving Stone. I realize these books mean nothing to you, but my point is that even 162 years in the future, people are fascinated by mountain men. He and his best friend made .50 caliber Hawken reproductions, they sewed buckskin leggings and shirts, and set out to cross the Continental Divide using your book, *Journal of a Trapper*. Your journal is one of the definitive accounts

of life in the Rocky Mountains. It's sold all over the world. This copy cost
$1.60, but the latest paperback edition sells for $15.00."

"Fifteen dollars? I can't believe it!"

"When my friends left they gave me your book so I could follow their
trip. I had a job in Texas that summer teaching horseback riding to girls. I
took your journal with me. They wrote and asked me to come west and
make the return trip over the mountains with them. In the meantime in
Texas we had a flood. I lost everything I owned: my money and my clothes
except the ones I was wearing. I found your book 100 yards from my tent,
water soaked, and covered with mud. I can't explain it, but when I found
your book I felt like you were there with me."

Russell watched the subtle expressions on her face as she recounted
the events that first connected them somewhere in time. She said earlier
she had loved him since she was twenty-two years old. He wanted to ask
her what she meant but the thought of asking such a personal question
made him uncomfortable.

"I joined my friends in Jackson Hole, eagerly anticipating the return
trip, but their romantic notion of the mountains had faded. They complained
of mosquitoes, of being cold, wet, and hungry, and they quit. They quit
before I had the opportunity to cross the mountains as they had promised."

"If they quit, how did they get home?"

"They got home in one of those inventions I'm going to tell you about
later. I've kept your journal all these years on my bookshelf, in one of those
plastic bags, secured with a rubber band, a rubber string, to hold it together.
The flood didn't do much for the binding. Anyway, jumping to the present,
about six weeks ago my best friend talked me into attending an Indian
powwow. I didn't want to go, but she taunted me until I said yes. At the
powwow I met an old Indian woman. When I first saw her I was awestruck
because she was surrounded by a golden radiant light."

"An invention?"

"No, more of a miracle. The old woman told me she had waited for
me all her life. She had been given a story by her great great grandmother
to hold in her heart until she met a woman who she would recognize because she, too, would be surrounded by golden light. I looked into her eyes
and could see my illuminated reflection."

Russell had sat by many a fire listening to yarns. Stories that were
meant to make a cold winter night seem warmer, or the untimely death of a
friend somehow more bearable, or the loneliness less painful, but he had
never imagined he would be sitting here with a beautiful woman, listening
to a story of the future. A story that intertwined his life with hers long after
his death, and pulled her back to him, years before her birth. He had read of

miracles in the Bible; water turned to wine, blind men gifted with sight, Lazarus raised from the dead, and barren women conceiving. Was this another of God's miracles? A woman named Sarah. A name from the Bible. Her name was Biblical, but his feelings toward her were certainly not religious in nature. What if she had fallen through this field of time and he had not been within ear shot? She would have been raped and killed, if not, left for dead. She would have been unprepared for the genuine threats that accompany life in the mountains in his time: grizzly bears, Indians, and men that had not seen a White woman since they came west. He didn't want to go to sleep tonight. He was afraid if he went to sleep he would awake the next morning and she would be gone. Her story, her voice, hypnotized him with its tone and tale.

"What was the story she held for you?"

"She told me we all have our own own path to find across the mountains. She said I had become lost from the journey I was destined to make. She went on to say there was a blanket that enabled a horse and its rider to travel across the seasons, and I had to find the blanket and resume the journey that was my destiny."

"What else did she tell you?"

"Nothing. When I returned the next morning I learned she had died during the night. Her story tied me in knots. It was too unbelievable even for the twenty-first century."

"You thought this was the journey you were destined to make?"

"At first I didn't know, but the more I thought about it I kept coming back to the anger and disappointment I felt when I missed the trip with my friends. Early one morning I thought I saw the silhouette of the Tetons in a cloud formation. I took it as a sign."

" . . . and your blanket, my blanket, how did you find it?"

"Do you know who His Crazy Horse is?"

"No."

"He's a Native American, that's what we call Indians now. I don't know if he's even been born yet, but he was a great chief of the Oglala Sioux. The U.S. Cavalry attacked a village, believing it to be His Crazy Horse's home. If I remember correctly, they were retaliating because His Crazy Horse refused to enter a reservation."

"What's a reservation?"

"Federal land set aside for the Indians to live."

"The government told the Indians where they had to live?"

"Ordered them. Threatened them. Herded them like cattle. His Crazy Horse sought revenge for the destruction of the village and led the Sioux and Cheyenne in a great war and defeated a Colonel, named Custer, and his command, in the Battle of Little Big Horn. There's a monument being built to him in the Black Hills. I went to see it and met an old man at a trading post. He sold blankets, pottery, and jewelry. I finally got up the nerve to ask him if he had ever heard of a blanket that would carry a horse and its rider across the seasons. He told me he had it!"

"You believed him?"

"No, I thought I was being ripped off . . . tricked. But there was something about him — about the place — it all felt very mystical. I took a leap of faith."

"How much did you pay for the blanket?"

"He told me I couldn't buy it; I had to trade something of deep personal value for it."

"What did you trade?"

Sarah smiled. "The small, blue, ceramic hippopotamus that was with your journal and the spirit blanket. After I gave the old man the hippopotamus he disappeared and returned with the blanket wrapped in brown paper. I didn't open it until I stopped for the night. When I unfolded the blanket I found the small blue hippo inside."

"I'll be," he shook his head, "he gave it back to you."

"Yes, and the rust-colored mark on the blanket is my own blood. It's all so unreal. As I left he warned me I had to make an offering in the direction of the four winds before I put the blanket on my horse to insure a safe return from my journey. I guess I did it wrong."

"You put the blanket on your horse the next morning?"

"No, I used it as a pillow that night but I never put it on my horse. The next afternoon I was attacked."

"Did you notice anything different that day?"

"Yes. Everything smelled different. Stronger. Fresher. Today I noticed the smallest sounds seemed extremely intense. But nothing else. It seems if a person went back in time 162 years, there should be a flash of light or something. I'm starving, why don't you check the rice."

Russell stood and walked to the fire. He used a sturdy stick to lift the hot bale of the pot off the fire. As he removed the lid the spicy smell of jambalaya filled the air. Sarah handed him her enamelware plate and a large spoon. He served them and put wood on the dying fire before he sat down across from her to eat. The fire popped and crackled as the flames consumed the dry timber. Maybe it was because they were both so hungry, but the cajun rice with the slivers of pepperoni was the best meal they had ever eaten. After a steady diet of elk and buffalo, Russell was overwhelmed by the savory meal that was so easy to prepare.

"This is delicious. I've had rice but not rice like this. What are these?" He pointed to the pepperoni.

"It's pepperoni. It's hard salami." The man doesn't even know the pleasure of a pepperoni pizza with black olives and extra cheese, she thought. "While I was coming west I thought how different my trip was from the pioneers on the Oregon Trail. We study westward expansion as an important part of American history. Lewis and Clark's exploration, Fremont, and the routes traveled by men like you opened the west. Soon, families will leave their homes by the tens of thousands to settle in the Willamette Valley, California, and the Pacific northwest coast."

"I've never thought of myself as a part of history."

They sat silent for awhile, finishing their second helping of jambalaya, watching the fire.

"I need to cache the food," said Russell. "It didn't occur to me last night. We don't need a grizzly coming into camp in the middle of the night while we're sleeping. I don't know the last time I ate so well. Thank you for sharing it with me. How are you feeling?"

"My head hurts, but not like earlier. I have a fair amount of aches and pains from hitting the ground and the horse stepping on me, but I'll survive. I am really tired."

Russell agreed, "It's been a long day. I can see how a person that has gone back in time 160 some odd years would be tired." He took their plates and cups to wash. Sarah was awestruck by his handsome features and his refined manners. Reading his journal, she had always thought of him as an older man.

"I'm going to water the horses and hang the food. Keep your pistol handy, but don't shoot me," he teased. He picked up his rifle and disappeared into the darkness.

She used the private moment to carefully make her way out of the firelight and relieve herself. She found a small plastic water bottle she had filled several nights before. She took three extra-strength acetaminophen. She pulled a wash cloth from her bag and used Russell's mirror to look at her reflection. Her eyelids were puffy from crying and the bandage held her hair tight against the side of her head. There didn't appear to be any more bleeding. Using the cool water and the wash cloth she washed her face, rubbed the terry cloth across her teeth, then washed her forearms and armpits.

I must be getting better, she thought. I'm obsessing about the way I look. She rolled up Russell's blanket, inside the spirit blanket that had taken her across the seasons, and placed it beneath her head for a pillow. She heard his footsteps and his voice as he spoke to the horses while he moved them to drink at the river. After a few minutes he returned. Sarah had already crawled into her bedroll. She sat up and handed him his white blanket.

"No, you keep it. It's going to get cold before morning. I have another blanket, and I'm used to the cold nights." He covered her with the three-point blanket; the three black stripes indicating it had cost him three beaver pelts.

Sarah looked at the stars and then rolled over, her back to Russell and the fire. "I wonder what time it is?" Before he could speak she added, "I forgot, you never own a watch."

Even when the words were spoken, Sarah didn't realize what she had said. Russell stood motionless, rooted to the ground as an unearthly chill ran through his body. He was thankful she had turned away, the fire was low, and his back was to her. He didn't want her to see the expression on his face when, for the first time, he suddenly realized Sarah knew all the details of his life. She knew his past and she knew his future. She had read the diary he had begun when he entered the mountains four years ago, and she knew the ending. It was true he had never owned a watch, and now she had revealed he would never own one in his lifetime. And what else did she know? Did she know he couldn't swim? Did she know he had rheumatism in his left knee? Did she know who he would marry and how many children he would have? Or did he die like many trappers and never leave the mountains alive.

"My God," thought Russell, "Sarah knows when I die."

"Good night, Osborne, thank you for everything."

"Good night. Wake me if you need me."

Chapter 13

In the morning Russell was gone. He needed a reason to leave camp. Hunting for meat was a necessity and an excuse. It was an exercise which gave vigor, health, and appetite to a hunter; to shoulder his rifle at daybreak on a clear cold morning and wind his way up a rugged mountainside of rocks and crags to hunt his meal. Many a time the wind had blown away his breakfast, when the game he was hunting caught whiff of him. He wrestled over whether or not to leave Sarah alone, but made his decision determined not to range more than a mile from where he had left her sleeping. He tried to awaken her before daybreak, to tell her of his departure and promise his timely return, but he wasn't sure she clearly understood the conversation.

It was a gorgeous morning. After four years in these Shining Mountains there were still days, special days, when it seemed the earth had just been created and Russell was Adam, blessed and wandering in God's rugged garden paradise. This was such a day. Even new, it seemed to Russell, a day was ancient with the earth's habit of turning over and over again. Sarah was right. There was a distinct smell in the mountains. He remembered one Sunday when he was ten years old, he had entered the new church his community had raised the week before. The lumber still oozed and smelled of its earthly roots. The congregation raised its collective voice in song while he inspected each timber, knothole, and splinter. His boyish thoughts dreamed of adventure and places far, far away from the preacher's lengthy sermon on Ecclesiastes.

Just as now, his thoughts were far away from the deer he had killed, dressed out, and was taking back to camp tied to the back of his pack horse. He had a woman waiting for him in camp. A woman who had been born years after his death. It was a sobering thought. He had surprised himself, settling in and accepting her story and their new shared reality so easily. He was not schooled in these new emotions. His days were filled with danger, loneliness, and fatigue. Sarah was a new kind of tension. A complicated tension of sexual excitement, self-consciousness, and disbelief. The hair stood up on the back of his neck when he remembered she knew the particulars of his life. He did not want to know. He would tell her so when he got back to camp. He wanted to know what the world was like in 162 years, but he did not want to know about his own life. He would make that abundantly clear upon his return. He would feel uncomfortable, from now on, when he wrote in his journal knowing his writing was a piece of American history. Why would anyone care about what he saw last year, the distance he traveled last month, or his description of a mountain antelope? He was not a classical or scientific tourist. He was a trapper rambling among the wild regions of the Rocky Mountains.

When Sarah awoke, rolled over, and turned toward the campfire, she found herself alone. Confused, she quickly sat up struggling to free herself from her bedroll. There was no sign of Osborne. Rising to her feet her first thought was to call his name. His horse and his pack horse were gone. Where was he? Where had he gone? Followed quickly by the thought, had he really been here with her at all? Russell had moved Cocoa, Walmart, and the other two horses to graze about fifty yards from camp. They stood contentedly side-by-side.

Looking down she found and a hand-written note carefully placed where she could easily find it.

Sarah. Tried to wake you. Gone hunting. Be back shortly. Protect yourself with that fancy pistol of yours. O. Russell

O. Russell.

Osborne Russell. In the bright light of day it still seemed impossible she had shared the last two days with him. Her fingertips lightly traced each letter, each word, elegantly written. How different his words looked in his own hand than printed on the pages in his journal. It was his first letter to her.

It was cold. Sarah placed small limbs on the coals and used her plate to fan the embers into a low flame. She emptied last night's coffee from the blackened pot and walked to the river. She cupped her hands and drank the icy water, within a few minutes her fingers were numb.

I'll need to bathe soon, she thought, trying to calculate how many days it had been since she last showered at Half Moon Lake. She smelled like she hadn't taken a bath in 162 years. She looked at the fire. Was it safe? Would the smoke be detected by another trapper or a scouting party passing by? Surely, he would have given her instructions not to rebuild the fire if it was dangerous.

Sarah's senses roared within her. The freshness of the cold air burned in her nostrils. Her fingers stung as the numbness began to leave and her blood began to circulate again. She narrowed her eyes to avoid the blinding light refracting off the water's surface. Absent were the sounds of dogs barking, traffic from the Interstate, sirens, and heat pumps cycling. The world sounded very different without machines.

Sarah returned to the small fire with the pot of water. She hung it from the chain as she had seen Osborne do the night before. She sat on the ground waiting for the water to boil. The water sizzled and steamed as it heated. Not even the handsome countenance of Russell, a fantasy she had tossed about in her mind for years, could stop Sarah from thinking about her family. She thought of the bumper sticker, *"Life Is What Happens To You When You're Headed Somewhere Else."* Somewhere else. Somewhere. Somewhere in Time. Had she gone back in time to meet Osborne Russell because he was a part of her destiny? How? Why? She remembered Margaret's advice not to deprive a story of its inner soul, but this was more than a story by a campfire, this was her life.

Only a month before, planning her trip with Russell's journal in hand, she navigated the Internet to try and find his journal on-line. At

www.xmission.com/~drudy/mtman/gif/ruslmanu.gif

she found the handwritten title page of *Journal of a Trapper* slowly appearing on the screen. A haunting chill went through her body as she sat in the dark reading the familiar words written in his hand. It was Margaret who suggested she have his handwriting analyzed. The idea intrigued her, and instead of laughing at the suggestion she paid a graphologist $30 for her services. The graphologist told her Russell was self-confident, outgoing, and sociable. He kept things inside and could be secretive and defensive. She characterized him as impulsive and strongly determined, with a tendency to worry about some things. She also said he had guilt feelings from the past and slight bitterness.

"Was he good in bed?" Sarah jokingly asked, amazed anyone could determine so much about a man's personality from one page of his handwriting.

"Well, he probably was, his handwriting shows he had a strong sex drive and was very physical and athletic." But his penmanship hadn't shown how masculine, rugged, and good looking Russell was in 1838; his strong features colored and lined by the weather and his time in the mountains.

"He had a tendency to exaggerate. He was intelligent, aggressive, and responsible," the graphologist continued. "He was also possessive. He didn't want to let go. When he became frustrated he was volatile, but he could hold his temper."

Sarah had known from the first time she read his journal that Russell was intelligent, artistic, and could express himself well. The woman mentioned he was spiritual. How could anyone live in the mountains and not be spiritual? The only contradiction in her analysis seemed to be her statement that he leaned on his family. After Russell ran away from home at sixteen, his family didn't know whether he was alive or dead. Perhaps his guilt feelings from the past, were leaving his parents and his eight brothers and sisters wondering what had become of him.

She had the urge to take out his journal and reread the details of his life, but a great sadness washed over her as she remembered some of the tragedies that befell Osborne before his death. Would her coming back in time, would their meeting, change his life? Change his death?

Sarah was Janus, the two-headed Roman god, that could see ahead and could see behind. She had somehow stepped through a doorway in time and found herself on the same path as a man that had been a part of her life since she first read his journal. She stood in the bright early morning sun with tears in her eyes as she began to mourn his death. She was oblivious to the grizzly bear that had entered their camp.

To bears any new odor signals a food reward. Although Russell had carefully cached the food from where they slept, it had not occurred to him a woman might have personal items that would bring a bear into camp. The bear smelled Sarah's toiletries: lotion, deodorant, shampoo, and sunscreen. He had easily picked up the scent 50 yards away.

It was Cocoa that alerted Sarah to the imminent danger. The horse lowered her head and let out a deep guttural noise followed by a high-pitched whinny and ran into the woods with Walmart close behind. Their hoofs pounded loudly on the dry ground as they made their retreat. Sarah jumped up and called out as the horses disappeared into the trees. Cocoa's erratic behavior was out of character. What was wrong? Sarah began to slowly turn 360 degrees, surveying the landscape around her. She saw the bear. She gasped and held her breath. She was paralyzed with fear. It was obvious the bear had seen her. He stretched his neck, sniffing the air as he approached. Sarah's mind raced, trying to remember what the Forest Service brochures said about bear body language, and trying to remember where Osborne had placed the .44 Magnum.

The great bear raised his body and stood on his hind legs. He was a shaggy, menacing giant, more than eight feet tall. She stood perfectly still while he tried to identify her, remembering this was a terrifying posture, but not an aggressive one. His jaws were enormous and were stretched wide open revealing his huge yellow teeth. His claws were caked with mud. Sarah began to talk speak softly in a monotone voice.

She stooped and groped inside one of her stuff bags, feeling for the flannel pillowcase where she kept the hand gun. She felt the canister of red pepper counter assault bear spray. She thought of the sales brochure, "Effective Within Twenty Feet," and Frank's comment, "It will burn the bear until you are dead." She pulled the canister from the bag.

The bear lowered his body, his ears back, and began making a moaning sound. He was about forty-five feet away. Don't kneel, the brochure instructed. Don't make direct eye contact. Try to find a suitable tree to climb. The bear began to pop his jaws, looking directly at her. She felt inside the second bag. She held the red pepper spray tightly in her left hand and popped off the cap. Her right hand felt the familiar softness of the flannel and the hard weapon inside. The grizzly seemed more agitated. Without looking she pulled the revolver from the pillowcase and stood with the .44 Magnum in one hand and the red pepper spray in the other. The bear let out a low growl and lowered his head. The 2,000 pound omnivore could easily close the distance between them in seconds. She didn't want to shoot him, she just wanted him to go away. She pulled back the hammer on the revolver with her right thumb. She hadn't been target shooting since Morgan died, and she had never fired expert.

Six bullets, she thought, only six bullets, what if I miss?

The grizzly let out another growl and charged, leaping toward Sarah. She dropped the aerosol spray and, grasping the revolver with both hands, shot twice. The bear let out a great bawling noise, tumbled, fell into a great heap, and reared, charging again; the adrenalin pumping through his enormous body.

Russell heard two shots that sounded like sharp, heavy cracks. He was only a couple hundred yards from their camp. He dropped the reins of his pack animal and spurred his horse toward the river, toward Sarah. She's in danger. I shouldn't have left her. Damn the food. I should have waited. What if something's happened to her? He would never forgive himself. He had just found her.

Crack. Crack. Two more shots. When the bear got up she could see his ear and the left side of his head was bleeding. She aimed again at his head, one bullet whizzing past him the other piercing his gapping mouth. His teeth shattered and blood poured from his jaws. The mighty animal fell to its belly, pawing at the ground, screaming as he tried to get to his feet. Sarah aimed at the top of his skull and shot twice. She was out of ammunition. The bear lay silent.

A thundering broke from the trees. Sarah whirled around as Russell charged, his rifle drawn, and jumped from his horse to stand by her side. He had seen her take the last two shots. He looked at her anxiously.

"Are you hurt?"

"No." she stood paralyzed.

"Good," he said, trying to make light of the situation which could have cost her life. "How much do you want for that pistol?" Let me give you some good 1838 advice — reload. Have you ever eaten bear meat before?"

"No, I've never eaten bear meat before! I've never killed a bear before! Hell, I've only seen bears in zoos!" She was trembling.

"Well, you're a natural. What's that?" He pointed to the can.

"It's red pepper spray. It's bear repellent."

"You're not serious." Russell reached for the can.

"I am serious and don't touch it. It will burn your eyes."

"How does it work?" he was highly amused and grinning from ear to ear.

"You point the can at the bear and spray it when the bear is twenty feet away. The spray burns him, and he runs away"

Russell threw back his head and doubled over with laughter. "It'll burn the bear until you're dead."

"Yes, I've heard that comment before, in my own century, thank you very much."

Russell walked over to his horse and mounted.

"Where are you going? Don't leave me, Osborne, I'm really upset."

"I've got to find my pack horse. I left him when I heard your shots, and I need to find your two horses."

Sarah watched in disbelief as he rode away.

"Sarah, reload, and don't worry about dressing out the bear, I'll do that when I get back."

"Thank you very much, Mr. Russell," she shouted after him as he turned to leave, blinking back the tears welling in her eyes from the after-shock of fear.

"And Sarah, you've really got the bark on you."

"The bark on? Is that some kind of off-handed nineteenth-century compliment?"

"It certainly is a compliment, M'am. It means you have a great deal of courage." He flashed her the most charming, winsome smile she had ever beheld, tipped his head to her, and rode away.

Sarah reloaded the .44 Magnum as Russell ordered. She raised her hand to her throat and jingled the small silver bell on the necklace Margaret had given her. She sat down, a safe distance away, and stared at her bear. He was magnificent. His great ragged fur was a rich variegated tapestry the color of chestnuts, brown sugar, and maple syrup. She wanted to touch him. She knew he was dead but she would wait until Osborne returned. She thought about Morgan, and the time she found a copperhead lethargically curled up on her desk at home one cool spring morning. She put on a pair of Morgan's Army boots, stood in a chair across the room, and shot at the snake with a BB gun. The copperhead, still feeling the sleepy effects of hibernation, slowly uncoiled and bled to death on her desk. When Morgan came home he replied, "Sarah, this would have made a great hat band if you hadn't shot so damn many holes in it." She wished Morgan could see her now.

She thought of her parents reading the newspaper and drinking their morning coffee. They thought she had gone across the country when, in fact, she had gone across time. She got up, refilled the water that had boiled away, and made a fresh pot of coffee. She searched the perimeter for downed wood and rebuilt the fire. She couldn't remember the last time she had gone four days without a bath; she smelled the strong, musky odor of her body. She rubbed patchouli oil on her arms, into her hair, across her breasts and her inner thighs. She brushed her teeth, washed her face with a baby wipe, and slathered on moisturizer, followed by sunscreen and lip balm. She combed her hair carefully, trying to avoid scraping and opening the tender gash on the side of her head. She finally sat, leaning against her saddle, and savored the strong, hot coffee.

Her mind seized upon the postcard her Father had sent her before she left, the postcard clipped to the passenger-side visor of her car, with the words from Kipling's poem

> *Something hidden. Go and find it.*
> *Go and look behind the Ranges —*
> *Something lost behind the Ranges.*
> *Lost and waiting for you. Go.*

Lost and waiting for me in time, she reflected. Philosophers had mused and speculated on the entire phenomenon of Time since the ancients. Some of the most popular television and film scenarios dealt with the theme of time. A few years earlier, while writing an article on Chagall, Sarah read a book entitled, *Man and Time: The Eranos Yearbooks.* Some of the essays in the book were fascinating theories on the concept of time. One of the theories was that time is an endless constellation of our lives, our wills, and our pasts. And that all of our individual journeys meet at the same mysterious Center, thereby uniting us. Another theory was there is no making history. The past and the future are verbs. There is a past and there is a past that has been passed beyond and transcended. The writers speculated that we are, "Not of our Time," but we are something better and greater: "We are our Time."

The Greeks believed the stars were moved by the gods, and all time was cyclical, returning perpetually upon itself. Their word was *anakuklosis*: eternal return. Why should time be anything but cyclical? The Christian year perpetuated the cycle; every Christmas Christ is born, every Easter Christ is crucified and resurrected. In the Bible time unfolds from Genesis to the birth and death of Christ in one straight line, but how long is the line? Why couldn't time revolve on a closed circuit? No event is then unique. Nothing is enacted once. The same individuals have appeared, and will appear at every turn of the circle. The revolution, like the steady ticking of an eternal celestial clock, drives time with no before, with no after.

She had never believed that time was a horizontal line with a questionable beginning and an undefined end. She had always asserted that man should be considered from a vertical perspective, in relationship to the whole of time, but she had never considered that there was a living stream of time. Sarah had been swept away in its current.

Russell returned within the hour. He had the horses in tow when he rode into camp. Sarah stood when she saw him, happy at his return.

"Is that fresh coffee I smell?" he asked as he dismounted.

"Yes it is, may I pour you a cup?"

"Please, M'am. I guess that bear was really dead, else he would have wandered off by now."

"Very funny," replied Sarah, handing him his tin cup filled with hot coffee.

Russell picked up the empty metal cartridges, examining them closely. "I've seen the paper cartridges the military uses, but never any metal cartridges like this. I'll be."

They sat for a few minutes without speaking, enjoying the peacefulness of the moment, the simple comfort of the hot coffee and, without speaking of it, the pleasure of one another's company.

"Osborne, while you were gone I was thinking about how I got here, how I could have gone back in time 162 years. Do you think that instead of going back in time that this could be eternity?"

"Those are mighty deep thoughts for so early in the day. Do you know Wordsworth?"

"Of course."

"Wordsworth said our birth is but a sleep and a forgetting, that our soul is but a sleep and a forgetting. And the soul that rises within us, our life's star, has had elsewhere its setting and cometh from afar. Not in entire forgetfulness, and not in utter nakedness, but trailing clouds of glory do we come, from God who is our home. Do you know that quote?"

"Yes, I do."

"If you, from 162 years in the future can't figure it out, then it goes without saying I'm having a hard time. But I have thought of it. I've hardly thought of anything else since I first saw you, and all I can tell you is that I believe eternity isn't some later time. I don't think eternity is a long time. In fact, it may have nothing at all to do with time. I believe eternity is here and now; it is this moment in our lives. Man marks time by his birth and his death. Our self-absorption implies there was nothing before our birth and nothing after our death. Plants fade, animals expire, only man dies."

There was nothing she could add to his thoughtful soliloquy except, "Even in 2000 we believe we can sit at a fixed point and comfortably look back at our past or gaze expectantly into our future. After traveling across the seasons, I would have to stay Time is a river. If I had to be swept away by its torrent, I'm glad I was swept back to you." She extended her hand and smiled. "It's a pleasure to meet you, Mr. Russell, I'm a great admirer of yours."

He smiled and shook her hand firmly. He had strong hands that were cool and dry like cracked leather. "M'am, the pleasure is all mine. Some things, seems like, were just meant to be." They held their handshake; her hand small in his grasp. She let go first, embarrassed by his gaze.

"What do you say I tell you about the first bear I ever killed, while I butcher yours here, if you will make us some breakfast, I'll cook supper tonight."

"I'll be happy to." Pancakes and maple syrup, she thought, that will impress him. "What does bear meat taste like?"

"A little like deer meat, I guess. Never really thought about it. In the mountains, sometimes, there's not much to choose from. You eat what you can get and often don't ask who's cooking it what it is, and where it come from. I've been so hungry that I've gotten up in the middle of the night and roasted more meat if I had it. One March the snow was so deep and the area was so destitute of game that we had to live chiefly on thistle roots for ten days. But I've found, to be acquainted with misery contributes to the enjoyment of happiness." He pulled a large knife from the back of his belt and walked over to the bear.

"That looks like a butcher knife."

"It is a butcher knife. It's a Green River knife, made by a fellow named John Russell, no relation. See," he showed her the blade, " J. Russell & Co. Green River Works, you plunge the knife to the stamp, Up to Green River, we say."

"Green River, Wyoming or Green River, Utah?" asked Sarah afraid of making another foolish comment.

"I beg your pardon? Green River, Massachusetts." He sharpened the large knife on a small whetstone. "This butcher knife saved my life last year. I was hunting mountain sheep and the rocks were covered with sleet and ice. I cut steps in the ice with this knife and climbed the most frightful precipices. I thought little of the danger during the hunt, but when I tried to go to sleep that evening my blood ran cold thinking of what might have befallen me. I vowed not to take the same risks again in such dangerous places, but I've broken my promise often. I find the sight of danger is less hideous than the thought of it."

Russell carved the bear with the skill of a surgeon while Sarah made breakfast.

"You were going to tell me about the first bear you killed."

"Well, M'am, it was 1834, the first summer I was in the Rocky Mountains. It was a couple of months after my first grand rendezvous at Ham's Fork on the Green River. It was early August, I believe, and it was right after we finished building Fort Hall. Fort Hall was the most lonely and dreary place I think I ever saw, but I did learn the Snake language while posted there. Mr. Wyeth and all the men, excepting myself and twelve others, left for the mouth of the Columbia River. I spent most of my time acting as campkeeper: guarding the horses, and keeping the fires. Those of us left were what you'd call raw hands, inexperienced in hunting game. In fact, I had never killed meat for my supper with a rifle. A few days after they left it soon became clear that if we were going to eat we had to kill something, so myself and three others, one of which was a Mulatto, left the fort to hunt." He got up from his work and began to dramatically act out the episode, gesturing with his hands and raising his voice.

"I approached a band of buffalo crawling on my hands and knees. When I got to within 80 yards, I stood up, took aim, and shot at a bull. The bull was wounded and all the other buffalo ran off. There I was reloading and shooting," Russell dramatically pantomimed his actions building the story, " reloading and shooting, until I'd driven about 25 bullets at him, in him, but mostly all around him. My bullet pouch was empty."

"Was he dead?"

"Lord no, he wasn't dead! I'd spent 25 bullets and the bull never fell. He stood riveted to the spot. I watched him for half an hour waiting for him to fall. Never did. I finally gave up and went back to camp. I'm trying to establish how raw a mountaineer, a greenhorn, I was. The Mulatto and I had traveled about six miles from the fort one morning a few days later, when we came upon a grizzly bear. It was near a group of willows and he was digging and eating roots. Claws all caked with mud, like these," he said, picking up one of the bear's huge front paws. "The Mulatto shot him through the left shoulder at about 100 yards out. I didn't know the true nature of these animals so I pursued him. The bear jumped into a thicket. I persuaded my companion to walk around the willows to make another trial. We had our rifles cocked and pointed at the bushes." Russell slowly skulked around the fire. "Then the bear sprang for us, not ten feet away, giving a hideous, sullen growl." He jumped back. "We took to running, and separated. The bear took out after me, but with the devil after me, I outran him."

"What happened?"

"The bear started after the Mulatto, he discharged his rifle, covering the bear with smoke and ball, but he missed. The bear again came bounding toward me. I jumped into a large quagmire. I was trapped. I had to face him. When he was ten paces from me he stood on his hind legs, his jaws open wide, and it seemed he was laughing at me, a kind of beastly laugh. My rifle was accidentally pointed toward him. I pulled the trigger without thinking and the ball pierced his heart. He leapt at me, gave a deathly howl, and fell dead."

"Your rifle was accidentally pointed at him?"

"Yes. I was lucky."

"So you were scared, like I was?"

"Scared? Heavens, yes, I was scared. And when it was over, I took it much worse than you did this morning. I trembled for half an hour. We butchered him and took the meat and skin back to Fort Hall. I secretly swore in my own mind never to molest another grizzly bear. Jed Smith had his horse grabbed by the tail and dragged fifty yards so they say, in another attack Smith had his ear tore off, and Jim Clyman sewed it back on."

"That's gruesome."

"But the most hair-raising tale I ever heard was of Hugh Glass, a trapper in General Ashley's 1823 expedition. Glass was attacked by a grizzly, a white bear or silvertip they're sometimes called in the mountains. When his ten comrades found him he was unconscious and covered in blood. The mighty beast was lying on top of him with his claws buried deep in Glass's flesh. His chest, his back, his scalp, his face, one shoulder, arm, hand, and thigh had been ripped to pieces; not less than fifteen wounds, according to those that found him. They thought for sure he would die during the night, but come morning he was still unfit for the grave. His companions made a litter of tree boughs and dragged him through rough country for several days. His lingering death put their own lives in danger, as the country was teeming with hostile Indians, yet they continued to drag him like a corpse on a bier.

"Major Henry was worried about the men he'd left in Blackfoot country. On the third day, or some say it was the sixth, Henry proposed the company continue and two volunteers, who were to be well paid, stay behind with Glass. Now I'm not saying the men wanted their patient to die, but it would have made matters considerably easier, and no one that had seen the extent of Glass' wounds would have reckoned him to survive. The two volunteers argued, but finally decided to take his possibles bag, his hatchet, knife, powder, shot, and, worse, his rifle. Sooner to forgive the taking a man's horse than a man's rifle. His keepers left him for dead. At night wolves gnawed at his bloody garments, and had it not been for the deserters leaving his pallet close to a spring, he might surely have died. He was driven by the will to live and his desire for revenge. He crawled on his hands and knees for days, unable to walk upright. His only weapon was his razor. Months later a man, whose head was so disfigured it made a brave man want to look away, approached Fort Kiowa. 'Hallo Bill,' he yelled. 'Thought I was gone under didn't you? Hand over my horse and fixens, I ain't dead by a cussed sight.'"

"I can't believe he survived such a horrible attack. The Forest Service says bears can sense a man's fear."

"Who's the Forest Service?"

"The people who run the forests. People pay to visit the mountains."

"People run the forests? Unbelievable," said Russell. "Pay for what?"

"Manage the forests. Maintain the roads. Look out for fires. Find people who get lost. Pay just to pass through and look around."

He shook his head. "I'm glad I didn't live so long." Silence fell between them after his casual remark. It had a sobering effect with its implications.

Russell finished butchering the bear and tied the meat in small bundles. The delicious smell of pancakes and hot coffee filled the air. The trees were teeming with noisy birds chirping at the top of their lungs. Russell went to the river to wash his butcher knife and the blood from his hands. He returned holding a red handkerchief.

"What's in the handkerchief?"

"The bear's claws. I'm going to make you a necklace as a trophy of your bravery. You should be proud of the way you handled yourself today."

"Else I'd be dead now."

"Yes, and I just found you. I'm not ready to lose you." That expression passed between them again. The wordless expression that they were destined to come together, but neither knowing why or how long it would last.

"Here are your pancakes."

"Thank you." Russell found his fork in his possibles bag and sat across from her. "Not bad to take," complimented Russell savoring the pancakes. "Not bad to take at all. Thank you."

"You're welcome."

"Where did you learn to shoot?"

"My husband taught me.

Chapter 14

Russell kept chewing, but the pancakes suddenly lost their sweet flavor and became a mouthful of thick dough. He struggled to swallow. Sarah was married. Of course, she was married, how could she not be married? She was so beautiful, but more than that, she was so wonderful. How could a man, even a twentieth-first century man, let his wife go alone on such a dangerous journey? It didn't make sense. If he didn't comment on her remark, or ask her any further questions, maybe he could forget she was married, and resume his fantasy that it was just the two of them alone in the world together.

Sarah got up and stretched her legs. "I'm going to get some water. Do you want more pancakes?"

"In the mountains we call them feast cakes."

"Feast cakes. I like that. Do you want more feast cakes?"

"Please, I don't remember when anything tasted so good."

She served them and walked to the river. He watched every movement of her body until her silhouette lost its definition and she disappeared into the bright sunlight reflecting off the water's surface.

Russell looked at the ragged pieces of blanket wrapped around his legs. They extended from his knees to his ankles and tucked into his last pair of deerskin moccasins. They were in shreds, as were the rest of his clothes. He had noticed early this morning, when he put on his blanket coat, that it had several holes. He had lost his black wool hat in the spring. His provisions were desperately low. He was out of sugar, tobacco, low on gun powder, and bar lead. He was also low on gewgaws: the beads, bells, and small mirrors the Indians were so fond to trade for. He didn't have any alternative but to take Sarah to Rendezvous and resupply.

Taking Sarah to Rendezvous presented all manner of problems. How was he going to explain her? Her clothes? Her supplies? Just her? He had often been the brunt of many a joke when he failed to seize an opportunity to lie with a willing Indian woman at Rendezvous. He could only imagine the look on Mr. Bridger's face, or Joe Meek or Captain Stewart, when he rode into the encampment with her. He could hear them now, "Russell, how did a ragged trapper like you get himself such a fine filly?"

He could leave her alone, go to Rendezvous for a few days, resupply, then return to her. That was an idea. But after wrestling with it, he decided it was too dangerous. There would be a crowd of Whites, as well as Indians, in the vicinity of the annual gathering, any one of which might discover her alone.

Returning from the river Sarah asked, "After we finish eating will you take a look at my head? Your mirror is so small I can't really see how it's healing."

"Yes, how are you feeling?"

"I feel stronger physically, but I'm sick when I think about my family. My mind gets into a knot when I start wondering where they are. Is my family still back there, wherever back there is? Or have they not been born so they won't be devastated when I don't come home. It makes me crazy. I used to always tell my Mother, "I know God is in control of my life, but I'm going to worry about it anyway." That's how I feel. I can't stop thinking about them."

Russell finished his last fork of pancakes. "Your coming here has made me think more about my own family. I haven't seen them since I was sixteen." He looked at her and asked, "Is that in the book?"

"I know you ran away from home when you were sixteen and went to sea, that's all."

"It's amazing how a man's life can be reduced to a few sentences and it all seems so simple. Sixteen isn't such a young age for a man to go out on his own. It's only called running away from home when you go against your Father's wishes. It's one of the paths boys travel to become men. When I told my Father I wanted to go to sea he was thunderstruck. I'm not sure he wanted me to be a farmer, but I don't think he believed I had the gristle on me to take the hard knocks of a sailor's life. This isn't all that interesting."

"It is to me."

"I was born in Bowdoinham, Maine, on an estuary of the Kennebec River. I grew up around water and I longed to go to sea. I haunted the waterfronts listening to the sailors tell of their adventures. Some of them were wounded, limping, missing a leg or an arm, or even blind, but their stories, of how they had fought for their very lives as they battled the merciless sea, were thrilling. I would go to Portland and watch the beautiful ships glide in; they seemed to be flying into the harbor like great-winged birds. One day, unbeknownst to my family, I tied all my clothes in a bundle, kissed my Mother goodbye, and struck out to find a ship that would hire me.

"My heart swelled the first time we set out to sea, but it wasn't many more trips before I learned why my Father had wanted to spare me a seafarer's life. There were times we had nothing much to eat or drink. We had birds, a few shellfish, and a precious few sodden biscuits, no other bread stuffs, but to us they were dainties. Often the seas boiled with violent storms, and we had to tie ourselves with ropes to keep from being swept overboard into the mouth of the sea. I tell you here in the mountains, I've been shot at by Indians, near starved, and near froze to death, but I've never been as lonely as when I'd awaken in the early morning and see the vast emptiness of an iron-grey sea. There were times when the horizon was indistinguishable and it appeared we were sailing off into nothingness. While I worked during the day, or stood watch at night, I thought about the beautiful countryside of Maine. I reconstructed, in great detail, every hill and field where I had played as a boy. It was on one of those lonely watches I decided there were many fields I had never entered, rivers with rapids and shallows I had not forded, and birds and animals I wanted to hold in the sights of my rifle. Stranded at sea I began to hear tales of the great West and of the Shining Mountains that rose so high they disappeared into the sky. I heard stories of the great rivers that had become roads to carry extraordinary men like Lewis and Clark to the far side of our country, and to another great ocean."

Sarah listened spellbound as Russell revealed not only details of his life which she had never known, but revealed how his dreaming of a life apart from the monotonous life of the settlements had led him to this place in the mountains which she now shared with him.

"One night, after a particularly bleak and troublesome voyage, I heard a siren's song and jumped ship in New York with the rest of the crew. I eventually wound up in Minnesota and Wisconsin, trapping for three years in the service of the Northwest Fur Trapping and Trading Company, but I guess you know all about that."

"Yes, but it's different now."

"Different because I'm a man and not just a book?"

"You were never just a book." He didn't say anything for a long time. For the first time it was apparent to Sarah that her life was not the only one that had spun out of control. She had been selfish in dismissing his feelings in all of this. How must he feel knowing she knew the date he was born, and when and how he died? They sat together without speaking.

"Is there a picture of me in the book?"

"No, there was only one known picture of you and it was destroyed in a fire many years ago."

"So, you didn't know how ruggedly handsome I was until we met a few days ago," he flirted self-consciously.

"I had absolutely no idea, but I thought you were older."

"What do you mean, older?"

"Older like me."

"You're not older than I am."

"Yes I am."

"No, women older than I am don't look like you?"

"How do I look?"

"Beautiful," he answered shyly. "You're the most beautiful woman I have ever seen."

"Thank you Osborne, right now I believe that's the nicest thing any-one has ever said to me."

Embarrassed, he quickly changed the subject. "Let me wash our plates and my hands again, and I'll take a look at your head. Do you think you'd feel like traveling a ways today?"

"Sure. Maybe it will help me take my mind out of that knot." Sarah guessed it was almost noon. The sun was high overhead. While she looked for her first-aid kit she thought about Russell quoting Wordsworth. What other poets and authors might they have in common although they were so many years apart in time? Shakespeare, certainly. Lord Byron. Nathaniel Hawthorne. John Milton. Benjamin Franklin. Edgar Allen Poe? Is Poe alive, she wondered, trying to place the dark poet in the context of time. James Fennimore Cooper had written *Last of the Mohicans* and would write *The Deerslayer*. Then there was Washington Irving and *The Legend of Sleepy Hollow* and *Rip van Winkle*. She must remember to tell him to read *Moby Dick* in a few years.

"Why are you smiling?" asked Russell when he returned.

"I'm thinking of all we have to talk about. All the things I want to share with you, and all the things I want to ask."

"When I was hunting this morning I was thinking about how every-thing is spelled out in my journal, and all the things you know about my life," he hesitated, "and my death. Thinking about it disturbs me. It ties my mind in a knot like the one you mentioned earlier."

"I told you it's different now. I'm not going to pull out your journal every day and refresh my memory on the details of your life. I've read your book over the years, but I didn't memorize every fact, every place you visited, and every mile you traveled. More than the details of your life, every time I read your journal it raised questions about you."

"What kind of questions?"

"Questions like how you became so intelligent."

"You think I'm intelligent?"

"I've always thought so. You make classical references in your writings; Phoebus, Oberon, Boreas, Elysian fields, Egyptian darkness. I had to look up many of your words. Your descriptions of the mountains are so beautifully and sensitively written. I always wondered how you became educated."

He was obviously pleased by her compliment. "I went to school, but it was my Mother who taught all nine of us to read by reading the Good Book. I've learned most of what I know by reading books. I enjoyed *Robinson Crusoe, Arabian Nights*, Swift's *Gulliver's Travels*. I've read all my life, even here in the mountains I borrow books from Fort Hall, the Hudson's Bay Company outpost on the Snake River above the mouth of the Portneuf. Chief Factor John McLoughlin sends them out of his circulating library at Fort Vancouver. Indians call him the White-Headed Eagle, trappers refer to him as a highwayman of former days. Sometimes I'll read the same book over and over until I get back to Fort Hall to return it." Sarah handed him the first-aid kit. He turned it end over end looking for the opening. Sarah pointed to the zipper.

"Pull," she instructed.

He pulled on the zipper and the teeth unfastened revealing the bandages and bottles inside.

"It's called a zipper. It'll be invented in a few years. See," she pointed to the fly of her jeans.

"Looks dangerous," he commented suspiciously. "Let's take a look at your head."

She handed him the hydrogen peroxide and ointment. He poured the peroxide over the wound as she tilted her head to the side.

"It's still raw, but it's healing nicely. We'll keep an eye on it for the next few days." He patted the gash dry and applied the ointment.

"There's one more thing," added Russell. "I want to know about zippers and all the other inventions, about plastic and dinosaurs, but I don't want want to know anything about my life, or what is going to happen to me. Do you understand?"

"Yes, I understand. I promise."

"Good. What do you say we ride out and I'll show you these Shining Mountains of mine."

"I'd like that."

Russell brought the horses . "Do you always tie your horses?"

"There's a proverb in the mountains that it's better to count ribs than tracks. In other words it's better to fasten a horse until you can count his ribs, than to let him loose to feed and end up counting his tracks after an Indian has made off with him."

They didn't talk while they worked, but occasionally they looked at one another out of the corner of their eye, like two self-conscious teenagers on a first date. Sarah found her gloves and put them in her back pocket. She reapplied moisturizer and sunscreen to her face. She couldn't wear a hat because it would rub and open her wound. She lifted Walmart's pad and pack saddle onto his back.

Sarah filled the white canvas panniers with the stuff bags of food, clothes, equipment, and her small two-person tent. She folded the flannel pillowcase around the .44 Magnum and placed it in her saddle bag which she carried over the pommel of Cocoa's saddle. She was genuinely pleased to be in contact with her horses again; like old friends, Cocoa and Walmart stood chewing and licking as she brushed them and readied them to leave.

Russell had two pack animals and two saddle horses; two buckskin, one bay, and a black. Sarah figured two of the horses belonged to the man Osborne killed the first day. One of the horses had a rusty Spanish bit and a crude saddle with huge wooden stirrups. A buffalo robe was rolled behind the saddle, and a hatchet and a five beaver traps were slung over the pommel. Both of the pack horses wore sawbuck saddles; wooden frames covered with rawhide. One of the pack animals was heavily loaded with a number of steel traps in a heavy leather sack, a wooden chest, and several bundles of furs. The other had panniers, and a rawhide box painted with decorative designs of green, red, and black. Tied to the pack saddle were the small bundles of bear meat and the deer Russell had killed. His equipment had seen hard service.

It was hot. Sarah took off her charcoal-gray wool sweater and tied it around her waist. She was finding conversation with Osborne awkward. The butcher knife was a good example, and her referral to states that were only territories. As much as she looked forward to sharing the technology of the future with him, she didn't look forward to explaining the mechanics of how things worked. As she was regaining her health and feeling better, she wanted to flood their conversation with questions and search for the answers together. But she hesitated, perhaps because rationally it still seemed like a dream, and by speaking too loudly or moving too quickly she would awaken from the dream and he would be gone.

While she waited for Russell to finish rigging the horses she walked over to the bear. The ground was stained with blood, especially from his enormous head where the bullets shattered his skull, and from his paws where Russell cut the claws. She knelt beside him, feeling his dense, thick fur with her fingers.

"Not too surprising he came into camp," said Russell approaching her, "there's plenty of cutthroat trout in that stream. Did you know grizzlies eat moths during the peak of the summer, and they make a humming sound when they lick their feet. It's the darndest thing you've ever seen," he said shaking his head. "Are you ready?"

They walked together to the horses standing patiently for their riders. Russell looked at the sky.

"We've been lucky with the weather. It usually rains, at least a shower, every day during the summer. Mosquitoes haven't been too bad the past few days either."

"We have a spray that keeps mosquitoes from biting."

"Like the bear spray?"

"Sort of, but you spray this on your skin."

"Does it work?"

"Depends on the mosquitoes."

"Keep it handy, where we're going you'll need it. We won't travel too far today, but I want to move, the bear is liable to bring in some animals tonight. We need to keep heading to Rendezvous. It's the mountaineers' annual summer gathering, our great wilderness fair, if you will. Only the trappers who have died during the past year won't be in attendance. It's one of our few rituals here in the mountains. It lets a man forget about the aches and pains of everyday life. It used to take seventy days to ride to St. Louis to trade our furs. Last year, 1837, the Rendezvous was at Horse Creek, off the Green River. Thomas Fitzpatrick brought in thirty wagons of supplies. Captain Stewart, Dick Summers, Robert Newell, Mr. Ewing, Mr. Drips, and Mr. Bridger were all there."

"Jim Bridger?"

"One in the same."

"I've visited his fort."

"He doesn't have a fort."

"He will." He looked at her blankly, she couldn't tell if he was irritated by her remark. "Who else was there?"

"There was a mixed multitude of Dutch, Irish, Scotch, English, French Canadians and Americans. There were full blood and half breed Indians from nearly every tribe that lives amongst the Rocky Mountains. General Ashley established the first rendezvous in 1825; that was way before my time. It changed the Rocky Mountain fur trade. He used his own men as hunters instead of trading solely with the Indians. He bypassed building an expensive fort that would be of no use when the area was trapped out, and he fixed himself to make two profits; on the trade goods he brought from

St. Louis, and second, on the furs he bought at mountain prices and sold at St. Louis prices."

"For the last thirteen years the fur companies, under one name or another, have been coming to meet us to get the furs we've trapped, as well as trade with us and resupply. The site requires an abundance of water and grass. Out here we have the misfortune of getting luxuries from the civilized world once a year, and then they are in such small quantities they only last a few days. Rendezvous is when we catch up on what's befallen each of us during the past year. Some receive letters from friends, public papers, and news of the day. We trade our furs for ammunition, food, bar lead, blankets, coffee, rum, tobacco, and other supplies. We also trade for clothes, of which it is apparent that I am badly in need. We have contests, tell yarns, tell lies more like it if the truth be known, play cards, gamble, and wrestle one another. Drinking is the order of the day; it's not uncommon for a free trapper, or any trapper, to get roaring drunk and spend a year's wages in just a few days. After five or six ounces of grog, that's when a man feels the richest."

"What's a free trapper?"

"A trapper that's off the company's hook. I am what you would call a company man. In 1834, Mr. Wyeth hired me to work for the Columbia River Fishing and Trading Company for a term of eighteen months. Despite my being somewhat inexperienced, I was paid $250. When my term expired I went to work for Jim Bridger and the Rocky Mountain Fur Company, but there are some trappers, free trappers, that are independent and don't work for the fur trading companies. They trap for themselves and sell to whomever they please. I have to be honest, I'm concerned about going to Rendezvous. How am I going to explain you? Who you are. Where you come from. How you got here. The way you look."

"You could leave me somewhere nearby."

"I thought of that, but it's too dangerous. We've got a few days, we'll think of something."

She pulled the gloves out of her back pocket and put them on. Russell held Cocoa's halter while Sarah mounted. He tied Walmart's lead harness to the pommel of Cocoa's saddle, she easily took control of him when she climbed into the saddle.

Russell mounted his horse. He sat powerfully and gracefully molded in the saddle, his figure strong and athletic. He rode out in front of her into the checkered sunshine and under the dark shadows of the trees. His powder horn, and a leather bag, was slung over his right shoulder and tucked behind him under his wide leather belt. His rifle rested across his thighs and against the pommel of his saddle. The mountains had not robbed him of the subtle refinement that perhaps only another educated person might observe. Russell was a trapper whose manner nor appearance disclosed his years on the rough and dangerous frontier.

Sarah couldn't wait to see his face when she told him a man had walked on the moon.

Chapter 15

Russell's idea of "we'll go just a ways," was a five-hour ride. From time-to-time he would turn around in the saddle and ask, "How are you doing back there?" She would wave and nod; he certainly wasn't coddling her. Even with sunscreen, Sarah could feel her face, neck and forearms burning. Her lips and her hands were dry. They stopped once to water the horses. Russell made small talk while the horses drank.

What is he thinking? she wondered.

Russell was thinking about the watch he would never own. His life was in a book. He couldn't put the thought from his mind. He was on his way to the Rendezvous of 1838. How many more would he attend?

His mind went back and forth between morbid curiosity and a gut full of fear. He kept an alert eye on the landscape watching for a scouting party or any of the other dangers that were inherent in life in the mountains. He keenly felt responsible for Sarah's safety. He mentally played out every dangerous scenario that could befall them, trying to plan how he would protect her. He had never lingered on the thought of dying before. Of course, he'd been scared to death, afraid that he was going to die, but he didn't worry about it. Russell's religious upbringing had taught him the Lord would grant him eternity for a righteous life. But if he died now, what would would happen to Sarah? Who would take care of her? Sarah could see the back of Russell's head as he rode ahead of her, but she could not see inside his heart and how she had already become a part of him.

As they rode across a landscape unlike Sarah had ever seen, she began to slowly realize there weren't any roads here, or a highway ahead where DuBois would be in 2000. There were no power lines or UPS trucks. No Best Westerns or KOA Kampgrounds. It also occurred to her that the first day she set out alone, she was not able to locate her position using the GPS because there weren't any satellites orbiting the earth. As for her "fancy pistol" as Osborne referred to it, she only had six more cartridges in the purple flannel Crown Royal bag.

"That's far enough for today," announced Russell getting off his horse. "We'll camp here tonight."

Relieved, but not wishing to appear a greenhorn, as Russell had referred to himself earlier in the day, Sarah asked, "Are you sure you want to stop? I can ride further."

"No, it would be smart to make camp. This is a good spot. Close to the river, plenty of grass, good cover in case of trouble."

She didn't offer twice. She slid off Cocoa, and immediately felt the stiffness in her knees. Russell had already unsaddled his horse and was hard at work on the second. Soon the saddles and packs were scattered and the horses picketed nearby.

"I'll gather wood," said Russell.

"I'll help."

"No, I'll do it, I'm not used to women doing such work."

"Look, you've taken great care of me, but I'm stronger and I'm not going to sit around while you wait on me. I just rode five hours, I believe I can help you gather firewood."

"Okay, but if you . . ."

"Osborne," she interrupted and said emphatically, "stop treating me like I'm going to break." He nodded; he could tell there was no changing her mind.

As they searched for firewood, Sarah asked, "How long does Rendezvous last?"

"It depends. Last year I arrived at the Green River on June tenth. Mr. Fontenelle and Mr. Fitzpatrick's supply caravan from Fort William didn't arrive until July 18th. Mr. McLeod and Mr. McKay, representing the Hudson's Bay Company, got there a few days before. I left a couple of days after Fitzpatrick arrived to hunt with five of my comrades at the head waters of the Yellowstone Missouri and Big Horn Rivers. I heard some stayed until after just August fifth. I should have stayed put too."

"Why?"

"We were traveling up the Green River, which we also call the Sketskedee, when we discovered a buffalo that had been freshly killed and butchered. The meat was neatly tied in small bundles, like the way I butchered your bear this morning. We found the trail of a scouting party of eight or so Blackfeet. I imagine they had seen us approach and had run into the bushes. We weren't too worried about it, supposing them to be small in number. We took their meat and tied it to our saddles. We hadn't gone much further when we discovered the savages hiding in a bunch of willow bushes. I reined in my horse and my friend, William Allen, began to secure the load on his pack horse. When I looked ahead into the bushes, which were about 150 yards distant from me, I instantly wheeled my horse around. I saw two guns pointed at me. Instead of a small scouting party, sixty or seventy Blackfeet jumped out of the bushes and ran toward us. My horse was shot by two balls and dropped from under me. I jumped on a comrade's horse and rode behind him to safety. We arrived at the Rendezvous about dark. The next time we set off from Rendezvous, heading up the Green River again, we traveled with Mr. Fontenelle's party."

"When we get to Rendezvous why don't we tell everyone I was captured by Indians and you rescued me."

"Captured by what Indians?" he asked, taken off guard by her comment.

"I don't know, just make one up,"she suggested casually.

"The only White women that have been seen in the Rocky Mountains are the wives of missionaries. Narcissa Whitman and Eliza Spaulding caused quite a ruckus at the Rendezvous of 1836; trappers attended Sunday services just because there were women present. They were gazed upon with wonder and astonishment by the rude savages they being the first White women ever seen by the Indians and the first that had ever penetrated into these wild and rocky regions. Besides, a woman taken captive by Indians wouldn't look like you, and how are we going to explain your clothes and your equipment?"

"I don't know. I haven't figured that part out yet."

"Well, let me know when you do." He reached into his leather bag and pulled out a round tin. When he opened the tin he gently lifted out a small charred piece of wood the size of his thumb. He made a small bird's nest of tree bark and thin dry grasses. Holding the flint in his left hand and striker in his right, he quickly brought the striker down sharply hitting the flint. Sparks flew as the hard objects met. One of the sparks came to rest on the charred wood and became a smoldering hot coal. He nestled the small, yellow-orange coal in the nest of grass and blew steadily and gently until it burst into flame. Within a few minutes the smell of smoke filled the air as the dry wood ignited. He thinly sliced the meat and impaled the strips on sticks angled out in front of the fire.

Russell pulled a white clay pipe from his bag.

"What else do you carry in your bag?"

"It's my possibles bag. Its got my personal property; everything necessary for me to stay alive out here, except my rifle." He began to empty its contents: bullet mold, awl, a small handsome knife with the letter *M* on the blade, a rectangular cherry wood box, a hand-forged screwdriver, fish hooks, a couple of small corks, a length of string, his small mirror, razor, and file. "This isn't much good," said Russell holding up his pipe, "I usually have a tin of Cavendish tobacco. I'd gratefully smoke some Indian tobacco right about now."

"What's Indian tobacco?"

"Shongsasha or kinnikinnick. The Indians make it by mixing their tobacco plant leaves with the bark of red willow trees or the bark of other plants. The formula depends on the tribe making it."

"I have tobacco," she reached in one of the panniers. "My friend Margaret gave it to me before I left. She said tobacco spit was an aphrodisiac to fish," she handed him the ziplock bag. "I have no idea what kind of tobacco it is, maybe it's Red Man."

Russell was astonished she would have tobacco in her possession. A woman who drank whiskey, a woman with tobacco. He filled his pipe careful not to drop a single leaf. He lit the bowl with a glowing stick from the fire. He took a puff and contentedly leaned back against his saddle. "Now I feel like one of the gentry. The moon's up early tonight," he observed, gazing at the early evening sky.

"Yes, I want to tell you about the moon. You said you wanted to know about modern inventions. I wanted to begin with transportation. It has changed dramatically in the last 162 years. Are you are familiar with railroads?" He nodded.

"Now we have machines that are like wagons, and can travel up to 100 miles an hour, although it's against the law to drive more than seventy miles an hour."

"Seventy miles an hour in a wagon?"

"We call them cars or automobiles."

"What makes them go?"

"Gasoline. It's a liquid fuel we buy by the gallon. You pour it in, turn a key in the ignition, and the car starts. The first gasoline-powered engines were invented about 1886. They looked like the old buggies that were pulled by horses, so they were called horseless carriages. They were crude by twenty-first century standards. When you asked me how I got to and from Wyoming, it was by car. It's not impossible to drive 800 miles or more in one day. We have Interstate highways, a paved road system, that connects cities all over the country."

He tried to visualize such a machine. It was difficult to imagine a wagon that would not shake apart when it reached such speeds.

"But it gets better. If you can only imagine, there are machines that fly in the air like a bird. In fact, they use the same principal of lift as a bird in flight. They have wings which are more curved on top than below." She tried to use her hands to illustrate air moving over the top of the wing. "As the plane flies, air going over the wing has farther to travel than air beneath. This means the air over the top moves faster, so the wing is pushed upward, which raises the plane. The first airplane was invented in 1903, by two brothers, Orville and Wilbur Wright in Kitty Hawk, North Carolina,. It flew only twelve seconds and traveled a little over 100 feet. The first airplane carried only one person, but airplanes today carry as many as 350 passengers. It's now possible to go from one side of the country, from the Atlantic Ocean to the Pacific Ocean, in only five hours in an airplane, in fact, you can fly to the other side of the world in only twelve hours."

Russell sat spellbound. It was fantastic. It was unbelievable. A machine that flew in the air like a bird.

"Have you ever flown in an airplane?"

"Many times."

"Were you afraid?"

"Sometimes, it depends on the weather, but it's more wonderful." She reached over and touched his hand. He was pleased by her gesture.

"Once man mastered flight we began sending machines into space that orbit, that circle, the earth. They're called satellites. Once we knew how to send up satellites we began sending out a type of airplane propelled by rockets, that carried men into space. Space ships." She couldn't explain how it all worked, past the principal of lift and that massive amounts of fuel ignited to cause a rocket to slip the earth's gravity, but he didn't seem to mind the lack of detail.

"Space ships have carried men to the moon. A man has walked on the moon. Can you believe it? I saw it happen and I still can't believe it!" She smiled, pleased that she had taken his breath away. "The space ship was called The Eagle, and when the man, we call them astronauts, first stepped foot on the moon, he said, "One small step for man, one giant leap for mankind."

"What a wonderful time to be alive. What year was that?"

"July 20, 1969. Can you imagine, that was only about sixty years or so after the first airplane flight. There's an American flag up there on the moon, or there will be."

"Now that's a yarn! I must remember to tell it next winter when we're froze in." He looked at the moon, it was huge, magnified by the earth's atmosphere. It rose steadily in the sky. "One small step for man, one giant leap for mankind," he repeated. "Machines that travel over land at 100 miles an hour. Machines that fly and can carry 350 people. Machines that go into space and carry a man to the moon. I can't begin to imagine what life is like in your time. What could be more splendid than traveling to the moon?"

"That's only the beginning."

They didn't talk much during dinner. They were both preoccupied with their thoughts, their feelings, and their new presence in one another's lives. The bear meat was good, although Sarah wouldn't have said it tasted like venison. She ate it gratefully, appreciating the strong animal spirit that she had faced earlier in the day. She had read that when Native Americans killed an animal they thanked the animal for giving its life that they might eat. She thought of shrink-wrapped ground beef in the meat department, and all the times she took a rotisserie chicken home at the end of a long day teaching. There was nothing romantic about having to hunt your food every day, it was serious business.

"You never really showed me the hippo you traded for the blanket."

She walked over and reached into her saddle bag for William, the blue faience hippopotamus. Seeing him always raised her spirits as she recalled the Christmas morning she found him in her stocking. She placed him in Russell's hand.

"It's clay that's been fired and glazed. These are lotus blossoms," she said, pointing to the incised lines on his body, "a flowering plant from Egypt. The original is in a magnificent museum in New York. In Egyptian mythology the hippopotamus is a supernatural animal with great power."

"How did you know this was what you had to trade for the blanket?"

"I didn't. I asked the man how much I had to pay for the blanket and he said I couldn't buy it, I had to trade something of deep personal value. My husband put him in my Christmas stocking one year."

Russell examined the small turquoise hippo, turning him upside down. "You traded him, and the old man gave him back to you?"

"Yes, when I unwrapped the blanket and I found him inside."

"Inside my blanket," thought Russell, "from 162 years in the future." "Do you have any more of that whiskey? I'm dry!"

"I have three wineskins; bring me your cup and I'll pour."

"I thank you," said Russell, handing her the hippopotamus. He sat down on the ground across from her, the campfire forming a fiery fence between them.

"I'd like to make a toast to your grizzly bear, Ole Ephraim. As the Bible says, Ephraim is wedded to his idols; leave him alone."

"To my bear," repeated Sarah raising her cup. They sat in silence enjoying one another's company, the strong Tennessee whiskey, and a quiet moment at the end of a long, tiring day.

Russell had promised himself he wasn't going to ask about Sarah's personal life, her marriage, and those she had left behind, but the whiskey loosened his resolve.

"Do you and your husband have any children?"

"No."

He said nothing more, not knowing her circumstances and not wishing to cause her to recount something which seemed painful for her. The darkness thickened around them. She stared into her cup trying to decide how much she was willing to disclose about herself. She doubted she would display Osborne's graciousness if the tables were turned, and it was he that had knowledge of the intimate details of her life.

"My generation was the first generation of women to effectively control when we were going to have children. It was called family planning or birth control, but millions of us used it not to plan our families but to fully enjoy sex without having to worry about pregnancy before we married."

Russell was both excited and shocked by a woman speaking of such subjects so forthrightly. He had heard married men talk of the fact they had consummated their marriages and fathered children, but they never discussed the events with their wives.

"We took pills and put little gadgets inside our bodies to prevent conception. When I finally married and my husband and I wanted to start a family, I couldn't get pregnant. It's not uncommon now, or should I say in the future, there are many women and men that are infertile. It's heartbreaking. My husband and I went to a specialist, a doctor that helps married couples with such things. Every day new medical procedures are discovered that help couples conceive. There were several things we were going to try but," her voice was weak and trailed off into silence. She began to cry.

Russell was confused. He didn't know what to say. He wanted to comfort her, to hold her in his arms and protect her. He walked over to where she was seated, her face buried in her hands. He put his hand on her shoulder. "I'm sorry I asked. I didn't mean to make you sad."

She stood and faced him, her face covered with tears. She put her head against his chest and cried. He wrapped his arms around her shoulders and held her tight. He could feel her body tremble, he could feel her tears soaking into his red flannel shirt.

"Sarah, I don't know anything about women," he apologized. "Not women in my own time and certainly not about a woman like you." He softly stroked her hair. He became aroused as he felt her breasts rise and fall as she cried. Embarrassed he moved his lower body away from hers. His face and his hands were hot and he could hear his heart beat in his ears. He inhaled deeply, savoring the sweet musky odor of her body. Despite his respect for her, he could well understand the lust the red-bearded man felt the day he met his death.

"You have graciously accepted my knowledge of your life, and it would be wrong if I was less than straightforward about my own." She rubbed her eyes with her fingers, and wiped her nose on her shirt sleeve, letting out a long sigh.

Russell wanted to kiss her before she moved away.

"My husband died three years ago."

Never suspecting this was the information she was about to share, Russell moved away from her. "Your husband is dead? This morning you said your husband taught you to shoot."

"He did, but he died three years ago. His name was Morgan. He died before we could try any of the breakthrough medical procedures and before we could freeze his," Sarah decided she didn't want to get into the details of modern science. "So, we were never able to have children." She took another deep breath. Her tear-stained face glistened in the golden light of the fire..

"How did he die?"

"He was a soldier. A real man's man. He was strong and masculine. A natural born hero. He was fierce in his loyalty and his patriotism. We had gone out to dinner at a restaurant. We call them fast food restaurants because of how quickly the food is prepared and served. It was about 5:30 in the afternoon. I remember the smell of chicken frying. It's odd how many details I remember. A group of girls had spilled a drink and they were trying to sop it up with a paper napkin. The drink poured like a sugary waterfall across the table and onto the floor. It was late spring, but it was hot in Georgia and even hotter because the room was crowded and poorly ventilated. I began to perspire before I saw the gun. Sweat ran down from my armpits and down the middle of my back into the waistband of my jeans.

Morgan noticed a young man, maybe seventeen years old, behaving very strangely. The military had trained him to have a keen sense of observation. He warned me to be alert, saying he was afraid something was about to happen. Within a few seconds the young man pulled a gun and announced he was going to rob the place. The young man was very jumpy and nervous. He waved his gun in the air and he spoke loudly.

Morgan put his hand on mine, to reassure me everything was going to be okay. Like everyone else, we sat very still, not talking, or moving. The manager instructed the sobbing cashier to give the money to the robber.

I remember watching a middle-age woman with a toddler in a booster seat. She had been feeding him fried potatoes, but her gaze was fixed on a young girl outside on a swing. The child fell off the swing and fell to the ground, hurting her knee. She pushed through the glass door and ran into the room crying for her Mother. Startled, the robber spun around in the direction of the noise and began to fire rapidly. The mother screamed her child's name and the cries of the child and her mother were joined by others in the room afraid for their lives. Morgan sprang out of his chair and grabbed the child in his arms, tucking her beneath his body and rolling to the floor. Glass shattered and more gunfire popped as the police stormed through the door shooting the gunman in the shoulder and through the chest. He fell backward and lay dying on his back. Morgan was shot four times while shielding the child from the bullets. The girl's mother and I reached Morgan at the same time. He was bleeding badly, the child was crying for her mother. He never let go of her." Sarah wept, her face grimaced with pain as she remembered her husband's tragic death. Morgan had been dead for three years, and she had buried herself with him.

"Even with the girl's mother at his side he never let her go until he knew she was safe. I tried to apply pressure and stop the bleeding but there was blood everywhere. He knew he was dying but he was worrying about me in those last few minutes. He said, "Sarah, do you know what I'd like for you to cook for me tonight when we get home? I'd like some spaghetti and meatballs and one of your famous chocolate cakes. Will you make it for me?" We would have never been in that stupid restaurant if I had gone to the store that afternoon and bought food for supper. My act of procrastination made our reservation and seated us at that table. It was my fault"

"No, it was not."

She stood, crying harder, as if her heart would break. She could hardly speak, " And you know what? That night after he died, when I went home from the hospital, I made that chocolate cake. Science can put a man on the moon, but they couldn't save Morgan's life." She gasped, "I can't get my breath."

He poured her a cup of water and stood beside her as she took in deep breaths trying to get control of herself. After a few minutes she began to calm. What a lucky man, thought Russell, to be loved by Sarah.

"You just thought Indians and bears were a problem, Osborne. You had no idea about the dangers of traveling with a crazy person."

"You're not crazy."

"I'm a wreck. Traveling through time has played havoc with my hormones."

"Hormones?"

"With my emotions."

"Your coming here has played havoc with my hormones too," he looked at her the way a man looks at a woman.

She wanted to march right over to Osborne Russell and kiss him. She wanted him to fold his arms around her again and hold her tightly against his body, but she couldn't even breathe through her nose. She didn't want to mix the emotion she felt remembering Morgan's death with the emotion she felt for Osborne. She wanted him to know she was in his arms not because she needed him to hold her, but because she wanted him to hold her.

Chapter 16

Sarah and Russell began traveling at daybreak, as the stars began to fade. While they rode they didn't try to make conversation. The few occasions they stopped, Russell schooled Sarah in mountain ways. He referred to life in the mountains as the "Rocky Mountain College." He showed her the dusty paths made by elk as they filed across the mountain side, snow-white trumpeter swans, and a bald eagle's nest high in a cottonwood tree. He pointed out wolf tracks, bear scat, and marmots; small white rabbits with little ears that made a bleating sound like a lamb.

"This is an active pond. Recently cut trees are one of the things we call sign of the beaver. People in the 1600s thought beaver hats held supernatural powers. They believed if you rubbed beaver oil onto your hair it would help your memory. We're all out here trapping because the Europeans want to wear fancy beaver hats. Ever see a beaver's feet?"

"Can't say I have."

"Their hind feet are webbed for swimming and one of their toes has a nail that acts like a small toothpick to extract wooden splinters from their teeth." He reached into his bag and pulled out a wooden box. "Both male and female have castor glands. When we skin the animals we remove the glands and hang them to dry. We use the castoreum to scent our traps I keep mine in this bait box of cherry wood.." He opened the box for Sarah to smell. She inhaled deeply several times. The castoreum was yellow and gummy, and smelled strong, musky, and faintly sweet.

"When skinned their hide is perfectly round."

"How much do you get for a hide?"

"Depends on the size. We measure the hide's diameter then double it; so a thirty inch hide would be a sixty inch plew. It also depends on the demand. The year before I got to the mountains, the American Fur Company destroyed the St. Louis Fur Company by giving the exorbitant price of $12.00 for beaver. I've gotten $6.00 for a large skin and $5.00 per pound. When I started out with Wyeth's expedition I heard tall tales that you didn't have to set your traps for beaver, they were so plentiful they jumped into your arms. Truth is, every year, they become more and more scarce."

He showed her the steel traps in his leather bag. "I carry five traps. Some carry more, but I try not to burden my animal with more than 75 pounds. I'll pack heavier if I'm riding in safe country, but I rarely travel in safe country."

She took one from his hand. "They're heavy,"

"About four to five pounds. We set our traps in the water, near the bank, about six inches below the water's surface. Beavers are very territorial. Whenever a beaver, male or female, leaves their lodge they dive to the bottom of the pond and bring up some mud, holding it between their forepaws and breast. They carry the mud to the bank and emit a small amount of castoreum on it. Other beavers passing by cover the spot with their mud and mark it with their own castoreum. Trappers throw a handful of mud on the bank, about a foot from the trap, and bait it with the castoreum. When the beaver comes out of his lodge he smells it, goes to remark the place and Whap!' His foot gets caught and springs the trap. He heads for the safety of deeper water and eventually drowns. They have a sort of down in their fur until late spring. In the summer we take it a bit easier, trap in the fall, and winter in one of the valleys."

During the heat of the day they passed a small mountain lake. She called to Osborne, "Could we stop, I'd like to clean up."

"Sure. We've made good time today. By day's end tomorrow we should be able to see the Absaroka Range. There's a point up ahead where you can see five mountain ranges. It's beyond belief."

"Do you want to unsaddle the horses?"

"No, just tie up your horses' reigns and let them loose to feed. I'll hobble mine."

Sarah pulled the GPS from her gear and walked over to Russell. "Remember last night I told you about satellites, the metal objects that circle the earth out in space? Well, we have machines, like this called a G.P.S., which stands for global positioning system," she handed it to him, "that enable us to know exactly where we are, our longitude and latitude, anywhere on the planet."

"Really? Show me how it works."

"Well, it won't work now because there aren't any satellites up there. The first day of my trip I turned it on and, when it didn't work, I thought it was broken. I prefer maps myself. I want to make you a present of the map I brought with me." She handed him the 36" x 24" map of the Bridger-Teton Forest safely encased in a map protector with brass grommets. Russell knelt and unfolded the map. He was like a small boy on Christmas morning, his eyes wide with delight at the sheer grandeur of each precisely drawn word and line.

"Why would a man ever need one of those contraptions when he had such a map? Oftentimes I take a star for my guide."

"Man has invented many things we don't need. My world runs too fast. Look here." She pointed to the Gros Ventre River. "This is where the Gros Ventre slide happened. Some time in the 1920s, it is one of the largest earth movements in the world. It sheared off the side of the mountain, which damned the river, but in two or three years the dam broke flooding the small town downstream. I started from the Tetons, up this road that runs along the river. When I planned my trip I used your travels in this area. You wrote that you traveled from Jackson Hole up the Gros Ventre River. I couldn't determine whether you crossed the Continental Divide over Sheridan Pass, to the north, or Union Pass, to the southeast."

He studied the map tracing each trail and river with his fingers, reading their names aloud. "Here's the Snake River, the Yellowstone River, some places have the same names. This is wonderful. Do these lines show elevation?"

"Yes, they're contour lines. The closer they are the steeper the grade." He smiled, pleased she knew such things.

"I've got a high-speed compass, too, but those haven't changed much in 162 years; except mine glows in the dark."

"You're kidding? Look, this is where we had Rendezvous last year." He pointed to a place on the Green River near present day Daniel, Wyoming. And, here's the place I told you about that's up ahead, where you can see five mountain ranges. I remember the first time I stood where the waters divide; one half running west to the Pacific, the other half bidding adieu and running east to the Atlantic Ocean. I sat alone in the shade of a spreading pine musing on the meeting of the waters."

Sarah marveled at his ability to express himself so eloquently. She thought about his poem, *Farewell to the Mountains*, written just before he left the mountains in 1843. Would she be with him?

"We come out off the divide here, across from the lower end of the Absarorkas; they're named for the Crow Indians, the "Bird People." We enter the Great Wind River plain, and follow the Wind River to here." He pointed to the confluence of the Wind River and the Popo Agie. "Riverton?"

"That's the town on the site today."

"This is the nicest gift I've ever received. Now I won't have to read the same book until I get back to Fort Hall. Thank you."

"You're welcome." She was happy it gave him so much pleasure.

Sarah didn't want to ask for special treatment, but a small fire and warm water would have been nice if he had offered. The small lake had an island of snow floating in the water on the far bank. She thought about how she was going to take a bath and wash her hair. She decided to change into her bathing suit and wear her denim shirt as a cover up. Although her black one piece suit was modest by modern standards, she didn't want to offend Osborne. She wrapped her toiletries, a wash cloth, and her bathing suit in her towel and excused herself to change.

"Where are you going?"

"I'm going to change into my swim suit. It's like an undergarment, you swim in."

"It's too cold to swim."

"I'm not going swimming, but I have to get wet to bathe and wash my hair." She unwrapped her black suit, he was shocked at its scanty appearance.

"And, people, women," he stammered, "wear this outside? Wear it in front of other people? In front of men?"

"Yes, and most of the time the suits are much smaller."

His face flushed. He grinned, lowered his eyes, and shook his head. She turned and walked into the trees to change. As she undressed she felt the stubble on her legs and the raccoon that seemed to be growing under her arms. Even traveling in Europe she could never get accustom to the profusion of women's body hair. She knew Margaret would say, "You run into a man and you start behaving like a teenager, all hormone driven and girlie-like." It was true. If she'd been alone in the mountains she would have never shaved her legs, but traveling with Osborne made her want to look her best, although it was difficult with the lack of supplies she'd packed. He said she was the most beautiful woman he'd ever seen. She would have probably plugged in a set of electric rollers and curled her hair if she had them.

Sarah pulled on her suit, the denim shirt, and headed for the lake. She could barely see Osborne down the shore line and through the trees. She stepped into the water. Within seconds her feet burned from the cold. She quickly splashed water on her body and hurried out of the water to soap her legs and shave. The afternoon sun was wonderfully warm. She took off her shirt and discreetly washed her upper body. She waded in again to wash the lime-scented shower gel off her body and to wet her hair.

In less than a minute, the burning returned as the cold began to rob her extremities of their feeling. She bent forward, dunked her head in the water, then flung her head back and ran out of the water. Russell heard the splashing. He stood to see where she was. He saw her, through the trees, standing in the sunlight washing her hair. Her head was covered with white bubbles. Her arms and long legs were bare. The swim suit, as she called it, clung to her womanly body and curved around her bottom and stretched across her bosom. He'd bedded women and never seen as much of their bodies. It was hard for him to believe that men could see so much of a woman and go about their business.

Sarah gingerly made her way back into the lake until she stood mid-calf in the water. She dunked her head under, trying to rinse the shampoo from her hair. She wanted to squeal and yip and yike but didn't want to worry Osborne. She dared herself to do it, held her breath, submerged her body, then sprang from the water and ran to the bank. She threw the towel around her, dried, and quickly put on her shirt. Her body was covered with goosebumps and her nipples were so hard they could have put someone's eye out. She vigorously rubbed her hair with the towel. Slowly the sun warmed her, she quit shivering and her body returned to normal. She wanted to spread her towel and stretch out in the sun. Instead she finished grooming and walked to where Osborne was sitting. He had just finished shaving. The sharp blade of his razor reflected the bright afternoon sun; it had a beautiful ebony handle.

"How was it," he tried hard not to look at her bare legs.

"Freezing, but now that it's over I feel terrific."

"What was that soap you used to wash your hair?"

"Oh, now, Mr. Russell, were you watching me while I bathed?"

"Uh, no, uh, yes. I was just making sure you weren't in any danger over there. Just making sure you were safe."

"It's called shampoo. It's soap for your hair. Don't you have shampoo?"

"Not like yours. Ours doesn't suds up like that."

"Smell." Sarah brought her face close to Russell and turned her head. Her wet hair brushed his face, and her body smelled fresh and sweet, like the mountains after a spring rain.

"Why don't you let me wash your hair."

"Wash my hair? No." He was emphatic and seemed embarrassed by her suggestion.

"Why not? Are you afraid of me?"

"Why would I be afraid of you? The way these clothes smell it wouldn't hurt to get them wet."

"You can use my towel."

Russell reluctantly agreed. He kept on his clothes, even his deerskin moccasins, removing only his half breeds; the blankets wrapped around his legs from his knees to his ankles.

"Do you want me to get a pot and pour the water over your head so you don't have to get all wet."

"Nah," said Russell. "I don't have cold feet."

"You will," she laughed.

She took the cap off the shampoo. Russell waded out, wet his hair, and returned to shore.

"Does that snow ever melt?" asked Sarah pointing to the island of snow bobbing in the lake."

"Sometimes not."

"Sit down on this rock, you're too tall for me to reach the top of your head without climbing on a ladder." She stood behind him and poured the shampoo into her hands. She began to work the soap into his wet hair and gently massaged his scalp, working the shampoo into a thick fragrant lather. She pulled her fingers through his long hair. He was warming up in a hurry.

"I've never washed a man's hair before. How am I doing?"

"I think you need to wash it a little longer."

After a few minutes Russell took off his shirt and suspenders and stood. He took some of the lather from his head and ran it across his chest, under his arms, and over his taunt stomach. Without suspenders his pants hung low on his hips. Sarah watched the muscles in his arms and stomach contract as he washed. She noticed the hair on his stomach as it thickened, darkened, and disappeared beneath his trousers.

Refreshed, they resumed their ride and traveled the rest of the day through meadows of wildflowers. Russell identified varieties she had never seen before: arrowleaf, Colorado columbine, fireweed, and glacier lilies. The sky was filled with a multitude of huge-winged insects and birds: black-billed magpies, white pelicans, yellow-headed blackbirds, and spotted sandpipers.

Russell would have ridden further but he was concerned about the weather. He found a stand of trees a safe distance from a fast-running creek. The last hour the wind had picked up, the temperature began to drop steadily, and there was a low muttering of thunder. Thick black clouds rose above the mountain peaks. A storm was about to succeed the hot, cloudless day. It began with a cool wind filled with the smell of rain, but within thirty minutes of setting camp, sharp incessant lightening lit the sky and thunder exploded, threatening from a distance. Russell took his axe and drove the picket pins in his horses' hobbles firmly into the ground with his axe. He shouted instructions to Sarah, as time grew short and the rain began to squall. She darted about gathering as much wood as possible, stacking it next to their saddles and panniers. There wasn't enough time to construct a lean-to of saplings or brush, so Russell took his largest piece of canvas and covered their belongings. Sarah arranged their possessions and the wood in a semicircle. She didn't suggest they set up her two-person tent and crawl in together to ride out the storm. The thought of crawling into the small tent and lying down beside him was more frightening than the storm. As the storm came closer the darkness increased; within minutes the sky was the color of India ink.

"Put on your warmest clothes, anything you've got, we're in for it." She pulled her gray wool sweater over her head and rifled in her belongings to find her J. Peterman duster. Russell put on his buckskin frock, leggings, and his blanket coat. They climbed underneath the canvas and sat inside the semicircle. He used his rifle, as a center pole, to pitch up the sides to form the upright of the primitive shelter.

"Hold this," he instructed as he tried to secure the edges of the canvas under the heaviest pieces of their equipment. The wind blew like a hurricane. The rain fell diagonally and within minutes it completely obscured the woods before them. It hit the ground with such heavy force it rose upward into a muddy spray. The horses turned their backs to the storm and stood in the fierce driving rain with their heads bowed, holding their tails like whipped dogs. Russell and Sarah crouched beneath the canvas. The temperature continued to drop and the torrential rain was followed by a blast of sleet and hail that felt like a storm of needles.

She huddled close to him in the darkness, without a roof over head, climate control, an umbrella, or storm windows, and she realized she was a fraud. A fraud created by twenty-first century innovation and convenience perhaps, but a fraud nonetheless. Not only had she crossed the Oregon Trail in an air-conditioned sports utility vehicle with a CD player, but she had armed herself against nature with waterproof matches, a pop-up tent, and her food neatly packaged in ziplock bags. For years she had given everyone the impression she was a survivor and now, stripped of her belongings, she stood face-to-face with who she was and who she was not. Her doctorate degree, impeccably framed on her office wall, was of no importance in 1838. The dog-and-pony-show she fervently performed at the university to lure students into an appreciation of art history was a hollow sound. In her possession were two horses that didn't belong to her, three wineskins of Jack Daniels, a saddle bag, two panniers and various personal possessions, red pepper spray, a .44 Magnum with six bullets, and William. And, of course, the blanket that had taken her across the seasons to Russell, a man that she had previously met only in that shadowy place between sleeping and dreaming.

The rain beat through the canvas; its heavy weight was suffocating. The wind whipped the makeshift shelter and rain drenched their clothing. They struggled to hold down the sides against the fury of the storm. It had been a long time since she had been wet and cold. Her hands, nose, and feet were numb and burned from the cold. In the rush she had forgotten to pull out her gloves. When the blue lightening broke the darkness, the rain stood in puddles like a thousand small lakes, as far as she could see.

Russell kept trying to gauge her spirits. After a long silence he smiled, turned to her and said, "It'll let up in a day or two, always does. Not like the snow. Snow comes and stays for months. I had a Snake Indian tell me once that thunder was a huge stone rolling across the sky. Another chief, called Comb Daughter by the Snakes and called Lame Chief by the Whites, said that thunder was a great blackbird. Once in a dream he saw the winged creature swooping down from the icy tops of the Rocky Mountains. When the blackbird flapped its enormous feathered wings over the lake, lightening shot upwards, from beneath the water's surface, into the sky. I've heard tell during winter camp, that some tribes have a mystic society of thunder fighters who take their bows and arrows, even take their guns, and fire at the rising clouds to frighten them down again."

"I had a professor of mythology who said the voices of the gods speak in the wind and the thunder, and the Spirit of God flows in every mountain stream."

"I wouldn't argue that," said Russell. "There have been times I know I've seen Him. Living in the mountains is like going to Sunday services every day. Sometimes it's an ambuscade with an Indian that preaches the sermon, or having your horse fall out from under you at a dead run and you figure yourself for sure dead, or it's an encounter like the one you had with your grizzly bear. But whatever it is, the good Lord's there with you."

The rain shutting off the world made it seem as though time had shifted even further. The storm, like the night after the campfire had turned to ash, left her alone with thoughts of the journey across the seasons; her journey across time. What sermon God was preaching to her? Was this journey historical purgatory where she had to "work out" one or more of her life's past confusions or errors. She genuinely believed the blanket was only a metaphor or an illusion, and it was God that had moved her from 2000 to 1838. She believed that God's hand had gently lifted her, and she tried to view the entire experience with a sense of faith.

Why was she here? What was she to learn? To do? To change? To see? She remembered her off-the-cuff reply to the frequently asked question about why she lived in Atlanta's bedroom community of Newnan. She always answered, "God sent me to here to learn something and when I've learned it, He'll let me leave." Was that true in 1838 as well? Had God sent her, moved her, shifted her, to learn something and when she'd learned "It" would He let her leave? And would she want to leave?

Russell seemed impervious to the cold as the rain ran through his hair, onto his shoulders, and his clothes. His blanket coat was saturated like a wet sponge. Lightening struck a tree nearby, cracking, popping, and bursting into flames. Sarah jumped. He put his arm around her shoulder and pulled her close to him. She freely accepted the unexpected gesture and leaned into the warmth and strength of his body.

"Everything's going to be fine, don't worry."

"Do you ever wonder why God brought us together?"

"Constantly."

"But why did He bring me here? Why didn't He bring you to me in my time?"

"Well, maybe it's because you wanted to change your past."

It was a brilliant thought, unscientific and speculative, but brilliant. Sarah wanted to change her past. Sarah wanted to control her future.

"What I think about more than your coming back in time is how long you'll be here . . . how long you'll be with me. When I wake in the middle of the night I'll walk over to where you're sleeping to make sure you're still there."

Since the first night they spent together she knew Russell was near her in the darkness, and that he was, scarcely sleeping, to be ready if she needed him.

"Sometimes I'll hear you move about," she said, "other times I'll wake up and I feel you lying there on the other side of the fire, watching me, guarding me."

"I promised I would take care of you." He looked her straight in the eye, "I take the vow very seriously. You're under my protection."

"You could sleep on my side of the fire. Then, when you wake up and see me lying next to you and you can go back to sleep."

"That would make some sense." He didn't say anything else, but was thinking about how he would feel lying within arm's reach of her.

It rained for hours while they sat in the driving rain and in the cold mud. It was well after midnight when the wind blew the storm away and the sky gradually cleared allowing the heaven's starry firmament to once again be seen from earth. Russell stood, pushing the heavy water-soaked canvas off them. They stared at one another's miserable appearance.

"I guess we'll have to take another bath tomorrow," he said. "I'll light a fire."

Sarah helped pull the limbs from under the canvas and stack them in a high pile on the wet ground.

"Leave a few pieces for the morning."

"Here," she offered. "These are waterproof matches. No need to work so hard when you don't have to."

Russell shredded some of the bark into thin fibers and sheltered the kindling with his left hand as he struck the match. The bark began to crackle. He patiently coaxed the small flame into a roaring fire which was a great comfort after the violent storm. Their camp was like a shallow lake; they walked in mud six inches deep while they took care of the horses and secured their belongings.

Sarah found her gloves and her flashlight. "Another handy invention," she explained as she turned it on and the light shone brightly. "It's powered by two batteries, but don't ask me how batteries work because it's just one of the many things that I, and so many others, take for granted. I'm going to walk to the river, get some water, and make us something to eat."

"Will you show me the batteries when you come back?" he shouted after her?"

Supper was Knorr's tricolored fusilli with creamy pesto sauce. She made the selection based upon the nine minutes it took to cook. She cooked two packages; they greedily ate every bite.

"Cooking has certainly changed," said Russell. "It's faster when you don't have to hunt it or grow it."

Their breath turned to steam in the cold night air, the heat of the fire made small clouds rise from their bodies as the heat dried their wet clothes from the outside. Russell looked at the mud, trying to decide where they were going to bed down for the night.

"I have a large plastic tarp. We can sleep on top of it and the water won't soak through."

"Do you want to change into dry clothes?"

She looked at her slime-splattered jeans and the mud caked on her hiking boots. "No, it would be too much trouble to change. I'll be all right by the fire."

They spread the blue plastic tarp and covered it with the space blanket she had packed. Russell watched curiously as the silver metallic surface reflected the fire light and crackled as she spread it on the ground.

"I'll explain in the morning," she promised. Sarah placed her bedroll on top of the space blanket. She took off her wet duster, pulled on her polar fleece, and then put the duster on again, afraid she would get cold during the night. She carefully stepped on the edges of the tarp with her muddy shoes. She lay down on the pallet, the fire warm against her back. Russell covered her with the Hudson's Bay blanket.

"I'll be right back." He disappeared into the darkness. She presumed it was to relieve himself. He returned in a few minutes, and lay down on the ground a couple of few feet from her.

"Good night, Sarah."

"Good night."

Their wet clothes were uncomfortable and they were cold. Sarah tried to keep from shivering but Russell heard her teeth chattering. He never got used to being cold, but he could wait it out until morning. A trapper couldn't carry enough to keep him warm; he learned to make do. He'd been colder, but he worried about her. She turned her back to him to face the fire.

He saw her tremble in the light of the campfire. He pulled her into his body and wrapped his arms around her, holding her close. He surprised her. Heavily clothed in layers of wet, muddy clothing, their position could hardly be construed as sexual, yet it took them a long time to fall asleep with their bodies lying so close together.

Chapter 17

"It appears Aeolus has contained the four winds," observed Russell as they huddled around the warm fire drinking their morning coffee. Their clothes and shoes were covered with mud.

"Aeolus? Wasn't he a friend of Hercules?"

"Yes, but he was also the keeper of the four winds: Boreas, Notus, Zephyr and Eurus."

"How do you know so much mythology? I don't even know the names of the four winds."

"A classical education, albeit humble, is very valued where I come from. Mythology is just another form of storytelling. It helps pass the time. I guess the idea of gods and goddesses living high atop a mountain is timeless."

"Tell me about Aeolus."

"When Zeus let loose the four winds and opened the floodgates of the sky, they brought about confusion and destruction; they were very powerful when they stormed together. Zeus chose Aeolus to be their keeper. Aeolus kept the winds in a hollow cliff far out at sea. The winds hated to be confined. They raged and howled. They stormed about Aeolus trying to break free of their prison. When one of the gods, like Poseidon, would summon a wind, Aeolus would take his spear and pierce the wall of the cliff and let out one of the winds. He would then seal the hole until the wind returned. Each wind had a different character."

She laughed and shook her head, "Do you realize that with all the innovations, discoveries, and history we have to discuss, we're sitting here talking about mythology! We are a pair! Please, finish your story."

"Eos, the Dawn, was the mother of the four winds. Eurus was the East Wind. He wasn't very important and wasn't summoned very often. Zephyr, the West Wind, was the most gentle of the four. His blowing swept the clouds from the sky and pleased all of Nature. Notus, the South Wind, was the most feared by sailors and travelers. Notus was so heavy with moisture that he spread a thick fog over land and sea, as water poured from his thick, tangled beard. Boreas, the North Wind, was the wild and icy wind. When he rushed out of the cliff, trees were torn apart by his wintry blast and waves rose up in front of him."

"I've been Greece to the Palace of Poseidon on Cape Sounion," interrupted Sarah, "where Lord Byron wrote his famous poem."

Russell stood, cleared his throat for dramatic emphasis, and recited:

Place me on Sunium's marbled steep,
Where nothing, save the waves and I,
May hear our mutual murmurs sweep;
There, swan-like, let me sing and die:
A land of slaves shall ne'er be mine —
Dash down yon cup of Samian wine!

He bowed ceremoniously and sat down.

"You know Lord Byron's poem?"

"I get the distinct impression you think all of us back here in the nineteenth century are intellectual primitives."

"No, it's just I never expected —"

"I'm no poet, but I can repeat a verse or two. Mr. Bridger can't read, but you should hear him recite Shakespeare. Speaking of Shakespeare, don't you think he should have written *Paradise Lost* instead of Milton? I can scarcely read more than a page or two of Milton at a time. An epic poet, certainly, give the man any title you wish, he's too correctly cold and classical in spirit for his theme. But Shakespeare writing *Paradise Lost*; what a poem he would have given to the world!"

After riding all morning, Russell dismounted to stretch his legs and check the pack animals. They stopped within fifty feet of a huge, hollow buffalo carcass, its decayed surface covered with black crickets.

"I've decided how we're going to explain your presence here in the mountains. I thought about it last night while we were waiting out the storm. We tell everyone at Rendezvous you're from Boston and you came to the mountains to find your brother, Seaborn Ratcliff. Your Mother died recently, and you came west to try and convince him to come home to Boston. Ratcliff came to the Rocky Mountains about the same time I did, in 1834. I know for a fact that he died earlier this year in a skirmish with Benj Johnson's boys."

"Benj Johnson's boys?"

"The Blackfeet. We tell everyone the last you heard from Seaborn was by a letter you received from Taos. You arranged transport to Taos in the company of a sympathetic St. Louis merchant. When you arrived you found people who knew Seaborn and they told you that if he was alive, he would make his way to the annual Rendezvous in the mountains. Since no one knew exactly where the meeting was to be held, you hired two men, who appeared to be gentlemen, to take you north to determine where the annual gathering was to be held. When these neer-do-wells forced their unwanted attentions on you, I arrived and rescued you. We'll say the men stole your baggage and that's why you're not dressed like a White woman. If we're in luck, Lame Chief and his village may be up ahead. I've spent time with them before. Very hospitable Indians, the Snakes, I spent Christmas with them one year. They will divide their last morsel with a hungry stranger without regard for where they will find their next meal. The Snakes believe the infernal deities live in the moon and the stars, but they are subservient to the Supreme Deity who lives in the sun. Most are very superstitious and will not smoke in the presence of a woman, or even a dog. They will sometimes turn their pipe around three times in the direction of the sun. I know enough of the Snake language to trade goods with them and to trade jokes. I have some claret seed beads, a few hawk bells, finger rings, and about an ounce of Chinese vermilion left to trade. Indians will trade almost anything for vermilion; it will usually bring one or two buffalo robes, sometimes three. I should be able to trade this ounce for some fancy Indian woman's clothes. Indians probably will never have seen a White woman before. You should create quite a stir."

"It's plausible."

"The best I can figure. We cache your things, except the three wineskins, of course, and after Rendezvous we'll recover them."

What then she thought, after Rendezvous? Where do we go then?

Russell was thinking the same thing.

"Kit Carson will be at Rendezvous. He's four or five years older than I. He's often spoken of his first expedition from 1829 to 1831, with Ewing Young. He called it his higher learning as a trapper and Indian fighter. He married an Arapaho girl, Alice, a couple of years ago. Last I heard they have one child, a girl, they named Adaline. Carson's likely to ask more questions than others regarding the goings-on in Taos." He checked the rope that strung the pack horses together and remounted.

"What should I tell him?"

"Tell him you imagine nothing's changed since he was there last. The men still consider honest labor a burden, and only work as a last resort. They spend their day sleeping, smoking, and gambling, and it's too dangerous to be on the streets at night. If he asks too many questions, just tell him you weren't there very long."

They rode hard. Late afternoon they arrived at the location Russell had been telling her about for two days. He was true to his word, Sarah saw the panoramic view of the five mountain ranges and felt their raw power. She had been drawn to the mountains as if they were a magnet. By rising above the dwellings of men she had left behind all low and earthly regions. She had climbed above herself. She had seen pictures of the earth from the moon, but she had never witnessed the infinite horizon line of the life God had given her. She felt as though God, like her Father when she was a small child, had hoisted her on His shoulders to gaze at His handiwork. She was reminded of Genesis, "On the second day God created the land, and it was good."

The mountains, each slightly different in their persona, were overwhelming in their size and grandeur; a great presence seemed to hover over the ranges. They possessed unimaginable mystery and splendor, and were the home of the fierce, powerful, natural elements beyond human control and the dangerous haunts of the gods. As far as she could see the horizon receded in the distance, revealing ridge after ridge of mountain ranges without end; a pathway to heaven, to the moon, and to the stars. Ruskin described mountains as great cathedrals of the earth, with their gates of rock, pavements of cloud, choirs of stream and stone, altars of snow, and vaults of purple traversed by continual stars. Soon Albert Bierdstadt would capture the rugged wildness of the Rockies in his paintings, and America would have its first glimpse of their majestic grandeur.

Perhaps it was the danger inherent in the mountains that fueled the mythology of their wild regions. Sarah was sure it was not simply financial gain that brought men like Osborne to the Rocky Mountains. Careless individuals did not live long; a slight mistake or a disregard for the weather cost a man his life.

"Think of the years that went by," said Russell in a whisper, "without any man watching."

It occurred to Sarah, as she watched him turn full-circle to once again admire the breathtaking view, that the mountains were his mistress. He worshiped her beauty and he took time and great care to explore her hidden secrets, and to pleasure her with his devotion.

"We're in luck," he pointed east.

Sarah saw a village of fifteen or twenty tipis. Their tall lodge poles rising into the sky looked like the teeth of a comb against the setting sun. Six young warriors rode at full speed to meet the them; their hair flying like jet black streamers in the wind. Feathers dangled from their horses' manes and tails. They yelled as they approached and exchanged words with Russell. They eyed Sarah keenly, turned their horses, and sped back to their village;

their shouts and yells fading as they rode away. As Sarah and Russell entered the Indian village small boys ran to greet them waving little bows and arrows. The entire village crowded around their horses eager to see their trapper friend and his White woman.

When the sun went down, half the sky was a fiery red. The young men left the village and returned driving a large herd of horses of every size, age, and color. Kettles were hung over camp fires. Young women were tossing children in the air on a buffalo robe. The coverings of the lodges fluttered in the wind. They were raised a foot or more from the ground to allow the air to circulate during the hot summer. Children enjoyed the last light of day, while their mothers visited and prepared the evening meal. The camp was filled with the low hum of cheerful voices. Sarah and Russell were escorted to a lodge in the center of the village.

The chief's lodge was the most weather-beaten in the village. Russell explained it was a demonstration of a democratic community; the chief never assuming a superior state. Old men and warriors of stature sat cross-legged on the ground with buffalo robes pulled around their shoulders. Several women and an abundance of children were present. A woman spread a buffalo robe for them, in the guests place, at the head of the lodge. Russell assumed a bold, self-confident posture in the midst of the throng.

Sarah had only seen the clothing worn by their hosts locked in glass cases in museums. Some had crests of feathers, and fitted tunics of antelope skin, fringed with the scalp-locks of their foes. A few of the men were armed with guns and long lances, but all had bows and arrows on their backs with sharp points of black obsidian. The bows were three feet in length and beautifully wrought from sheep, buffalo, and elk horn. They were fastened with deer and elk sinews and ornamented with porcupine quills. Furs, robes, blankets, and painted cases of rawhide were the domestic possessions of the lady of the house. A long red pipe, and an impressive quiver of otter skin with bows and arrows, hung on the interior poles.

The chief began a highly agitated tale. Sarah sat silently, watching his animated gestures without the slightest idea what he was saying. He told Russell about a recent attack on two of the village's young men by a war-party of Blackfeet. One of the young men was wounded when shot with the enemies' arrows. The other was chased up the side of a mountain, surrounded by his attackers, and scalped alive. They cut the tendons of their captives' wrists and feet and threw them in a fire, pinning them in the flames with long poles, until they burned to death.

Russell responded in a sympathetic tone to his host's story.

"What did he say?"

"They've had some trouble with the Blackfeet," he answered without elaboration.

The talk and laughter continued for what seemed to be an eternity. Russell pointed to Sarah and tugged on her shirt and pants. The Indians laughed loudly. She displayed good humor, as the object of the private joke. Russell unfolded a remnant of a red wool blanket and placed it on the ground in front of him. All eyes in the lodge, old and young, strained to see the trade goods the trapper offered. Wrapped inside the blanket was an ivory comb, a pocket looking glass, blue cut beads, white seed beads, hawk bells, and vermilion. The chief's wife eagerly approached the make-shift storefront and began to inspect the merchandise. After a few minutes she made her selection, and began haggling with Russell. Pleased with the bargain, she clutched her new treasures to her flattened bosom and secured them under a robe behind the jovial crowd.

Sarah noticed a litter of seven rust-colored puppies sleeping together in a heap, nestled among the buffalo robes. A woman entered the gathering, carrying a mallet of stone, affixed to the handle by a covering of rawhide. She grabbed one of the puppies by the hind leg and carried him yelping out of the entrance of the lodge. In the doorway the woman swiftly clubbed the animal in the head until it was dead. Russell's expression never changed. He put his hand on Sarah's, patting it nonchalantly, speaking to her in a whisper through a forced smile.

"A dog feast is the highest compliment to be offered a guest. It is considered an insult for a stranger, White or Indian, to return any portion of the food which is offered him. If we don't eat all that is set before us we'll have to take the remainder with us when we leave."

Sarah nodded, smiling back at him, and at their hosts. Through a hole in the back of the lodge she could see the woman, holding the puppy by the legs, swinging it back and forth through the fire until all of its hair was singed off. She looked away when the woman unsheathed her knife and began to butcher the dog into small pieces, dropping each piece into a kettle to boil.

In a short while, the woman returned with a large wooden dish filled with meat, and a cake of dried meat and fruit pounded together and mixed with buffalo marrow. The women had prepared a boiled flour pudding with dried fruit and a sauce of berry juice and sugar. They ate from crude wooden bowls. Their gracious hostess served them with a ladle from a big-horn sheep. Sarah took a deep breath and reminded herself that she had eaten horse in Greece, guinea pigs in South America, and alligator in Florida, but she had never eaten an animal whose mother slept unsuspectingly in the room.

When the men began to fill a pipe with tobacco and chased the dogs out of the tipi, Sarah excused herself and walked to the lodge their hosts had prepared them for the night. A dim sea of smoke blanketed the village. Their lodge was a huge, old tipi, rotten with age, discolored by time, rain, and storms, but to Sarah, it was a palace after sleeping in the mud the night before. Entering the tipi she found a central blazing fire. On one side was a single bed of buffalo robes laid together and a pillow of whitened deerskin stuffed with feathers and ornamented with glass beads. Russell had neatly placed their saddles and equipment around the circular room. A kettle of water hung over the fire. Sarah got her soap and a wash cloth . She carefully removed the kettle from the fire and dipped the cloth into the steaming water. It was too hot to touch. She took off her sweater and denim shirt and began to wash herself when the cloth was cool enough to handle. The hand towel felt heavenly as she rubbed the warm cloth up and down her arms, across her face, and her breasts. She rubbed lotion on her badly sunburned face and neck.

"Sarah! Look at this foofarraw!" Russell burst into the lodge carrying the dress he had traded for. He found her standing, bare breasted, by the fire. She immediately crossed her arms to cover herself.

"I beg your pardon," he was ashamed and embarrassed. He turned his back and hurried toward the lodge door.

"Osborne, please, don't leave."

He stopped at her command, but did not turn to face her. "I humbly apologize, I didn't mean to walk in on you. I should have announced myself."

She stepped toward him. His eyes were cast downward. Still covering herself, she walked in front of him, placing herself between him and the door. She never imagined this would be the night she would make love with him. She had enough experience to know their first sexual encounter was going to be over quickly. After a moment, and several deep breaths, Sarah uncrossed her arms and dropped her hands to her side. She took the dress from his hands.

Russell tried to keep his gaze locked in hers, but he was unable to keep from lowering his eyes to her breasts. He was embarrassed he knew nothing about lying with a woman. The few times he had taken advantage of the opportunity, it didn't last long enough for him to hardly recollect what had happened. He didn't want to be rough or to hurt Sarah, but he wanted to take her and he wanted to take her now.

Her hands were covered with the lotion she had been applying to her face and neck. She reached for his calloused hands and placed them on her breasts. He inhaled deeply and exhaled trying to slow himself. With the sweet tenderness of a husband touching his bride for the first time on their wedding night, he lifted the weight of her breasts in his hands. They were cool and soft. Her nipples were the largest he had ever seen. The cold night air made them hard in his hands.

"Have you ever done this before?" she asked softly.

"Yes, but I don't think I did it very well."

She stepped closer, her heart beating so hard she felt Osborne could have seen it leaping beneath her breast if he had looked closer. She touched his handsome face with her hand, she felt the tautness of his neck and jaw, and raised her lips to his. His lips were dry, she moistened them with her tongue. She opened her mouth for a stronger taste of him. She felt his body rise. He pressed his mouth against hers. Their standing shadows on the tipi wall spun around him. He placed his left arm around her waist and pulled her into the firmness of his body. He let go long enough to roughly pull his red flannel shirt over his head; he heard it tear.

Sex. Real sex, not masturbation or sheer imagination was all coming back to her. The soft, slow dance of tongues and lips, the heat of the skin, and the involuntary shuddering as a woman's body begins to respond to her lover's touch. She pulled him from the shadows into the amber light of the fire. She let go of his hand and reached into the kettle, wringing the hot water from her wash cloth. She brushed it over his mouth and face, bringing it down over his throat and across his chest. The water ran down his body. She wet the cloth again and ran it across his abdomen and along the waist of his trousers, squeezing to allow the warm water to cover him. She unbuttoned the top two buttons of his trousers. Russell was both shocked and aroused by her sexual confidence. Sarah dropped the cloth and bent over to open the bottle of moisturizer. She squeezed the milky lotion into her hands and rubbed it on his chest. She slowly moved her breasts against him covering herself with the lotion on his body. Russell closed his eyes and hunted for her mouth as he held her tightly with one hand and caressed her upper body with the other.

Sarah took her hands and ran them just below Russell's waist. His muscles quivered as her fingers dropped farther beneath his trousers and she lightly touched him. He bore down harder on her mouth. He opened his mouth for a deeper kiss; she opened her hand for a deeper touch. An uncontrolled tremor ran through his body. He threw back his head like a drowning man gasping for air. He held onto Sarah's shoulders afraid his legs would buckle beneath him. She braced herself against him and held him until he dropped his head to her shoulder. She lightly kissed his face and brushed back his hair.

"I've loved you almost all my life," she whispered.

He kissed her passionately. "I will love you the rest of mine." He led her to the robes their hosts had prepared for their bed. She stepped out of her jeans and pulled the blankets over her. Russell added wood to the fire, picked up his rifle and pistol, placed them by their bed, and lay down beside her. She was self-conscious when he pulled back the blanket and looked at her. God, she wished she had the body she possessed when she was twenty; the body she had wielded like a sword. She moved her body beneath him as though she had made love to him all her life. She moved her hand between them to help him find his place.

The night became a dream, and the terms past and future lost their meaning. As Sarah laid beside Osborne she realized her attempt to count, measure, and control time was futile. The "present" was a gift. Somehow God had given her a gift, a long-playing dream. She prayed, no one would call her to awake.

They talked until the early hours of morning about microwave ovens, telephones, organ transplants, submarines, and electricity. They discussed the Alamo, the Civil War, weapons of mass destruction, and how the United States government would soon condemn the Indians to an imprisoned life on reservations. Lying side by side they laughed and whispered, sharing stories of their childhood.

He came to her twice during the night.

Chapter 18

Russell awoke early, despite the late hours he and Sarah had kept together. He had the smell of her on his face and on his hands. He lay beside her a long time listening to her breathing, and watching her sleeping face as the tipi began to fill with the first light of day. He threw a few small timbers on the fire and walked to a nearby lake to fill the kettle with water for her to wash. How he looked forward to their privacy and another opportunity to make love with her.

The village began to crawl with women of all ages emerging from their lodges to begin their toilsome day of labor. Several of the women giggled and hurried away as he greeted them, speaking much too quickly in their native tongue for Russell to understand their humor. The Chief's wife approached him, wearing one of her newly acquired brass rings, and presented him with their morning meal, juicy hump ribs from a buffalo cow. After the Chief's gruesome story about the Blackfoot attack on the two young men of his village, Russell was in a hurry to get to Rendezvous and enjoy the security and safety that only came in numbers.

"Today will be a hard ride, Sarah. You may never want to see a saddle again."

"What's the hurry?" After the cordial greeting they had received from their hosts, she had hoped they might remain a day and rest; remain a day and enjoy the seclusion and intimacy of the night before.

He hesitated then told her the reason for their hurried departure. "The truth is this country's swarming with Blackfeet."

"The Chief's story last night?"

"Yes, I started not to tell you, but I think you should know. The Blackfoot tribes consider any of us, Hudson's Bay Company men, American Fur Company men, all enemies. They call white men 'Napikwan.' They hate us not only because we're robbing them of their resources, but for giving aid and comfort, by way of trading, to their enemies: the Crows, Flatheads, Snake, and Nez Percey. Their enemies hate them. If a Blackfoot woman is taken prisoner on a raid, she is carried back to camp and handed over to the mothers, wives, and sisters. I've heard the women vomit on their captives, cursing while they butcher them with hatchets and knives. There are three Blackfoot tribes, each is politically independent, but they speak the same language, share the same customs, intermarry, and make war on common enemies. Together, the tribes comprise the strongest military strength on the northwestern plains."

He repeated the Chief's story. "The Blackfeet are feared by the bravest white man. Their tribes were the first in their part of the country to own both horses and guns. With their mobility and firepower, they rode ramshackle over their rivals and soon the choicest buffalo grounds were theirs. There was a group of mountaineers, back in 1821, returning from trapping a fine collection of beaver pelts on the Yellowstone. In mid-May when they were traveling downstream, they encountered some thirty-eight Blackfeet, who professed to be friendly, and allowed them to pass without incident. But fifteen days later, as the trappers were riding through a narrow pass, some three hundred to four hundred vicious warriors descended upon them. They cut one of the men to pieces, another man's chest was pierced with dozens of arrows. Five other whites were killed and four wounded. In addition to their carnage, they carried off at least $15,000 worth of property. In 1832, a Blackfoot named Eagle Ribs, was sent westward from Fort Union with letters for Henry Vandenburg, a principal clerk of the American Fur Company. The Whites mistakenly fired upon Eagle Ribs and his party, believing them to be hostile Indians. In the ensuing battle, Vandenburg's horse fell and he was pinned beneath. Vandenburg was mortally wounded, his body stripped of flesh, and his bones thrown into the Jefferson River. And, that's the reason I want to leave after we eat." He kissed her awkwardly.

"I'll be ready."

The entire village came out for their departure, just as they had swarmed around them when they arrived. Their hostess presented them a generous gift of boiled buffalo tongues as they mounted their horses to leave.

By mid-morning they could see the craggy faces of the Absaorka Range over a wide meadow. The meadow floor looked like a Persian carpet woven with wildflowers. Sarah saw the tracks of animals where their hoofs had crushed the sunburned grass. The Absaroka Mountains looked like gray, granite-faced owls scowling across the Continental Divide at the graceful elevation of the Tetons. The Snake Indians call the Tetons "The Hoary Feathered Fathers," Russell told her. The Absaroka's looked like the bones of the earth.

"Mr. Fitzpatrick was showing Captain Stewart the land of "Absaroka" a few years ago and the Crows robbed him of everything he owned, personal and profit alike. The furs got into the hands of the American Fur

Company. Fitzpatrick never felt quite the same about the Crows or the fur company after that episode." Russell helped pass the long day telling her stories about life in the mountains, and about the good friends his life often depended upon.

The ground was easy to travel. The huge open meadow was rimmed on either side by dark evergreens. The ground was soppy and muddy with melting snow that still measured eighteen inches in some places. They followed a shallow stream. She was thirsty. How she had taken for granted life's real creature comforts: a bathroom and a plentiful supply of hot water from a faucet. Russell was on edge. He was always alert, but today he was visibly worried.

As they began their descent from the mountains Sarah saw the crested, rolling foothills of the Wind River Basin. The change from the mountains to the Wind River basin, a high desert landscape, was as different as night and day. Sparse vegetation colored the landscape with muted colors of celery, orange, tan and yellow. There was a sense of desolation. There were dark red cliffs on the right with evidence of rock slides, and snow-covered mountains on the left. The ground resembled a sand painting of plum, rose, and cocoa. The sun was hotter, the wind was still. For the pioneers, Wyoming was a cruel reality of battering rivers, hostile Indians, and perilous mountains. They left their names on trailside rocks and their dead in shallow graves. In her time, Minuteman missiles were buried in the Wyoming desert floor in bunkers of steel and concrete.

"What's that?" pointed Sarah. It appeared to be a dark moving cloud cast over the landscape.

"Buffalo."

"I've only seen buffalo in zoos, a couple hundred thousand are alive today."

"It's no wonder with the value young braves get for a tanned hide; their mothers or their wives do all the work. They can buy a cheaply made trade gun for one buffalo hide. Buffalo are amazing animals. One bull will feed many hungry men. Indians prefer the meat boiled. They cut it into foot-long lengths and cook it using one the buffalo's stomachs as a pot."

"One of the stomachs? How many stomachs do they have?"

"Five. They make plates from the shoulder blades, cups and bowls of their horns. They even use their tails for whips and fly swatters. Indian women can use every piece of the animal until there's nothing but a stain of dried blood on the ground, but how much they use depends on what they need and how much time they have. Two and half year old cows are the easiest to kill and are the most tasty."

"Some people in the twenty-first century think the wearing of animal fur is immoral?"

"What's immoral about it?"

"Killing an innocent animal just to wear its skin."

"You're jawing me?" Russell stopped his horse and began to tell her a story.

"I was trapping with three others on the Yellowstone. We were encamped on a stream that ran in a southwest direction into a lake. On each side of the valley, which was about a quarter of a mile wide, rose a bench of land about twenty feet high running parallel with the stream and covered with pines. The pines immediately behind us were thick with logs and fallen trees. Two of my comrades, one a Canadian, went hunting in hopes of shooting an elk. The third, Mr. White, lay asleep. I took a bath in the lake then returned to camp. I pulled off my powder horn and bullet pouch and laid them on a log. I took my butcher knife and began to cut pieces from a bale of dried meat we had spread in the sun. After eating I arose, kindled a fire, and sat down to smoke my tobacco pipe. My comrade, Mr. White, was still asleep. I cast my eyes toward our horses, which were feeding in the valley, and saw the heads of some Indians within thirty paces of me. I lunged to my rifle but an Indian had my bullet pouch and powder horn in hand. We were completely surrounded.

"The air was filled with their horrid yells. Blackfeet swarmed everywhere carrying their battle axes and showering us with arrows which flew like hail. White was struck on the right hip joint and I was struck in the same place, and on my right leg above the knee. The Indian who shot me sprang towards me with his axe uplifted. We cocked our rifles and started through their ranks fleeing into the woods. With great effort, we made a stand fifty yards further and crouched in the logs and bushes. I was faint from the loss of blood. We determined to kill those that sought to kills us, and then die like men.

"About twenty, well armed with fusees, bows, and battle axes passed within fifteen feet of us, but did not look our way. We sat motionless until the rustling in the bushes had died, then we slowly made our way to the lake. White began to wail, "I cannot go down to the water for I am wounded all over and I shall die." He was a young man who had been reared the pet of his family, and had never learned much of anything but gambling and horse racing. I crawled down to the water on my hands and one knee and after an hour brought some water back to him in my hat. He continued his lamenting, "Oh, dear, we shall die here! We shall never get out of these mountains!" To which I replied angrily, "If you persist in thinking so, you will die." He had only a slight wound on his hip, but he was entirely without clothing except his hat and shirt. I pulled off one of my leg wraps, a piece of blanket, to cover him."

Sarah listened intently to his story, and marveled how he was able to survive under such dangerous conditions, and to be one of the fortunate trappers that left the Rocky Mountains alive.

"The next morning White found two sticks for me to use as primitive crutches. My leg was swollen and very painful. White carried my rifle and we tried to make our way back to our encampment, hoping to find our two missing comrades. We found the Canadian very agitated and afraid, swearing he would never again leave our sight. He told us the Indians had come back to camp and he had been separated from our other comrade, Elkridge, and had not seen him since. The Indians had carried everything away, or had cut it into pieces. The only thing remaining was a sack of salt. I bathed my wounds in salt water and made a salve of beaver's oil and castoreum. It eased the pain and drew out the swelling. We made a fire, hoping our missing trapper would see our signal. We left directions on a tree at our encampment detailing which route we would take to get back to Fort Hall. It rained during mid-day. My lame leg was bent considerably and so swollen my knee joint was stiff. I could only bear half of my weight to walk.

"The Canadian succeeded in killing an elk which provided us with plenty of meat, but we were almost destitute of clothing. I had on a pair of trousers and a cotton shirt that were wet from the afternoon rain. I wrapped the deerskin around me and felt prouder than a Monarch with his imperial robes. The night was very cold and we made a large fire of pitch knots. We were alternately burning on one side and freezing on the other all night. I only slept four hours but it was longer than I had slept at any other time since I was wounded. The next day we killed an elk and I was able to make a pair of moccasins of raw elk hide. Two days we traveled without eating, and we were much fatigued due to want of sleep. We spent many cold and tedious nights descending Teton Mountain, and it took us days to get back to Fort Hall. The point of my story is that sheep, elk, deer, buffalo, and bear, supply us with clothing, bedding and lodges, while the meat of the same animals supply us with food. What could be immoral about that?"

"I didn't say it was." She was embarrassed her off-the-cuff comment had angered him. "Did you ever find your companion?"

"Yes. He showed up a few days later at the fort. He'd found a trail over the mountains he'd made the previous summer." His voice was terse. "I'd challenge any of your high and mighty twenty-first century men to come out to these mountains and live a week. They couldn't do it. They'd be the center of attention at a scalp dance, I reckon, while their scalp was dangling from a pole. I expect they never sleep on anything but beds of down, or recline on anything harder than silken cushions. I am not a counselor or a philosopher, but I have learned my lessons from experience. Our way of life is not immoral, it is of the highest honor. I'd like to read those who think otherwise a page in the Good Book."

His comment ended the conversation. There was no way she was going to begin a discussion on gun control.

The wide landscape flattened to a moonscape of grasses, rocks, and blowing dust. Sarah's face was tight; her lips burned, her buttocks numb. She stood up in the stirrups to try and stretch her legs. The Wind River followed the soft swell of the land, narrowing and widening, like a liquid ribbon winding across the land. The clouds in the distance looked like snow-covered mountains. Mid-afternoon Russell stopped and dismounted.

"You need to change into your dress and we'll cache your belongings here."

"Why here?"

"Because there's nothing here. Nobody passing by would be any the wiser."

He was right. It was a stretch of indistinguishable high desert. Russell began to dig a hole while Sarah took the panniers from Walmart.

"Your saddle, too. You can use your attacker's saddle, it's crude but preferable to riding without. Leave out the whiskey," he smiled for the first time that day, "at day's end we will partake of it together." They agreed to keep her .44 Magnum, wrapped in the flannel pillowcase, in his possibles bag.

Sarah helped Russell place her belongings in the deep hole. He turned his back when she took off her clothes and changed. She had to tug hard on the dress to pull it down over her body which was wet with perspiration. The dress was exquisite. It was made of the skins of Big Horn Sheep, which Russell explained are softer than elk. The dress was embroidered with beads and porcupine quills dyed a myriad of colors.

"I'm never going to hear the end of this," said Russell, his back turned to her.

"What do you mean?"

"I don't exactly have a reputation with the ladies. My comrades are going to whoop it up when I ride into camp with you."

"How do I look?"

He turned to face her. "Like Venus."

"How do I tie these?" she asked, holding up the leg wraps.

"Like mine; I'll show you." He knelt and wrapped the blankets around her bare legs from her knees to her ankles. He would have much preferred removing her clothes instead of helping her dress. He helped her slip the embroidered moccasins on her feet as if he she was Cinderella and he, her handsome Prince. It had been a long time since she felt like a Princess.

"Sarah, we never talked about last night."

"Do we need to talk about last night?"

"Do you know how I feel?"

"Yes, I do."

"Remind me to recite Lord Byron's *She Walks In Beauty Like The Night* when we reach our destination."

"I'll do that."

She was encouraged when Russell finally told her they were near the Rendezvous site. They swung south to reinforce their story that he had rescued her from her assailants coming up from Taos to find her brother, Seaborn Ratcliff, at Rendezvous.

Russell stiffened. "Sarah," he spoke in a low voice. "Loose your pack horse's rope."

Without questioning, she released Walmart.

"Look over on that ridge line. Do you see the riders? I'm assuming the worst until I see a white flag, or the face of a friend. Ride, full speed, to that shallow ravine ahead. Ride out now!"

Sarah slapped her heels into Cocoa's side. The horse fired like a ball from a cannon and flew across the sagebrush to the only cover afforded by the desert plain; a shallow ravine created by the shifting riverbed. She could hear Russell behind her, and the sound of the horses' hooves beating against the ground as if the earth was a hollow ball. She heard shrill cries and screams behind them. When she reached the deepest part of the ravine she dismounted and released Cocoa. Russell jumped from his horse's back, pulling the reins down over his horse's head. He reached into his saddle bag for the flannel pillowcase with Sarah's pistol.

From within a cloud of dust, forty or fifty Indians on horseback careened toward them, closing the distance with the impending fury of the Four Horsemen of the Apocalypse. Russell thrust the .44 Magnum into Sarah's hands.

"Get behind me," he ordered.

"Like hell, I will. I'll fight beside you."

"You have six bullets, make them count."

They stood side-by-side. A hundred yards out front one of the Indians dismounted, stood defiantly, and cursed loudly.

"Are they Blackfeet? What is he saying?"

"He's calling me a coward. He says I should be dressed in a woman's clothes."

"What's he doing?"

"I know what he's doing, but I've never seen an Indian behave in such a manner."

The Indian stripped off his blouse, pulled up his breech clout, stood naked and aroused himself until he ejaculated. He had fierce black eyes, and a large mouth with thin lips. He looked like a thoroughbred race horse, with his nostrils flaring. He had a broad chest and the muscles under his bronzed skin stood out like twisted wire. The Indians on horseback yelled and raised their arms over their heads. He mounted and turned his horse's head toward them. His face was hideously painted in alternate lines of red and black. He led the swiftly charging warriors with barbaric grandeur and strength. Each time he raised his right arm and waved his hand, it was perceived by his legion to be a royal gesture. They responded with wild cries of rage and encouragement, answering with blood-chilling yells of exultation. They rode into battle like bold centaurs.

Sarah looked at Russell. She imagined he was worrying something was going to happen to him, and she would be alone."

"Osborne."

"Yes," he never looked in her direction.

"I've read your journal. You don't die today." She offered the unsolicited prophecy in a small attempt to build their confidence, and, by saying it aloud, to somehow stack the odds in their favor. He placed a handful of lead balls in his mouth.

The Indians divided and charged up the riverbed. They crashed upon them like an angry wave that breaks after hurling itself on a mighty rock where the sea meets the shore. The mounted warriors swept down upon them at full gallop. Their raven hair was long and hung loosely around their necks; a narrow lock of hair, cut square, fell over the bridges of their nose. Most of their menacing faces were painted red, and some were painted with yellow ochre. Their horses had halters of hair; their stirrups and saddle pads were made of buffalo hide stuffed with elk hair. They came in a wall of dust. They verbally assaulted Sarah and Russell with loud, hoarse cries of obscenities, while the crack of their fusees and balls whirred over their heads.

The ravine provided a fair breast work. Sarah and Russell crouched low, leaning forward, with their knees well under them, as the wave continued to crash upon them. Russell fired his rifle, reloaded, and as they circled and closed in, he took aim and fired his pistol, killing an Indian within twenty feet of them. Sarah stood from her crouching position as one of the Indians, holding his horses's bridle in his left hand and his rifle in his right hand, lunged forward from seventy feet away.

"Get down," Russell ordered.

Sarah held her position. Gripping the revolver with both hands, she fired. She shot the Indian's horse in the neck. Its front legs buckled. The speed of its hind legs put its enormous body into a forward spin, crashing and rolling into the ravine. She heard bones splinter, snapping and cracking as they shattered. She didn't know if it was the bones of the man or the bones of the horse but it made her wince and look away from the rider caught in the momentum of the horses' fall. The Indian fell, crushed and broken beneath the horse's weight. Sarah had killed a man. She killed another.

Their enemies rained bullets upon them. The ranks of charging warriors came forward, answering each ringing war-whoop with louder, wilder yells. A new brigade charged into the battle, shrieking and yelling, attacking from the southeast.

"I've been in worse situations," said Russell without expression, "at least they haven't set fire to the dry grass."

Some twenty Indians and twenty Whites joined the noisy fray waving their arms in frantic and threatening gestures.

"Look Sarah!" he shouted, startling her as much as the charging Indians, "we're saved, they're friends!"

"Thank God, I only have two shots left."

Their dress and appearance could scarcely be distinguished from the attackers. Many rode without saddles, which illustrated the haste with which they had taken to arms. Among mountaineers, the man who made the greatest display of animal courage; the man who advanced fastest, farthest, and first, rose highly in the estimation of his brethren. They met the war cries of the Indians with a response only rowdy trappers could give. They rode into the swarming nest of Blackfeet with such speed and fury they could not reload their rifles. It was difficult to know which war party was the most crazed with the smell of battle. The Blackfeet warriors began to retreat at the onslaught of reinforcements.

As one of the trappers rode by he flashed a broad smile and tipped his beaver cap to Sarah and Russell.

"You got a ball in there, Mr. Russell? Glad to see you made it. I'll be damned, you got yourself a woman! And a White woman at that!" His voice trailed off as he charged the fleeing Indians.

For a few minutes they were alone. Perspiration stood on their faces from the late afternoon heat and the pitch of the battle. She handed Russell her pistol to conceal. He wrapped his arms around her and held her close. They didn't speak.

The cracking of the guns ceased. The victors returned leading Russell's and Sarah's horses. Their resonating voices greeted him with boisterous laughter. They leapt from their horses, slapping him on the back, and questioning him about the altercation. Sarah stood close beside him while the men crowded around them. She was uncomfortable by their stares; she felt like she was standing inspection, their eyes looking her up and down. She blushed a bright red on her face and neck.

"You boys have game spirit!" said Russell. "You had them running across the land like hunted rats among the ruins of an old building."

"We heard rumor there was a party of Bug's Boys, and we decided to take the fight to them rather than wait for the savages to surprise us, or try to steal our horses while we slept." Their gaze was fixed on the White woman in the white sheepskin dress standing by Russell's side. He wanted to put his arm around her and claim her, but instead offered a hurried explanation for her presence in the mountains.

"Gentlemen, this is Mrs. Sarah Hanley."

They nodded respectfully.

"Mrs. Hanley was on her way up from Taos, headed to Rendezvous, when I found the two escorts she hired to guide her behaving in a very ungentlemanly manner. I have put her under my protection, and have offered to help in her efforts to find her brother, Seaborn Ratcliff. Some of you know Seaborn, he came to the mountains about the time I did in 1834. The last Mrs. Hanley heard from her brother was by way of a letter she received from a merchant returning to St. Louis from Taos."

The expression on some of the men's faces was grave. Many had heard rumor of Seaborn's death, but since they could not confirm the heresay, they did not put a voice to their suspicions, nor did they offer words of encouragement.

"We haven't seen your brother at the encampment, M'am, but perhaps there will be someone at Rendezvous who can give you news of his whereabouts." They stood like bashful school boys in her presence.

"Well, come on," said Russell. "Can't you boys see by my clothes that I need to see my haberdasher immediately."

"Big doings at the marrying of the rivers this year. Thomas Fitzpatrick didn't make it to the mountains. Drips and Sutter brought twenty horse carts loaded with supplies. Monsieur Pierre Chouteau has changed the name of the American Fur Company to Pierre Chouteau and Company. He got here with 75 men and 150 mules in his supply train. He also escorted a group of missionaries and their wives. They had to camp a couple of days on the island because the river was it so high they couldn't ford the Popoesia.

There's a rumor the fur companies won't be extending credit this year since many trappers have stayed away because they can't pay their debts."

"How much for beaver this year?"

"$5.00 per pound. And, Captain Stewart's here again this year! He's undertaken a bold project. He's brought along some fancy young artiste to paint pictures of us to take back to Scotland. I reckon we'll all be hanging in some museum in Paris, France one day."

"I reckon," said Russell, wondering if, in fact, their daring lives in the mountains would be reduced to oil on canvas.

When they rode into the massive encampment, they were met with the firing of rifles. There were all manner of men, every one strong in appearance: tall, short, heavy, thin, mostly clean-shaven, yelling at the top of their lungs. The air smelled strongly of sulfur. The blue smoke from their rifle blasts blew back over the noisy crowd. The Indians beat hide-covered drums and fired their weapons, singing, and dancing around the newcomers. Their bodies were brightly painted and they were scantily clad. Even at the outer perimeter of the annual gathering, word spread quickly that another White woman had arrived at Rendezvous.

"Good to see you, Mr. Russell." A tall, distinguished man with an intelligent face and sad eyes made his way through the crowd and placed his hand on Russell's horse's bridle. "I thought you'd moved to Fort Yukon and were trapping for the Hudson's Bay Company, riding around in one of those baidarkas."

"No, Sir, Mr. Bridger, I plan to outlast you in these Shining Mountains. How long's it been now since you came west?"

"Well, Mr. Russell, do you see that mountain over there? When I came here it was just a hole in the ground." He tipped his broad-rimmed black felt hat to Sarah, "M'am."

"Sir, do you have a square of canvas you might lend us? We're badly in need of a lodge."

"I think between us we can accommodate you." Bridger looked at the White woman in Indian woman's clothes. An American legend was standing before her. He motioned for Russell to lean toward him. Not wishing to upset her, Bridger quietly told him what Russell already knew; Seaborn Ratcliff had been killed earlier in the spring. He left the telling of the sorrowful news for him to give her in private.

They constructed an A-frame tent over a pole lashed between two trees. For privacy, Russell wrapped the back with a smaller piece of canvas. They camped on the bank of the Wind River opposite a small island that had been formed by the river's current. Huge logs of driftwood bobbed like corks in the deep water. The river bank dropped off sharply and was deeply undercut by the appetite of the strong, swift current.

Mosquitoes swarmed around them, humming and biting like ten thousand poisoned needles. Sarah and Russell waved their arms, frantically trying to drive them away. It wasn't until the cold air descended from the mountains that the hellish pests were driven into the leaves and grass for shelter.

Sarah wrapped his white wool blanket around her shoulders and walked to the river. Down deep in the cold, dark mirror the stars looked like diamonds that had been cast into the river. She could see the Wind River Range in the distance where the earth reached up to touch the sky; the peaks seemed to dissolve in the air. Trees covered the snow-capped mountains like dark green lichen growing on a mossy rock. Some of the white clouds looked like they were painted on a background of blue flecked with gold, others flew by like wispy ghosts in the wind. Against the evening sky, the intricate silhouettes of the trees resembled fancy black lace. As nightfall edged out the day, the shadowy forms of ridge and pinnacle disappeared into a silvered mist. Floating across the encampment was the loud talk, laughter, and shouts of men. The evening fires burned brightly within their lodges and resembled golden luminaries that had been carefully placed across the landscape. The monotonous thumping of the Indian drums rose and fell; an occasional sharp yell, followed by a chorus of voices, filled the air.

Russell joined her after he picketed the horses; he stood behind her watching another day together set with the sun.

"Look," she pointed, "a falling star."

"You told me during the attack I wouldn't die today."

"Yes, I'm sorry, I just thought . . ."

"No, don't be sorry. It encouraged me. I know I told you I didn't want to know anything about my life, but I want to ask you one thing, and I want you to please, tell me the truth."

"All right. What do you want to know?"

"Do I ever marry?"

Of all the things he could have asked, why did he want to know the answer to this question? She didn't turn around but answered softly, "No, you never marry."

He stood behind her a long time. He wrapped his arms around her, pulling the blanket snugly around her body to keep her warm. When she finally turned to face him he had the saddest expression on his face.

"What's the matter?"

"If I never marry, it must be because you eventually return to your own time."

Chapter 19

The full moon set against the scarlet glow of the morning sky. There was a transparency to the sky, as if each molecule in the atmosphere was a crystal magnifying dawn's light. Russell left early to take his large bundle of beaver and otter pelts to trade. He strained against the heavy weight of the pack as he left camp and walked to the transient community to resupply. There was a rumor the American Fur Company was having difficulty paying $5.00 a pound for beaver and wanted to lower the price to $3.00.

"These are Ashley beaver," he bragged, "I won't settle for less than top dollar."

After he left, Sarah finished her coffee and enjoyed the peaceful serenity of the morning. It was quieter than any other time since their arrival. She was awakened often during the night by the loud shouts of men, the howling of wolves in concert, and the noisy braying of the horses and the mules. She slept lightly, despite the many miles they traveled the day before. She dreamt for the first time since she had crossed the seasons. Waking, she tried hard to recall her dream, but all she could remember was a song; a strange song whose notes and intonations were more of the spirit than of sound.

She hoped she would see Jim Bridger again today. He was a venerable figure of a man, keen-eyed, tall, and upright. He was older than Osborne, and had a commanding aura of leadership about him, more importantly, he had a look of good faith in his face. The way Osborne talked about Bridger, Mr. Bridger he always referred to him, it was obvious he inspired confidence and was well-liked and highly respected by the men.

She remembered Osborne's surprised look when she casually remarked she had visited Fort Bridger; a fine restoration of the original near Mountain View, Wyoming. She remembered how overwhelmed she felt standing in the deep ruts carved by the wagons traveling the Oregon Trail as they stopped to rest at the fort, and then passed on to the new territory. Bridger occupied the fort until he was driven from his holdings by the Mormons in the 1850s.. As she recalled from U.S. history, Bridger was the first white man to visit the Great Salt Lake and believed it to be the Pacific Ocean.

At nine o'clock in the morning four missionary wives: Mrs. William Gray, Mrs. Mary Walker, Mrs. Myra Eels, and Mrs. Sarah Smith, came to visit Sarah and to pay their respects. They were aghast when they saw her dressed in a white sheepskin dress; an Indian woman's clothing! Overnight the news had reached them of her arrival at Rendezvous, her unfortunate experience with her escorts from Taos, and the sorrowful news of her brother's death. Sarah eagerly accepted the mince pie Mrs. Gray brought as a welcome. They greeted her sympathetically and suggested they bow their heads in prayer.

"Sarah, may we call you Sarah, or would you prefer we call you Mrs. Hanley?"

"No, please, call me Sarah."

"You poor, poor thing having to endure such hardship, and be met with such devastating news that your brother is dead. And those nefarious men stole your baggage? Mrs. Walker, we must sew her some proper clothing."

"Of course. I'm almost finished with my riding dress. If would be no difficulty at all. You must be dreadfully warm in that costume."

"We were told Mr. Russell came upon you in your dilemma. My dear, you are welcome to stay in any one of our tents where you will have suitable privacy. I'm sure your husband would be appreciative to Mr. Russell for rescuing you, but . . . "

"My husband is dead."

"Oh, my, my, how tragic. Your husband, your Mother, we heard has recently passed, and now your dear brother."

I'm sure you're interested in my privacy, thought Sarah. You're wondering what I'm doing in that small lodge all night with Mr. Russell. Despite their provincial nature, she was happy to have them visit. Their attention made her feel at home and, somehow, cared for.

The women wore cotton dresses with leg-o'-mutton sleeves and high waistlines. They wore shaped shawl-like neckerchiefs around their shoulders of cotton gauze; some were printed, but Mrs. Walker's had a colorful embroidered design around the edges. Mrs. Smith was wearing a white apron with Battenburg lace, but the other women had sturdy, solid color cotton aprons, much better suited for working. Their pockets were on the outside of their dresses and tied by ribbons around their waists. Their calfskin shoes looked like ballet slippers with pleated toes, leather looped backs, and ribbons.

"I appreciate your kind offer, for the dress, and the invitation of a place to stay, but Mr. Russell has saved my life on more than one occasion. I feel very secure in his company. I have found him to be of the highest moral character under all circumstances. He has generously agreed to escort me back to Taos to make the return trip to St. Louis with a merchant caravan. I'm sorry I can't offer you ladies a place to sit."

"Oh, we are used to having to stand or sit on the ground. Mr. Rogers complains about it dreadfully," said Mrs. Walker. "He yearns for a house and a civilized life." They found a spot of shade and sat down under a cottonwood tree.

"Is Mr. Rogers a missionary?

"Gracious, no, Mr. Rogers is our assistant. He is accompanying us to Oregon. I'm rather happy here! My health is good, and our animals are in better order than when we started."

Mrs. Eels, who had only nodded her head in compliant agreement, joined the discussion for the first time. "Well, I'm not happy, and Mrs. Smith cries half the time. Last night, in the middle of the night, the noise of drunken men and barking dogs awakened us. Mr. Eels went to the door of our tent and found four men swearing and blaspheming. They wanted to settle their accounts with Mr. Richardson. They said they meant us no harm, and proceeded to try and persuade Mr. Eels to sing with them. Can you imagine! Mr. Eels told them he did not know their tunes and, finally, they went away.

"There's noise from guns and yelling every night," added Mrs. Smith. "The men are either mad, intoxicated, or both."

"Captain Drips, Mr. Wood, and Mr. Fontenelle all have Indian wives," chimed Mrs. Eels. "They came to visit us all dressed in their finery. Their children can even read a little. Fifteen to twenty mountaineers and Indians came to our tent dancing, beating their drums, and firing their weapons. They looked like emissaries of the devil worshiping their own master. The trappers were dressed and painted like Indians. It was horrible! I cannot imagine that White men, brought up in a civilized land, can appear to do so much to imitate the Devil!"

"In my opinion," said Mrs. Smith, "these trappers take great pleasure in dressing their Indian brides but do little to care for their minds. Captain Drips has two wives."

"Didn't Mr. Walker preach just the other day on judgment?" Mary Walker tried to end the downward cycle of the conversation, but her three companions would not hear of it.

"Mr. Smith told me he heard Dr. Newell won a woman on a wager last year, and he was already married to a Flathead woman! When Dr. Newell learned his wife was coming to Rendezvous with Mr. McLeod and his party, he sold her to her previous owner for one hundred dollars. Can you imagine such a thing! Why, I received an Indian caller yesterday wearing nothing but a buffalo hide. I didn't understand a word he said, but he presented me with a butcher knife and a red feather. I had to accept them, of course."

"Mr. Rogers estimates we've traveled 1,100 miles since we left Westport," interrupted Mrs. Walker, in another attempt to change the subject. "We had to encamp on the southwest side of the Popeasia when we arrived; the river was too high to ford. Do you know on our trip I had the opportunity to meet Meriwether Lewis Clark and Jefferson Clark, the sons of George Clark, the famous explorer. The two brothers were traveling with the fur company."

"And, did you know, a gentleman from Mr. Bridger's party told me of an unprovoked attack by the Blackfeet Indians on another tribe. Fifteen souls went to the bar of God and eternity," said Mrs. Smith, clasping her hands in a gesture of prayer. "One of the Indians begged for his life after he had been wounded, but the Blackfeet dragged his body away and cut him to pieces. Dreadful!"

"The four of us will work together to make you a dress," said Mrs. Walker, standing to leave. "We'll make one with long sleeves so your arms won't get blistered."

"Yes," agreed Mrs. Smith. We'll make you a dress. I have three others to make, but I'll sew yours first. I'll even add a few ruffles."

"You are all very kind."

"And you must come take tea with us," invited Mrs. Gray.

"I have a tin baker," said Mrs. Smith, struggling to stand after stepping on the hem of her long dress. Sarah offered her hand. "Last night we had rice pudding, without eggs, but it was very good."

"There is no Sabbath in this country; no time to give rest to the body and food for the mind, but we do have two public services every day. Brother Walker will lead us this evening, and Brother Eels will hold worship services in the open air under the cottonwood trees. The heat is so oppressive midday. You must join us for services tomorrow."

"All right."

"Do you sing? The men and the Indians love to hear us sing."

"Yes, I sing."

"Then you must sing for us. Mrs. Smith has a lovely voice. Yesterday she sang, *Yes, My Native Land, I Love Thee*."

"Thank you for the compliment, Mrs. Gray. We'll cut your dress out today, Sarah, after we finish handing out Bibles."

"Thank you all very much for coming." Sarah watched them walk away, the hems of their long dresses dragging across the ground. What a mess it must be when it rained, she thought.

She had to flatten her body against a cottonwood tree to conceal herself while she stood to urinate. She was hot and sweaty. The white sheepskin dress clung to her hips; by the time she got the dress up and pulled off her underwear she was standing bare buttocks, the dress gathered around her waist. After she finished she threw her underwear into what was left of their morning fire and fanned the smoldering coals until they burst into flame. Without underwear she could modestly squat the next time.

She was restless. When would Osborne return? She didn't want more company; certainly not an Indian clad only in a buffalo hide bringing her a gift of a butcher knife and a red feather. Yet she wasn't comfortable striking out on her own. She'd wait. She had the uncomfortable feeling she was being watched. She looked through the small stand of trees, across the grove and the encampment. No one was approaching.

She turned and discovered a man on horseback watching her from across the river. He looked like a statue among the rocks and trees. His eyes were riveted on her. A sudden, unexpected gust of wind rushed through the grove, sending a chill through her body, and loudly rustling the leaves on the trees.

At the river's edge, 150 paces from her, he first believed she was an Indian. He watched her. He saw the way she looked naked from the waist down. She was White. He had never seen a White woman. The fact she knew he had seen her naked excited him.

Menelah had not stolen a woman in a long time, but on the occasions he had done so, he eventually returned the woman as a present to her rightful partner. In most instances the husband's vengeance fell asleep and he was content with the return of his property. He knew it was a pitiful and mean-spirited practice, but he didn't care. He was used to being given what he wanted, or forcibly taking it. Out of the several dozen women he had stolen he never paid for one, and no husband dared to lay any finger of violence upon him. He could snap his fingers in the their faces defiantly, and become more aroused by their indignation and humiliation than by the taking of their wives. Despite his reprehensibility, he was followed into battle by young men and followed into bed by vermilion-cheeked women.

He was one of thirty Crow warriors that had grown to manhood together. This was his protection. His rivals feared him, and should anyone challenge him it would conjure the anger of his brethren and many fierce hearts would thirst for the challenger's blood. But though he had the allegiance of his brethren, he was confident that his chances of victory rested upon his own merits. He was indifferent to the gaudy ornamentation favored by other Crow warriors. He knew the strong conformation of his body was enough to win him favor. As sinister as he was, he had an air of gallantry about him.

Sarah was startled, then she was furious. The anger surged through her body causing her temperature to rise and her heart to beat furiously. She knew how long he had been there. The bastard. On several occasions during her life she had been sexually intimidated or threatened. After the paralyzing fear, she always felt violent. Her memories, her humiliation, her shame, and her fury, replayed within her. She glared at him and stood defiantly as he crossed the river on a large, cream-colored horse. She was shaking by the time he stopped his horse in front of her.

"Where is your husband?" His voice was deep and strong, it resonated like the deep notes of a pipe organ. He had a strongly proportioned and powerful body. His legs and chest were bare and smooth without body hair. He had a large scar that ran from the left side of his neck across his chest to underneath his right arm. He had a bow and a quiver of arrows over his back, ornamented with colorful feathers and with the scalp locks of his enemies. His handsome face was not painted, and his long, black hair was loosely pulled back at the neck. He wore moccasins rubbed a mossy green. His horse did not have a bridle, but a braided cord of hair lashed around the horse's jaw. His Apollo-like body, a deep rich bronze, was not impressive to Sarah who felt she had been violated by his unannounced arrival. Her teeth were clenched, her hands balled into fists.

"Sarah!" Russell hailed her from behind. She turned to see him carrying an armful of packages, he was walking quickly to close the distance between them. Her anger turned to embarrassment and shame.

"What's going on here?" Russell recognized his face.

"Nothing, he just crossed the river."

Menelah had a superior expression of defiance and superiority on his face. He rode past the trapper without a word.

"Did he frighten you?"

"No," she lied, "he just startled me. I wasn't expecting anyone to come across the river."

"His name is Menelah; he's a Crow warrior with several young wives. Their tribes have greatly been reduced by outbreaks of smallpox, just like the Blackfeet. They're handsome Indians; both the men and women are very tall and well-proportioned. Prostitution of their wives is very common; if a stranger wishes he can always be accommodated with a wife. They refuse to drink alcohol. They call it "White man's fool water." They believe if they drink they will cease to be a Crow and become a foolish animal. Stay away from him, he's as savage as a meat axe: half Indian, half-devil." Convinced by her explanation that she was simply startled by the intruder's unannounced arrival, Russell hurriedly began to show her what he bought with his year's wages.

"We're rich, Sarah, at least today. "

God, how she loved him. He was flushed with pride and excitement. He placed each item in front of her for inspection and her approval.

"Rum. Brown Havana sugar. New shirts for me: another red flannel, my favorite, and a fancy navy calico. A seven-inch butcher knife. A wrapper blanket for leggings. A new black wool hat. A cross-cut file. Rifle flints. Four pounds small bar lead. Two pounds of Dupont gun powder. Plug tobacco. Three sacks of flour. Dried apples, peaches and pears. Sea salt. Black ink powder. A quill. Fool's cap paper. Young Hyson tea. Coffee. Black pepper. Soap. Chocolate. Black woolen half hose. A pair of duck trousers. A gun worm. And to trade with the Indians: A paper of hawk bells. Carnelian fine beads. Seed beads. Blue beads. Cut glass beads. A bunch of mock garnets. Vermilion."

"And, I bought these for you." He handed her two packages tied with string. Pleased and surprised, she opened the smallest and found a light blue French chintz shawl, a turkey red handkerchief, a sheer, rectangular black silk scarf, an ivory comb, and ten yards of blue ground calico.

"The presents are wonderful." She picked up the sheer black silk scarf and draped it around her neck and shoulders.

"Mr. Rogers, the assistant traveling with the missionaries, suggested we ask one of the missionary wives to sew you a dress."

"They came this morning and offered to sew me what they considered a suitable dress." She unwrapped the larger package to find a brilliant green wool blanket. The wool was lush and soft. The three black stripes were a price tag, indicating he had traded three beaver pelts for the blanket.

"I couldn't ever figure out why you made such a fuss over my blanket that first day, but I thought maybe you'd like one of your own." For a minute he thought she was going to cry.

"The Hudson's Bay Company still makes these blankets. It's the oldest chartered company in North America."

"Figures, the way they break down all their opposition. They sell their goods for less than a quarter the price charged by their competition. The secrecy surrounding the location of Rendezvous this year was to prevent them from interfering with trade. If the blankets are made in your time, what's so special about them?"

"I guess I was waiting to meet someone who would know this green wool blanket means more to me than a ring of diamonds. Why don't we go inside our lodge and get out of the hot sun?"

"Inside? Now? " He was shocked she was suggesting lovemaking in broad daylight. "I'm not sure how much longer we'll have privacy. The men have kept away out of respect for your loss, but they're itching to come call on you."

"Then we'll have to hurry." She picked up her blanket and led him to the shade and privacy of their small lodge. He went willingly.

Chapter 20

"What are you thinking?" asked Sarah. Russell's earlier euphoria had been replaced with a sense of melancholy. He was gazing down river at the mountains in the distance.

"I can't imagine myself living among quiet men."

"Why would you think you have to live among quiet men?"

"It's too dangerous for you here. In the last week you've been attacked by a White man, Indians, and a grizzly bear. I can't risk anything happening to you. In a couple of days we need to head back to Missouri or on to Oregon with the missionaries."

"Osborne, I don't want you to change your life for me."

"Your arrival has changed my life."

"I can live in the mountains. I can learn to trap and shoot. I can learn to hunt. I know I'm green around the gills, as you call it, but I've got game-spirit, too."

"Of course you do, I've never seen a woman handle herself so well, that's not the point."

"It's not time for you to leave the mountains. You're a part of history. My coming here must not change that!"

"Your coming here has changed me. I'll not have you endure such hardship. I don't want to be a part of history, I want to be a part of you."

She didn't know whether to curse or cry, so she walked a distance from him to clear her head and to prevent saying something she would regret. He didn't follow her; he went to water the horses.

"Sarah, Sarah," called Mary Walker, making her way across the open field to the riverbank where she stood. She was accompanied by a distinguished gentleman who looked older than his years.

"Sarah, this is Mr. Elkanah Walker, my husband."

"Mrs. Hanley, I'm pleased to meet you, we are all so sorry for your loss."

"Thank you, Mr. Walker."

"These horrible mosquitoes," Mrs. Walker complained as they swarmed around her face. "They'll be a dreadful nuisance the next couple of hours. We cut out your dress today, and we went through our meager collection of fashion, and brought you suitable attire to wear until we finish your dress. It's rather plain, but missionary wives aren't known for their millinery and other finery."

Sarah graciously accepted the green chemise and linen skirt.

"We let out the hem of the dress because you're so much taller than any of us, but the linen skirt should do nicely. I'm sorry we didn't have a cloak to spare. How have you been managing at night when it's cold?"

"I wrap a blanket around me, or I sit very close to the fire. You are very kind. Please thank Mrs. Eells, Mrs. Smith, and Mrs. Gray for me."

"Please do come for tea tomorrow; anyone can point you to our camp."

"I would be delighted. Thank you again."

Mr. Walker took his wife by the arm and escorted her across the open field as ceremoniously as if they were attending a formal ball. They waved at the cloud of mosquitoes that engulfed them.

She went inside their small lodge to change her clothes. The dark green dress fit her snugly at the waist and across her upper body. She wrapped the sheer, black silk scarf Osborne had given her around the back of her neck, crossed it in front, and tucked it into the bodice. She tightened the linen skirt with the ties on both sides. The back of the dress fastened with hand-forged hooks. How fashion would change with the invention of the zipper and velcro. She fixed her hair with the ivory comb, and pulled the blue French chintz shawl around her shoulders. What she wouldn't trade for a tube of black mascara, lip gloss, and a mirror where she would see both of her eyes at once.

Several dozen men on horseback rode up to Russell and rode off as suddenly as they had appeared. Russell walked slowly back to camp.

He looked at her dress.

"The missionary women?"

"Yes, how do I look? Do you prefer me dressed as an Indian woman or a White woman?" She pivoted to show him the back of the dress.

"I like you better undressed." His face flushed crimson. The words flew from his mouth. "I beg your pardon, I shouldn't have been so crude."

She took his hands. "Don't be sorry you said it, I'm not. Will you fasten the hooks?"

"Well, you look wonderful," he stammered, "in either one."

"Osborne, didn't you tell me Rendezvous was a party?" She was trying to resolve the earlier tension between them. "Let's stay in the safety and company of your friends for a few days. When it's time to leave, we'll decide together where we're going. What do you say?"

"All right, but I'm still going to worry about it."

"I'll help keep your mind off your worries."

"And, speaking of friends, we're going to have a crowd here within the hour. Your period of mourning has expired. The men want to call and pay their respects. I told you this afternoon it would be hard to stall them off, even those with good breeding."

"What can we offer them?"

"Don't worry, with the plenty around here today, no one will go hungry or dry."

Within the hour they were besieged by a whimsical throng of visitors, both civilized and savage, parading into their modest camp with armloads of food and drink. A noisy concert of shouts, howls, barks, yelps, and laughter, rose from the revelers and mingled with the swarms of mosquitoes in the early evening air.

"The demonic hubbub is highly complimentary," he said, "an honor intended for you.." He let out a loud yell to answer their greeting.

The Indian warriors were dressed in breach clouts and their bodies were gaily painted. They energetically shook their rattles and beat their drums of animal skins drawn over hoops. The lively multitude of men, women, and children were clad in all manner of dress ranging from motley garb to fantastic costume. The procession was led by Jim Bridger, wearing a helmet and suit of steel armor.

"That's Captain Stewart alongside Mr. Bridger." A distinguished looking gentleman in a full set of buckskins, with fringe on the arms of his shirt and down his leggings from waist to ankle, walked beside Bridger. He had a full head of dark curly hair and a thick moustache with long sideburns that almost reached his chin.

"He's from Scotland; an English nobleman, with a wild love of adventure. I first met him at Rendezvous in 1836 when he arrived with quite an entourage and his own wagon pulled by four mules. He gave Mr. Bridger the armor, it's like the armor worn by English lifeguards. The men really like it when he wears it, and dub him, 'Sir James.'"

"Evening, Mrs. Hanley. I hope you don't mind our early arrival at this difficult time for you. We are sorry for the loss of your brother."

"Thank you, Mr. Bridger."

"I would like to introduce you to Sir William Drummond Stewart. He fancies our way of life here in the stoney mountains." The noise of the crowd was so loud it was difficult to carry on a conversation.

"Pleased to meet you, Mrs. Hanley," said Captain Stewart with a thick Scottish brogue. "It's been a couple of years since we had the pleasure of woman's influence at Rendezvous. I expect you'll be the bright star of this encampment."

"I understand you have an artist with you, Captain Stewart. Is it George Catlin by any chance?"

"No, M'am, Mr. Alfred Jacob Miller, is the artist in my employ. He's referred to as the American Raphael in Paris. I wanted a competent artist to sketch the remarkable scenery and incidents. I found him in New Orleans. He had just returned from a year of studying abroad in Europe. I'm taking him back to Scotland to my home, Murthly Castle, to paint large murals, of the field sketches he's made chronicling my travels in the west."

"Will he be joining us tonight?" Russell was surprised by Sarah's overt interest in the young artist at Rendezvous.

"No. Mr. Miller has a general lack of martial spirit and very little mettle to him. I owe it to the fact he was not properly brought up. Last week he was sitting on the wagon sketching in his portfolio and I began to suggest what he should sketch, and he answered, "If I had half a dozen pair of hands, it should have been done." To which I replied, "That would be a great misfortune. It would be very expensive in the matter of kid gloves." He retires early, and often hires others to do those duties which he despises, such as rounding up the horses. I expect you can easily meet him tomorrow if you so desire."

"We're going to need a healthier fire, Mr. Russell, if we're to cook this fine elk tonight." Tied to the rump of a roan horse was a fat bull with huge antlers. "Fat on his back will measure three or four inches, I'll wager," said the young proud hunter who offered the elk for the feast.

The occasional firing of rifles as a means of a toast, startled Sarah. The sharp crack sounded more like a cannon blast than the throaty sounds of a shotgun. The blue smoke from their rifles hung in the early evening air like fog. A beardless man, below medium height, with brown, curling hair emerged from the crowd.

"Mr. Carson. Good to see you."

"Gentlemen, I'm just happy to be here. Little Gray and I can usually find our way wherever we're headed, but we looked for the main camp on a tributary of the Green River but all we found was a herd of buffalo. My wife and daughter are with me."

"This isn't the first time you've been late to Rendezvous, Carson. How about 1831 when Fitzpatrick hired you in Santa Fe to help him get the supplies to Rendezvous."

Kit Carson. Jim Bridger. Osborne Russell. They were all men, real men, not worn, dusty biographies filed alphabetically on a library shelf. America's fascination with its heroes had transformed them into mythological proportions. Sarah would have supposed Carson to be over six feet tall, with the build of Hercules, and a voice like the roar of a lion, in fact, he had a voice as soft and gentle as a woman. After lighting his pipe at the fire he walked quickly into the shadows, out of the bright light of the campfire.

"Mr. Fitzpatrick hired forty of us in Taos, not Santa Fe," corrected Carson. "Fitzpatrick arrived in Lexington in May, and was too late to buy supplies. He had to follow Smith, Jackson, and Sublette to Santa Fe. We traveled along the range of the Rockies to North Platte. Got there in September as I remember. Both seasoned and new recruits alike waited at Willow Valley for Fitzpatrick to arrive from St. Louis."

"I sent out a small party to look for them," added Bridger. "We had exhausted the stock of goods we had on hand. We were out of blankets, ammunition and knives. We were scarce on traps, but the saddest state of affairs was the depletion of our stores of tobacco and alcohol. We broke up for the fall hunt after waiting several weeks. We left without supplies and learned later Fitzpatrick was very much alive but on the wrong trail.

We weren't resupplied until Fraeb got the sorely needed goods to us in the fall. No furs were taken back to St. Louis that year. Fitzpatrick left them in the mountains and Sublette took them in the next year."

"Tell the story about that mule you lost, Carson," shouted one of the men.

"Not much to tell. We were buffalo hunting and one of our mules got the notion he'd rather be a bison than a mule and ran off with the herd. We sent several men out after that mule, but we never recovered the animal. I guess he decided the life on the prairie was a good one."

Turning to Sarah, Carson said, "I heard you traveled here from Taos, M'am. That's a long, hard trip under the best of circumstances, which I understand you did not have. You were certainly fortunate to get as far as you did and be found by the Judge, here."

"The Judge?"

"Mr. Russell. We all have nicknames out here. Joe Meek's called Major; George Ebbert's called Squire; we call Mr. Bridger, Gabe, but the Crow Indians call him Casapy which means Chief of the Blankets."

"Russell's name is well-deserved," said Bridger, raising his cup in a toast. "He talks like a book. He is a man of education, refined feelings, and virtuous habits, and one who always remains true to his principles. His life has not been marked by a single conspicuous error."

"Here, here," said Captain Stewart. "His manly face is the mirror of uprightness, simplicity, and kindness of heart."

"Here, here," the men cheered, raising the kettle in a merry toast.

"I appreciate the toast, gentlemen, but I don't know why I can't be called by the name my dear Mother gave me. Osborne means god bear and the ferocity in such a name suits this lost Maine boy just fine. At Fort Hall,

Mr. Ross, Mr. Nott, Mr. Evans, and the others never could remember my name."

Individual bonfires were lit within forty yards of their lodge. Each of the splintered groups set about the cooking of their meal, their merriment, and their liquor. Their rowdy voices tangled together as they rose in the early evening sky. Two men shouldered a barrel of rum and proceeded to fill several copper camp kettles to the brim, and pass it from man to man. Some of the men threw wood on the fire while others butchered the red-haired elk. The children played hide and seek among the trees as the sun set deeper and the air began to cool.

"It's more like a family reunion than a Rendezvous this year; wives and younguns all over the place, and missionaries," grumbled a man with sharp, prominent features and a face like a piece of old leather. "I tell you it's not like it used to be in these stoney mountains. This may be the last year we all get together like this. Times are changing. I guess we can all go north and trap with the Russians. Not like 1833 when the three fur companies were spread out for ten miles along the Green. You've never seen such a saturnalia! You'd think men who had been rivals during the year would display hostility, but with hunting season over, they gathered in good humor, cordial reconciliation, and maudlin endearment."

"Captain Bonneville was there and Nathaniel Wyeth. I came with Robert Campbell, he'd just formed the St. Louis Fur Company with William Sublette," said Stewart. "We left Lexington, Missouri in early May, with $15,000 worth of supplies."

"That was the year Ben Harrison's Pa sent him to the mountains in hopes he'd curtail his frequent habit of drinking."

"Ah, and a fine influence we were on the man," said a trapper with a broad German face and a bristly red beard and moustache, tipping the copper kettle as he took his turn at the bar. He followed his drink with a hearty belch and handed the kettle to Sarah to pass to Russell standing beside her.

Without thinking Sarah raised the kettle and took a mouthful of the sweet rum. When she lowered the huge copper goblet the men were looking at her in gaping astonishment. Trying to make light of the embarrassing situation where she had carelessly shone the spotlight uncomfortably on herself, she said simply. "I'm dry," and took another drink.

A howl of laughter and knee slapping gave rowdy approval. She passed the kettle to Russell who laughed at the attention she had unwittingly called to herself. It was good to be with his friends; to share a campfire with meat roasting over it, and a full camp kettle of rum passing freely. He was proud of Sarah. He had made it abundantly clear she was under his protection, and he needed no competition for her attention. Tonight he had made up his mind. He was taking her to the Williamette Valley.

"1833? Wasn't that the year the wolves came into camp?" asked a trapper wearing a white blanket coat, a broad hat of black felt, shabby moccasins, and trousers of deerskin.

"It was mad dogs or wolves, which I cannot say, but I believe it to be the latter. Nine persons were attacked in Drips and Fontenelle's camp and three in ours. The blood-curdling screams rang out from the men. All of them were bitten on the face. George Holmes was badly bitten on the right ear and face. We were in the habit of sleeping in the open air, and never took the trouble to put up the tent except in bad weather. The demons came into camp for three nights. Captain Bonneville told me the story of an Indian who had been bitten by one of the animals. The Indian was out riding with a party and he began to lag behind. When his friends entreated him to move faster, he waved them on and asked them not to approach him. He leapt from his horse and began to throw his body violently from side-to-side rolling on the ground, gnashing his teeth, and foaming at the mouth."

One of the men, who had paid his respects to the camp kettle each time it was passed, unexpectedly fell to the ground on all fours and began to thrash, howling, and working his alcohol-laced saliva into a thick, bubbly foam that hung from his mouth in long strands.

"Aye, twas no joke. The Indian repeatedly warned his friends of the danger: to stay away lest he might bite them. His friends went for help, but when they returned they found only his horse and his accoutrements. He was never seen again. One of the men from the Rocky Mountain Fur Company was also bitten. In a few days he showed symptoms of hydrophobia. As night approached, he broke away from his companions, rushed into a thicket and was never seen again. I heard Joe Meek say that several more died on the way back to St. Louis, but I don't know it to be so."

"Aye, and Joe Meek was so drunk he would have killed the mad wolf that bit him," said Stewart. "Our orders were not to shoot in camp for fear of accidentally killing someone. Word was the animal was killed by someone in Fontenelle's camp. I tell you 1833 was the last good year, for with 1834 came the spoilers - the idlers, the missionaries, and the hard seekers after money."

"Where is that wag, Meek, tonight?"

"You mean the gay, daring, prosperous, and handsome, Joseph Lafayette Meek? He's back at camp trying to patch things up with his wife. She's rowing him up Salt River. He graduated from being a valiant hunter and trapper a long time ago to the vices of camp life, especially the one of conviviality. In other words,, Joe's very often a powerful drunk."

Sarah listened. The rowdy trappers stood together, laughing, talking, Some men leaned against the cottonwood trees, their charged rifles never out of arm's length. She said nothing, not wanting to call any more attention to herself, or make a remark that would raise an eyebrow, like her tipping of the camp kettle. The fact that Russell had appeared at Rendezvous with a White woman, no matter what the explanation, seemed to be a cause for celebration, met with much surprise, or perhaps more accurately, much astonishment.

"Richardson, Stevens, and some of the others are going buffalo hunting tomorrow, Mr. Russell. Do you want to join us?"

"Certainly. I can't understand how kings, nobles, and gentlemen can derive so much sport and pleasure in chasing a fox or simple hare all day. I prefer the pleasure a hunter experiences when he and his horse are hunting the noble and stately bison."

"Where do you plan to winter this year, Russell?"

"I thought I'd make my way over to Fort Bonneville. It's not very crowded in the winter." The men laughed loudly.

"Yes, sir. I do believe you could find winter accommodations at Fort Nonsense, Judge."

The good-humored stories flowed as freely as the alcohol. The juicy haunches hung over the glowing embers of the fire. The delicious smell of food filled the air. The men unceremoniously cut pieces of the meat with their butcher knives. When darkness fell the landscape was illuminated with bright moonlight. Spangled stars hung in the branches of the cottonwood trees like a million white twinkling Christmas lights. With all the parties safely in camp the atmosphere was relaxed. The numbers gradually dwindled, with only a few remaining at their fire. Each Indian, each trapper paid their respects to Sarah before leaving the gathering.

"Good night," said Captain Stewart with a firm handshake. "Better keep your eye on her, Mr. Russell. Joe Meek is liable to take up residence in your camp once he makes her acquaintance. Joe's not bashful and full of jaw as a man can be. I can see him donning his best trapper's toggery and parading before your tent. Remember the attentions he lavished on Narcissa Whitman? I don't remember her turning down an opportunity to hear one of his tales." He leaned over, winked, and whispered, "Remember, Mr. Russell, in a woman's eyes strong liquors be."

"I can't believe Kit Carson was here tonight!" said Sarah after everyone finally left. "Why does he stand away from the fire?"

"He doesn't want the fire light to show his position in case there are Indians around. It's one of his peculiarities, but not an ill-founded one. To hear him tell, it's kept him alive on more than one occasion. At night he uses his saddle as a pillow, and arranges it as a form of barricade to protect his head. He sleeps with two pistols, half cocked, always in the exact same place, so, if needed, he can lay his hands on them without thinking. He sleeps with his rifle at his side, under his blanket. Carson is one of the most honorable men in the mountains. He's a man of peace. He's also devoted to his wife and daughter. He avoids quarrels at all costs, but when a fight is unavoidable, he's a foe to be reckoned with. He can whip any man's weight in wild cats.

"A few years ago at Rendezvous there was a huge Frenchman in Captain Drip's party, named Shunar. He was overbearing and very strong; a great bully who whipped just about any body he was displeased with, and that was nearly everyone. It was the end of another day of great indulgences at Rendezvous. Shunar mounted his horse with a loaded rifle and challenged every man in camp, regardless of nationality: Dutch, Spanish, American, even his own French countrymen, it made no difference to him. There were several in camp that could have defeated him, if they'd a mind to, but they were all afraid of him.

"Carson had enough of it and told him if he continued to talk in such a manner, he would rip his guts. He also told him that he was the worst American in camp, with which no man present would have taken issue. All of this took place in front of everyone at camp. Carson seized a pistol, mounted his horse, and galloped up to Shunar, demanding to know if he intended to shoot him. They were so close their horses were touching. Shunar drew his gun, all the while telling Carson he wasn't going to shoot. Carson was prepared to fire, and allowed him to draw his gun. They both fired at the same instant. We heard only one report. The muzzle of the Frenchman's rifle was near Carson's head when it fired. The ball passed his head and the powder burned his eye. Shunar was shot in the hand, through the wrist and the ball passed through the arm above his elbow. Carson reached for another pistol, and Shunar pleaded and begged for his life to be spared."

"And did he spare his life?"

"Of course, Carson would have never taken the fight to him if there had been another way, but the man had already flogged two or three men that day for his amusement. Tell me, did you have a good time tonight?"

"Yes. I guess missionary women don't tip the camp kettle."

"Not that I've ever witnessed. Are you ready to retire?"

"I'll be in shortly. It's such a beautiful night."

Menelah had stood within seventy-five yards of Sarah all evening. He had thought of nothing else since he first saw her in the early afternoon. The smell of her fear aroused him. Looking into her eyes he could see she was different from an Indian woman. There was a confidence, a strong defiance, and a fire that shone brightly although she was afraid. He wanted to touch her hair and run his hands over her and inside her, discovering the subtle differences in her White body, and the Indian women he had taken. After his unexpected encounter with her, he returned to his camp outside Rendezvous, and took one of his wives into his lodge, stripped her, and took her roughly; imagining it was the White woman on her knees in front of him. He cursed at his young wife when he was finished, yelling at her to get out. He lay on his back, exhausted, looking upward at the bony skeleton of lodge poles that supported his tipi. He decided to return in the night.

He watched the lively scene of drunken trappers. He watched the White woman standing beside the trapper.

Sarah had felt uneasy all evening. She was not in the habit of being afraid. It made her feel vulnerable and angry; a hostage in its grip. The night seemed to move around her. She stared into the darkness trying to find what she was looking for, or find what was looking for her. She moved out of the light of the dying fire, disappearing, like Carson, into the safety and the darkness of the shadows. She stood motionless. She heard Osborne's deep, rhythmic breathing, and knew he had already fallen asleep. She stood with her back against a cottonwood tree, nuzzling into the dry vines which hung like party streamers from the top of the tree. She heard a hideous chorus of lonely wolves, the dying hum of conversation from the encampment, and faraway, the shrill whistle of an elk.

She thought she heard him. She thought she saw him move. She thought she saw the night shatter into small pieces and the blurred silhouette of a man or an animal, moving effortlessly and silently, as if the inky darkness was his habitat. But did she? Was she still terrified by the sudden appearance of the uninvited man with the powerful countenance, and the serious and sinister expression? She stood riveted. She could hear herself breathe.

He slipped silently up behind her, touched her hair, and quietly whispered in her ear, "I will take you from your husband."

She spun around and saw him towering over her, his dark, handsome face close to hers in the night.

"And I will kill you," she promised in a solemn whisper.

He laughed and disappeared. It was a frightening, evil laugh that filled her with a cold terror more frightening than the bear, more frightening than the Indians attacking, and more frightening than the huge red-bearded man who tried to rape her. Somehow she knew it was true.

He was going to take her from Osborne.

Chapter 21

"A penny for your thoughts?"

"I beg your pardon?"

Russell walked toward her leading his horse, saddled to go buffalo hunting. He held out his right arm and offered a closed hand to Sarah.

"I said, a penny for your thoughts?"

Sarah extended her arm and Russell dropped a coin into her open hand. She brought the coin toward her face to examine it more closely.

"A penny?"

"Sure, it's a penny! The currency of the mountains is beaver, furry banknotes, but I still like the feel of money in my pockets. Isn't one cent still a penny in 2000?"

"Yes, but it's so big. This penny is larger than our quarters." In the center of one side of the coin were the words *One Cent* surrounded by a garland of leaves and the words *United States of America*. On the other side was the profile of a woman with a crown in her hair that read *Liberty*, and the date *1838* beneath her figure. She handed it back to him.

"No, it's yours. Keep it."

"Thank you." She held the penny tightly in her hand.

"What are you thinking?"

"I'm thinking from the ashes of these campfires cities will rise. All of you who have fearlessly ventured into the unknown wilderness, climbed impassable mountain heights, crossed dangerous rapids, and risked your lives in these Shining Mountains — it is your courage that will open the way across our country. It began when Jefferson appointed Lewis and Clark, and it will continue in a few years when Fremont is hired by the United States government to survey the west, but it would not have happened so soon in our nation's history, if it wasn't for men like you and the men here at Rendezvous."

"It's a might hard to get used to the thought of being a part of American history. Are you sure you don't mind if I go hunting?"

"No, of course, I don't mind, what's it like hunting buffalo?"

"There are two methods commonly practiced, running and approaching. Running is the most dangerous. The hard part is reloading at a full gallop; some trappers keep three or four balls in their mouth. The Indian method of using bows and arrows has many advantages over firearms. An Indian on horseback has more lives than a cat! The landscape of the prairie is not a level; there are animal holes, sagebrush, ravines, and hollows. If a horse, at full gallop, falls into one of the burrows or into a ravine, the hunter is sent over the horse's head with such speed that he's most likely killed. The approaching method is done on foot and does not endanger the horse or the rider. The hunter must understand the animal, be mindful of the terrain and the direction of the wind, and be skillful in using his rifle. Sometimes buffalo are so stupid a man can walk right up to them in full sight, and even shoot three or four, before the rest of the herd will retreat. Their lethargy makes for very little sport in killing them.

"It's hard to describe the feeling you get when you see such a mass of wildlife. I've seen herds pass rapidly on a distant plain and appear like the dark shadow of a cloud; their rounded backs crowded so closely together the earth appears to be a surface of uniform blackness. It's grand! Your heart beats faster. Sometimes you can hear them in the distance. It sounds like a dull and confused murmuring. In the early part of the day, when the herds are feeding, they are in constant motion. The columns of dust rise as their heavy hooves hit the ground and as they roll in the grass. When there is a battle among the bulls you can hear the clattering of their horns and their deep, hoarse bellows. The bulls always run at the back of the herd to protect the females.

"Sometimes the Indians will butcher the buffalo and place their heads lying with their faces toward the east. They believe if they face the heads in the direction of the sun's rising, the buffalo will rise. If they place the heads toward the sunset, the buffalo will go down. They often place several heads in a circle, and will pray, sing, and smoke in hopes the buffalo will increase in number. After a successful hunting expedition, they will very often offer the best pieces of meat to the Great Spirit. I'll never forget the first time I drank mountain cider."

"What's that?"

"A beverage. When I was new in the mountains I was hunting with some well-seasoned trappers and they killed a buffalo. One of the men took his knife and cut the belly of the bull to expose its great stomach. Its entrails were still twisting and crawling. Quite a site! The hunter plunged his knife into the stomach and a fountain of gelatinous green juices poured out. I've seen men drink blood directly from the heart of an animal, and one trapper, Dead Horse, sucks the fluid from the eyeballs and keeps them in his medicine bag."

"Osborne! That's disgusting. It's too early in the day for your gruesome stories."

He rushed to finish his story. "I guess you don't want me to go into the details of how men eat boudins for amusement?"

"No! Please, go hunting, I'm going to tour the encampment today and talk to Mr. Miller. I wish it was George Catlin or Karl Bodmer, I'm more familiar with their paintings of the west."

"Are you coming Mr. Russell?" Richardson, Stevens, and a dozen other men rode up on horseback.

"Yes." Russell picked up his rifle and turned to Sarah, "Watch yourself today. Don't wander off alone. Promise me."

"I promise."

The men rode toward the northeast. Sarah reached to put her new penny in her pocket, but discovered there were no pockets sewn into her dress. She tied it into one of the ends of her black silk scarf for safekeeping. Osborne hadn't mentioned leaving the mountains again this morning at breakfast, nor did she tell him about the threatening return of Menelah. She didn't want to risk Osborne confronting him or risk what might ensue.

She realized she had nothing to protect herself. The .44 Magnum was in Osborne's possibles bag. She hurried toward the vast Rendezvous encampment to find safety in numbers. If she couldn't find Mr. Miller she would stay with the missionary wives all day and attend both morning and afternoon services. She saw the white canvas tops of the wagons as she approached.

The early morning was fresh, beautiful, and bright with sunshine. The encampment was quite a little town; a lively and animated scene. White lodges and tipis were scattered across the landscape. Hundreds of horses and mules grazed in the distance. Mongrel dogs bayed loudly and discordantly whenever a hunting party rode into camp. There were approximately two dozen carts, and a great tent was set up in the middle of a huge open field. It was as busy a marketplace as the Greek agora in ancient Athens. The merry trappers congregated while the goods were opened. It reminded Sarah of the children's nursery rhyme, "When the pie was opened the birds began to sing." The company representatives sorted and weighed the otter, beaver, and muskrat hides. Indians dashed about, yelling, howling, and whooping. The long, black hair of the Indian women was braided and gaily-colored ribbons were tied into the plaits of their hair. They proudly carried armfuls of blankets, cloth, embroidered moccasins, and other trade goods.

The Indian children swarmed like bees, running to the river where they splashed and screamed in the rough, foaming shallows of the river.

The air was filled with the hum of conversation, boisterous laughter, and the rhythmic crack of splitting wood. Smoke from the fires rose in the cool morning air. The residents were taking advantage of the brief time of the day when the wind and the sun pose a gentle presence. Saddles, packs, and plunder lay about the camps. Men sat around their fires cooking and drying meat, making moccasins, and cleaning their firearms. It was a pleasant time of busy idleness. As Sarah passed the camps, the trappers rose to their feet and greeted her enthusiastically, offering her coffee, or a biscuit. She graciously refused their hospitality, but stopped to talk and to enjoy their good-natured stories of freezing, suffering, being shot at and chased by Indians, and their other daring adventures.

She had been nervous about attending Rendezvous. She was afraid the men would ask her questions and her unrehearsed answers would unravel the story she and Osborne had carefully crafted, or someone would mention his name and her love for him would show clearly on her face. But the men didn't pry. Although a stranger, an unexpected guest, they welcomed her presence with genuine concern, respect, and cordiality. This splendid summer morning she was aware she had not only gone back in time, more importantly, she had gone back in history. In the twenty-first century men didn't look like these trappers, soldiers, perhaps, but not university men. Danger, deprivation, and hardship strengthened the look of a man who had survived the dangerous gauntlet. The men wore the brand of the mountains on their faces, some wore the brand on their scarred bodies.

Some of the men were sleeping under the wagons, after standing guard in camp from midnight to early light. At four in the morning the appointed camp keepers loosened the horses' pickets for them to feed. Every camp had its own guards, the men explained, to protect its occupants and to protect their horses and their property from being stolen by unscrupulous neighbors.

"We don't get many occasions to live fat," explained a rough-faced trapper with a strong and compact physique. An old calico handkerchief was tied around his head. His buckskin tunic and pants were blackened and polished by grease and by hard service.

"Can any of you gentlemen tell me where I might find Mr. Miller, the artist employed by Captain Stewart?"

"I'm no gentleman, Mrs. Hanley, but I can tell you where you won't find him. You won't find him doing any work, or buffalo hunting with the other men. Mr. Miller has a rather delicate nature, and doesn't take to our rugged life here in the mountains. I'd allow he won't mind a pretty lady interrupting his work, but he doesn't much like our standing around watching. Try down that way about 100 yards," said the grizzled trapper pointing east.

As Sarah walked east through the encampment she heard the shrill yells and angry screams of an old Indian woman. She was as ugly as one of Macbeth's witches. A tattered deer skin covered her shriveled body. A man, Sarah assumed to be her husband, sat cross-legged in his lodge smoking his pipe in silence. Unable to get her husband's attention despite her violent rage, the woman charged their lodge and, one by one, removed the poles supporting the tipi. The lodge fell like a house of cards, burying her husband beneath the hides and poles. The angry woman saddled her horse and rode out of camp. When his wife's loud curses had faded, the man slowly emerged from the ruins, broke off a three-foot length from a lodge pole, mounted his horse, and galloped off to discipline his angry and unruly spouse.

"Don't let me startle you," said Sarah as she approached the artist from behind. Miller was hard at work on a sketch of the encampment below. He turned toward the sound of her voice. He seemed surprised she was not one of the missionary wives. He set aside his work and stood in a fine display of civility. He was dressed in a long-sleeved linen shirt and tailored wool trousers. His long, dark hair fell to his shoulders, his moustache was combed and trimmed. He was exceptionally clean.

"I'm sorry to disturb you, Mr. Miller, but I heard there was a painter in camp and I was curious — like most of the camp, I suppose." She extended her hand, "My name is Sarah Hanley." He bowed at the waist, took her hand, and kissed it lightly. She was surprised by his courteous gesture.

"Captain Stewart told me you are from New Orleans."

"No, Sir William found me in New Orleans, but I am originally from Baltimore. I established a studio in New Orleans in 1834, when I returned from studying in Europe. I had been getting along quite well as a portrait painter, but his offer was too good to refuse, although I find this way of life rather undesirable. A fish out of water, I am. And you, Miss Hanley, where is your home? You don't have the look of a missionary wife about you."

"I'm from Boston."

"What are you doing so far from home?"

"My Mother died recently and I came searching for the whereabouts of my brother. He left the predictable life of Boston society several years ago to seek adventure in the west. I confirmed yesterday that he died earlier this year."

"My sincerest respects. This must be a terrible shock, having to endure this life of privation here in the wilderness. You must be an exceptionally strong woman to undertake such a difficult journey. Please, take my seat." He gestured to his canvas folding stool.

Miller was working on a field sketch of an encampment of Indians: a group of Indians in painted robes standing together on a bluff. On the flattened plains in the foreground other members of the tribe were cutting meat into slices and laying it on a framework of sticks, supported by poles, over a low fire.

"I finished this one yesterday." He pulled out a large watercolor. Sarah admired the work; a parade of Indians gathered in the foreground of the painting to honor the arrival of the supply train. It showed an Indian riding in front, followed by the main body of the camp. Miller had captured the magnificent design of the Indian's clothing, and the bright red vermilion painted on their bodies and faces.

"I wonder why sculptors have not come west to make use of these magnificent Indian models. They travel thousands of miles to study Greek statutes in the Vatican, but here at the foot of the Rocky Mountains are as fine forms stalking about with a natural grace, never taught by a dancing master, as ever the Greeks dreamed in their happiest conceptions. They had better make haste; Indians are melting like snowflakes in the sun."

"Your paintings are obviously influenced by European Romanticism, Mr. Miller."

"You display some knowledge of the fine arts, Miss. Hanley" he remarked with a tone of superiority. He was visibly curious about her background and shocked by her reference to Romanticism. Her first impression was to blast him with her "knowledge of the fine arts," as he so condescendingly categorized her comment, but she decided to behave herself. Over the years she had become accustom to such sexist comments in scholarly circles.

"And just what is your definition of Romanticism?"

"Well, unlike the French Academy, which is a classical program intended for wide public acceptance, Romanticism rests on the individual artist and his desire for autonomy. It doesn't concern itself with public acceptance. That is why the movement has been splintered with a plurality of styles, your paintings stress dramatic emotion and ideal beauty, like Wordsworth's writings. Your imagery conjures a sense of nobility in the humblest lives."

Miller looked dumbfounded. She could not resist continuing her soliloquy.

"The subject matter of your paintings, by virtue of your being one of the first artists to paint the west, takes the spectator to a remote time and place very different from their own. Like Gainsborough, your brush work is fluid, rhythmic, and evokes a wistful mood."

"I am a great admirer of Delacroix," remarked Miller.

"I am, too. Did you see *Liberty Leading the People* when you were in Paris?"

"Yes."

"Isn't the power and strength of the bare breasted Liberty raising the French flag unbelievable? His triangular composition and dark palette are reminiscent of Gericault's *Raft of the Medusa*, don't you agree?"

"Yes, but may I ask how are you familiar with such works?"

"Ah, Mr. Miller, the advantages of a classical education and the opportunity to travel abroad. Doesn't it make you wonder just how art will evolve in the centuries to come?"

"I've never really thought about it. What do you suppose artists will be painting in the twentieth century?"

Sarah smiled, "Or the twenty-first?"

He never talked down to her again. He showed her drawings for other paintings, *Antoine Clement, The Great Hunter, Bull Boating on the Platte River, and Landing the Charettes*. His watercolors were spontaneous and charming. The foreground was strong and detailed, and the atmospheric background disappeared into a vast nothingness which left the viewer enchanted by what might lie beyond the gauzy mountains in the distance.

"To date, this summer, I have produced over one hundred sketches and watercolors of Indian life, landscapes, buffalo hunts, and these unconventional trappers! Look at this sketch of Chimney Rock."

Sarah and Miller spent a pleasant morning and early afternoon together. Several trappers passed and took notice of the young artist and Mr. Russell's woman. Mid-afternoon Sarah returned to the main camp to take tea with the missionary wives.

The relaxed atmosphere of the morning had been replaced with noisy sports and raucous festivities. The heat was oppressive as the sun rose higher overhead. Their rifles leaned against trees in the nearby shade, the metal too hot to touch. Trappers played games of hand, and played mad pranks on one another as they sang, danced, ran, jumped, and shouted. In their drunken condition, they were as crazy a set of men as Sarah had ever seen at a fraternity party at Ole Miss. They had the confidence they could buy all the world in thirty minutes, or fight all the world, one-at-a-time. Sarah wondered if Mrs. Walker, Mrs. Gray, and the other two missionary wives had ever ventured into the bedlam of howling, swearing, and screaming. One trapper, with a little black pipe stuck in the corner of his mouth, sat cross-legged in the hot sun, splicing a trail rope with a mischievous look-ing knife, others were lying in the grass swapping stories and smoking.

Sarah easily found the missionaries' camp. The four women greeted her as if she was a visiting head-of-state. They were rushing to finish her dress. The tents of the four formed a small, private encampment, well out of the fray and hoopla of the main camp. They offered her a cup of tea and a bowl of rice pudding.

"You will attend afternoon services with us today, Sarah?" A question phrased in the form of a subtle command by Mrs. Gray.

"Oh, yes, and you must sing. Anything you choose will be lovely. I told Mr. Rodgers to spread the word today that you would sing this after-noon. Everyone is so looking forward to your joining us. This morning we had eight men hear the sermon."

"There is no Sabbath in this country," remarked Mrs. Eells. "Not like at home. No time for the body and the spirit to rest. I wonder if those back home truly appreciate all they have, and appreciate all we have left behind for the Lord."

"I'm sure it is much appreciated," replied Mary Walker, always posi-tive in her remarks and conversation. "Stand up, Sarah. I want to measure this hem on you."

"Afternoon, ladies," greeted a tall, bearded man with mirthful eyes, long, black hair, a generous smile, and not one spoonful of bashful in him.

"Good afternoon, Mr. Meek. Have you met Mrs. Hanley?"

"No, M'am, I have not had the pleasure. Mrs. Hanley, how do you do?"

"Very well, thank you, Mr. Meek."

"Mr. Meek, where is your home?" asked Mrs. Walker politely.

"My home is in Virginia. I came west at fifteen. My father, a slave holding planter, said I was headstrong and lazy, and M'am, he was right."

"Mr. Meek," addressed Mrs. Gray. "Before we reached Rendezvous we heard rumors you had been killed."

"Oh, yes, M'am, it's true. I've been killed many times!"

The missionary women giggled, falling under Meek's charming spell as he told bias tale after tale of his adventurous life in the mountains. He eventually excused himself, alluding to a powerful thirst, and was allowed to depart only after promising to attend afternoon worship services.

Russell, Richardson, and the others returned after a successful hunt, carrying the choicest pieces of meat on the backs of their saddles for the evening meal. When Russell did not find Sarah, he returned to the main encampment. It did not take long for the news of where she had spent her day to reach him. Jealousy was a powerful new emotion for Russell. He knew it was unreasonable, but the fire in his gut burned just the same. Of course she would be interested in the painter, they most certainly had a great deal in common. Captain Stewart mentioned Miller had traveled in Paris and Rome, they had both probably visited many of the same places. He was angry with himself for leaving her. Why would she be impressed with a few pieces of fresh meat compared to the talents of the young painter. He had lost almost an entire day with her. He purchased a pint of rum and sat down in the shade of a tree.

"Talk around camp is Mrs. Hanley spent most of the day with the young artist, Mr. Miller," Meek taunted Russell. "Is that why you're so grum? She's with the missionary women now, I left them about an hour ago. Is this a weeping drunk or a roaring drunk?"

"I'd like to give that artist a good drubbing. A man whose hands are stained with paint and not the color of honest, hard work, I set no store by. And, I'm not getting corned, I'm just drinking."

"Ah, we'll join you then," said Newell. "We can share a smile of Old Orchard before worship services. I promised Mr. Eells I would attend this afternoon. I understand Mrs. Hanley has agreed to sing. Should be quite a congregation of trappers in attendance if that be the case."

"A man should not depart from the way in which he was brought up," quoted Russell from the Bible. "I might make an appearance at services myself."

The three friends sat together in the shade talking about the last year, the decline of the beaver trade, and the winter to come.

"Ermatinger says Chouteau will leave Rendezvous this year with only 2000 beaver and otter skins," said Meek.

"Come, Joe," Newell shouted to Meek. "We are done with this life in the mountains - done with wading in beaver dams, and freezing or starving alternately. Done with Indian trading and Indian fighting. The fur trade is dead in the Rocky Mountains, and it is no place for us now, if ever it was. We are young yet, and have life left before us. We cannot waste it here; we cannot or will not return to the States. Let us go down to the Wallamet and take farms. What do you say, Meek? Shall we turn American settlers?"

"Not before we attend afternoon services," said Meek, offering a hand to Russell to help him up from the hardened ground.

Mr. Eells began preaching the word of God from Psalms 66. It was a wild and motley congregation, best described as curiosity seekers. They were politely attentive as the pastor read from his worn Bible:

Bless our God, O peoples,
let the sound of his praise be heard,
who has kept us among the living, and has not let our feet slip.
For thou, O God, hast tested us;
thou hast tried us as silver is tried.
Thou didst bring us into the net;
thou didst lay affliction on our loins;
thou didst let men ride over our heads;
we went through fire and water;
yet thou hast brought us forth to a spacious place.

Sarah stood with Mr. and Mrs. Walker, Cornelius Rogers, Mrs. Smith, Mrs. Gray, and Mrs. Eells. She saw Osborne standing to the right, some fifty feet from her. The missionaries were fine upstanding examples of churchgoers, even when the church was the great outdoors under God's spacious firmament. They led the singing of several hymns and then Mrs. Walker asked Sarah to sing. She'd thought about the request since Mrs. Gray made the initial command earlier in the day. Her favorite hymns were Christmas carols, not appropriate for July. She settled on *Amazing Grace*, although she had no idea whether it had been written by 1838. She could always tell them she heard it for the first time in Boston and, perhaps, it had not had time to find its way into churches across the country, certainly not to the mountains. Her voice began softly, hesitantly, and rose in the late afternoon air, its tone and sincerity, an inspiration to all present as they heard the words of the beautiful hymn for the first time.

Amazing Grace, how sweet the sound
That saved a wretch like me
I once was lost, but now I'm found
Was blind but now I see.

'Twas grace that taught my heart to fear
And grace that fear relieved
How precious did that grace appear
The hour I first believed.

Through many dangers, toils, and snares
I have already come
'Tis grace has brought me safe thus far
and grace will lead me home.

When we've been here ten thousand years
Bright shining as the sun
We've no less days to sing God's praise
Than when we first begun.

As Russell watched her sing he felt emotions that rendered him ill. The raw pain of loving Sarah, wanting her, left him feeling vulnerable and weak. He would not share her tonight.

Thunder growled and roared like a battery of cannons in the distance. The leaves of the tall cottonwood trees rustled with a sudden gust of the hot summer afternoon breeze. Someone yelled, "band of buffalo in the valley," and the congregation dismissed itself before Mr. Eells could give the benediction. The trappers left quickly to find their horses, rifles, and ropes. Russell walked to Sarah and took her by the arm, to escort her back to their camp.

"I want to leave tomorrow. We're resupplied, and we'll have plenty of provisions to get us where we're going."

"Where are we going? I still don't think we should leave the mountains."

"We'll take it one day at a time. Tomorrow morning I'll say our good byes and explain that I've decided to take you back to St. Louis myself, rather than taking you back to Taos. We'll head north and retrieve your belongings. Today, before I was out of sight, I regretted leaving you. I wasn't worried about your being alone. I just wanted to be in your presence. When you were singing, I wanted to walk over and take you in my arms; not exactly what a man should be thinking about when he's in the house of the Lord."

He pulled her into a small stand of trees, into the shade and out of the prying eyes of others. He leaned her against a tree. His lips gently kissed the nape of her neck and each side of her throat, dozens of soft kisses, moving up behind her ears and down her throat again. He turned her face to his and pressed his lips to hers, softly at first, then more firmly, deeply probing her mouth with his tongue. His touch filled her with passion and warmth. He wrapped his arms around her, pulling her close to him as their kisses became more passionate. He moved his hand down her back and rested it on the lowermost part where her buttocks began to swell into their shape. He held her tightly for a long moment, then whispered, "I love you. I need you."

They stood in the cottonwoods for a long time, kissing one another, holding one another, until they could go no farther without more privacy.

They walked hand-in-hand toward their small lodge, unconcerned with who might see the magic that flowed between them.

"Remember our first day together? You asked me if I was an angel? The way I felt when I picked you up and carried you to your bed could hardly be described as angelic. The first time you rode away, hurt and confused after you were attacked, I was afraid I was never going to see you again. I still wake in the middle of the night, with you lying naked beside me, to make sure you are really here."

"Osborne, I will always be beside you."

III.

God knows no distance.

Charlezetta Waddles

Chapter 22

A steady rain fell during the night. It coaxed the spent lovers to sleep. The soft, monotonous pattering of summer rain shut out the world beyond their lodge, the world beyond their embrace. True to his confession, Russell woke several times during the night to reassure himself Sarah still lay next to him. Comforted, he listened to her rhythmic breathing; she sometimes made a sleeping sound like a cat purring with relaxed contentment. He gently placed his right hand on the curve of her waist as she lay on her left side, her back and buttocks spooned into his chest and abdomen. As she slept he buried his face in her hair, deeply inhaling the smoky scent of her. He tenderly kissed the salty skin on her neck and fell back to sleep thinking he had never known such happiness.

In the morning when Sarah and Russell awoke there were shallow pools as far as the eye could see. The clouds rested on the tops of the cottonwood trees. Oblivious to anything around them, the two were embracing tenderly when the four missionary women carefully made their way across the muddy field and interrupted their intimacy.

"We're sorry to come so early, Mr. Russell, but we wanted to bring Sarah her dress so she could enjoy a change of clothes today." The women were clearly shocked and embarrassed they happened upon the lovers during a private moment.

"Good morning, ladies, won't you join us for a cup of coffee?"

"Oh, no thank you, we just finished our breakfast," Mrs. Walker stammered. "We're so used to waking early when we're traveling, it's impossible not to rise before the sun comes up."

"You have been so kind; I appreciate all of your hard work. The dress is absolutely beautiful. I'm glad you brought it because we are leaving this morning. Mr. Russell has agreed to personally take me back to St. Louis, and I have accepted his gracious offer."

"That is so gallant of you, Mr. Russell," commented Mrs. Eells. "After everything Sarah has had to endure, I'm sure she will feel much safer, despite the obvious dangers, knowing she is under your protection."

"We are leaving ourselves, tomorrow morning," interrupted Mrs. Smith, with more animation on her face than Sarah had seen before. The thought of leaving the mosquito-laden river bottom seemed to agree with her. "We are leaving with the Hudson's Bay Company, and heading on to Walla Walla. We hear it is a lovely place. I am most anxious to live in a location where my dining table is not the ground!"

"I hope you have a safe trip," said Sarah, "I wish you Godspeed." They each quickly embraced her and, again, commended the young trapper on his unselfish and high-minded act of personally escorting her back to the States. Sarah could only imagine their conversation as they remarked about finding her in Osborne's arms. Their visit was pleasantly short and a great relief to Russell, the high-pitched overlapping voices of the four women reminded him of a crowded coop of pigeons.

"I'm going to go see Mr. Bridger, Meek, Newell, and some of the others, and explain we're leaving today. Do you want me to tell your artist friend, Mr. Miller, goodbye for you, or would you prefer to tell him in person? He may be heartbroken if he doesn't see you again!"

"If I spend another hour with him, I might influence the entire evolution of art. I'm going to walk to the river and get some water to wash before I change into my new dress."

"Do you want me to help you down? The river is strong here and the bank is extremely undercut."

"I can manage. If it's a problem, I've got sense enough to wait until you get back. This dress is very beautiful, but I have to admit, I'll be glad to change into my own clothes."

"Might not be such a good idea. With the number of people leaving here in the next few days, we're likely to run into company."

"I can always wear your clothes," she suggested as a shocking possibility. "Go say your goodbyes. I'm going to think of something I can do to persuade you to let me wear my clothes with zippers again."

"I can think of a couple of things you could do to me that would be very persuasive."

"Go!" She pushed him toward the open meadow. She took her wash cloth and made her way down the river to find a safe place to reach the water's edge. The morning was crystal clear and fluid. It seemed she could fall forward and up into the flowing sky and the drifting clouds. About thirty yards away she saw two Indian women and decided to crawl down the steep bank at the same point. As she approached, she noticed one of the women was very old, and looked vaguely familiar. The other, a young woman, looked to be eighteen.

She nodded, "Good morning." She didn't know whether they could understand her. The rocks were warm and rough to the touch. She slipped crawling down the muddy bank, its surface made slick as glass by the night's rain. The young woman spoke to her elder. Even though Sarah couldn't understand what they were saying, there was no doubt in her mind that they were talking about her.

"She does not understand why you do not desire her husband," the old woman said slowly, acting as an interpreter.

"I don't understand."

"Her husband, Menelah, the great Crow warrior. She says all women desire him whether they are stolen from their husbands or whether they go willingly."

Sarah could not believe this innocent girl was the bride of such evil. "Tell her I have my own husband, I do not want hers. Is she Crow?"

"No, she is from the Bannock tribe. She was stolen from her family by Menelah, but she loves him and she does not wish to return to her family. The girl is very young. My old eyes see more clearly, but I do not need my eyes to see. The differences in you are deeper than the white of your skin. I see another color. I see the gold light of the morning sun that surrounds you."

A wordless, mystical communion passed between them. It was as though, at that moment, it was another earth, another sky, beyond the world of men. Although they stood by the mighty Wind River, it seemed they were walking through mist and clouds on a pathway that could have easily carried them, in one direction to the icy surface of the moon, and in the other direction, to the fiery surface of the sun. A divine infusing of the natural world gave all things around them the sense of eternity, the sense that the world could last forever. When Sarah crossed the seasons, going back 162 years in time, she was unaware that anything had changed. But now, standing beside the woman, she felt time had shifted again. Sarah studied her familiar features carefully; the deep, magnificently etched lines in her bronzed face.

My God, this is the woman in my dream! This is the woman standing beside me in line while we were waiting to sign our names in God's book. The woman nodded, pleased Sarah had recognized her. She didn't speak for a long time.

"Death has a great power over man, but love is stronger. God knows no distance. Death has no sovereignty over love. There is a sweetness and a purity that ultimately prevails. The door to the invisible has been made visible to you. It is not an illusion. All people live on the fringe of eternity, but you have been granted a great blessing. Always remember what you have seen is not an illusion. No matter what happens, do not doubt what you have experienced is real. Time has erupted for you because you belong to something ancient. What now lies within you echoes the power of the earth."

Sarah tried to speak, but no sound came from her lips. She had many questions. She wanted answers. Do I have a choice? Will I be allowed to stay with Osborne and live the rest of my life with him? Where is my family? Have they been born? Are they ahead in time waiting for me? Are they worried about me? If I stay what will happen to them? Why can't I stay?

The woman repeated, "God knows no distance. Your family is with you now, as surely as I am with you now. I have been with you a very long time, sometimes walking beside you, sometimes ahead, sometimes appearing in your dreams to foretell how your life will not be like the lives of others. You were correct sensing long ago that there has always been something waiting for you in Time.

"Do not be afraid. You have come far. You have trusted your heart and you have carved your own path across the mountains. You are no longer lost. You have resumed the journey that was your destiny. You are no longer alone. You will never be alone, Sarah. Remember. Do not be afraid. Sometimes a woman thinks she hears a song, or she thinks she remembers beautiful words, and she weeps for the beauty she almost knew. You have become part of the Mystery. You will weep because you have heard the song and because you will remember the words. You will weep because you know the beauty."

The morning sun burned through the thick gray haze that blanketed the landscape. The glare of the bright-white sunlight reflected off the river's surface, scalding her eyes with its intensity. Sarah blindly walked toward Osborne standing in camp.

"I was getting worried until I saw you at the river with that young Indian woman."

"There were two women. There was an old woman, too."

"Really? I've been here awhile; I only saw one. I already packed the horses, but I left the lodge because I thought you might want to change inside. There are plenty of people about this morning."

"Only one woman?"

"Yes, a young woman. Are you all right? Do you feel sick?"

"No. Where's the spirit blanket?"

"I put it on Cocoa. Sarah, what's the matter?"

"I do feel a little sick."

"Do you want to stay another day? We can wait and go tomorrow. There's no hurry."

"No," she stated emphatically. "I want to go today. I want to go now. It will just take me a few minutes to change clothes." She couldn't remember whether she had washed herself or not. "Will you unfasten these?" She turned her back to him; he unfastened each hook exposing her bare back.

Russell watched her disappear into their small lodge. He was worried and concerned by her disoriented behavior. She must be sick. It wasn't like her to act so confused. It wasn't a long distance to where they had cached her belongings, an easy four-hour ride. Instead of continuing north, the way they had come to Rendezvous, they could head west and camp at one of the foothills of the Wind River Range. It would be a beautiful place to spend the night. They could stop sooner if she became ill, but he felt her spirits would improve when they recovered her plunder.

Sarah emerged from the tent. The dress was made of silk. The vertical-striped pattern, in graduated shades of mustard yellow to medium brown, made her look even taller and slimmer. She was tan from the days in the hot sun. Again, she turned her back to him to fasten the six sets of hooks. The back of the dress had drawstring gathers at the center back with a tie closure.

"Women certainly can't live alone in this day and age. They could never get dressed!" She tried to focus on their day ahead, be positive in her tone, and not worry him. "The missionary women really outdid themselves with this dress, didn't they?"

"Yes, you look beautiful. I know that complicated attire has to be uncomfortable and hot. If you'll endure it four more hours, we'll have you back in those breeches with zippers," he promised, trying to brighten her spirits. "But those zippers won't be nearly as much fun for me since you can manage them alone." She was looking back toward the river bank where she had talked to the old woman. "Sarah, do you hear me?"

"Yes. Zippers. You said zippers."

Cocoa stood motionless while Russell helped Sarah into the saddle. It was hard to mount with the bulky, heavy dress. Russell tied Walmart and the other pack horses together. They rode northeast around the perimeter of the annual gathering. Despite their efforts to leave inconspicuously, they were hailed by all who happened to see them pass. It seemed the leaving would take more time than the traveling.

"Here, Mr. Russell," said Jim Bridger, handing him a brass telescope, "this will help you be on the look out for squalls."

"Don't forget you still have a bill at Fort Hall for that fiddle you have waiting for you," said a man in a huge buffalo robe that could have fit a man twice his size.

"Miss Hanley," said Alfred Jacob Miller, taking his well-manicured hand and holding hers to Russell's chagrin, "perhaps we'll next meet on the Champs Elysees in Paris. Please, if you ever get to New Orleans, I would much enjoy visiting with you again." Miller's bold action galled Russell.

"Best be going," said Russell. "Can't make talk all day."

"And, Mr. Russell," said Captain Stewart, firmly shaking Russell's hand, "if I don't see you again in the Rocky Mountain College, you are always welcome at my home in Scotland. It would be my distinct pleasure to show you its majestic wonders. In fact, you might be surprised and feel right at home. I plan to take an assortment of plants, birds, and animals, perhaps even a herd of buffalo with me when I return home."

Russell stopped from time-to-time trying to gauge Sarah's spirits and her physical condition. Neither of them spoke while they retraced their path north, once again following the Wind River. They stopped briefly when they reached the shallow ravine where they fought side-by-side during the attack of the Blackfoot.

"Now it's my turn to ask you, what's the matter?" For the fourth or fifth time during the day Russell was looking across the landscape with the telescope Mr. Bridger had given him. "Do you see Indian sign?"

"No, I don't see a thing, but the hair's been standing up on the back of my neck all day. I can't explain it. I guess I'm just beginning to stand guard again after enjoying our safety at Rendezvous. There's nothing to worry about. Are you feeling better? You appear stronger."

"Do your eyes ever play tricks on you out here?"

"Tricks? Do you mean do I ever see things that aren't really there?"

"Yes, exactly."

"Sure. A kind of mountain sickness we call it. It can be brought on by being overly tired, by being sick, or too much grog. It passes. What do you think you're seeing?"

"This morning there were two women at the river, not one. An old woman and the young woman."

"I'm sure there were. The old woman probably left before I returned. I'm sure you weren't seeing things. Don't worry about it."

Russell's explanation wasn't a comfort. It took four hours to reach the nondescript location Russell had selected to bury her belongings. She waited anxiously as he pushed away the dry soil and loose rocks to expose what, to Sarah, was hidden treasure. She felt oddly comforted by her arti-facts from the future. She tore into them before he could help her shake off the dust. She impatiently sorted through her green stuff bag for her jeans and denim shirt.

"Please, help me out of this dress. I am sorely wanting the feel of my own clothes."

He unfastened the hooks on her dress, just the sight of her bare back and buttocks excited him. He turned to give her privacy.

"Do you think it's really necessary to look the other way while I un-dress, after all we've shared together?"

"Yes, M'am, I certainly do. If you want to get where we're going today, it's best I keep my back turned to you while you undress."

The loose shirt allowed the air to circulate freely, cooling her body temperature immediately. She pulled on the jeans. "I wish I could remem-ber who invented the zipper, I'd drink a hearty toast to him tonight." She put on her socks and tied her shoes. After wearing the beautiful, but unpadded mocassins, the heavily cushioned soles felt wonderful on her feet. God bless, Timberland, she thought.

Russell got the horses, repacked their equipment, and began to resaddle Cocoa. "Do you want to keep the spirit blanket under her saddle, or do you want to put it in one of your bags?"

"Let's keep it on her. I owe a great debt to that blanket. It brought me to you. Do you still have William?"

"Yes." He produced the small, blue faience hippopotamus from his possibles bag. "And I have your pistol. How many shots are left?"

"Two."

"You never showed me how it fires."

"There's nothing to it. You keep pulling the trigger until you're out of bullets."

"Ball and powder all rolled into one," observed Russell. "Kind of takes the sport out of it."

"Save the sport for the buffalo. I just wish I'd brought more. After these two bullets are gone, we might as well throw it away."

"No, we need to save it to show our children, to prove their Mother really came from the future."

She could hardly speak. Her throat tightened, saliva gushed into her mouth like a faucet turned on, and tears welled in her eyes. She pursed her lips together, tightening her jaw. Tears ran down her face. He folded her tightly in his arms; she felt his heart beating in his chest. She was safe and well-protected, as if nothing in the world could harm her.

"You said you would always be beside me, Sarah, do you promise?"

"I promise."

He looked at her face, wet with tears, as if he was seeing her for the first time. She was so beautiful, but she looked so sad, as if her heart was breaking. He kissed the hot tears off her cheeks and gently brushed her hair back behind her ears.

"What did I do before I found you, Sarah?"

"Well, for one thing, you got more sleep." They both laughed breaking the overwhelming emotion they felt. She wiped her face with her shirt tail. He handed her a red handkerchief to blow her nose.

"This isn't the handkerchief where you've been keeping the grizzly bear claws?" she asked before putting it to her face.

"Whoa, you're the one with the bark on! What's a little grizzly bear gristle to a soon-to-be trapper like you?"

Russell kept a sharp eye out for trouble as they rode. His German pistol was tucked in his belt, and his rifle was balanced on his thighs. He passed the time thinking about the night ahead with Sarah. Her mind wandered as they made the easy ride northward. The widely extended high desert prairie was beautiful and verdant. The soil was sandy and made a crunching sound under the heavy weight of the horses' hooves. The country was bisected by small streams that were lined with shrubbery and thickets of brush. How closely the nation's highways would follow its mighty rivers. The sun beat down upon them. They had been spoiled by the cool shade of the cottonwood groves. Sarah was thankful they did not have a full day's ride ahead of them. Throughout the afternoon she saw mule deer grazing on the short, tough, grass-covered landscape.

By the afternoon position of the sun in the sky, it was late in the day when they reached the location Russell had chosen. The Wind River foothills were thick with evergreens: Douglas fir, Englemann spruce, and Lodgepole pine. The lofty granite face of the mountains looked like the Hall of the Mountain King; wondrous, magical and frightening. Russell unsaddled his horses and picketed them in a spot generous with vegetation. Sarah let Walmart and Cocoa loose to forage for their evening meal.

The two leisurely set camp, walking hand-in-hand, halfheartedly looking for firewood, and enjoying the relaxed pace at the end of their day. Russell took out his knife and carved their names and the date on the rock face. He picked her a small bouquet of Indian paintbrush, meadowlarks, and sourdock for their supper table. Later, he pulled his cardboard-covered journal from his possibles bag, and for the first time since the day they met, he began to write. His head was bowed in heavy concentration.

In three or four minutes he was finished. He stood and moved to return the book to his bag.

Not wanting to pry, but dying of curiosity, Sarah could not keep from asking, "What did you write?"

Russell read his brief entry: "*During our stay at the Rendezvous it was rumored among the men that the company intended to bring no more supplies to the Rocky Mountains and discontinue all further operations. This caused a great deal of discontent among the Trappers and numbers left the party 21st We travelled up the Wind river about 30 Mls and encamped.*"

"I like the subtle "We" part," she remarked.

Russell put the book in his bag and found his flint and steel to start a fire. Sarah sat on the spirit blanket near him. The heat of the day gradually began to disappear. The fire crackled and hissed as the dry branches went up in high flames.

"Yesterday I saw an American flag. It had twenty-five stars."

"Must be an old flag, the new flag has 26 stars. Michigan was granted statehood in 1837. How many states are there in 2000?" He began to understand why such a simple thing as seeing the American flag had produced her bewildered response.

"Fifty. The last two states were Alaska and Hawaii."

"The island in the Pacific Ocean?"

"Yes."

"Well, I'll be."

"What would you like for dinner?"

"Just boil some water and throw in a couple of those packages of rice. I'm hungry. Anything you make will be well appreciated. The fire's well on its way, I'll move the horses."

"How about something strong to drink?" she called after him.

"Fine by me. I didn't give up drinking today."

She found a package of rice with sun-dried tomatoes and the wineskins of Jack Daniels. She sat by the fire. She poured herself a generous drink, raised her cup and made a toast.

"To the future," she said aloud. She wrapped the spirit blanket around her shoulders, tucking it in her jeans to keep it in place. The setting sun began to change the color of everything; the mountains, the open prairie to the east, and the deep forest of trees to the west. Her right leg fell asleep from sitting cross-legged on the ground. She stood and began to walk around to return her circulation. Russell moved his horses, and was leading Walmart and Cocoa. Sarah watched every step he took, every movement he made.

He talked to the horses, as if the two noble beasts could understand every word he spoke.

Could she ever truly be objective about what would happen to him during his lifetime? Could she let history take its course; the history outlined in his journal? Or would her presence in 1838 alter history, changing his life and what would befall him? She had never opened *Journal of a Trapper* after the first day she met him. Would he change his mind and one day want to compare his handmade journal to the paperback copy she had treasured since she was a young woman?

The two lovers had been lost to the world all day; each pondering their deep love for the other. They did not observe the reason Russell had been apprehensive. They did not notice the naked, spectral figure of Menelah skillfully stalking them, undetected, as they crossed the open plain. He watched, at a long distance, while she changed her dress. He sneered when the White trapper turned his back while she disrobed. After he had taken her, he would keep her, tied like a mongrel dog outside his lodge. He would lie between her legs whenever it was his pleasure. If he could not eventually see desire for him in her eyes, he would take her eyes from her.

He slipped into the cover of the forest and waited in the dark shadows until Russell left, and he could take her easily. He pulled his long knife from its sheath. If he could not steal her, he would kill her, letting her red blood gush from her body as the trapper watched. She was easy prey. She saw nothing of the natural world around her; her eyes were filled with the sight of Russell, her heart was filled with her love for him.

In ten silent steps he was upon her; grabbing her and violently pulling her against him from behind. He lay his left hand over her open mouth to silence her surprised scream, and brought his sharpened knife to her throat beneath her jaw. He rubbed himself against her from behind, as she struggled. His butcher knife glanced her throat. He saw her blood on his hand. He buried his teeth in her neck and licked her blood with his tongue.

Russell, hearing her frightened cry, quickly covered the ground between them, his pistol drawn. He was terrified. He was not afraid to die, but he could not bear to watch her die. He saw the frightened look in her eyes. He saw the blood on her neck and on the face and hands of Menelah.

"Ah, your husband has heard your cry, and has bravely come to rescue you. If you fight me, the last thing you will see is the painful look in his eyes as he watches the life drain from your body and soak into the earth of his beloved mountains." He took his hand from her mouth, and reached across her chest, defiantly grabbing her right breast.

"Where are your comrades now? Where are they when you need them, trapper? Back there at your summer feast, drunk like stupid animals? I have many wives, but I want yours. If you are fortunate I will return her to you when I tire of her. I can see by the fire in her eyes she is too much woman for you."

Sarah was repulsed by him. He kneaded her breast roughly, intentionally hurting her and angering Russell. He pushed his stiff penis against her from behind. She remembered Osborne calling him a half breed: half Indian - half Devil. She was terrified, and, her attacker was correct, she could not look at Osborne's face while he watched her die.

She locked eyes with him. Her voice exploded from her mouth so loudly it startled both men. "Mr. Russell, do you have a ball in there?"

Menelah, with his knife at her throat, tightened his hold, angry she did not seem more afraid. Her eyes never left Osborne's. She raised her right leg, and forcefully drove the right heel of her heavy hiking boot onto the bridge of her attacker's bare foot.

He loosed his violent grip and reeled backwards in pain. He briefly regained his balance and grabbled Sarah as she struggled to get away, but she was too quick. She sprang from his grasp. Menelah only succeeded in pulling the spirit blanket from her shoulders. Furious, he threw the blanket into the fire. Russell fired his pistol. The ball lodged in the Indian's left shoulder, he cried out cursing, and fell to the ground. Russell pulled his rifle over his shoulder and took aim, but the rifle misfired. Menelah tightly gripped his knife, readying for the fight.

Sarah didn't see the blanket begin to disintegrate in the flames. Her only thought was to reach Osborne, to find safety in his arms. She saw the expression on his face change from one of fear to one of panic. She turned and looked behind her and saw Menelah on the ground. She saw the blanket burning. She began to feel it burning, the hot flames rising inside of her. She fell into Russell, hitting him forcefully, holding him desperately. He caught her in his arms.

"Osborne! Don't let go of me!" She couldn't breathe. She was suffocating as if the smoke was the only air she could inhale. She began to choke and claw at her throat to loosen the invisible cord that was tightening around her neck. She began to sob, calling his name over and over when she could catch her breath. Her body began to go limp. She looked into his handsome face one last time, trying to memorize its every line and feature. She could see his heart breaking. She breathed her last breath; deeply inhaling the familiar scent of him, and the scent of their Shining Mountains. She felt his strong arms holding her, and then she was gone.

Russell couldn't hold her tightly enough. No matter how he tried he could not keep her from slipping from his arms, falling away from him into the darkness.

"Trapper, I told you I would take your whore from you!"

He heard the cruel laughter of his enemy, taunting and cursing him. The wounded savage was struggling to mount his horse, knife in hand. Russell stumbled to reach his possibles bag, pulled Sarah's pistol, and aimed. He charged Menelah, uttering a scream so primal he felt his chest, like his heart, would burst. He fired.

Menelah was hurled from his horse by the bullet's fierce blast. For the first time in his life he felt terror as the bullet ripped through his body. He fell hard, and lay on his stomach in a limp, broken pile. Russell stood shaking with blind fury and sorrow. Menelah struggled to raise his body with his last strength. He pushed himself up and rolled onto his back. The blood spurted from his open heart forming red bubbles, then spilling across his naked chest. He looked at Russell with horror and surprise; the look of a man who knew he was dying. He gasped and muttered something indistinguishable in his native language. Whether it was a prayer or a plea it did not matter. Gone was the mocking tone in his voice, only the rattling sound as death filled his lungs. Russell watched him die slowly and painfully. Although he was already dead, Russell raised the pistol and shot him between the eyes. He fell to the ground on his knees.

It was the blood of the savage devil, Menelah, and not the blood of his beloved, Sarah, that soaked into the earth that day.

Chapter 23

The hospital room had two poorly colored, poorly conceived, and poorly executed lithographs on the wall. Sarah, despite her pain, couldn't help notice how dramatically the hospital's idea of fine art differed from her own. She felt edgy. Everyone kept telling her to calm down and relax: her doctors, Margaret, her family. She looked at the clock on the wall and thought, Time doesn't mean much to me anymore. She had been rushed to the hospital the night before.

It was when she was alone that everything closed in on her. It was very difficult for her to maintain composure, and step back into her life as if nothing had happened. She had to carefully measure what she said, and how she said it to prevent causing those who loved her, concern about her mental stability. The last months had been a blur. The doctors originally said it was stress, dehydration, exposure to the elements and shock. The doctors were right, but they had left out the most significant part of the diagnosis. Her heart was broken.

Two backpackers found her suffering from exposure, and helped her out of the mountains. She wasn't far from Highway 287, she could have made it herself, but she didn't want to move from the last place she touched Osborne. In the hospital, all she could remember was crying and praying, and crying and praying, then cursing, because she had been ripped from his arms and from his life. She kept hoping a portal would open and he would step through, to once again hold her and place her under his protection. Why couldn't magic, why couldn't miracles happen more than once? Why couldn't she cross the seasons of time again and live the rest of her life with him? She knew wherever he was, he was frantic to know she was safe.

When the doctors examined her in the emergency room, they saw the massive bruises on her breast and the knife wound on her throat. They suspected she had been the victim of a sexual attack and asked if they could do a rape kit, but she refused. She knew they would find semen, but it wouldn't be the semen of an attacker. It was the gift of her lover that had taken her so tenderly and claimed her as his.

God bless Frank. He arrived within four hours after he received the call from the backpackers that the Wyoming Highway Patrol had taken her to the hospital in Riverton. He must have dropped everything at Half Moon Lake, hitched the trailer, and driven like a mad man to make it to the hospital in such a short time.

Frank hadn't worried about the length of time Sarah had been in the mountains. He had strongly encouraged her to take her time and enjoy this once-in-a-lifetime journey across the Wind River Range. As he sped to her bedside, a terrifying chill ran through him as he remembered standing beside her that beautiful July morning and holding the mysterious blanket with the strange rust-colored mark.

He was horrified when he saw her. He entered the room quietly while she was sleeping. He wanted to hit the something or the some one who had done this harm to her. Her face was sunburned and her lips cracked and blistered. The doctors had bandaged her throat and her left arm. What in God's name had happened to her? When Sarah awoke she found Frank standing by her bedside. She hadn't seen her mirrored reflection, but she imagined by the concerned look on his face, that the news wasn't good. He shook his head in dismay, but he never pried, and she never said. He sat by her bed all night. He held her limp fingers in his strong, scarred hands; during the night he heard her crying.

The doctors released her in two days with strict orders for her to rest and delay the long, strenuous drive back to Atlanta. Frank took her and the horses back to Half Moon Lake. Chef Ron made her sumptuous meals, but she yearned for her handsome trapper and a roasted buffalo rib heavy with grease. Every morning Frank helped her from her cabin to the lodge and left for his day's labors. She sat on the deck all day and stared across the inky lake and the forest-covered mountains. He returned each evening when the air began to cool, smelling of sweat and horses, with a hand-picked bouquet of wildflowers. She cried. He wrapped a blanket around her shoulders and sat beside her, saying nothing.

"I don't remember how I cut my left arm, Frank."

He wondered what she did remember. He was furious when he thought of the person who had hurt her and hurled her into such an emotional state.

She had to summon all her strength to call her parents and pretend she was having the time of her life in Wyoming. She told them she was extending her trip to relax at Half Moon Lake after her strenuous ride on horseback. It took her longer to call Margaret. She knew Margaret would know, by the trumped up tone of her voice, something was wrong. When she finally called, Margaret immediately offered to fly to Wyoming and drive her back to Atlanta. Sarah didn't argue. She knew she wasn't well enough, emotionally or physically, to make the trip alone.

She began the fall semester like a woman walking in her sleep. She was tired and moody. She was down right angry. Margaret called her every day for several weeks and finally suggested Sarah see a psychiatrist, a doctor, or both.

"I'll come check on you every day. I'll call you every day, but I can't bring Osborne back and neither can you. Please, go to the doctor and make sure you don't have Rocky Mountain Spotted Fever or other strange disease. If the doctor says you're in good health, I'll leave you alone."

She had been blessed with a life of good health. Her emotional and physical malaise since she returned home was unwelcome and debilitating. She agreed to submit to a routine physical to satisfy her own fears as well as Margaret's. She hated doctors. Not doctors, but the whole sickness thing. "Pee in a jar. Roll up your right sleeve. Make a fist. Put your feet up in these stirrups. This may be a little cold. Cough. Take several deep breaths for me. Step up on the scales for me, please. This may be a bit uncomfortable."

After she dressed, it took her doctor forty-five minutes to return to the examining room. She read every trivializing article in a nine-month old issue of *People* magazine.

"I thought you'd forgotten me."

"I didn't mean to take so long," said the doctor when he finally returned, "but I wanted to double check some of the test results, and make sure I was familiar with all of your options."

"What options?"

"Well, Sarah, just to be straight about it, pregnancy for a thirty-nine year old woman is a very high-risk situation. I'm sure you understand there is a one in twenty chance that your baby may be born with"

She interrupted him, "I'm pregnant? Are you sure?"

"Yes, I am."

"Are you really sure?"

"Yes, Sarah, I'm really sure. You didn't have any idea?"

Osborne's love had breathed hope into her lifeless body. His love had given her a glimpse of eternity and had blessed her with the child she had always wanted. The child she had never been able to have. As the months passed she thought about the night they consummated their love in the soft amber firelight of the discolored tipi. Her body began to swell with her love for him. After her amniocentesis Sarah knew she was pregnant with a healthy baby boy. As Osborne's child grew inside of her, she pondered the love she felt for both the father and the son.

It was 5:00 p.m. by the clock on the birthing room wall. Sarah had been in labor for hours. When Margaret rushed her to the hospital the night before, the doctor kept her overnight and, the next morning, broke her water to induce delivery.

"I'll be back at lunch," her doctor promised, "after my morning appointments. This baby should be born by noon."

But the baby wasn't born by noon. Nor one o'clock. Nor two o'clock. The early morning contractions were no worse than heavy menstrual cramps. The meddlesome nurses hovered over her checking her blood pressure, seeing how far she was dilated, and reading the cumbersome fetal monitor strapped around her huge belly. Another digitized machine displayed the strength of each contraction. The readings meant nothing to her, but after ten hours of labor, she could tell by the expression on Margaret's face that she was concerned. Their six weeks of natural child birth classes had not adequately prepared the two over-educated, middle-aged women for this moment. Sarah heard herself screaming and hoped her parents and Frank, waiting outside, could not hear her cries of pain, and her cries for her baby's father. The pain was unbearable. The contractions became stronger and more violent.

She thought she heard the doctor ask, "Can you hold on a little longer? We'll have this baby born in the next twenty minutes." She felt her body ripping from the inside out.

Margaret leaned over, gently touched her shoulder, and whispered, "Go to the mountains, Sarah. Dream of the mountains, and the places you will one day take your son." She smiled weakly. She had the shiny 1838 penny Osborne had given her clutched tightly in her fist.

She closed her eyes and slipped out of the hospital room. She flew like wild geese fly swiftly home after a hard, long winter. She crossed the country, skimming the wide expanse of the plains, until the pinnacles of the mountains rose in the distance. She traveled until she found the parting of the waters at the Great Divide. She saw icy mountain streams, freed after winter's frozen blast, rush west to the mighty Pacific, and rush east to the Atlantic. Again she saw the Grand Tetons, the Hoary Feathered Fathers, that presented a lofty mountain face like no other heights in the world. She raced along the Gros Ventre River, its crystal surface sparkling like the Queen's diamonds. And there, on Dry Cottonwood Creek, she found her brave mountaineer, standing young and strong, under the Wyoming summer sky in their Shining Mountains.

Sarah heard a sharp cry. The smiling nurse placed a beautiful baby boy on her breast. She wrapped her arms around him, touching his warm, sticky body for the first time. She looked into his screaming red face, and saw Osborne.

"What name have you picked for this handsome boy, Sarah?"

Her body trembled. She was exhausted from her long-suffered pain and overcome with emotion. It took a long time for her to answer the simple question.

"His name is Russell.."

Chapter 24

"What did the doctor say?" whispered a distinguished giant of a man standing in the doorway of the small, dark hospital room.

"He said it shouldn't be long now. He's resting comfortably. Thank God for that. He's not suffering."

"Has he said anything?" The tall man looked at his gold pocket watch to check the time. His fingers were thick, his hands big and sturdy.

"Not a thing."

Russell heard his friends, Walt and A.B., whispering but he didn't care to listen to what they were saying. He knew he was lying on his deathbed, and the thought did not disturb him in the least, in fact, it was rather a comfort after such a long illness. He lay, paralyzed from the waist down, his arms at his side, his fists tightly clenched. He lay warm in his metal hospital bed beneath the old and discolored green Hudson's Bay blanket he bought for his beloved Sarah, fifty-four summers ago.

A day didn't pass he didn't think of her. Some days he remembered her sense of humor and the sound of her laughter. Some days he remembered how brave a woman she was; eating dog meat, standing down the fearsome grizzly bear, and standing down the devil: Menelah. Some days he remembered the expression on her face and the sound of her voice when she sang "Amazing Grace:"

> Through many dangers, toils and snares,
> I have already come
> 'Tis grace has brought me safe thus far
> And grace will lead me home

Some days he thought of how beautiful she was whether she was wearing her trousers with zippers, the Indian women's clothing he had proudly traded for her, or the White woman's clothes which, in his opinion, covered too much of her body. Some nights, many nights, he remembered their lovemaking.

Even at his advanced age, some nights his body would stir for her. He looked back and laughed at his inexperience their first night together. She had so gently led him, never embarrassing him about his clumsy, eager manner. She had given herself freely and generously whenever he desired her, which was often. He remembered the smoky, musky smell of her body that lingered on him. He remembered the look on her face, the way she would clench her jaw, when he pushed deeply into her, pouring himself inside her, pouring his heart out to her. He remembered watching her while she slept as the first light of morning streamed onto her face. Sometimes in his dreams he would pass her in the night.

He remembered everything. Every day. Every sunrise. Every sunset. Every meal they shared. Every cup of whiskey they raised. Every wonderful story of the future she told him. Every dream they dreamed. Every promise. Most of all, he remembered her promise that she would always be beside him, and throughout his life he strongly felt her presence.

Sarah had been adamant it was not time for him to leave the mountains, otherwise, he would have left after she was gone. He stayed, keeping his journal, until 1842. He continued to borrow books from Fort Hall, and took pleasure in the comfort he found in his Bible. He believed God brought Sarah to him. There wasn't a night that went by he didn't say a prayer thanking Him for her. Not a night that went by he didn't ask God to watch over her and keep her under His protection.

As he was preparing to leave the mountains for the Willamette Valley, he stopped to gaze at the wild, romantic scenery of the mountains. It was that evening, when the sun was gently gliding behind the western mountains and casting its gigantic shadows across the vale, he remembered Sarah remarking that he would one day write a poem before he left the mountains. He sat down under a tall pine and took a last farewell view of the country he loved so much. He was not content to merely be a humble journalist. He knew Sarah would one day read his poem and he took great care to frame his thoughts into rhyme and wrote his last impressions of the Shining Mountains.

The Hunter's Farewell

> *Adieu ye hoary icy mantled towers*
> *That ofttimes pierce the onward fleeting mists*
> *Whose feet are washed by gentle summer showers*
> *While Phoebus' rays play on your sparkling crests*
> *The smooth green vales you seem prepared to guard*
> *Beset with groves of ever verdant pine*

Would furnish themes for Albions noble bards
Far 'bove a hunters rude unvarnish'd rhymes

He reached Oregon in September, 1842, traveling with Dr. Elijah White, a Federal Indian sub-agent, and his emigrant party in one of the first covered wagons migrating to Oregon.

He often wondered how much Sarah knew would come to pass during his lifetime. Did she know he had rheumatism in his knees? Did she know he couldn't swim? Did she know he could read French? Did she how about his accident? The knowledge of so many painful things must have hurt and worried her. If she had stayed, would she have let him go to the mill race in Oregon City in June, 1843? An explosion blasted a sixty-pound piece of rock and struck him on the right side of his face. It knocked him six feet backwards and struck him unconscious. Nine particles of rock, the size of wild goose shot penetrated his right eye, leaving him blind in that eye forever. After the mining accident his health was never the same. He was often glad Sarah never saw him like this. He knew she would always hold the memory of him as a strong, young trapper wandering in the Rocky Mountains.

And she was right. He never married and he never owned a watch.

During his convalescence he studied law. He earned the nickname given to him by his fellow trappers, "Judge Russell," after he served on the bench of the Supreme Court. He was one of the original trustees of Pacific University at Forest Grove. In 1845, he was a candidate for the Governor of Oregon, but late in the race threw his support to the candidate that went on to win the office.

In 1848, he caught gold fever with the rest of the country. It was the most alive he had felt since leaving the Rocky Mountain College, but it wasn't the same and it didn't last. He took a partner and went into business running a provision store and a boarding house. They later expanded and bought and operated two trading vessels between Sacramento and Portland. His partner absconded with all of the company's money and he was financially ruined. He spent the remainder of his life paying off his creditors, and it had been a long life; he had celebrated his seventy-eighth birthday in June.

Russell fell asleep, or he thought he fell asleep. The room was quiet. He had been in the county hospital eight years, admitted with what the doctors called "miners rheumatism." His two loyal friends had taken a respite from their long vigil at his bedside. He closed his hand tighter. He was waiting for Death to come this silent night. He was not good at waiting. He remembered waiting for Sarah to return after she disappeared. Of course, he knew she would not, but he could not leave where he last held her in his arms. He sat at the place for three long days and three long nights. He kept thinking, "She found her way to me, perhaps she can find her way back. I must wait for her. If she comes back, and I'm gone, she'll be alone and she will never find me." The fourth day he raised his two calloused, sunburned hands to his face and wept. He could endure his grief no more. The tears rolled down his cheeks like hard summer rain. His throat was as tight as if the devil had him by the throat. His chest heaved, trying to pour out what he could hold in no longer.

A few days after she disappeared he pulled her pistol, the map she had given him, and her worn copy of *Journal of a Trapper* from his possibles bag. The binding was broken and held together with rubber string. It was sealed in one of her plastic bags named after zippers. Just holding it in his hands made him feel close to her. He stared at the cover a long time. He admired the painting of the three trappers riding on horseback. He didn't open the bag. He didn't want to read the book. It was impossible not to notice the dates: 1834 -1843. After holding it a long time, he built a fire and burned it. He buried the gun. He kept the map. The clear bag melted and the pages went up in flames. As he watched it burn he remembered Sarah's story of the summer flood when she was a young woman, and how she lost everything she owned in the raging current except his book. She told him how she cried when she found his water-soaked *Journal of a Trapper* deep in the woods, and how she felt he was there with her, tightly holding her hand; just as he believed, at this minute, Sarah was with him, as he lay dying, holding his.

It was worrisome to him that *Journal of a Trapper* had not been published. Before 1848, he sent it to an agent in New York, with instructions that the copyright be given to his younger sister, Martha. He had to accept, on faith, that it would some day find its way into print after his death, and eventually, across the seasons, Sarah would one day hold a copy for the first time. She would be unaware how her life would change because of that small, paper book written so long ago.

He never attended another annual summer gathering. When he would see men who met Sarah at the Rendezvous of 1838, they always asked what had become of her. It was hard to keep his rising sorrow choked down inside, but he would muster his greatest sense of theater and say, "Gentlemen, she was just too fine a lady for a backwoods trapper the likes of me." They would all laugh and heartily agree with him and the subject would be dropped.

He lived long enough to see some of the things she told him come to pass, but there were some things she had not told him. She had not mentioned that the famous explorer, Meriwether Lewis, committed suicide. It came as a great shock to Russell, but as the years passed, and the clean morning smell of the Rocky Mountains became a distant memory, he understood Lewis' sadness that he and Clark had rendered the Unknown into the Familiar. He remembered Sarah saying it was from the campfires of trappers cities would rise. And they did. It was a new frontier opened by time. The way west was no longer known as Sublette's cut-off or Sublette's trace, but the Oregon Trail. By 1843 Fremont had touted the ease of moving through South Pass and, the same year, one thousand people, made the trip west. Senator Thomas Hart Benton promoted the idea by saying it was a "utopia, three crops a year and every baby was healthy." In reality, the trip to Oregon took six months, traveling fifteen miles a day, and one in ten died on the perilous journey.

Ever once in a while he'd hear of the goings on of a fellow trapper. Newell and Meek, true to their conversation at the Rendezvous of 1838, left the mountains in 1840 and journeyed to Oregon and settled as farmers on the Tualatin plains on the Willamette River. In 1843, Meek was made sheriff of the territory, and, the boy who had left home at sixteen unable to read and refusing to learn, was elected twice to the legislature. After the tragic massacre of Dr. Whitman, his wife, and others, Meek was elected a special messenger to Washington to ask for protection of the colony. He had written Russell a letter describing himself as "envoy extraordinary and minister plenipotentiary from the Republic of Oregon to the Court of the United States," and though "ragged, dirty and lousy" on his arrival he was warmly welcomed by the popular voice and dubbed, "Colonel." In 1843, Russell, Meek, Newell, and forty-nine other men, stood on a bluff overlooking the Willamette River at Champoeg, Oregon and voted to organize the first provisional government west of the Rocky Mountains.

Mr. Bridger built his way-station, Fort Bridger, on the Oregon Trail in southwestern Wyoming in 1843. Word spread Bridger offered generous hospitality and reliable advice to those passing by his door, some of which included: Wyeth, Bonneville, Whitman, Parker, DeSmet, Fremont, the Donner Party, Brigham Young, and countless others making the pilgrimage across the wide, perilous country. Bridger farmed awhile after the Mormons drove him from his holdings in 1853. Last Russell heard, Mr. Bridger was acting as a guide, accompanying the Rayolds Yellow Stone Expedition.

The sun had set. He was cold. He pulled the faded green wool blanket around his neck. Outside the curtainless hospital window, Russell could see the quarter moon rising against the Egyptian darkness of the late summer sky, soon it would be the edge of dawn, a new day. He had never lain with a woman under a moonlit sky since his last night with Sarah on the Wind River. Throughout his life his love for her burned, like a fire banked for the night.

Men will walk on the moon, he thought. How different his daydreams had been having the privilege of knowing so much about the future. How different his life had been since he heard the anguished cries of a hurt and confused woman. He remembered how he thought his heart would break that first day when she struggled to mount her horse and rode away. He remembered how his heart broke that last day when she slipped out of his arms, fading like the last misty smoke from the evening's campfire and disappeared in his arms.

The sound of glass breaking immediately brought the two friends to Russell's bedside.

"Get the doctor, A.B."

"Osborne?" The tall man reached out and gently touched his dying friend's shoulder.

Russell saw the concern and sadness on his friend's face. "Don't worry over me, Walt. I'm going home. I'm going back to my Shining Mountains and wait for my girl. Did I ever tell you about Sarah, Walt? She's the prettiest girl you've ever seen. I want to get her something pretty at Rendezvous this year. Did I ever tell you one day men will walk on the moon? They will. My Sarah told me."

The grieving man watched him breathe more and more slowly, holding his hand, until he breathed no more. Osborne Russell was dead. Tears welled in his eyes as he looked at the weathered face of the honorable man who was more than a brother to him, he was his friend.

In the dark he saw something lying on the floor by Russell's hospital bed. He stooped down and picked up the broken pieces of a small, blue, clay hippopotamus.

Epilogue

Osborne Russell died August 26, 1892.

He died in the Placerville County Hospital. Russell is buried in an unmarked grave in the hospital cemetery. His death notice appeared in the *Placerville Mountain Democrat* on September 4, 1892:

"Russell — at the County Hospital, August 26, 1892,
Osborn Russel (Judge), a native of Maine, aged 78 years."

Peter H. Burnett, the first governor of California and a friend said of Russell upon his death,

"All his comrades agreed he never lost his virtuous habits, but always remained true to his principles . . .
He is a man of education and refined feelings."

Osborne Russell never married and he never owned a watch.

ISBN 155212625-0